Sweet Holy Motherfucking Everloving Delusional Bastard

ABOUT THE AUTHOR
jeromesegundo.com

ABOUT THE TITLE
268*

ABOUT THE SUBTITLE
286*

Sweet Holy Motherfucking Everloving Delusional Bastard

a clearly labeled work of fiction*

Jerome Segundo

illustrations by
R. Priest

TILLERMAN PUBLISHING
BOSTON

This book is a fictional memoir. Any similarity between
the characters portrayed herein and any person—living, dead,
or as yet unborn—is purely and entirely coincidental.

Published by Tillerman Publishing
www.TillermanPublishing.com

Segundo, Jerome
Sweet Holy Motherfucking Everloving
Delusional Bastard / Jerome Segundo—1st ed.

ISBN-13: 978-0-9882085-1-3
ISBN-10: 0988208512

First Edition
J I H G F E D C B A

UNDEDICATED

Foreword

Year 8 | Summer

In the naïveté of my youth, I believed that love reigned as the most powerful of human traits. "All you need is love," as some one-hit-wonder band from the '60s used to sing.

But then I studied the Holocaust in high school and realized that the survival instinct trumped all.

At various times since, these minor epiphanies were successively supplanted, as I considered the drive for food or sex or money to be the defining element of humanity.

But now, at age 30, I see the error of my ways. If there is one characteristic that exemplifies humankind, it's our innate and infinite capacity for self-delusion.

Our ability to reassemble facts to better fit our personal narrative, our propensity for rewriting our individual history as casually as a shopping list, transcends all other attributes. We rationalize the irrational, reconcile the irreconcilable, and controvert the incontrovertible to justify our actions or to place ourselves in a more flattering light. We narrate and star in our fanciful, self-aggrandizing stories. And, more astoundingly, we tell the tales so convincingly that we believe them ourselves.

I admit, it's an odd point to bring out at the start of a memoir—instilling doubt as to the veracity of all that follows. But I consider acknowledging this tendency the critical first step in my personal "self-deluders anonymous" program.

I've tried my best to be honest and true as I peel back the layers, but stripping one oftentimes just reveals another. Even my delusions are deluded.

-Jerome Segundo

Prologue

Year 5 | Winter

In the interest of a coherent narrative, certain parameters must be established from the outset:

One: A jailhouse journal this isn't. Those seeking tales of cellblock degradation and penetration will have to look elsewhere. In composing this memoir, I'm simply taking advantage of the abundant time afforded me while housed in state-funded accommodations to write down my thoughts, clarify my thinking, and gain perspective on certain life events.

Two: Neither is this a confessional. There's nothing to confess; the evidential facts are well-known and not in dispute.

Three: Nor is this my *mea culpa*. Yes, I'm a convicted rapist. But the verdict was the malformed product of a binary system of jurisprudence that proclaims either guilt or innocence and ignores the plight of those caught in between. A reasonable case could be made that I am *both* guilty *and* innocent. Or *neither* guilty *nor* innocent. I'm still grappling with the issue myself. My internal jury's still out, so to speak.

I should also state, just briefly because I don't want to dwell on the incarceration aspects of my story, that prison isn't so bad. I got lucky, if one could call it that, and wound up in a minimum-security facility in the Upper Midwest. My fellow inmates fall into two categories: drug possession and white collar crime. Most are actually decent guys who either liked to get high and got stupid about it or tried to cook the books and got stupid about it. So I guess one could say that stupidity is the chain that shackles us together. There are a few assholes, of course, but then there are assholes everywhere. Why should prison be any different?

In fact, the worst part of my whole crimes-and-misdemeanors experience was probably the local lock-up where they kept me for three days until my bail hearing. Popular perception notwithstanding, prison does teach valuable lessons. In my case: avoid getting arrested on a holiday weekend.

Initially, I was the only inmate in the barren four-cell holding area at the police precinct. The accommodations, as expected, were no-star: a seatless, tankless, waterless toilet caked with fecal scum; a wooden bench bolted to the floor against a gray cinder block wall; poor light; horrible acoustics.

At the time, I hoped my quandary would soon be relegated to a black humor anecdote recounted at the bar. That hope, it turns out, was illusory.

During my second night, just as I was dozing off on the bench, the cops hauled in a noisy drunk and stuffed him into the cell next to mine. Thankfully, the steel bars framed only the front of the cage; solid walls separated the cells and blocked the inmates' view of one another.

"Hey, what are you in for?" the drunk belched.

I considered a couple of phony offenses—jaywalking, parking in a handicap zone—but decided to play it straight.

"Rape."

"Statutory?" he asked with what seemed like a hopeful lilt.

"No, just plain old garden-variety rape. You?"

"DWI, third offence. I'm up shits creek, skating on thin ice."

"Hope you don't fall through," I said.

At my arraignment, the state argued that I was a threat to the community, a predator in the midst of God-fearing, law-abiding citizens. Meanwhile, my lawyer showed up late, mumbled a lame counter-argument, and rushed out afterward with a curt, "I'll be in touch." Bail was set at $25,000, about $24,950 more than I had in the bank.

My friends Dave and Graham came up with my bail money the next day. Unfortunately, my liberation was short-lived. A mere week after posting bail, I was transported via ambulance from a hospital, where I was recuperating from injuries sustained in a freak entomological attack, to the courthouse.

Although I arrived at my post-indictment arraignment in a wheelchair, I decided against milking my condition for sympathy and, bucking the advice of my attorney, changed my not-guilty plea to *nolo*.

The judge handed down a schizophrenic sentence. Citing the seriousness of my offense, he locked me up for five-to-seven. Yet noting my lack of a prior record and extenuating circumstances, he sent me to a minimum-security prison. I can get out in three years with good behavior, and my inclination at this point is to be good.

The prison shrink suggested I write about the events leading up to my present circumstance. Having abundant hours to fill over the next few years, I readily agreed. Also, I figured cooperating with the mind doctor might earn me points with the parole board.

Most of my story will take place within a brief, albeit event-filled, two-year span, from graduation to incarceration. What happens after jail is anyone's guess. If it's interesting or pertinent, I'll throw it into an epilogue.

I should note that some of the events documented in this memoir actually take place in my absence. These scenes have been pieced together based on accounts from those who were present. The dialogue may not be verbatim, but I think I captured the gist.

In the meantime, a man's cell is his castle. When I'm not transcribing my brain waves on the prison library computer, a pathetically outdated model, I'm regaining my touch at ping-pong. I'm also enrolled in a writing course taught by a volunteer from a nearby community college, reading classic paperback novels, and studying botany. And steering clear of the assholes.

Okay, I've already broken my vow to avoid the prison memoir genre. *Mea culpa.*

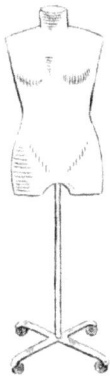

Chapter 1

Year 1 | Autumn

As I innocently strolled down the city street, a vision arrested my progress. There before me stood a figure of unparalleled beauty.

What, exactly, is the rationale for putting erect nipples on storefront mannequins? In simpler times, dummies were tan, smooth, featureless figurines. Now they seemed more lifelike than most people I knew.

This troubled me on several levels, prudery not being one of them. What bothered me was the allure, the fact that these dummies could actually stir a response in me. Equally depressing was the fact that these mannequins desired me as much as any living woman on the planet. But worst of all was the realization that I'd sunk to a new low. Checking out the mannequins in a storefront window was just one step removed from ordering a life-size blow-up doll on the Internet.

The overall effect was an unfamiliar sensation of self-awareness, disconcertingly uncomfortable, like underwear two sizes too small.

I caught a glimpse of my reflection in the glass, an optical illusion that superimposed me into the window display. I saw myself standing beside the mannequin, so close we could practically embrace.

A bee circled and landed on the plate glass window. It, too, was now projected onto the scene, appearing to alight directly onto the mannequin's cheek. Instinctively, to save her from this threat, I reached out to brush the insect away. The bee went into a frenzy and stung my finger. I cursed, swatted it to the ground, and crushed it under my shoe with a distinct crunch.

The dummy was unmoved by my heroism.

A disheveled street person shuffled by. "Shame on you," he said. "Never kill a bee."

"I've figured out what's wrong with my life." I sat on a barstool next to my friend Dave at "13," a long, narrow pub with the grand good fortune of being located at 13 Thirteenth Street. I pressed my throbbing finger against a cold glass of beer.

"Jerome, I could've saved you the trouble," said Dave, nursing a lager. "You're 22 years old. You've been out of college five months, and you've still got no job. You haven't had a girlfriend since eighth grade. You're as stupid as this coaster and as ugly as the pimple on my butt. Does that pretty much capture it?"

"You forget to mention I've got no friends," I said. "At least none who are sympathetic."

"I may not be *sym*pathetic, but I am pathetic. At least give me partial credit."

"Fine. Partial credit to the pathetic friend."

Dave adopted a self-satisfied smirk, as if he had just scratched a winning lottery ticket or something.

Thirteen was our favorite watering hole. Dave and I, along with our mutual friend Graham, started frequenting the place when we first met at college a few years prior. As the only pub in town where we could reliably get an underage drink, the establishment commanded our loyalty during our early undergrad years, an allegiance that endured once we came of age.

A long wooden bar, buffed by countless sleeves, occupied one side; snug booths lined up against the other. A row of tables ran between the two.

I rubbed my welt. "I need a woman," I said. "In the worst way."

"Don't you mean in the best way?"

"Well, yeah, both ways I guess. Anyway, it's gotten bad. I passed a clothing store on my way here and found myself checking out the mannequins in the window."

"No shit!" said Dave, suddenly sitting up and brightening. "You do that too?"

"Wow," I said. "What a relief! I thought I was the only one."

"You are," he said, reverting to his slouch. "Pervert."

Dave Deng was one of those rare people who knew exactly what he wanted—nothing—and who had it all—also nothing. At 5-foot-10, 190 pounds, he was a bit of a doughboy, with a roundish face and pleasant-enough features. Peered at in just the right light, he sported a vaguely Asian air, many generations removed. His black hair was unruly even when combed, which it wasn't, and at least three months beyond the expiration date of his last haircut. Dressed in an extreme casual style, he favored clothes that looked slept-in and were a size too big. He wore imposing sneakers, loosely laced. The overall impression was distinctly one of *I don't give a damn*, which he didn't.

Inexplicably, Dave always seemed to have a girlfriend or three. It was an enduring mystery. Just about the only positive attribute I could discern was his hygiene, which was admittedly first-rate. Yet cleanliness seemed a slender thread to hang a long string of girlfriends from. But I couldn't deny his street cred, and I needed to draw upon his wisdom. It pained me to ask, but I did anyway. "I don't get it, Dave. What do women see in you?"

"Jerome, there's a perfectly reasonable explanation why women are drawn to me. I'm just not sure you'd be able to comprehend it."

"Hey! *Yo comprendo* with the best of them."

"Okay, then," said Dave. "Question. How many girlfriends have you had in your entire life?"

"I don't know. Like, one and a half."

"Exactly! You may be too green for this."

I adopted a pained look, which elicited the desired effect.

"All right," he continued. "I'll share some wisdom, but you must be discreet. This is powerful information."

"Not to worry."

"You think of me as kind of a crude dude, don't you?"

I mulled over the question. Dave had an unnatural obsession with bodily functions. His every-other utterance was punctuated with profanity. He was oblivious to the finer aspects of life. "Yeah, I'd say that was pretty accurate."

"Well, that just shows what an unobservant motherfucker you are, Jerome. Because if you paid any attention at all, you'd notice that I am never, ever crude in the presence of a lady."

"That's your secret? Women are attracted to you because you refrain from belching in their company?"

Dave raised his hand. "Please. Allow me to continue. It's all about respect. Women are the superior gender in every measure that matters. They know it, and they need to know that you know it. You're so busy licking plate glass windows that you don't even realize how you come across. Women can smell desperation a mile away."

The pub door swung open, admitting a shaft of painfully bright light and a blast of chilly autumn air. Graham sauntered into the barroom.

"Have you ever seen anyone walk so erect?" asked Dave. "It's like he's got a steel rod shoved up his ass."

"Finishing school," I said. "They made him walk around the room with Miss Manners sitting on top of his head."

"Gentlemen," said Graham, settling onto a high stool at the corner of the bar. He spotted the napkin rolled around my finger. "What happened to you?"

"Bee sting," I said.

"That's a coincidence."

"How so?"

"I've been researching bees lately. Thinking about getting myself a hive. Saw an article about it in *Country Gentleman*."

"Don't you need some acreage for that?" asked Dave. "Last I checked, you lived in a frigging condo."

"Common misconception," said Gray. "City apiaries are all the rage."

Tall and thin, Graham Earling wore a black cashmere v-neck sweater over a gray cotton jersey. His blue jeans bore a crisp crease down the front, all the way to his sockless ankles and spit-shined penny loafers.

"Did every dickhead iron their jeans at prep school or just you?" asked Dave.

"It would be inaccurate to describe these trousers as ironed," said Graham. "They have been professionally dry-cleaned and pressed."

Graham looked disdainfully at the foamy lager in the two glasses on the table. "I don't know how you lads can drink that swill."

"First of all," said Dave, "we aren't lads. We're dudes—dee-double-oh-dee dudes. Two, Budweiser is the king of beers, a royal title that a Brit wannabe like yourself should appreciate."

"David, I find it difficult to concentrate when you move so carelessly from the ordinal to the cardinal," said Graham, grabbing my beer, taking a sip, and making a face.

"Yeah? Well, I find it annoying when you throw bird-watching non sequiturs into the conversation."

Graham flagged the waitress. "A pint of bitter."

An anglophile to the extreme, Gray affected a British lilt, spread Marmite on his white toast, and drove a Land Rover. He claimed to have involuntarily picked up his accent during a semester abroad program.

He turned to Dave and me. "What's new, gentlemen?"

"I was just giving Segundo here a talking to about womankind and respect," said Dave.

"Ah, yes," said Graham. "Respect. Essential to meaningful relationships with the fair sex. And subject of great personal expertise, I might add."

"You don't say," I said.

"I do say," Gray said. "Here's a little quiz to test your respectability, Jerome." He paused as the waitress delivered his pint, then intently watched her backside as she sashayed away. "If a naked woman walks into your elevator, what do you do?"

I tried to imagine my response. A sense of lightheadedness overcame me. I was instantly tongue-tied.

"All right then," continued Gray, "here's a hint. You don't start groping her once the doors close."

"Is it just me and the nude lady? Or are there others in the elevator?"

"Just you two."

"Well, considering you as the source of the question," I said, "I politely invite her to tea?"

Dave snorted. "Jolly freaking good!"

Graham was unfazed. "If a naked woman enters your elevator, you look her straight in the eye, never breaking your gaze, and you say, 'Those are truly exquisite earrings you're wearing.'"

I was awestruck at the brilliance of Gray's approach. The nonchalant attentiveness. The coy compliment. The casual panache. "Genius," I said with genuine admiration.

"Cheers," said Gray, lifting his glass before taking a swig.

Dave looked at us both incredulously. "If that perverse little story represents your idea of respect, I suggest you guys invest in a couple of parachutes. You, my foolish friends, are in for a fall."

"Don't be ridiculous, Dave," I said. "What good is a parachute in an elevator?"

"To respect," said Graham, again hoisting his pint.

"Empty," said Dave curtly, flicking his fingernail against his glass and leaving it sitting on the table.

"To respect," I said, raising my pint to clink with Gray's. Favoring my stung finger without realizing it, I lost my grip. The beer slipped from my grasp and crashed to the floor, exploding on impact.

Chapter 2

Year 2 | Winter

In hindsight, my choice of sociology as a major was probably not the savviest move I ever made. Out on the street, looking for my first post-collegiate job, I quickly understood that I was qualified to do only one thing: teach sociology. To a new generation of students. Enabling them to go forth. To teach sociology.

Yet even that depressing realization proved invalid. Teaching, I discovered, required a master's degree. My bachelor's looked feeble, and my C average wouldn't even land me an interview at the local adult education center, never mind a *real* school. Not that anyone was taking sociology courses in adult ed.

I didn't have much work history to fall back on. The summer between my junior and senior years, I had toiled as a piece-rate factory worker. Five days per week, seven-and-a-half hours per day, five thousand-some-odd times per shift, I picked up a flat piece of spade-shaped metal, inserted it into a slot, stepped on a foot pedal, and, with a spine-shuddering thump, transformed it into a curved piece of spade-shaped metal.

Three months of that brutal monotony made me understand the primary benefit of summer jobs: learning exactly what careers to avoid. I vowed to go on the dole rather than work in another factory.

After graduation, parchment in hand, I took the summer off to celebrate my awesome academic achievement. In the fall, I began the quixotic task of applying to businesses all over the region, from fast-food restaurants (didn't pan out) to dry cleaners (rife with nepotism) to bowling alleys (all the pin-setters were robots).

Filing an unemployment claim looked like my best option. But then another crushing disappointment set in. It turned out that prior employment was a prerequisite for unemployment; i.e., one needs to first *have* a job in order to get paid for *not having* a job. What kind of an idiotic system is that?

Autumn passed into winter, and the chill deepened my funk. Things were getting desperate enough that I seriously considered asking my folks for a bridge loan. I concocted a lesser-of-two-evils scheme: either they lend me a few thou, or I move back in with them. Faced with the unsavory prospect of me on their doorstep, my parents would surely pony up the capital to tide me over until my dream job materialized.

But how to make the ask? Face-to-face was out of the question—too up-close and personal. Email seemed the other extreme—impersonal and easily ignored. The telephone creeped me out—I didn't want to hear my father's disappointed silence on the other end of the line, the absence of disapproval being a particularly devastating form of disapproval. So I decided to go old-style and put pen to paper. It took several drafts, as my handwriting skills had severely atrophied in the electronic age, but I finally got something down that didn't look like it was written by a dyslexic first grader. I folded the letter and tucked it into an envelope. As I licked the flap, a slicing pain seared my tongue. A drop of my blood adorned the seam like crimson sealing wax.

* * *

Dave and Gray decided a change of scenery would lift my spirits, so they proposed a ski trip.

"Fresh powder," said Dave.

"Fresh air," said Gray.

"Fresh ale," said Dave.

"Fresh ski bunnies," said Gray.

"And, if I know Graham, he means fresh bunnies in every sense of the word," said Dave.

"How many senses are there?" I asked.

"More than you can handle."

"Guys, just one problem," I said. "As you both continually remind me, I graduated eight months ago and still don't have a job. I'm broke."

"Don't you worry, little buddy," said Dave, putting his arm around me. "I've got you covered."

"Thanks, skipper."

We left Friday night for the three-hour tour north. Other ski resorts were closer, but they were more hill than mountain. One hundred and fifty miles represented the minimum journey required to reach a quality slope. We were forced to rent a car, since Gray's Land Rover was in the shop, Dave's motorized egg beater wasn't worthy of the trip, and my car, well, I didn't have a car.

The rented sedan had no roof rack, but the back seat split sixty/forty, folding down to extend the trunk. Three sets of skis of varying vintage jutted into the cabin: Gray's spanking new, sleekly contoured pair; Dave's five-year-old, well-used set, received as a Christmas present from his parents just before he went off to college; and my ancient sticks, constructed from some sort of archaic material—I think it's called wood—handed down through generations, with rusted bindings and numerous nicks and gouges.

"You'll need to stay at least ten feet away from us at all times," said Dave. "I can't be seen with any dickhead who'd wear those lame skis."

"Certainly not a problem for me," said Gray.

"Why, thank you, Graham. I appreciate your support," I said.

"Support? Oh, sorry, you've misconstrued. You won't be anywhere near me because you lads will be choking on my snow-vapor."

Gray drove; I sat shotgun. Dave settled in with the equipment in the back. A conspicuous hiss emanated from the rear seat.

"David," said Gray. "If you insist on emitting flatus, at least do us the courtesy of ventilating."

"I.e., crack the window before you crack your cheeks," I added.

Dave took umbrage. "As the old saying goes, you guys don't know my ass from my elbow. The only thing I cracked is this beer." He displayed a can of lager while letting out a hearty belch. "Anyone care to join me?"

I reached for the offered can.

"Correct me if I'm wrong, but isn't there an open container law in this jurisdiction?" said Graham. "I suggest you lads dump that lager and switch to soda for the duration."

"The hell we will," said Dave. "As Charlton Heston once said, 'You'll have to pry this beer out of my cold, dead hands.'"

"Charlton Heston?" I said. "Who's he?"

"Not sure. I think he was a pitchman for adult diapers," said Dave.

"If he drank less beer, maybe he wouldn't be incontinent," said Gray.

I hit the window button and dropped the glass halfway, admitting the frigid air. "This, my good friends, is how a gentleman passes gas." I produced a highly audible emission.

"Is this to what we have stooped?" asked Gray, getting all petulant on us.

Gray often took on an air of offended sensibility. Indeed, in light of all his prim protestations, corrections, and objections, one might have concluded that he wasn't particularly fond of me and Dave. Yet I'd contend that beneath Gray's stuffy exterior lived a vulgarian dying to get out. It showed in the slight curvature of a smile that he couldn't suppress; in the glint of his eyes even as he disparaged and disavowed the crass behavior of his *déclassé* friends.

"Did you know that every fart has its own signature aroma, unique like a fingerprint?" said Dave. "You can tell a lot about a person by their farts."

"You don't say," I replied, quickly rolling up the window. "Pray tell, David, what do you read in this bouquet?"

"Must we?" pleaded Gray, to deaf ears.

"Okay, my farting friend, you're on," said Dave, lifting his head and sniffing the air like one might a fine Cabernet Sauvignon. "I discern that your gastrointestinal p-h is a bit on the acidic side. The pungent fragrance is suggestive of a cruciferous vegetable; I'm guessing broccoli or Brussels sprouts. And there's a rancid aftertaste that implies red meat. The science is a bit imprecise here, but I'll take a flyer on a Big Mac."

"Yow!" I said, reaching back and high-fiving Dave. "I had a burger and broccoli last night! You are a freaking freak!"

"Thank you. Thank you," said Dave, bowing his head while cascading his hand through the air. "What can I say? Just a little talent I've cultivated through the years."

"I'm not even going to speculate as to how one might cultivate that talent," said Gray.

"I can't believe you ate something healthy like broccoli," said Dave.

"Bad luck," I replied. "The fry-o-later was down. Won't happen again. As noted, it didn't sit well with me."

"Here, try this," said Dave, handing me a small white pill bottle. "Beano. I don't leave home without it."

"That would make a good advertising slogan," said Gray.

"Already taken. Here's a better one," I said, popping a couple of the fart pills, then holding the Beano bottle aloft. "*Break bread, not wind.*"

"Almost," said Dave.

"How about this?" said Gray, snatching the bottle and brandishing it. "*Melts in your mouth, not in your pants!*"

Realizing that he's stooped to the level of his uncouth friends, Gray quickly tossed the bottle back to Dave and clenched his teeth to fight off a grin.

* * *

We rented a two-bedroom slope-side condo and pulled straws to determine who'd sleep on the living room couch. I came up short.

"Hey, isn't this trip designed to get me out of my funk?" I asked. "For the sake of my mental health, shouldn't I get one of the bedrooms?"

"No fucking way," said Dave. "You can only take this wounded bird shtick so far."

Judging from the shopworn feel of the place, we weren't the first twenty-something skiers to rent this condo. Countless cigarette burns spotted the beige living room rug, despite the prominently placed "No Smoking" signs. A sooty stain arose from the fireplace, discoloring the brick and mantle. In the kitchen, cabinet doors hung askew, and several drawers were missing handles. The contents of the supposedly fully-equipped kitchen had been thoroughly pilfered, with little more than a couple of coffee cups and assorted useless cooking utensils remaining. Wisely, we brought along the only truly essential item—a bottle opener.

The night was still relatively young, ten-ish, so we headed down to the lodge for a drink. As we stepped out to the edge of the floodlit trail, a pack of thoroughly inebriated skiers whooshed by recklessly, emitting war-cries as they careened down the mountain.

We slip-slid along the edge of the trail in the frigid air as snow guns blasted plumes of crystallized vapor into the sky, creating a dazzling display in the spotlight beams.

Arriving at the lodge, we stomped up the split-log stairs, stamped our boots on the metal grate outside the doorway, and ambled in. A large brick fireplace dominated the room, smack in the middle with openings on four sides. What appeared to be a genuine fire roared from within, its heat radiating all the way to the entrance.

The place was moderately full, befitting the sluggish ski season and the unpromising forecast. We worked our way through the milling *après*- and pre-ski crowd, the former being characterized by their wind-chapped faces; the latter by their city pallor.

Three unoccupied seats awaited us at the bar. "Is it just my imagination," I said as we settled in, "or do we spend an inordinate amount of time together in bars?"

"I consider it entirely ordinate," replied Graham.

Signs advertising various drinks were plastered around the room. One in particular caught my eye. *Try our new hard cider. It's better than ever!*

"That sounds promising," I said to the 'keep. "I'll take the better-than-ever cider."

"False advertising," said Dave. "It's an empty promise."

"What are you talking about?"

"The phrase, 'It's better than ever' is a comparison. Like 'I'm better than you at ping-pong.'"

"Or, 'Gainsborough is better than Titian,'" chimed in Gray, momentarily looking up from an appetizer menu.

"But 'it's better than ever'"? said Dave. "What does that even mean? How do you compare something to 'ever'? Have you ever tasted 'ever'?"

"Never," I said.

"Case closed," said Dave.

"Ever, never, whatever," I said. "I just want a drink."

"To the extent I can follow this meandering stream of illogic," said Gray, "it appears you gentlemen are arguing a meaningless point. It's an elliptical phrase. There are words implied but unstated."

"That's stupid," said Dave. "Why would they deliberately leave words out of an ad?"

I was also dubious of Gray's pedantry. "What is missing, oh knowledgeable one?"

"'It's better than ever' is the elliptical version of 'Our newly released product is better than it has ever been in all its previous incarnations in the illustrious history of our company,'" said Gray.

"There's more words between the lines than on the lines," I said. Disillusioned by the whole discussion, I canceled my cider and ordered a beer.

"Elliptical, schmiptical," I muttered.

After a couple of drinks, I suggested we retire to the game room for a little pool and ping-pong. "I assume you mean billiards and table tennis?" said Gray. I resisted the urge to smack him.

Two woman wielded pool cues at a table near the back of the drop-ceilinged, wood-paneled room; another three green-felt tables stood vacant. A couple of ping-pong tables were arrayed by the door. I chose the closest and challenged Dave and Gray to a round-robin tournament—games to eleven, serve transfers on lost point, winner holds table.

"Why would you bastardize the well-established rules of a century-old game?" asked Gray.

"Yeah, you wouldn't change the dimensions of a baseball diamond, would you?" said Dave.

"They lowered the pitcher's mound in the late sixties," I replied.

"Okay, bad example. You wouldn't change the value of a shot in basketball."

"Three-point rule, NBA, 1979," I said.

"Oh, yeah? Well, you wouldn't allow a triple-axel in a ladies figure skating short program."

"You would as of 2010," I said.

"Okay, shut the fuck up," said Dave. "Let's play."

Dave and I paired for the first game. I toyed with him, unleashing a potent combination of spin and straight serves, followed by an array of fore/aft and starboard/port sequences that left him flailing and frustrated. We ended the match at 11-3.

"Next victim!" I announced.

Dave sulked and skulked out to the bar to grab another round. Graham picked up Dave's paddle and promptly dropped it. "This racquet is saturated with perspiration!"

"Speak American," I said. "Repeat after me: The paddle is covered in sweat."

Gray wiped the handle on a handkerchief he produced from his pocket, looking not unlike a maid polishing silverware. Sporting an unconventional grip that portended either a high level of skill or total unfamiliarity with the game, he held the paddle upside down, with the handle jutting through his index and middle fingers and the face of the racquet over his palm.

"Unorthodox style," I noted.

"It's the Guizhou Grip, popularized by the Chinese table tennis Olympian, Wu Huang."

"Don't say," I said.

"Yes. Wu Huang has won more gold medals in table tennis than the next five players combined."

"You misunderstood. When I said, 'don't say,' I meant, 'don't say.'"

Gray put up a much fiercer battle than Dave could muster. His long limbs neutralized my left-to-right, shallow-to-deep strategy, as he barely needed to move his feet to reach the ball. Where I had Dave lurching and panting, Gray showed no strain.

My spin serve proved similarly ineffectual, with Gray hitting counter-spin returns that bounced crazily from the reversed English. This forced a new strategy. For several consecutive turns, I used the longest point-to-point measurement on the table—the diagonal from my right corner to Gray's opposite corner—delivering laser serves that barely cleared the net and touched down at the extreme tip on his side. If the technique is well-executed, after a bunch of identical serves in sequence, the recipient subconsciously shifts his physical and mental orientation to that side, setting him up for a quick baseline serve to the reverse corner that more often than not yields an ace. I teed Gray up with five consecutive diagonal serves before baselining him. He didn't stand a chance. "*That* won't happen again," he said through gritted teeth.

Gray and I swapped the lead several times as we neared the eleven point victory threshold.

"Got to win by two," I said at 9-9.

"That's fine. You just continue improvising rules as the game progresses."

"Hey! That's a well-established rule."

"Establish this," said Gray as he smashed the ball mercilessly to my backhand corner. 10-9.

By this time, Dave had returned with the drinks. "You guys take this game w-a-a-a-y too seriously," he said.

"Shut the fuck up," I replied.

Gray's serve. His delivered a shot with heavy topspin that landed at my right edge and virtually fell off the table. I anticipated his tactic and lobbed the return to his deep right edge, forcing him to actually move off the center of the table. He uncharacteristically sent back a poorly placed shot and then scrambled to get back into position. The high bounce allowed me to set up a slam. I windmilled, tensed, roared, and then oh-so-delicately dinked it over the net. Gray emitted a counter-scream, dove in desperation, and crashed to the floor with the ball spinning just out of reach.

"Deuce!" I yelled triumphantly, jumping and slicing my paddle through the air.

"Truce," said Gray from the floor. "I think I broke my wrist."

I strode over to view the damage. "Of all the pathetic tricks to avoid defeat, this is the worst. Get up so I can put you out of your misery!"

"I'm serious," said Gray. "I'm hurt."

The injury appeared non-life-threatening, but the wrist did start to swell. Gray decided to withdraw to the condo to lick his wounds.

"To be continued!" I taunted him on his way out of the game room, waving my paddle in his face. "You can't retreat from defeat!" Gray knocked my paddle to the floor with his good hand.

Dave and I decided to switch to pool. The two women across the room were just finishing, collecting the billiard balls into the wooden triangular rack on the table. I was feeling unusually amorous. "How do I look?" I asked Dave, slicking my cowlick and tilting my head toward the women.

"You want the brutal truth or the sugar-coated version?"

I was offended by the inference but decided to take it like a man. "Both barrels," I said.

"Okay, let's work top to bottom. Number one, your hairdresser should be fired for malpractice."

"Uh, 'barber,' if you don't mind. And what's wrong with my haircut?" I ran my fingers through my hair, scanning the room in vain for a reflective surface.

"The cut is fine; it's the color. That fucked up, off-brown dye job has no equivalent in nature."

Dave was right about the look but wrong about its origins. Despite appearances to the contrary, I had never actually dyed my hair. Yet my head sprouted a virtual swatch card of brown hues, darker at the roots, lighter at the ends, umber at the back, ochre at the fore. The irony hit me every time I gazed in a mirror: I needed to color my hair to make it look like I didn't color my hair.

"Number two, your eyes are jaundiced."

Nailed again. I hadn't been to the optometrist since sophomore year, and my contacts needed replacing. They were so old, they'd yellowed.

"Three, your nose is too long and too skinny."

I was tempted to protest this assessment, as I'd always considered my Greek nose to be one of my finer features, chiseled in form and noble in character.

"Four, your hands are effeminate."

I held my hands before me in disbelief, ruing the absence of manual labor in my life. Okay, maybe I should go easy on the moisturizer, but who wants chapped knuckles?

"Five, your feet are disproportionately large."

"Wait a minute!" I said. "Don't you know about the correlation between foot size and penis size?"

"My size nines have never led to a complaint," said Dave. "Six, you're gangly—all elbows and knees. Seven, you're taller than me, but your slouch makes you look shorter. Eight, your overall physique resembles the 'before' picture in a body-building magazine."

I was exhausted by the time he finished. "That's it?" I asked. Dave gave me a thumbs-up and a grin.

I paused to let the assessment sink in.

"Just as I thought," I finally said. "Ruggedly good looking."

I quickly checked my shoulders for dandruff just seconds before the women sauntered past to replace their cues in the rack. I winked at Dave. He mouthed something unclear; maybe the word 'no'?

"Excuse me," I said to the better-looking one. "I've been watching you from afar and I must confess, I admire the way you handle that stick. Firm, yet gentle. Shy, yet confident. Watching you play pool is, dare I say, like watching you make love."

The woman paused, stunned, then suddenly flung her stick in my direction, narrowly missing me. It clattered to the floor. "Shove it up your ass!" she said. They stormed out of the room.

I turn to Dave, palms up. "What did I say?"

"Segundo, you got no couth," said Dave, shaking his head in disbelief and then grabbing me by the lapels. "Listen up, asshole. You should never, ever open a conversation with a sexual remark, no matter how clever you think it is."

"'I like how you handle that cue stick' isn't clever?"

"It's a fucking door closer. It's a suck-all-the-air-out-of-the-room remark. It's a guaranteed dead-end."

"Okay, okay. You've made your point."

We retreated. On the way out, I glanced toward the corner where the two pool players joined a couple of other female friends. Before I averted my gaze, I felt their searing glare.

The next morning, Gray arose first. The smell of coffee wafted toward the living room, invading my senses. I slowly surfaced from my dreams, becoming increasingly aware of cramps and aches in my neck, shoulders, and back. I cursed the fraternizers and fornicators whose abuse had transformed my couch into its current sagging, smelly, battered shell.

Hauling my blanket around my shoulders, I shuffled into the kitchen. Gray stood by the sink, coffee cup in hand, wrist wrapped in a bulky ace bandage.

"How's the wound, slacker?"

"Shouldn't hinder me on the triple black diamonds," he replied.

"This mountain has triple diamonds?" I said, trying to hide the panic in my voice.

"It does indeed," said Gray.

Dave ambled into the room. "You should have seen this suave bastard in action last night," he said to Graham. "The women were scurrying from him like roaches flee a shot of Raid."

"Lively metaphor," said Gray. "But not particularly flattering to the female sex."

"Well, Graybeard," said Dave, "it pains me to say this, but you're absolutely correct. My apologies to all of womankind. Let me rephrase: They were avoiding him like a biker avoids a pothole."

"Weak," I said.

"Like an accountant avoids the IRS," said Dave.

"Better," said Gray.

Dave looked pensive for a moment before his face lit up. "Like a thoroughly repulsed woman avoids a completely repugnant guy!"

Dave and Gray fist bumped.

Despite Gray's nagging, we didn't get out of the condo until about ten. The weather proved better than forecast, with the sun making frequent stabs though the cloud cover.

"To the top!" said Gray.

"Hold on," I said. "How about we warm up on an intermediate slope?"

"Remember when we promised you ski bunnies on this trip?" said Dave. "This is what we meant." He pointed to a tame little incline served by a T-bar. "Bunny slope."

"Fine!" I said. "You bastards want to push the limit, I'm right there with you. If I can whip your butts at ping-pong, I can conquer a few black diamonds."

"As I recall," said Dave, "you and Gray ended the night tied. Hardly a butt-whipping."

"Have you looked at his wrist?" I asked. "Indicative of a total whup."

Dave eyed the bulky bandage. "More like a total wuss."

"I'm sorry?" said Gray indignantly. "Your propensity for switching sides mid-debate is indicative of a lack of personal conviction."

"This ain't no debate," I said. "Just a simple examination of the evidence. You took a beating. Literally. If not, um, literally."

"I'll see you back at the table this evening," said Gray. "We'll settle this like men."

"That'll be a first for you," I said as we slide-strode toward the lift.

For some unknown reason, the boys relented and agreed to tackle an intermediate slope that originated three-quarters of the way up the mountain. Light snow fell as we hopped off the lift. I turned and saw the valley below, patchworked between light and shadow, the falling flakes glittering in the sun, a glorious, breathtaking sight. I wondered why anyone would actually ski down the hill rather than stay up top and just revel in the spectacle.

As we started our descent, Gray moved well ahead, Dave fell into the middle of the pack, and I trailed along, my creaky skis holding me back. The moderately challenging slope featured a narrow path, a few switchback turns, and some steep drop-offs along the edge. It had been a couple of years since I'd skied, so I proceeded conservatively, concentrating on closing my bow legs and making my soggy turns crisper. When I arrived at the bottom, Dave and Gray were waiting impatiently. Gray pretended to check his watch.

"That would be a more believable gesture if your wrist wasn't swaddled in an ace bandage," I said.

"My velocity was supreme, wrist notwithstanding," he replied.

We squeezed into a triple chair and headed for the top. I wasn't feeling ready for the summit, but my manhood was at stake. The snow picked up as the sun ducked behind the thickening clouds, and the temperature dipped noticeably on the ascent. "Did anyone check the thermometer at the base?" I asked.

"It was minus-five degrees Celsius," said Gray.

"Oh, shut up, you pretentious bastard," said Dave. "Why can't you just call it twenty degrees like everyone else?"

"If it were twenty degrees, I'd be skiing in my Bermuda shorts," replied Gray.

We reached the summit. Four trails descended, one single diamond, two double diamonds, and one triple diamond, splayed out neatly like points on a compass.

"Hit the triple?" asked Dave.

"Not me," I said. "I need to ease my way up."

Keen on getting their runs in, Gray and Dave spared me any razzing and immediately dropped onto the trail and out of sight. I took my time, adjusting my gloves and admiring the view before skating over to what appeared to be the least challenging double-D trail. I probably should have tackled the single diamond first, but I felt intense pressure to get my form back so I could keep up with them in subsequent runs, somehow forgetting that I never had much form to begin with.

The double diamond trail was steep, peppered with moguls, and treacherously spotted with sheens of ice. Worse yet, the steady snow left a thin veneer over the frozen bits, masking the hazardous conditions.

I stood at the lip of the trail wondering which I valued more, my macho pride or my survival. I was thankful that Dave and Gray weren't there to help me with my decision.

On impulse, I tilted forward over the edge and quickly regretted it. The moguls were deep and tightly packed, making turns on my long skis difficult. I managed the first cut and barely executed the second, turning awkwardly, picking up unwanted speed. I couldn't slow down. Careening toward the edge, which dropped off steeply into trees below, I had no choice—I bailed, a desperation move with no chance for a graceful fall.

My hip bounced off one mogul; my ski hit another and popped free of its binding. With no built-in brake prongs, it took off on its own, bounding crazily between and over the moguls as it gathered momentum. It might have continued all the way down the mountain but for a sharp turn in the trail. The wooden slat rocketed into the woods and disappeared into the deep whiteness.

I broke into a sweat despite the temperature, a combination of exertion and fear. Looking back up at the lip of the trail, about fifty feet above me, I noted thankfully that the initial drop-off was so steep that skiers-by were unable to view my fallen frame.

Losing a ski offered one major benefit—it spared me the indignity of continuing. I looked disdainfully at the other slat, remarkably still strapped to my boot. I released it and stood. Hoisting the ski like a javelin, I fired it down the hill. The recoil caused me to slip and fall back into the depression.

The ski wended its way through the moguls far more skillfully than I had managed. Approaching the bend in the trail, it didn't continue in a straight line into the woods to join its twin. Rather, it somehow negotiated the turn and continued on out of sight.

I imagined my ski arriving at the base lodge and coming to a halt at the feet of my friends. With mock concern, Dave tries to get the ski to tell him where I am. The ski is unresponsive. Dave threatens to throw it into the nearby fire. Dave and Gray and all the beautiful ski bunnies surrounding them laugh mercilessly at my expense.

Suddenly, a loud whoosh filled the air as a skier vaulted past, mere inches from my squat position. She screamed an obscenity as I scurried sideways toward the far edge of the trail.

Time to reassess. Me: butt perched in a mogul hole like I'm sitting on an icy toilet seat. Ski #1: at least 150 yards away, lost in the woods. Ski #2: location unknown; possibly still slaloming its way down to the base.

Nowhere to go but up. I grabbed my poles, stood, turned uphill, and forcefully jabbed one of the spears into the surface to aid my climb. The tip failed to penetrate the ice, bending under the impact. Windmilling like a softball pitcher, I flung it into the woods. The effort again landed me on my ass.

Facing downhill, I raised my right ski boot and brought my heel down forcefully. It broke through the ice. I pushed myself uphill until my knee was fully extended, repeating the process with my left leg: lift, smash, push. Slowly, painstakingly, I made my way up toward the start of the trail, scurrying backwards on my rear, looking like some sort of demented mountain crab.

At the top, the ice disappeared in favor of hard-packed snow. I stood and walked clumsily toward my salvation, the summit lodge, sitting on the mountaintop like an oasis. I reached the door covered in sweat.

The restaurant contained just a smattering of patrons due to the 11 a.m. hour. A few tables were occupied; the bar was empty. I clomped over to a stool midway along the length and a young, fit, good-looking bartender approached. "Drink?" he said.

"If you insist. I'll take a bloody Mary, double shot of Absolut, extra spicy, garnished with a shrimp."

"I can do everything but the shrimp. How about a nice organic celery stalk instead?"

Mixing with practiced skill, he placed the cocktail before me a mere thirty seconds after my order. I took a hard pull on the straw and contemplated my predicament.

Riding the lift back down would be unthinkable, except that I just thought of it. What if I feigned injury? That would make my return more respectable, heroic even. Maybe the ski patrol could cart me down on their skimobile. Probably unwise. I'd been harassing Gray about his injury and could expect him to return the favor in spades.

The bartender stood nearby, polishing glasses and hanging them on a rack. I looked around the restaurant and saw two attractive women, thankfully not the same pair as last night, engrossed in conversation at a table across the room. A broad-shouldered man sat with them, his back to me, mesmerized by something on his phone.

Finishing off my drink way too fast, I signaled for another. I clutched it and swiveled to face the exterior of the restaurant, looking out the wide windows. The cotton-ball clouds obscured the scenic view, but I found the lazy falling flakes soothing.

I stole a few glances at the women, still chatting animatedly, still ignored by their phone-obsessed companion. I wondered what could possibly be more interesting than the two lovely women he was with.

Resisting the temptation for a third drink, I re-donned my cheap winter jacket, slid back into my ski boots, and marched outside like a

Clydesdale. I passed several people on their way in, the restaurant filling up as the noon hour approached.

With a clear plan, probably alcohol-inspired, in mind, I walked purposefully to the ski rack, scanning the selection. One pair was cable-locked, the rest left unsecured by good, trusting souls.

Understanding that this was no shoe store, I knew I had limited time to properly size myself. I pretended to limber up for my next run, lifting my boot toward a promising binding, attempting to gauge the fit. Too small. I lowered my leg, raised one arm over my head, and leaned sharply to the left, continuing the stretching ruse. As I did so, I shuffled discreetly down the line. Another pair, a gleaming set of brand new, racing-striped Elan skis, caught my eye. I raised my boot to line up against the binding, and this one looked like a match. Just as I eased the pair from the rack, a tap landed on my shoulder, eliciting a jump and grunt like a startled animal.

"Excuse me, but how do you like those Elan skis?" asked a female voice. "I'm thinking about getting a pair."

I turned and saw a woman, fresh of face, cheeks flush from the cold, light blue eyes peeking out from under a knit cap. Her countenance bespoke beauty and purity. Mine, petty thievery. She had interrupted a crime in progress, only she didn't know it.

I stammered in reply, unable to form a coherent sentence. She looked at me with bemusement. I finally composed myself. "I'm sorry. You caught me by surprise," I uttered.

"I saw you stretching," she said. "Do you do yoga?"

"Um, yoga? Well, uh, yes. Yes, I do. I'm kind of a yoga freak. I'm a yogi, actually."

"That's impressive," she said without a trace of sarcasm.

"Um, well, not officially. I'm actually an apprentice yogi. I'm expecting my certificate from the Maharishi any day now. Once I finish my course. Online. Yogi dot com."

She looked at me expectantly, then turned her gaze to the skis.

"Oh, right, the skis!" I blurted out. "I love 'em! Best skis ever! Highly endorse them. Recommend them to all my friends. And family. And co-workers. And now even strangers!"

"Oh, wow, that's, um, great," she said. "Thanks so much." She walked toward the restaurant.

"And they're top rated by *Consumer Reports*!" I yelled to her. She turned and gave a little half wave.

Before she was out of sight, I dropped the skis onto the hard-packed snow, where they landed with a resounding thwack. I stepped into them and my boots, thankfully, clicked snugly into place. Grabbing the poles, I started ski-striding toward the single diamond trail in a furious blur of synchronized arm and leg movement, wanting to get away from the lodge as quickly as possible. The building receded behind me.

The single diamond trail wound around the back of the mountain instead of dropping straight down like the three others. With less verticality, the conditions were vastly better, as the snow cover hadn't been blown away. I cut back and forth smartly, which surprised me, given the debacle on the other trail. Perhaps downing a couple of drinks relaxed me and made my motions more fluid. Or maybe the pricey contoured skis improved my form. Whatever the reason, I thoroughly enjoyed my run, despite the wind whistling past my muffled ears and biting at my unprotected eyes. I should steal some goggles, too, I thought.

Halfway down, the trail cut under one of the lift lines. I scanned the chairs and saw Dave and Gray on the ascent. Yanking off one glove, I put my middle finger and thumb to my lips and blew a shrill whistle. They looked my way, and I waved. As they passed overhead, Dave yelled, "Wait for us at the base!" I gave them the thumbs up.

Dave turned back in his chair and peered at me again. "Hey! Where'd you get those skis?"

"What?" I yelled, cupping my hand to my ear.

"The skis. Where'd you get those skis?"

"Can't hear you! I'll see you at the bottom!"

I turned downhill and sped off.

Chapter 3

Year 2 | Winter

As I got closer to the base, my pulse quickened. Had my victim
sounded an alert? Would the ski police be waiting to cuff me?

The roar of a snowmobile arose from nowhere, nearly driving
me off the trail in alarm. I lurched to a stop at the edge, lost my
balance, teetered, and almost toppled over. A bright red machine
zoomed by, towing a long sled with a mummified woman strapped
onto it.

I resumed my descent. The base lodge came into view, and the
terrain flattened. I scanned the area for official-looking types but saw
no one. Weaving among the thickening crowd of skiers, I headed
toward the ski racks farthest from the main entrance to the lodge.

I slid to a stop and aimed my pole tip at the binding release tab
at my heel, intent on abandoning my stolen skis as quickly as
possible. "Hey!" yelled a man standing by the apron deck that
surrounded the lodge. He pointed my way and started running

awkwardly in his ski boots toward me. I jabbed my pole at the binding tab, missing once, twice, then hitting. My foot popped free. As the man neared, his face weirdly contorted in a half-grin, I grabbed my pole with two hands and brandished it like a jousting spear. One ski on and one off wasn't the most advantageous stance for a confrontation, but I was stuck. In fight-or-flight mode, I was ill-equipped for either.

As I readied to defend myself, he yelled "Celia!" and ran past, not even noticing my aggressive pose. He roughly embraced a woman behind me, enveloping her in a bear hug.

I quickly lowered my weapon, crouched, and manually released my other binding, leaving the skis and poles on the ground where they fell. I lumbered toward the lodge.

Suddenly, a spray of snow hit my legs. I looked up to find Gray nearly upon me and Dave close behind.

"Jerome, you do realize it's poor form to leave your skis on the ground like that?" Gray asked.

"Spiffy looking sticks," said Dave. "Where'd they come from?"

I lurched back toward the rack. "Oh, these?" I said, picking up the skis and poles and tucking them between two dowels. "I, uh, rented them. My skis just weren't cutting it."

"Sweet," said Dave. "Where are you going? Don't you want to take another run?"

"Nah, I need a break," I said. "Going to get me a hot chocolate."

"Makes sense," said Dave. "Drive 150 miles to go skiing, then spend the day in the lodge. Did you bring your knitting?"

"Maybe I did," I said petulantly. But they had already moved out of earshot, gliding toward the lift. I stomped into the lodge bar, my day on the slopes officially over.

When Dave and Gray returned to the condo hours later, they found me fast asleep on the couch. Their clatter startled me awake. Groggy, I had no clue whether the dim light represented dawn or dusk.

"Slacker! Get the fuck off that couch before I knock you off," yelled Dave.

"David, my good man. Let's observe the maxim about sleeping dogs and let him lie," said Gray.

"That dog don't hunt," said Dave. "Don't ski either."

"You're mixing the metaphors," replied Gray.

"Actually, old chap, he's not," I said, flinging the blanket aside. "Your metaphor involved untruthful canines—dogs lying—and Dave's involved lazy canines—dogs not hunting. Slander and sloth among dogs. Completely compatible metaphors."

"Damn straight," said Dave. "Those metaphors were as unmixed as you'll ever find." He fiddled within a kitchen cabinet and extracted bottles of vodka and tonic. "Unlike this pitcher of drinks," he said, simultaneously pouring from each.

I shuffled off to the bathroom, flipped up the toilet seat with my foot, liberated my member, and fired away. Unfortunately, I was still groggy and my aim was untrue. The spray saturated the toilet seat, the tank behind it, and a swath of the floor. I noted that my yellow urine on the blue linoleum created an appealing shade of green, so the artiste in me decided not to spoil the effect by wiping it up.

I flushed and then attempted to wash my hands but couldn't seem to coax hot water from the tap. My impatient twisting wrenched the handle from its stem, prompting me to give up and wipe my hands on my pants. Thankfully, my blue jeans didn't turn green. Meanwhile, the toilet continued to run until a jiggle of the handle finally silenced it. I huffed at the state of the facilities. If I had chipped in on the rent of this dive, I probably would have been pissed off at its deplorable condition.

We knocked back a couple of drinks, chasing them with two bags of Doritos. Gray was feeling his oats—or whatever grain is used to distill vodka—and was keen on settling our ping-pong match, so we donned our outerwear and headed for the lodge. Just outside the condo door, I pulled an orange knitted cap from my pocket and yanked it down to my earlobes.

Instead of stumbling down the slope this time, we were led to a nearby footpath by Dave. "Found this secret little trail on my mountain map," he said with pride more appropriate for having discovered a trade route to China.

Dave splayed his crank-powered flashlight across the trail. "Hey, look at this!" He pointed his beam into a little clearing off to the side. "Cool."

Gray and I trudged over for a peek. "What?" I asked. "It just looks like a pile of animal shit to me."

"Where you see a heap of dung," said Dave, "I see a detailed identification marker. You can learn a lot about an animal by its shit. Not only the type of animal, but its diet, health, and ecosystem."

"Pray tell," said Gray.

"This, my friends, is fox scat. Although it looks like a loosely rolled marijuana cigarette, let me strongly caution you against smoking it."

"Duly noted," said Gray.

Dave poked the shit with a stick. "If you look closely, you'll see feathers and bones imbedded within the fecal matter, indicative of bird consumption. Judging from the size of the bones, I think we can presume a small ground bird, like a bobwhite, rather than something larger like a turkey or pheasant.

"Notice how the scat is right out in the open. Some animals hide or bury their shit. The fox, on the other hand, uses it as a territory marker. I would also dissuade you from emulating this particular practice. Tends to turn off the ladies."

"Illuminating lecture," I said. "Shall we proceed?"

We resumed our hike with Dave still in the lead. "When I was a kid," he continued, "I'd spend hours in the woods looking for animal droppings. I could identify an animal by its excrement the way other people can ID a bird by its call."

"So shit is the birdsong of the intestinal tract?" I asked.

I heard Gray sigh heavily behind me.

"Oh, by the way, Jerome, you owe me a huge thank you," said Dave.

"I do?"

"In your absent-minded stupor, you left your rental skis out on the rack. Gray and I saw them after our final run. I did you the favor of returning them to the rental place."

"You *what?*"

"At great personal inconvenience, I dropped them off at the ski rental. A beer or two at the bar tonight would be reasonable compensation."

"Damn it, Dave! What did they say?" I asked, voice rising. "Did you give them my name?"

"Of course, you ungrateful S.O.B. Otherwise, how would they know they were your skis? I gave them your name, phone number, email address, social security number, and mother's maiden name."

"Dave, this is no joke!" I said. "Exactly what did you tell them?"

"Well, truthfully—"

"Never trust a man who starts a sentence with 'truthfully,'" said Gray. "His next words will invariably be a lie."

"Okay, *actually*, then," said Dave. "In fact, I didn't 'say' anything to them. The place was just about to close, so the guy told me to stick a note with your name on them, and they would check the skis in in the morning."

"So they didn't actually check them in yet?" I asked.

"Nope. The skis are standing in the corner by the door."

"Shit!" I said.

"I fail to comprehend your response, Jerome," said Gray. "If those skis were stolen, you would have been responsible."

"They *were* stolen," I said. "And I *am* responsible."

"*No comprendo,*" said Dave.

We entered the lodge. The packed room vibrated from the cacophony of voices. Skiers stood shoulder to shoulder. The fireplace roared. A band ran a sound check in the corner, the drummer striking his drums, cymbals, blocks, and bells in sequence, a single tap upon each. The guitarist fingered atonal, seemingly random riffs, while a roadie conducted a monotone volume check.

Dave grabbed my sleeve. "What do you mean, the skis are stolen?" he yelled into my ear.

"Can't! Hear! You!" I replied.

We grabbed our beers and headed for the stairway. A sign at the top said, *No Alcoholic Beverages Beyond This Point*. We blew right by it.

The decibel level dropped with our descent. Below, we found the ski resort retail district, with an information desk, ski lessons booth, ski shop, and related services, all shuttered for the night. I sat at a bench by the info desk and took a long draw on my beer.

"So here's the deal. My crappy old skis weren't working out. I needed a way to get down the mountain, so I, um, *borrowed* that pair from outside the summit lodge."

"You absconded with someone else's equipment?" asked Gray.

"No, dickhead," said Dave. "Didn't you hear the man? He *stole* them!"

"SHHHH!" I said. "Let's try not to broadcast this, okay?"

"What do you mean, your old skis weren't working out?" said Dave.

"I took a spill and broke out of my bindings. One ski shot down the mountain and straight into the woods."

"Probably went looking for someone who knew how to use them properly," said Dave.

"Considering the age of those skis," said Graham, "that person would have to be deceased."

Dave and Gray attempted a high five, but missed.

"Okay," said Dave. "That accounts for one ski. The other?"

"Flung it," I said despondently.

"Flung it?" asked Dave.

"Flung it," I repeated.

"Say no more," said Gray, in a moment of uncharacteristic empathy. "I've done the same with golf clubs, tennis racquets, fishing poles—"

"Golf carts," said Dave.

"Ahem. Cart, singular," said Gray.

"Driven straight into the water trap by the thirteenth hole, if I remember correctly," said Dave.

"Let's not go there," said Gray.

"Not an option," replied Dave. "You've been banned, remember?"

"Uh, guys?" I said. "Can we get back to my problem, please?"

"Right," said Dave. "So there you are, sprawled out on the slope, ski-less."

"Yup. I wasn't too far down the trail, so I hiked back up to the summit lodge, knocked back a couple of drinks, snatched a pair of skis, and headed for the hills."

"And now you find yourself on the most-wanted list," said Gray.

"I wouldn't be on anybody's list if boy-genius here hadn't attached my name to the stolen merchandise."

"Don't fret over it," said Gray. "There's no such thing as the perfect crime. Even the most sophisticated criminal leaves a clue or two behind."

"Sophisticated criminals don't have dolts for accomplices," I said.

"Accomplice?" said Dave. "How can I be an accomplice when I didn't even know a crime was being planned?"

"Will you keep it down?" I said in a loud whisper. "The crime wasn't planned. It was a crime of passion."

"*Passion?* What, you had a carnal desire for those skis?" said Dave.

"What our petty thief means to say is 'crime of opportunity,'" said Gray. "It was a spur-of-the-moment decision, entirely out of character, which he deeply regrets." Gray turned toward me. "You should be taking notes. Your lawyer may want to use this for your defense."

Beers in hand, we walked over to the rental shop. "There they are!" said Dave in a stage whisper. "Right by the door."

I tried the handle, but, no surprise, it was locked. A wide customer service window, directly beside the door, was protected by a roll-down metal grate. Gray rattled it and found a fair amount of play. "Look!" he said, pulling the grate toward him. "Can you fit your arm in there?"

Suddenly, a man came out of the men's room opposite. He gave an odd stare toward the three of us clustered around the window and then continued on his way.

"Let's regroup," said Dave. We reconvened at the bench around the corner.

"We need lookouts," I said. "Dave, you position yourself at the top of the stairs by the bar. Gray, you go to the foot of the staircase on the far side of the building. Check your phones. Any reception?"

"Four bars," said Dave. "Not unlike the jail cell you may find yourself in."

"Three," said Gray.

"I'm good too," I said.

"The evidence suggests otherwise," said Gray.

"Just for the record," said Dave, "we're now officially accomplices."

"But not accomplished accomplices," said Gray.

"And not compensated accomplices," said Dave.

"Indeed. We're uncompensated, unaccomplished accomplices," said Gray.

"Could you two please shut the fuck up?" I said.

Before we headed off to man our posts, I opened a three-way conference call. "Gray, can you hear me?" said Dave into his phone.

"I can," said Gray. "But only because you're right beside me. I haven't dialed in yet."

"We should synchronize our watches," said Dave.

"First of all," I whispered into my phone, "you don't wear a watch, and neither do I. Second of all—" I looked at my phone, then snapped it shut. "Second of all, there's no timing involved. I simply grab the note off the skis. You guys alert me if someone's coming. Let's not overly complicate this."

I reconnected the conference call, plugged in an earpiece, and dropped my cell phone into my pocket. We moved into position.

"Guard Dog One, checking in," said Dave over the line. "Bad Dog, do you read me?"

"Roger," I said.

"Guard Dog Two, reporting for duty," said Gray.

"Check," I said. "Stand by, ready alert."

I reached the corner and peered around. Coast clear. The rental shop was thirty feet down on the left. Just as I was about to sprint over, my eye caught a security camera perched above the men's room door, directly opposite the rental shop.

"Code red," I said into the phone. "There's an eye in the sky. I'm taking it out."

I flattened my back against the wall and sidestepped toward the camera. A crackling came through my earpiece. "Shouldn't we reserve 'code red' for emergency situations?" said Dave. "And what does 'eye in the sky' mean?"

"It's a security camera," I said. "Code yellow. Moving in to disable."

"Guard Dog Two here. I feel compelled to mention that destruction of private property may be considered a felony if the value exceeds a certain dollar amount. Such as an expensive security camera."

"Roger," I whispered. "Not destroying. Disabling."

As I neared the camera, I took the knitted cap off my head. I pantomimed a throwing motion a couple of times for practice when I noticed a label on the inside. *Jerome Segundo*. I cursed my mother and ripped it out.

I feinted once, twice, then let the hat sail. Bull's eye! The cap landed softly, enveloping the camera.

"Bad Dog to Guard Dogs. Target neutralized."

I sprinted to the metal grates. The door stood just to the left of the window, with a two-foot-wide counter inside the room, separating customers from staff. The skis leaned against the counter on the customer side.

I pulled the grate toward me with my right hand, creating a small opening for my left hand to slip through. The positioning proved awkward, as I needed to reach around to the left, essentially requiring my elbow to bend backwards. I tried holding the grate with my left and reaching in with my right, with a similar degree of difficulty. I grunted from the exertion.

"Guard Dog One to Bad Dog. What's that noise? Are you okay?"

"Minor snafu," I said. "Stand by."

I sat and pulled off my hiking boot. Standing half shod, I yanked on the grate and jammed the boot in. Freed from the need to become a human pretzel, I pressed my face and body against the wall, thrust in my right hand, and reached around. I could observe my disembodied hand through the glass, my fingers tantalizingly out of range of the note taped to the skis. I slid toward the grate to extend my reach. Inches to go. I got on my tiptoes, stretching every tendon from my shoulder to my fingertips.

"Oh my freaking God!" squealed a female voice. The sound startled me. My elbow hit the boot. It popped out of place, and the grate snapped shut, entangling my arm.

I turned my head to see a vaguely familiar-looking female standing by the door, pointing at the stolen merchandise. "Those skis!" she said.

"Code red! Code red!" said a voice in my earpiece. "Female approaching from outpost one!"

"Those are my boyfriend's skis!" said the girl in a high-pitched voice. "They were stolen this afternoon. Oh my God, I can't believe I found them. Those skis cost 1,200 dollars!"

"Twelve-hundred dollars?" I said in disbelief. "Damn!"

The girl looked at me as if for the first time. "Um, what are you doing?" she asked. Cheek pinned against the wall, sleeve snagged on the security grates, I appeared the very definition of red-handed.

"Would you mind?" I asked, nodding toward the grate. "I'm kind of stuck here."

"Oh, I'm sorry," said the girl. "I was so excited about finding the skis I didn't even see you!" She pulled on the grate, and I extracted my arm, slightly tearing my shirt in the process.

"Bad Dog! Bad Dog! Come in! Can you hear me?" crackled my earpiece.

"Bad Dog, over and out," I said into the microphone. I ripped the piece from my ear and stuffed it into my pocket.

"I'm sorry?" said the girl.

"Oh, just my friends making a prank call. Juvenile stuff." I stuck out my hand. "Jerome Segundo."

"Oh, um, Michelle Perth. Nice to meet you." She looked at me quizzically as I stood rubbing my arm. "I don't get it. How did my boyfriend's skis wind up here? And what were you doing just now?"

I replied in a rambling, rapid-fire stutter: "Oh, well, I, um, truthfully, I found your boyfriend's skis in the woods earlier today and I dropped them off here so they could be returned to their rightful owner but I realized later that I never gave my name to the rental guy and I thought I should in case your boyfriend wanted to thank me or give me a reward or something although I didn't know he was your boyfriend at the time so I came back here to put a note on the skis only the place was closed so I was reaching through the grate to tape the note onto the skis—really slick skis by the way; ride like a dream I hear—see, the note is right there on the skis—when you came by and scared the crap out of me and—"

"Yo! Bad Dog!" yelled a voice from the end of the hall. Michelle and I turned to see Dave running toward us.

"Tally ho!" shouted Gray, approaching from the opposite end.

"What the hell happened to you guys?" I asked, momentarily forgetting about Michelle's presence. "Fall asleep at your post?"

"Sorry," said Dave sheepishly. "I just went over to the bar to grab a beer when this lovely lady waltzed by, apparently on her way to the powder room." Dave turned to Michelle. "Hello. David Deng. Pleasure to meet you." He extended his hand.

"You too," said Michelle, shaking it.

"You wouldn't happen to be a dancer, would you?" asked Dave. "I couldn't help but notice how gracefully you moved down the staircase."

"Well, actually, I did dance a bit when I was younger," said Michelle, faintly blushing and clearly pleased.

"She has a boyfriend," I said to Dave.

"Yes I do!" said Michelle brightly. "And your friend Jerry here found his skis!"

"Jerry?" said Gray and Dave in unison.

"Yes, Jerry found my boyfriend's skis! In fact, he was just attaching a note with his name on it when I came by."

Dave and Gray shot me accusing looks. I smiled and tilted my head charmingly. "What can I say? Heroism comes naturally to me."

"How did you ever stretch so far to attach the note?" asked Dave. "That's fantastic. Must be your reed-like arms."

"Yeah, I'm sort of a superhero," I replied.

"My boyfriend is right upstairs in the bar!" said Michelle. "Come meet him. I'm sure he'll want to buy you a beer at least!"

"At least," said Gray with an ominous tone.

We moved toward the stairway when Dave nudged me. "Your eye-in-the-sky?" he said.

"Oh, yeah." I ran over dribbling an imaginary basketball, jumped in classic Jerry-West-logo style, twisted 360 in midair, dislodged the cap with my fingertips, caught it on its way down, tripped, tumbled, somersaulted, and bounced up, cap in hand. I rushed back to join my friends.

Michelle led us through the boisterous crowd toward a picnic table at the far end of the room. Two unnaturally bulked up men sat on a bench with their backs to us, one scrutinizing his cell phone, the other deep-kissing a woman seated kitty-corner to him. Dave elbowed me as we approach. "We've got some serious 'roid rage potential here," he said. An empty bench ran between the long edge of the table and the back wall.

Michelle rushed over. "Benny! Benny! You won't believe it! I found your skis!"

Michelle plopped herself into a chair beside her boyfriend. Gray, Dave, and I stood awkwardly in the background as Michelle told her tale. "... and Jerry here, he's the one who found them!"

With Dave and Gray discreetly shoving me at the small of my back, I moved forward and extended my hand. "Jerome Segundo." Benny's grip nearly buckled my knees. His forced smile revealed perfect, gleaming teeth. I rode along for a couple of vigorous pumps, then attempted to extract my hand. Benny was unrelenting.

"So, how'd you happen to wind up with my skis?" he asked.

"Well, um, Benny, truthfully—"

"Yeah, Jeromeo, I'm a little unclear on the details myself," said Dave. Gray jabbed him with an elbow.

"Jeromeo?" said Benny. "I thought Michelle said Jerry."

"Yeah, no, it's actually Jerome. My friends are just trying to be funny in an ironic, sarcastic kind of way. Seeing as cause I don't have a girlfriend at the moment."

Benny kept squeezing.

"Um, could I have my hand back now?" I asked.

Benny released his grip. "No girlfriend, huh? What do you think of my girlfriend?"

"Benny!" said Michelle, giving him a little shove. He tensed and glared at her.

"She's gor—, uh, she's beau—, um, I'm sure she's a perfectly adequate girlfriend," I said.

"We really must be going," interjected Gray. "Early curfew tomorrow."

"Ski team," said Dave.

Michelle's girlfriend extricated her tongue from her boyfriend's mouth and whispered something to him. He suddenly improved his posture, narrowed his eyes, and scanned me from head to toe.

"And what team would that be?" asked Benny, lip curling. "You boys don't exactly look like athletes."

Gray stiffened. "Beg pardon?"

"That accent," said Benny, rotating his head on his massive neck to lock in on Graham. "What are you, some kind of illegal?"

"No, no, he's total Americano," I replied quickly. "That's a mid-Atlantic accent. His mother's from Boston; father's from Liverpool. His accent wound up smack dab in the middle of the Atlantic Ocean."

"Yeah. Notice the drowned vowels," said Dave.

"And the saturated diphthongs," I said.

"Actually, I attended university in London for a spell," said Gray. "Picked up a bit of the accent during my stay."

"Bloody contagious, that accent," said Dave, affecting his best Cockney lilt.

"Spot on," I said in mock Liverpudlian. "Contagious like the bleedin' flu."

"So, you guys are Brits," said Benny. "No hard feelings, even though we kicked your red-coated butts in that war, right?" Dave, Gray, and I looked at each other.

"Okay, you English bulldogs," said Benny. "Sit!"

We remained standing.

Benny moderated his tone a bit. "Hey, the least I can do is buy a beer for the guy who found my skis, right? Sit!"

In sequence, Dave, Gray, and I slid along the open bench, our backs against the wall.

"So," said Benny, casually cracking his knuckles, "tell me. Exactly how did you wind up with my two-thousand-dollar skis?"

"Two thousand? Michelle said they cost twelve hundred."

"Whatever," said Benny.

"Well," I said, "I was riding up the chair when I spotted something just off the trail in the woods."

Benny's bulky buddy leaned over and whispered into his ear.

"I wasn't quite sure what it was," I continued, "so I skied down that way to check it out. Lo and freaking behold, it's your bright red, spanking new Elan skis, stuck in a snow bank. I suspect the guy who stole them planned to come back after dark to fetch them. Probably didn't realize that you could see them from the lift."

Benny glared at me through slitted eyes.

"Hey, if you want to stake out the spot later tonight," I said, "my friends and I will be glad to join you."

"Yeah, surveillance," said Dave. "Our specialty."

"You didn't happen to be up at the summit lodge today, did you?" asked Benny.

"Summit lodge?" I replied. "No, nope, not me. Don't even know where that is."

"I'd hazard a guess that it's at the top of the mountain," said Gray, unhelpfully.

"Cause Gloria here"—Benny nodded toward his buddy's girlfriend—"says she saw you up there sitting at the bar."

"Nope, couldn't have been me. I never drink before noon. And I never drink alone."

"Who said anything about the time?" said Benny.

"Or about being alone?" said his friend, uttering his first audible words since we arrived.

Dave leaned forward and asked, with a slight edge to his voice, "What, exactly, does the summit lodge have to do with your stolen skis?"

Benny leaned in from the opposite side and replied in a matching tone, "That's where they were stolen from, dickhead."

Gray put down his mug with a solid thump. "Why, pray tell, would my good friend here return your skis *and* put his name on them if he were trying to steal them?"

Michelle tugged on Benny's shirt. "Benny, you need to calm down," she said. "Remember what happened last time."

"Benny, Benny, Benny," I said. "You are one suspicious dude. If I wanted to steal your skis, I'd already have them posted online instead of bringing them to the lost-and-found. This is the thanks I get for doing the right thing?"

Benny turned a shade of purple. Veins sprouted from his temple. He rose from the bench, grabbed the underside of the table, and thrust it into Gray, Dave, and me, pinning us against the wall. Our beers careened down the slope, splattering us on their way to the floor. Benny's goon friend joined in, pushing his barrel chest against the table edge, doubling the pressure. Bar patrons turned their heads and instinctively moved away from the commotion, creating our own little island of antagonism. The noise level dropped in anticipation of a brawl.

"You were saying?" said Benny.

We were trapped and helpless, our arms immobilized, our legs flailing pathetically.

"Listen to me, Benny," I said in a choked voice. He and his friend eased off slightly. "The bartender's calling the police. Unless you want to tell the cops how those steroids and syringes wound up in your duffle bag, you better ease off."

Benny growled and increased the pressure. I gasped as the air was forced from my lungs. Michelle pounded against Benny's bicep. He elbowed her away. Benny's friend was the first to comprehend. "The cops? Benny, that's not good."

Benny gave one final shove, then released. The table dropped to the floor. Dave, Gray, and I all inhaled sharply.

Benny grabbed Michelle's arm, picked up his duffle, and turned to his buddy. "C'mon, we're out of here." They pushed their way roughly through the crowd.

A wave of palpable relief washed over our end of the room, and the noise level inched back upward. We sat there, licking our wounds.

"I guess we're the saturated diphthongs," I said morosely, sopping the beer from my shirt.

"'Steroids and syringes'?" said Dave. "How'd you come up with that?"

"Lucky guess," I said.

Neither Gray nor I could muster any enthusiasm for our ping-pong rematch. Although we agreed to call it a draw, we realized the unspoken truth. We were both losers.

Chapter 4

Year 2 | Winter

The afterglow of the ski trip was short-lived. One can only revel in the joys of petty thievery and abject humiliation for so long. Inevitably, it's back to harsh reality.

The letter I composed to my parents seeking financial support sat unmailed on my table. My bank account exhausted, I was down to the balance in my spare change jar. Time for decisive action. I grabbed my last fistful of coins and marched to the post office to buy a stamp.

"First class, please!" I said authoritatively to the clerk as I handed over my envelope.

He dropped the letter onto his digital scale. The display flashed between 1.0 and 1.1 ounces several times before settling on one ounce even.

"Right on the cusp," said the clerk. "A hair more and it would have cost you two stamps."

"My lucky day," I said. As I fished for the change in my pocket, my good fortune continued—a penny to spare. I pushed the coins across the counter. The clerk tore a stamp from a sheet and dropped it onto the scale alongside the letter. The weight of the stamp tipped the balance. The readout again flashed between 1.0 and 1.1 and this time stopped on the higher number.

"Whoops, looks like you're going to need another stamp after all," he said.

"Wait a minute. The letter itself weighs exactly one ounce, right?"

"Yeah?"

"And only after you added the stamp did it weigh more than an ounce, correct?"

"What's your point?"

I wasn't ready for the question. What, exactly, was my point? I was stumped. This felt fundamentally wrong, but I couldn't articulate why.

"Um, my point is, if I mailed this letter without a stamp, then it would only cost one stamp to mail the letter."

"You can't mail a letter without a stamp."

"No, you don't understand. It's your stamp that's making my letter too heavy. Without the stamp, it would be just fine."

"Like I said, buddy, you can't mail a letter without a stamp."

"What if the stamps that you sold weighed three pounds each? Would I have to pay postage for a three-pound letter?"

"Listen, pal, I got no time for your hypothermial what-ifs. I got a line of people waiting behind you. Are you going to buy the stamps or not?"

"Damn it! I don't have enough money for two stamps!" I grabbed my letter off the scale, swept the change back into my palm, and stomped toward the door. Just before exiting, I turned back toward the postman. "And it's *hypothetical*, you idiot!"

An elderly woman entered through the door I was holding open. "You're hypothetical, dear," she said.

* * *

Down to my final coins, unable to even buy two stamps, I trudged home dejected. As I kicked open the door, my basement studio seemed even gloomier than usual. Dim light struggled to gain entrance through the grimy half-height window. I made a mental note to wash the window followed by the quick self-realization that I never would.

Dropping my phone on the coffee table, I noticed a missed call on the display. Must have come in while I was going postal. The message was from Dave, informing me that one of his colleagues had slipped on the ice and taken a bad fall, with the blow partially cushioned by three months off and a nice worker's comp check.

I called Dave back, and he encouraged me to apply. "Jerome, they haven't even advertised the freaking job yet. You can totally head off the competition."

"I don't know," I said. "I never pictured myself as a flower boy."

"That's flower 'man,' my friend. And the job is as respectable as they come. *Uno,* cool uniform. *Dos,* short shifts. *Tres,* only nice people order flowers. And *quatro,* the van smells great."

To prove the desirability of the position, Dave invited me to join him on a delivery run the next day. I reluctantly agreed.

All night long, I dreamt of flowers. I delivered sorrowful arrangements to widows, sensuous roses to the smitten, and recuperative flora to hospital patients. By the time morning came, I was exhausted.

Seven a.m. sharp, Dave pulled up to my apartment and tapped the horn. I opened the door to the delivery van, and an overwhelming blast of fragrant air accosted me. "Man, it smells like a hooker working overtime in here."

Dave relocated a potted plant from the passenger seat. "You'll be loving the scent in no time."

I appraised my tour guide. Aside from a pink pastel golf shirt with a flower logo on it, Dave sported his usual attire of baggy jeans and well-worn sneakers. "Hey! I thought you said the flower boys got spiffy uniforms to wear."

"You don't consider this shirt spiffy?"

"More like prissy."

"You know, my first day on the job, my boss warned me about dickheads like you. He said that the manhood of flora transport specialists would be called into question by certain ignorami. He said hold your head high, look your critic in the eye, and hand him a rose."

Dave pulled a flower from a suction-mounted vase on the dash, locked his gaze with mine, then thrust the bloom toward me.

"This ain't no rose," I said, squinting at the bright yellow petals. "Even I know that."

"Sorry. I can only give away surplus and rejects."

I stifled a yawn and reclined my seat a click or two. So far the job had two strikes against it—the obscenely early hour and the ridiculously feminine shirt.

"Prepare to turn right," cooed a mellifluous voice from the navigation system.

Dave explained the set-up. "Our dispatcher plugs all the delivery addresses into the computer and uploads them to the van. Then my co-pilot Fiona tells me where to go, so to speak. No maps, no muss, no fuss."

"No brains," I said. "You watch—map reading will be the next casualty of the digital age, along with spelling and phone number remembering. People won't be able to find their way to the corner store without a GPS whispering in their ear."

"What corner store?"

"Right. Bad example. They won't be able to find their way to the local Wal-Mart."

"Have you ever tried to read a map while driving?" asked Dave. "It's a fucking accident waiting to happen."

"Have you ever looked at a map before you started driving, figured out where you are going, then driven there?"

"Hell no. Not for years."

Dave plucked a cup of coffee from the holder and handed it to me. "Black with seven sugars, right?"

"Close enough," I said, taking a sip.

"Okay, Jerome, before we get too far along, we should make sure you're cut out for this kind of work. You'll need to take the standardized florist test."

Captive in the passenger seat, I had little choice but to participate.

"Question one. What's the most popular gift in the world?"

Suspecting a trick question, I rapidly considered various demographic and sociological angles before replying. "McDonald's gift cards?"

Dave slapped his forehead. "Flowers, you dumbass! Flowers! People gift more flowers than the next three categories combined!" He let out an exasperated sigh. "All right. Q number two. Don't blow this one."

"Not a chance," I said, determined to get it right.

"What's the most popular subject in the history of painting?"

"Latex versus oil?"

"Not house painting! Fine art painting!" said Dave, employing several more decibels than necessary. "The muse! The subject!" His hands gripped the steering wheel tightly.

"Sheesh, calm down. I don't know. Buxom Rubinesque women?"

"Jerome, you're shitting me. You're kidding, right? It's fucking flowers, for God's sake! How could you miss it?"

"Sorry, I'm not my best at seven a.m."

Our first stop was a nursing home. Dave pulled to a stop under the entrance canopy of a low-slung building with a faux brick exterior. From the back of the van he lifted a rolling cart, a contraption clumsily retrofitted with iron rings to hold vases and pots, into which he loaded two startlingly colorful bouquets plus dozens of daffodils. With a nod, he indicated I should follow.

The sliding doors of the facility opened with a whoosh, and we entered to a stale, faintly medicinal smell. Dave greeted the receptionist heartily and handed her a flower. He nodded toward me. "This is Jerome Segundo, my assistant." The gal and I murmured pleasantries.

"So, I'm the assistant flower boy?" I said as we rolled down the corridor.

"Assistant *to the* flower boy, Gareth."

I didn't get the remark. Dave constantly dropped inane cultural references into his conversations, bits of dialogue or microfacts gleaned from comic books, TV shows, and movies. For all I knew, Gareth could be the Greek god of flowers. I had long since given up trying to sort it out. It was easier to just let his comments pass.

"Good morning, ladies and gents!" announced Dave in a loud voice. "Beautiful day!" He sauntered down the hallway, smiling, greeting, gently high-fiving, and passing out single daffodils to outstretched hands.

"Mrs. Sampson, how are you today?

"Mr. Doubleday, good to see you!

"Ms. Kennedy, here's a little stalk of sunshine!"

Ms. Kennedy put her hands over her ears. "David, I'm not deaf you know!" she yelled. She lowered her voice. "Course, just about everyone else is."

Dave grabbed two bouquets from the cart and cradled one in each arm. "I've got to deliver these to a couple of rooms. You keep handing out the daffodils."

I grasped a fistful and worked my way down the corridor, zigzagging between rooms on the left and right. "Get your daffodils!" I barked like a ballpark hawker. "Fresh daffodils!"

Each room housed two residents. Although an attempt was made to personalize the space with photos and knickknacks, an institutional feel pervaded. Maybe it was the cheap, wood veneer dressers. Or the metal, hospital-ward-style beds. Or the beige walls dotted with empty nails and yellowing tape. A depressing air hung over the place, like smog over a city.

Until I walked into the room, that is. When I showed up, flower in hand, faces brightened. "New haircut?" asked one elderly man, eyeing me intently.

"Whole new body!" I said.

"Thank you, David!" said a woman in another room, hunched in a chair by the window. "Hey, wait a minute. You're not David!"

"I'm Dave's assistant flower boy," I replied.

"Well, young man, work hard and one day you'll get promoted to a position of authority and prestige, just like David!"

"Yes, ma'am."

I met Dave back in the corridor. He eyed the single flower remaining in the cart. "We missed somebody," he said. "Let's see, fifteen rooms equals thirty residents. Plus one for reception. We brought in 31 flowers, but there's still one left." He scanned the rooms as we walked back toward the entrance.

We approached a room with only one name on the door. A metal bracket intended for a second name was empty. "Oh, fuck," said Dave in a low, concerned tone. He crossed the threshold. "Mrs. Jackson. How are you?" A gray lady sat on the edge of a neatly made bed, hands folded in her lap. "Where's Mrs. Peters? She didn't—?" Dave's voice trailed off.

Mrs. Jackson nodded slowly. "The service is on Thursday morning," she said in a wavering voice.

Dave went over and gave her a hug. "I'll be there." He took the last flower, tucked it into a bud vase, and placed it on the dresser. "I'm so sorry."

We rolled our empty cart down the worn, faded carpet and out the front door. Back in the van, Dave sat for a moment. "Mrs. Peters was a sweet old lady," he said. "Although I guess it's good you saw that. You should understand that delivering flowers isn't pure, unmitigated joy. There are some depressing aspects."

Dave prompted Fiona for our next destination. "In one-quarter mile, turn left," she said in an inappropriately upbeat tone.

"How often do you deliver to the nursing home?" I asked.

"Once a week. We have a standing order for two bouquets from a couple of asshole sons trying to ease their guilt about never visiting their mothers."

"What about all those daffodils? Who sends those?"

"Oh, that's my own little initiative. After my first delivery, I couldn't go back with flowers for just two people while a couple of dozen residents got nothing."

"You pay out of your own pocket? Thirty flowers a week?"

Dave nodded.

"Must eat into your wages," I said.

"Continue on this road for two-and-a-half miles," said Fiona.

I scanned the carnival of colorful blooms in the back of the van. Rather than being uplifted at the sight, I was burdened. This huge collection of blossoms was merely flowers to me. With my gross ignorance of the natural world, I couldn't identify any of the varieties. Sure, I would probably know a rose or a tulip if I saw one, and, thanks to our last stop, a daffodil, but that was the extent of my knowledge. Perhaps dandelions, too, but I suspected nobody was delivering those.

I pondered a bit more and, to my growing dismay, recognized that my woeful ignorance extended to flora taxonomy. Not only couldn't I name the variety of flower, I wasn't even sure if flowers came in varieties. Maybe species? Or were species restricted to animals? Class, phylum, kingdom? Who the hell knew?

There was simply no escaping the vastness of my stupidity. I looked at the trees whizzing past outside the van. I could spot a maple, but only thanks to Toronto's hockey team. Birch, I knew. And I could probably nail a generic pine. Sycamore? Beech? Linden? Not a chance. Rousseau said a person can't truly know something until he can name it. I can't name diddly.

"Rerouting," said Fiona, with just a hint of irritation in her voice.

"Frig," said Dave. "Missed my turn."

Ignorance, I decided, ain't bliss. I made a silent vow to increase my knowledge of the world, starting immediately. "Dave, I need some remedial instruction." I swept my arm in an arc toward the cargo bay. "What do you got back here?"

Dave perked up at the prospect of enlightening me. He tilted his rearview mirror to reflect the panorama. "Do you want to start with the single species or the combination bouquets?"

"I *knew* it!" I said triumphantly.

"Knew what? We haven't even started yet."

"I knew there were *species* of flowers, as opposed to, say, *kingdoms* of flowers."

"A frigging genius, you are. Okay, whatever." Dave drained the dregs of his coffee and cleared his throat. "Hang on for a wild ride through the world of flora. Closest to you are potted perennials: peony, periwinkle, and lavender. These sell well in the winter. Customers will generally keep them indoors until spring, then plant them outside.

"Next are the bulb flowers—hyacinth, lily, narcissus, gladiola, and tulip. These samples are all cut, but they're also popular garden flowers. You plant the bulbs in the fall to bloom in the spring."

"Got it."

"Farther back, more bouquets. The rose, of course, is king. Carnations and chrysanthemums show up in many mixed bouquets too. Then you have your ubiquitous gerberas."

"Never heard of them," I said.

"That's the genus. You've definitely heard of the species below it: sunflowers, daisies, and asters. Staples in many a bouquet. They've been so extensively hybridized that they come in a massive, some would say garish, array of colors."

I was impressed. "How'd you ever learn so much about flowers?"

"Osmosis," said Dave.

"Is that like photosynthesis?"

"Sort of."

"Seriously, how do you keep track of all that kingdom/phylum stuff?"

"Crazy people can't order fresh garden salad," said Dave.

"Huh?"

"It's a mnemonic phrase: Crazy people can't order fresh garden salad. Stands for kingdom, phylum, class, order, family, genus, and species."

"Wow, that's good," I said. "Except crazy doesn't start with a K."

"I know. It's a crazy spelling."

"I have a mnemonic phrase stuck in my head from fifth grade," I said. "Most great statesmen have never committed blatant perjury."

"Fucking eh," said Dave. "Totally mnemonic. What's it stand for?"

"Can't remember."

As we tooled down the back road, I repeated the taxonomic mnemonic in my head. Krazy people can't order fresh garden salad. Krazy people can't order fresh garden salad. Krazy people can't order fresh garden salad.

Dave hummed a low tune.

"Remind me," I asked. "How long have you been doing this job?"

"Well, I started freshman year in college, so going on five years now."

"And how long do you plan to stick with it?"

"Indefinitely. It's good work. I like it. I see no reason to change."

I suspected as much. Since I first met Dave in college, he'd been a do-just-enough-to-get-by kind of a guy. No ambition. No grand vision. Satisfied with what he's got.

"But Dave, isn't this kind of a dead end? Are you going to schlep flowers for the rest of your life?"

"Oh, for Christ sake, Jerome! You sound like my fucking parents. You aspire to something greater? Then by all means, go for it. But leave me out of it. I've got a stress-free job that makes people happy and pays the rent. What more could I want?"

"Dave, you live with your parents. You don't pay rent."

"False on both counts. I live in an apartment above my parents' garage. A *detached* garage, I might add. And I do pay rent. Ten percent of my earnings."

"That's your rent—ten percent?"

"Yep."

"So if you earn ten bucks in a month, you pay one dollar in rent, no questions asked?"

"Impressive arithmetic. Did you do that in your head?"

"That's a cozy arrangement. Why work at all?"

"In work, there's dignity. And speaking of dignity, you can go fuck yourself."

We traveled in silence for a few minutes, until Fiona chimed in, "Your destination is 100 yards ahead on the right."

I saw nothing but trees on either side. "Private home delivery," said Dave. "Exclusive neighborhood. Rich as cow manure."

That was the beauty of Dave. I'd have a heated exchange with him one minute; the next minute, it was forgotten. Either he had short-term memory problems or he forgave quickly. Either was fine by me.

We turned into a long and winding driveway, marked only by a granite stone obelisk bearing the number 169. At least I think it was granite; maybe marble? A quarter mile in, a large home came into view. Dave wheeled around a circular gravel driveway, the tires making a satisfying crunching sound.

We stopped at a grand façade flanked by Dorian columns. At least I think they were Dorian; maybe Ionian? The phrase Ionian pentameter came to mind. Architecture? Poetry? Music? I hadn't a clue. My brain was a maddening jumble of cultural illiteracy.

At the rear of the van, Dave pulled out a dozen red, long-stem roses. "Plus one black rose," he said. "Genetically modified."

I whistled. "Dazzling. What, exactly, does the single black rose symbolize?"

"Usually it's a cry for forgiveness. It means, 'I'm a good-for-nothing bastard. I'm sorry. Please take me back.' Nine times out of ten, it's from a man trying to make amends."

"The hidden psychology of flora," I said. "I'll never look at a bouquet the same way again."

Dave pressed the button. Eight bells chimed in Big Ben sequence inside the foyer. As we waited, I appraised the premises. A thin layer of snow covered an expansive front lawn that gently sloped away from the house toward a small, concrete pond. Next to the water, a grove of nearly identical trees—a small apple orchard perhaps? Or maybe pear trees?—stood in tidy rows. Through the denuded branches sat a tennis court, its net slightly sagging. "Honestly! You'd think the groundskeeper would have brought in the net for the winter," I said with faux snootiness.

"One would've thought," agreed Dave.

After thirty seconds, he pushed the bell again. "Must be the butler's day off," I mused.

We were about to leave the flowers in the portico when the heavy inner door swung open. Through the ornate, wrought iron outer door we saw a woman, apparently in her early thirties, wearing a terrycloth robe and a towel wrapped around her head.

"Flower delivery!" said Dave with the good cheer of an ice cream man.

She looked critically at us, then at our wildflower-festooned van. "ID?"

Dave tucked his official florist identification card, hanging from his neck on a lanyard, through the ironwork. She glanced at it, then looked at me. "And him?"

"My apprentice," said Dave.

The woman unlocked the wrought-iron gate and pushed it gently toward us. We stepped back to let it swing by, and Dave extended his arm to offer the flowers.

"Come in. It's freezing out there," said the woman.

In the foyer, twin staircases curved elegantly upward, joining at a top landing overlooking the entranceway. A crystal chandelier sent fragments of light skittering across the polished wood floor and the bright white walls. A large parlor with overstuffed furniture was situated through an archway to our left; a library with floor-to-ceiling bookshelves behind mullioned glass doors to our right.

"Is there a card?" she asked. Dave handed her a small red envelope, which she tore open haphazardly. "That bastard!" she said, almost instantaneously. "If he thinks this is going to patch things up, he's stupider than I thought." She ripped the card decisively, repeatedly, bordering on maniacally, until the tiny pieces fell like snowflakes to the floor.

We stood awkwardly for a moment as the woman fumed. Finally, Dave broke the silence. "Shall I put these roses in water for you?"

"You can flush them down the toilet for all I care!" she said, eyes afire. She took a deep breath. "I'm sorry. He just makes me so angry."

She looked at the bouquet and ran her hand along one of the stems.

"Careful of the thorns," said Dave.

The woman turned on her heel and walked toward an archway under the balcony. "This way."

Dave dutifully followed, and I brought up the rear. The woman glided through double swinging doors to reveal a massive kitchen. Painted clay tiles covered the floor; a huge island dominated the center; gleaming copper pots dangled from a rack. The back wall contained a sweep of windows overlooking a patio and a kidney-shaped swimming pool, drained and glittering with snow and ice.

The woman's towel-turban had loosened. As she reached up to rearrange it, my eyes were drawn to her shapely figure, accentuated by the terrycloth robe. I realized I was staring and averted my gaze before she noticed. Out of the corner of my eye, I thought I saw her discreetly widen the cleavage on her robe.

As Dave filled a large glass vase with water at the sink, the woman sidled up next to him. She steadied the glass container as he began to insert and arrange the long stems, her right breast pressing lightly against his bicep. "Let me tell you what my soon-to-be-ex-husband did, and you can tell me if I'm overreacting."

Suddenly, the woman remembered I was in the room. "Um, I wonder if you could get your apprentice to clean up that paper in the foyer?" She fished a dustpan and brush from under the sink and handed them to Dave, who shuttled them over to me. "Grunt before glory," he said in a whisper.

I exited. The door swung closed behind me, and the woman's voice diminished to a murmur. Back at the grand foyer, I took my time sweeping up the scattered bits of paper. I was nearly done when Dave appeared in the doorway.

"Um, this is kind of awkward, but would you mind waiting for me in the van?"

"Oh wow!" I said, keeping my voice low and trying to curb my enthusiasm. "You didn't mention the fringe benefits!"

"Don't be a dickhead, Jerome. She's in a lot of emotional pain, and she needs to talk it through."

"Uh-huh. I'm sure she does." I scooped up the rest of the paper, handed the pan and brush to Dave, and winked at him. "Take your time, my friend," I said. "However long you need to provide that, *ahem*, emotional support."

I headed for the van. The massive oak door clicked shut behind me.

I was reclined in the passenger seat, dreaming fragrant dreams, when Dave returned. He hopped into the van, turned the key, shifted into gear, and started rolling down the driveway before I'd shaken the cobwebs out.

"We need to make up for lost time," he said. "Fiona, where to?"

"Calculating route," she replied.

I raised my seat to the upright position and strapped myself in. Dave hummed an off-key tune to himself. I was annoyed by his smug good mood.

"Okay, true confession time, Davy boy. I want every steamy detail."

"Jerome, remember when you asked me to reveal the secret of my success with women?"

"Of course I remember. The Aretha code: R-E-S-P-E-C-T."

"Correct. But that was only one of the principles. I would have told you more, but you didn't seem ready to advance to the next level."

"I needed to kiss before I could screw?"

"Perhaps, but counter to the spirit of my advice."

"I needed to smile before I could laugh?"

"Closer."

"I needed to play Raffi before Rachmaninoff?"

"That sounds about right."

"Okay, maestro, start conducting."

"Rule number one: respect."

"Got it."

"Rule number two: trust."

"Don't got it."

"Here's a real-life example to illustrate rule number two. Even if I had helped to ease Nadia's psychic pain—"

"Nadia?"

"Over her husband's affair—"

"Her husband had an affair?"

"By making mad, passionate love to her on her satin sheets in her four-poster bed, which, for the record, I did not, I would never betray her trust by revealing such intimate information to anyone."

"You dog!" I said. "Wow. Nadia on satin sheets. That must have been incredible."

"Jerome, you're totally missing the point."

"Oh, no I'm not! The point is, I need to get my job application in right away before somebody beats me to it. Fiona, take us home!"

A buzzing sound arose from the back of the van. I glanced over my shoulder but saw only flowers. Dave seemed not to notice.

We returned to Dave's apartment after our hard day's work. It was only noon—he worked a five-hour shift—but it felt like six p.m.

Dave moved into the apartment above his parents' garage during his junior year in high school and never left. Why would he? Except for the self-respect and independence aspects, it was a sweet deal. He paid almost nothing for rent, didn't worry about maintenance or repairs, raided his parents' refrigerator whenever he felt like it, and had his dad do his laundry, his parents having one of those quirky marriages where the man shares equally in the chores.

The place fit Dave's personality: an orange shag rug popular during a decade known primarily for its poor taste; kitschy yellow plaid curtains that his mother made; a motley collection of hand-me-down furniture from countless generations of Dengs.

Despite its random thrown-together look, Dave kept the place tidy. "My girlfriend likes a neat apartment," he explained. I had no idea which girlfriend he was speaking of.

Cracking a beer, I glanced into the small bedroom off the living room and saw an impeccably made bed. "Just get discharged from the Marines or what? Looks tighter than a condom."

"Hospital corners," said Dave. "The secret to a well-made bed. Plus I just changed the sheets, so they're more snug than usual."

"You change your sheets? Jeez, that's impressive. I don't think I've ever changed mine."

Chapter 5

Year 2 | Spring

I got my flower-boy application in quickly, but my speed proved irrelevant. The florist's son preempted me. My fantasy of workdays lined with satin sheets vanished, and the vice grip of unemployment continued its unrelenting clench.

My gloom teetered on the brink of despair when I finally caught a break. I was watching the Humiliation Channel on TV, where a white guy was getting verbally abused by his black girlfriend for leaving the toilet seat up or something. As he groveled shamelessly to get back into her good graces and warm bed, I cringed at the spectacle and felt embarrassed for my gender. Thankfully, the phone rang and broke the thrall. It was the human resources director at the Sunshine School, a residential and educational program for handicapped children. I had interviewed there over a month ago during an energetic flurry that had me filling out applications at a hardware store, a deli, and a pizza joint.

The offered position was entry level, requiring only a high school diploma and a willingness to learn on the job, but I didn't mind being over-qualified. It was gainful employment, and every penny of the lowly wages they paid was a penny I wasn't making before.

"Come, meet the students!" the teacher exclaimed as I entered the brightly decorated classroom clutching my freshly inked employment papers. In a corner, a boy of indeterminate age sat on a frayed yellow rug, head cocked, with the middle digit of his right hand thrust deeply in his ear and the fingers of his left waving rhythmically at the fluorescent light. The teacher reached down to dislodge one hand and calm the other.

"I'm Maura Wood, the head teacher," she said as I walked over. "I'm sorry we haven't met. I was on vacation when you interviewed."

I extended my hand. "Jerome Segundo."

"That's an interesting last name," said Maura, squeezing my hand a bit longer than social mores might indicate. Her palms were warm, soft, and dry. "Hispanic heritage?"

"Actually, I'm as Anglo as a Saxon," I replied, not knowing what I was saying or what it might actually mean. Maura, graciously, let the inane comment slide. "My family's original surname was Whittaker, but my father thought it was boring and unromantic. He was Jerome Whittaker, Junior, so he changed his name to Jerome Segundo, Junior."

"So that makes you Jerome Segundo the third," said Maura.

"I guess it does. Jerome Segundo Tercero. Has a certain ring to it, no?"

Around the classroom, six students sat in various states of repose: at a table handling textured carpet squares; at a water tray manipulating floating plastic toys; at a desk wearing stereo headphones set at a volume that might be deemed deafening under other circumstances.

The classroom had an exaggerated, sensory-overload feel to it. Gaudy paint coated every stick of furniture. Coarse sandpaper lined one storage shelf; smooth Plexiglas covered another; a knobby bathtub mat lay upon a third. A plug-in air freshener emitted a lavender scent of vertigo-inducing potency. A vibrating recliner sat in a corner, all abuzz despite being unoccupied. Posters filled with dizzying optical illusions papered the walls.

The boy at Maura's feet almost instantaneously resumed his fiddling, and his teacher again leaned over to redirect his attention. As she did, the front of her blouse billowed out to reveal two bare, perfectly shaped breasts. I was momentarily mesmerized. I couldn't tell if Maura caught me staring, but if she did, she seemed unfazed. I blushed. "Um, those are truly exquisite earrings you're wearing," I stammered.

"Thanks," she replied. "They're starter studs. Just got pierced."

I smiled awkwardly.

Maura gestured toward the child. "This is Danny."

It was just my second encounter with the students of the Sunshine School, the first being during the interview process. Getting acclimated to their strange appearances and bizarre behaviors would clearly take some time.

"What's he doing?" I asked.

"That's what we call 'self-stimulation,'" said Maura. "He's compensating for his limited hearing and lack of sight by massaging his ear canal and exciting his retina. It's very common among our population."

She flashed a sly grin. "But then, I suppose even normal people engage in self-stimulation once in a while."

And that was all it took. A sensuous glimpse, a coy remark, and a mere two minutes into my employ, I was smitten.

The children at the Sunshine School embodied a devastating array of disabilities: varying degrees of deafness, blindness, and mental retardation being only the most obvious, cruelly augmented by a grab-bag of psychological diagnoses.

Maura and I reviewed the case files at the end of my first day. "Schizophrenia, bipolar disorder, hyperactivity, attention deficit disorder, paranoia, xenophobia," she said. "Just about the only condition I haven't encountered here is penis envy."

I shot her a surprised glance.

"At least, not in the students," she added.

Attractive and lithe, Maura's every movement bespoke "experience." Walking across the room, brushing back a wisp of hair, crossing her legs, everyday acts became sensuous when performed by Maura. Her black hair, tied in a loose ponytail, framed a face unusual in structure and composition—high cheekbones that appeared a cross between Native American and Asian, and eyes so dark one could barely discern between pupil and iris. Favoring tight jeans and loose blouses, she demonstrably eschewed under-attire on her upper torso, and I suspected, or at least fantasized, a similar practice regarding her lower.

The school was part of a dying breed: a medium-sized facility for about thirty children, a cradle-to-grave program that housed, fed, schooled, and worked its clientele. In size and function, it sat somewhere between the large state institution that was in the process of being phased out and the small community-based residence that was starting to command the bulk of taxpayer resources.

With its pittance pay, demanding work, and difficult population, the school attracted workers who were usually young, single, and idealistic. Teachers needed full degrees and certification, but the qualifications slipped precipitously when it came to the second-tier workers—the classroom aides, the evening attendants, the overnight crew.

Maura held a bachelor's degree in elementary education, an almost irrelevant qualification in this rarefied environment. The institution preferred a special ed degree. Maura landed the job on the promise to continue her studies, but two years later, she had yet to sign up for a course.

Given my rookie status, Maura felt I could benefit from some after-hours tutelage. She had scheduled a performance evaluation of one of the evening staff for that night, and she invited me to come by and pick up a few pointers.

I arrived at the school at the scheduled hour and found the dormitory door ajar. A sound carried faintly from the opposite end of the long hallway, the muffled cascade of running water. "Hello?" I yelled.

A heavy-set attendant poked her head out of one of the dorm rooms. "Looking for Maura? She's in the bathroom with April."

The rectangular-shaped bathroom encompassed three toilet stalls, two sinks, and a bathtub cordoned off with a six-foot divider. I approached the swinging door to the sound of splashing on the other side. I tapped twice and paused. No reply. I urged the door open gingerly.

Maura stood with a white terrycloth towel draped around her neck, dangling over her red silken blouse like a scarf. She wore a gauzy skirt that reached almost to her bare feet. I inhaled the bath-scented air. April, seven years old but appearing much younger, flailed contentedly in the bubble-filled tub, looking like she was buried in a snow bank. Her sightless eyes roamed indiscriminately about the dimly lit space.

"You're alone?" I asked.

She nodded. "Martin called in sick. I'm helping out with the bathing duties."

"I see." Heading off an awkward pause, I commented randomly, "That's a beautiful blouse you're wearing."

"Thank you," said Maura. "It's a Japanese *millefleur* pattern. The fabric is incredibly sensuous to the touch. Here, have a feel." She leaned toward me.

Despite my inexperience, I was no fool—I recognized a come-on when I heard one. My hand trembling slightly, I reached for the lapel near Maura's shoulder blade, slipped my fingers inside, and rubbed the material between my thumb and forefingers. "Lovely," I murmured, adopting my best textile-connoisseur tone.

Sliding my fingers in a bit deeper, I slowly drew my hand down the lapel, pretending to examine the delicate material as it passed through my grasp. The back of my hand lightly caressed Maura's upper torso, following the curvature of her form. Her skin was impossibly soft, more so than the satiny fabric. I paused at the first button, deftly released it from its loop, and continued my deliberate descent. At the apex of her breast, I gently stroked her nipple. Maura pressed her body into mine, kissed me warmly, and teased my tongue. Reaching behind me, she clasped my buttock and pulled me into such a tight embrace I could no longer tell where my pelvis ended and hers began.

This rush of erotic sensation abruptly ended as April gurgled loudly. Maura quickly uncoupled and stepped back to attend to the child.

Wisps of steam arose from the water as Maura knelt before the tub and started affectionately splashing and cooing at her student. A pale band of skin shone between the tail of Maura's blouse and the waist of her skirt. I fumbled with my own garments for a moment, then genuflected noiselessly behind her.

Maura rose from her haunches and, still on her knees, stretched across the tub to retrieve a bar of soap. I lifted the hem of her skirt to discover, with joy but not surprise, no additional impediments. I scooped a handful of soap bubbles from the tub and generously lathered my erect penis. As Maura leaned back, she gasped softly and paused. She then descended slowly, purposefully, settling down with exquisite liquid ease. She arched her back; I kissed her neck. I reached under her blouse and feather-caressed her taut belly. As she relaxed fully, I felt as if I myself had slid into the warm, inviting waters of the tub.

Maura lifted herself up as if to wash the child's hair, then rocked back. She reached up repeatedly to address April anew, first with bubbles, then with toys. Finally, she dropped all pretense of engaging the child, closed her eyes, and held on to the edge of the tub.

Lost in her timeless rhythm, she ebbed and flowed like a tropical tide. I washed ashore on her wave.

Chapter 6

Year 2 | Spring

The classroom seat was so low that my knees were level with my chest, so narrow that, were I to stand, the chair would follow, stuck to my butt like some bizarre appendage.

Opposite me at a similarly diminutive table sat Katie, a deaf, blind, developmentally delayed child, age ten but with the stature of a five-year-old. She had no eyes, just hollowed-out sockets. My initial encounter with her had evoked a horror-film-like response, which I managed to keep bottled up, but after a few days on the job, I was only mildly disturbed rather than completely freaked out.

Between us on the table stood a wooden box with three openings in the cover: square, circle, and triangle. Beside the box sat wooden blocks of corresponding shapes.

Maura walked by and dropped a plastic bag filled with M&Ms on the table. "Primary reinforcers," she said. "Every time Katie shows a desired behavior, give her one of these."

"I get the reinforcer part," I said. "But primary?"

"Primary refers to elemental human needs like food; things that are inherently reinforcing. For our purposes, anything you can put in your mouth is a primary."

She took a single candy out of the bag and fed it to me. "If you get my drift." Maura caressed my cheek, then moved across the room. I couldn't help but follow her shapely frame as she departed.

I turned back to the child and picked up the square. "Okay, Katie, let's start with this one." I placed the block into her hand. She turned it over several times, then put one end into her mouth, sucking on it like a popsicle. I reached out and gently pulled her hand down. "No, Katie, it goes in the box." As soon as I let go, the piece reverted to her mouth. Again I drew her hand away. "Here, let me show you." I took the saliva-covered block, dropped it into the box, and wiped my hand on my jeans. "See? That's how you do it."

Katie, of course, didn't see. Or hear. The absurdity of giving auditory and visual cues to a deaf and blind child dawned on me. I looked around. Luckily, Maura was across the room and didn't notice my ineptitude.

"Okay, Katie, let's try again." I couldn't help myself. I had to talk to the students, even if they couldn't hear me. I took Katie's left hand and guided it toward the box, directing her to feel the overall contours of the container, then moving her fingers to each of the openings. We traced each shape.

Still manipulating her hand, I helped her pick up the circle. We moved in unison toward the box. "Okay, let's try this hole first." We attempted to fit the circle into the triangle slot, followed by the square opening. "Darn," I said. "Doesn't seem to fit. Okay, let's try this last hole." With my fumbling help, she finally dropped it in.

"Yes!" I said triumphantly, raising my arms into the air. Katie sat expressionless, unaware of the magnitude of her accomplishment. I placed an M&M in her palm; she consumed it in a millisecond.

"Okay, now you do it alone," I said, passing her the triangle shape. Katie rolled the piece around in her fingers, then attempted to shove it into her mouth. I was ready, though, and pulled her hand away. She resisted; I countered. The tussle devolved into an arm-wrestling match. Katie was surprisingly strong, and I struggled for control. Finally, she gave up and rested her hand, still holding the block, on the table. I eased my grip. Stalemate.

Then, in a sudden burst, Katie flung the block at me, swept the box to the floor, and stood with a jerk, sending her chair tumbling. She emitted a loud yell and fell thrashing to the floor.

I sat motionless, stunned by the sudden turn of events. Maura came over and surveyed the scene. "Making good progress, I see."

"Actually, she did manage to put a peg in a hole before she melted down," I said.

"Entirely on her own?"

"Pretty much."

"Wow! That's a first. We'll have to record that on her progress chart."

Maura pointed to the clipboard on the wall. At the top of the page the words KATIE and SHAPE BOX were printed in large block letters. A line graph showed months along the horizontal axis. Numbers arose along the vertical, starting at zero and culminating at three. A long flat line ran adjacent to the zero.

"Wow," I said, gazing at the chart. "You've been doing this exercise for how long?"

"Two years," said Maura.

"And today is the first time she ever got one in?"

"That's right. You must be an exceptional teacher." She gave me a little pat on the head. I beamed with pride.

"What do we do about this?" I asked, looking toward Katie, still lying on the floor, sucking her thumb and thrashing intermittently.

"Just ignore her."

After our seven-to-three shift, Maura and I hopped a streetcar two stops to an Irish pub. The dark room stood empty, save the bartender and one lone patron smack in the middle of the long bar. It took a minute to get acclimated after coming in from the bright sunlight. We groped our way toward a booth and sat on opposite sides of the table. I tamped down the urge to sidle alongside Maura to take advantage of the lack of light and patrons.

The 'keep ambled over. Maura ordered coffee; I asked for a stout.

"When it comes to working with severely disabled children," said Maura, "you enter a different time dimension. You can go months, if not years, without seeing a hint of progress."

"Jeez, that's depressing. Two years to learn how to stick a peg into a hole. I can't get over that."

"Depressing? Are you kidding me? You were part of a major milestone. That was the equivalent of a toddler's first step."

"Actually, I have a confession to make. Katie didn't quite do it on her own. She had a little help. I sort of guided her hand."

"What? I thought you said she did it independently."

"Well, she did," I said. "Independently with assistance."

I drank my beer glumly, aware that Maura was disappointed in me. "We'll have to revise the chart," I said. "The data has been falsified. You could get kicked out of the Special Educators Guild."

"If there were such a thing."

We sipped our drinks in silence.

"What's the point?" I finally asked.

"What do you mean?"

"Why are we even teaching her how to fit a shape into a hole? What's it leading to?"

"It's prevocational."

"It's not prevocational," I said. "It's prenatal."

Maura smiled.

"Seriously, what are we training her for?"

"I don't know," said Maura. "Putting keys into locks? Fingers into dikes?"

"Isn't there something more relevant to their lives that they could be taught? Isn't this just busy work?"

"Oh, it's more than busy work," said Maura. "It's what keeps the school afloat."

"What do you mean?"

"When the wealthy benefactors of our little nonprofit make their annual visit, they need to see the students engaged in constructive tasks. If they come in and Anson is light-gazing by the window or Danny is masturbating in the corner, do you think they're going to write that big fat check that sustains the organization that pays our salary?"

"So basically, we teach them the shape box to ensure that we continue to have a job teaching them the shape box?"

"Something like that."

I whistled. "Wow, the cynicism of that concept just boggles the mind."

"It's true of everything we do," said Maura. "The matching, the sorting, the beads, the Legos, the water play. It's all designed to keep up appearances and keep the donor dollars flowing."

"That's totally disillusioning," I said.

"Actually, there's one other benefit," said Maura. "Every minute they spend engaged in classroom activities is a minute they aren't banging their heads against the wall."

She sipped her coffee.

"You have no idea how costly it would be to keep repairing those walls," she said dryly.

Chapter 7

Year 2 | Summer

I rendezvoused with Maura outside The Smoky Escargot, a recently opened, fabulously trendy restaurant. She walked up briskly, slightly out of breath.

"I forgot to tell you," she said. "Judith is pregnant."

We were meeting Judith Spanner, Maura's best friend, for dinner. I tried to muster some enthusiasm for this news about a woman I had yet to meet, but the joy was elusive. "You didn't tell me she was married either," I said, awkwardly pecking Maura on the cheek.

"Don't be a dork. Of course she isn't married. She was artificially inseminated by an anonymous donor. She's a strong, independent, single woman. And she'll make a great mother!"

A "doth protest too much" remark took insipient form in my brain, but I judiciously shunted it aside.

The place was most definitely a "stretch" restaurant, in two senses of the word. One, the prices were well beyond our means. But Maura wanted to splurge, and to accommodate her desires, I was prepared to empty my bank account of my newly acquired wages. And two, the fare was far outside of my realm of experience. I'd never consumed a snail in my life. In fact, the very thought of a slimy mollusk slipping down my throat repulsed me. Were it not for Maura's insistence, I would have remained blissfully unaware of the pleasures of this French delicacy.

We retired to the bar to wait for Judith. "Okay, tell me a bit more about your friend so I'm not totally ignorant."

"Would that there were a correlation, my love," said Maura.

"Huh?" I replied.

The waitress approached and looked directly at Maura. "A glass of mid-list chardonnay for me, and a Shirley Temple for my underage friend."

I straightened out the order, produced the necessary identification, and sent the waitress on her way.

"Okay, here's the cheat sheet on Judith," said Maura. "She's fabulously gorgeous, incredibly intelligent, and charming to a fault."

"How will I ever tell you two apart?" I said. Maura beamed at the remark, while I made a mental note to inform Dave of my rising suaveness quotient.

Maura and I traded small talk while nursing our drinks. Fifteen minutes after the appointed hour, a woman entered the bar, looked around expectantly, brightened when she saw Maura, and waddled over. She was clad in a leather skirt that hung to mid-shin, patent leather boots, the tops of which nearly met the skirt hem, and a leather vest over a sleeveless white T-shirt. Her straw-colored hair was pulled back so severely it served as a de facto facelift, stretching her skin over a gaunt, but not unpleasant, facial framework. She had a large leather bag strapped over her shoulder.

"Judith, I'd like you to meet Jerome," said Maura. "Jerome, Judith."

"You must have slaughtered a whole herd to come up with that outfit," I said with a smile, trying to keep the charm-offensive alive. Unfortunately, the charm portion failed.

Judith scowled. "In fact, except for a recent binge on steak *tartare*, I'm a strict vegan," she said in a voice redolent of whiskey and cigarettes. "This purse comes from the bark of the cork oak tree; my vest is made from kelp; and my skirt is pure naugahyde."

"Yikes, sorry," I said. "Just trying to lighten the atmosphere."

"Speaking of atmosphere," said Judith, darting her eyes nervously, "can I smoke in here?"

"I hope that's a joke," said Maura. "Surely you're not smoking with child?"

"I've cut way back," said Judith, fidgeting with an unopened pack.

"You know, I don't believe I've ever seen a skirt with a pregnancy panel," I said to Judith, admiring how the garment cleverly accommodated the basketball-sized bulge at her waist.

"I designed it myself," said Judith, warming a bit. "Let me tell you, sewing naugahyde is a bitch. I must have broken a dozen needles on my machine."

I looked more closely. "Wow, velcro attachments."

"Astute of you to notice," said Judith. "I can swap in progressively larger panels as my belly expands."

"Innovative," I said in what I hoped was a sincere tone.

We flagged the *maitre de* to be seated, and he led us from the bar to the dining area. The romantically lit restaurant simply oozed good taste. Comfortably spaced tables, draped in white cloth that grazed the floor, dotted the airy room. Large planters of immaculately maintained ferns were sprinkled throughout, offering color and privacy. In lieu of traditional artwork, the walls contained an eclectic collection of antique mirrors—oval, rectangle, square, and full-length; cracked, mottled, and spider-webbed; all housed in frames ranging from the spartan to the ornate. As I turned my head, I could see Maura's visage from about seven different angles.

The patrons, almost to a one, were white, middle-aged or older, and clearly well-to-do. Our ne'er-do-well air contrasted strikingly, no doubt compelling our host to sit us in a far corner away from the more-distinguished guests.

"I could go for a glass of wine," said Judith, settling into the cushy velvet seat.

"It's one thing to kill your own brain cells," Maura observed. "Quite another to kill the unborn's."

"Yeah, yeah, I know. Can't blame me for fantasizing, can you? In fact, barely a drop of alcohol has passed through these lips since the rabbit died."

Still holding the pack of smokes, Judith tamped them nervously against her palm. "Would you please put those things away?" said Maura. "You can't smoke in here, and you shouldn't smoke anywhere. Why do you even carry them around?"

"I find them calming," said Judith, trying in vain to shove the pack into her overflowing handbag. To make space, she clamped the top shut with two hands and gave the entire bag a violent heave-ho, resettling the contents sufficiently to wedge in the cigarettes.

The waitress approached. Surprisingly, she neither introduced herself nor elucidated the evening's specials, instead offering a mono-syllabic and -tonal query, "Drinks?"

I quickly scanned her name tag. "Well, uh, Celeste," I said, "I'd like a glass of the house Chablis."

"Your second-best chardonnay," said Maura. I gave her a look that said, in so many words, that if she kept climbing the price list with each successive drink, there would be nothing left in the kitty for food. She either missed or ignored my facial subtleties.

"Do you have any fake wine?" asked Judith, glancing down at her protruding belly by way of explanation.

"Certainly, madam. Red, white, or blush?"

"Oh, any color's fine," said Judith with a wave of her hand. "They all taste like crap."

Judith and Maura chatted about onesies and breast pumps. Channeling Dave, I refrained from making any crude remarks and instead excused myself to the men's room.

"So, what do you think?" said Maura as I disappeared around the corner. I paused to listen, just out of sight.

"About what?" said Judith.

"About Jerome!"

"He's awfully young. Robbing the cradle, are we?"

"He's only three years younger than me!" said Maura, mildly offended.

"Kind of a dull boy, isn't he?"

"My, my. Pregnancy making you cranky?" said Maura. "He's not dull at all. He's sweet. He's naïve. He's like a blank canvas. I see him, and I just want to take out my watercolors and paint!"

They changed the subject, so I abandoned my eavesdropping post.

The waitress arrived with the tray of drinks just as I was returning from the toilet. "To new friendships!" I said brightly, raising my glass.

"To new babies," said Maura.

"To nannies and wet-nurses," said Judith.

We touched glasses. Judith and Maura sipped demurely. I took a too-large gulp.

Suddenly, a woman stepped briskly to our table. "Excuse me," she said, addressing Judith in a schoolmarmish tone, "but I couldn't help noticing your condition. Are you not aware of the dangers of fetal-alcohol syndrome? Do you have any idea the damage you're doing to your baby with that wine?"

Judith froze, shocked into speechlessness. Maura appeared calm and composed, except for a look in her eyes that I'd never witnessed—a rising inferno.

"Why thank you so much," said Maura in a falsely pleasant tone, "for protecting the rights of the unborn. I'm happy to tell you, and I'm sure you'll be relieved to learn, that this"—she pinged Judith's wine glass with her petite butter knife—"is non-alcoholic wine. I would note, however, that this matter falls not within your purview, so with all due respect, I cordially invite you to—"

She paused dramatically.

"—FUCK OFF!"

Heads turned. The vigilante gasped and lurched backward. Maura emitted a low guttural sound and brandished her mini butter knife, sending the woman scurrying away.

We sat in astonished silence for a moment. Then Maura broke the quietude. "How gauche," she said in her finest British accent, batting her eyelashes. "How positively barbarian!" We raised our glasses to toast the heathen's retreat.

"The indignity of it all," Maura said, fuming. "I must have a word with the manager about this."

"Maybe you can get us a free meal out of the deal," I said.

Maura went off in search of the complaint department, leaving Judith and me in an uncomfortable void. I cleared my throat, shifted in my chair, and swallowed a sip of wine. After scrutinizing my fingernails for a while, I turned my gaze to Judith, who had taken on a slightly ashen pallor.

"You don't look so good," I said. "Don't let it bother you. That woman was way out of line."

"It's not the woman," said Judith through gritted teeth. "It's morning sickness."

"But it's seven-thirty at night," I said. Judith glared at me, groaned, and hunched over slightly, clutching her belly.

"So," I said, "tell me about the father."

Judith shoved back her chair and sprinted for the ladies room, or as much of a sprint as a nauseated, impregnated, lopsided, cowboy-booted, naugahyde-bound woman can make.

Maura returned and theatrically dusted the imaginary dirt off her hands. "Drinks are on the house!" she said triumphantly. She eyed the vacated seat. "Where's Judith?"

"Bathroom. Morning sickness."

Maura looked perplexed.

"You can get morning sickness any time of day, you know," I explained.

"Darling, don't graze in unfamiliar pastures. You might get indigestion."

Judith returned, still looking peaked. "I'm sorry," she said, clutching her bag with unnerving intensity, "but I can't stay. The smells in this place are overwhelming."

I stood. "A pleasure meeting you—both," I said, gazing at her belly. Judith nodded grimly, and then Maura walked her outside to fetch a cab. I gestured to the waitress for another, hopefully still free, round.

Maura reappeared just as the waitress was depositing two fresh drinks. "Poor thing. She feels like crap. She's going straight home to bed."

"She seems rather high-strung," I said.

"She can be intense. And somewhat quirky."

"You don't say."

Maura perused the menu and informed me that she'd be ordering for us both. I agreed with one caveat. "Just stay away from the weird stuff."

"Might be difficult. I'm afraid they don't have cheeseburgers on the menu."

"They don't? I thought the French were big into cheese."

"They are. But not the individually wrapped, rubberized, day-glow orange, dairy-deficient junk food that you erroneously refer to as cheese."

"That's a totally unfair characterization," I retorted. "I'm fully aware that cheese comes in other forms besides American singles."

"Cheese in a can doesn't count," said Maura.

"Fine. Enlighten me. Order away."

Maura ticked off her selections for the waitress: oysters on the half shell and sautéed escargot for *hors d'oeuvres*; braised spring lamb rubbed with rosemary for herself; filet mignon for me. "And could you bring back the wine list?" she asked sweetly. "I'd like something a bit more upscale."

Whether it was the thought of slimy sea and land creatures commingling in my abdomen or the fear of an astronomical wine bill that sent my stomach churning was unclear.

"Shouldn't you be easing me gently into this new realm of gastronomic delights?" I said. "And, just out of curiosity, is it true that the oysters are alive when you slurp them down?"

"That's what gives them their sexual potency," said Maura. "A dead oyster doesn't provide the same, shall we say, *uplifting* experience." She rubbed my leg with her bare foot.

The appetizers arrived. The live ones looked dead, cadaver gray, embalmed in their own little casket shells, chilling on a bed of ice. The dead ones looked alive, tiny glistening soldiers, ensconced in their armored whorls, marching waist-deep in a pool of herb butter.

"A purist will eschew the *accoutrements* and eat the oyster in its natural state," said Maura. She jabbed the creature with a miniature metal pick and broke its death grip from the shell interior. "*Bon appétit!*"

I watched intently as she lifted the half-shell to her lips, tilted her head back, and tippled the contents. I couldn't tell if she was masticating, tonguing, or gargling with the creature, but clearly she was savoring the experience. She swallowed with a satisfied look. "They go down smooth," she said. "And they never complain."

My turn. I tried to evict the little body from the only home it had ever known, but it held fast. I fumbled with the pick, attempting to get a purchase. Doing so, I tipped the shell precipitously.

"Careful!" intoned Maura. "Those are precious juices!" She took the pick and deftly liberated the oyster. I eyed it warily.

"For my virgin experience," I said, "I may need to accessorize." I spooned on generous dollops of hot sauce and horseradish, then added a massive squeeze of lemon juice.

Maura could barely contain her disdain. "You've ladled so much crap into that shell, you won't even be able to taste the oyster," she said.

"Exactly," I replied.

I hoisted the vessel with trepidation and ingested the entire contents wholesale. The helpless mollusk, dressed up for its execution, felt nary a bicuspid on the way down. Murdering it with stomach acid rather than grinding it to death with my molars may not have been more humane for the condemned but certainly more palatable for the executioner.

Maura watched me with excited anticipation. "So? How was it?"

"It, um, tasted like salsa without the chip."

Maura looked crestfallen. "You know, these are expensive items. The least you can do is eat them properly!" She knocked back another one.

I did chew the snails, if only to hang onto some semblance of manhood. They neither enthralled nor repulsed. They had a rubbery texture that was essentially tasteless but for the herb butter, garlic, and soy sauce they were soaked in.

Maura, on the other hand, was positively enraptured. She moaned orgasmically with each plump little morsel that she popped into her mouth. Her eyes rolled, then closed. She wore a look of ultimate contentment.

When the last shell was empty, Maura looked at the plate with longing and regret. After a moment, she sat erect in her seat. "Tell me your wildest fantasies," she said.

I realized this was no *non sequitur.* For Maura, one sensual experience flowed seamlessly into another. She again gently ran her foot up my trouser leg.

"Okay, let me think for a sec."

Our lamb and beef entrees arrived while I was organizing my thoughts. "Okay, got it," I said. "Number one, making love with twin supermodels. Number two, riding a horse on a tropical beach."

"Oh, Jerome, you devil. How about merging the two? Picture it. Mounting a horse with naked supermodel twins. All three of you on one beast, one in front of you and one behind, charging through the surf."

"I suppose I could accommodate that modification," I said.

"You know, legend has it"—she lowered her volume and leaned across the table—"that a naked woman can derive a great deal of pleasure astride a galloping beast."

Her bare foot slid past my knee.

"Is that so?" I murmured, caught up in the fantasy.

"But you know what?" She suddenly raked her toenails down my leg. "It's bullshit! Another case of male fantasy run amok. Trust me when I tell you that horse's hair is coarse and itchy, and being thrown violently up and down on its bony spine is no picnic either."

"The bitter voice of experience?" I asked.

Maura quickly returned to fantasy mode. Her foot resumed its caress, tickling the inside of my thigh.

In our few months together, Maura and I had become insatiable lovers. Bedroom or restroom, it didn't matter. We had a mild exhibitionist streak—we loved to grope in public. We never actually wanted to be seen with her hands in my pocket—which she scissored out of one pair for improved access—or mine up her skirt—no alterations required—but we wanted to *almost* be seen, hurrying back into a semi-respectable position whenever passers-by came into proximity.

What I only realized later was that Maura hadn't chosen this restaurant for the ambiance or cuisine. She picked it for the tablecloths. Not their brilliant whiteness, luxurious thickness, or frilly edging either. Rather, for the length. The fabric extended nearly to the floor.

Maura slowly traced a meandering pattern that got ever-closer to the intersection of my legs. "Something's come between us," she said. "Anything you can do about that?"

It took me just a second to decipher her meaning. I unbuckled, unclasped, and unzipped, making sure the tablecloth had me adequately covered. I had recently adopted her habit of no underwear, which quickly proved its merits. Her foot resumed its journey, now unimpeded. As I looked across the table at her, Maura locked in my gaze with an odd intensity.

I pried off my shoe with my opposite foot, then reached down and swiftly removed my sock. Maura wore a long, cotton print skirt. I drew circles on her calf with my toes. She widened the aperture between her knees. I tickled her uppermost, innermost thigh, then began to massage her clitoris. Soon, my big toe was thoroughly moistened.

While all this was going on down below, up above we described for each other the pleasures of the meal as we consumed our entrees. From afar, we looked like lovers engaged in earnest conversation. Maura occasionally put down her fork, rolled her eyes, and moaned quietly but emphatically. "Is the lamb really that good?" I asked. "I simply must have a taste."

We managed to finish our main courses and order dessert, all the while stimulating each other under the table. Finally, Maura could take it no more.

"Is anyone looking?" she asked. I discreetly scanned the room. We were tucked in a corner near the back, and no one, it seemed, had a direct, unobstructed view.

"No, you're free to writhe and moan as much as you—" I stopped mid-sentence. Maura was gone.

I gave a quick start when something deliciously warm and wet engulfed me from under the table.

"Maura!" I whispered through clenched teeth. "You can't do this!" I said, wanting her to stop, wanting her to never, ever stop.

She continued, slowly, lovingly, lusciously.

Somehow, despite the trance she put me in, I caught a movement out of the corner of my eye. The waitress approached with our desserts. "Don't move!" I whispered. "She's coming!"

The server placed my plate in front of me and Maura's before the vacant chair. I looked up sheepishly. "Ladies room," I explained, nodding toward the empty setting. "She'll be right ba—aaaakk!" I yelped as a sharp pain emanated from my loin, a stray incisor, no doubt. The waitress looked at me oddly before striding away.

Maura resumed her oral caresses. Soon, she dexterously urged the last drop of passion from me. She must have somehow simultaneously pleasured herself, for when I gave her the "all clear," she popped up in her seat like a happy jack-in-the-box, fully composed and serene. "Lovely bouquet," she opined, swirling the wine under her nose. "Should complement that little appetizer quite nicely."

In the glow of the after and the wine, we savored our desserts one sweet bite at a time. Maura consumed a chocolate torte; for me, half a roasted pear with vanilla ice cream. I fed her a sample of mine, and she returned the favor.

The waitress arrived with the bill and, for the first time all evening, focused her attention on me. I handled the black leather folder with trepidation, hoping that my meager wages would cover the expense. I knew that the outcome hinged on Maura's deal with the manager. All that expensive wine would surely break the bank.

I cracked the folder and took an involuntary breath at the charges: one glass of nonalcoholic wine plus six glasses of increasingly expensive vintage pushed the bill easily into three figures even before the food was tallied. I scanned the register tape with rising dismay. The appetizers, main course, and desserts added up to the equivalent of a month's salary. I was about to enter full-blown panic mode when my eye reached the bottom of the bill—a credit for all the beverages. I had it covered!

"It's on me," I said, slipping my card into the folder and crisply snapping it shut. My bank account had been ravished, but then again, so had I. Every penny I had to pinch was worth it to indulge—and participate in—Maura's sexual-gastronomic fantasy.

"Thank you. That's sweet of you," she said.

"No, thank you. I'll never think of 'eating out' in quite the same way again."

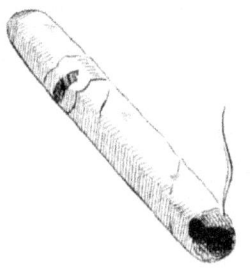

Chapter 8

Year 2 | Summer

"*Jesucristo*, this room reeks," said Dave.

We took up a spot by the door in Pope's Pub, possibly the only remaining smoky bar in the city. Public tobacco use had been legislated out of existence, but this place found a profitable niche flouting the law. The proprietors paid a fine every so often, but smokers flocked here like crows to road kill, more than offsetting the penalties. The room was always packed.

"I love the smell," I said. "Reminds me of my childhood. My mother used to smoke three packs of Marlboro's a day."

"Fine for you. Doesn't your sister have asthma?"

"Yeah. Every time she has an attack she gets all nostalgic too."

We nursed our Guinni, the white foam mesmerizing as it cascaded down the inside of our glasses, drinkable lava lamps. Dave read the sports page on his mobile phone while I tried to break the

beer's hypnotic spell by sucking off the foam. It was a losing cause—
the head was too thick and creamy. I signaled the waitress for a
spoon.

Midway through our second pint, I needed a bathroom break.
The men's room—larger, nicer, and cleaner than my apartment—
sported a trendy industrial design with corrugated metal walls,
stainless steel basin sinks, and a five-foot galvanized trough instead
of individual urinals. A long mirror hung over the *pissoir*. My uric acid
streamed against the hard metal, almost evoking a gurgling brook in a
sylvan glade, but not quite.

After a quick shake and tuck, I snagged my fly on a thread. I
was still attempting to zip when I returned to the table.

"You planning to drink with that unwashed hand?" said Dave,
observing my groin-area machinations.

"These hands?" I placed my palms on the counter, then lifted
them while holding my fingers flat. Eight knuckles cracked loudly in
unison.

Dave cringed. "You motherfucker. The only reason you do that
is to annoy me."

"Untrue," I said. "It's a range-of-motion issue. If I don't
periodically crack them, my fingers feel stiff."

"You'll know stiff when the arthritis sets in," said Dave.

The threat of that debilitating joint disease had done little to
dissuade me from years of near-obsessive knuckle cracking, any more
than the prospect of lung cancer breaks cigarette addiction. I'd been
a compulsive cracker since the seventh grade, when I first realized
that spontaneous joint pops in response to normal movement could
be deliberately reproduced. The recoils of my classmates soon forced
the habit underground, or, more accurately, under desk, where I
would interlock my fingers and turn my palms outward, clearing my
throat at the exact moment to mask the sound. The surreptitious
nature of the act made it even more pleasurable, so much so that the
supremacy of this particular form of self-stimulation remained
unchallenged for two years, until finally surpassed by my discovery of
the joys of masturbation, which, at its essence, is just the
manipulation of another joint.

I rotated my wrists to extract a final pair of pops.

"See that woman over there?" I asked, tilting my head toward a solitary female across the room.

"That fabulously good looking woman?" said Dave. "Why? Planning on accosting her with one of your patented charm offensives?"

"Not a chance," I said. "In fact, she's not nearly as pretty as she looks. From here she's gorgeous, but I walked past her on the way to the loo, and she got less appealing with every step. Pock-marked skin. Bleached hair. Bloodshot eyes."

I took a long draw. "So which is it?" I asked, wiping the foam from my lips with the back of my hand.

"Which is what?"

"Is she attractive or ugly?"

"Well, obviously, she's ugly."

"What if I never walked past her, and we only saw her from this vantage point? She'd remain beautiful in our eyes."

"She is what she is," said Dave.

"Okay. So I go into the men's room. A bright bare bulb hangs above the urinal. Totally harsh light. I look in the glass while I'm taking a leak, and I can see every crease, blemish, and pore on my face. Makes me look grotesque."

"Reality is a cruel mistress," said Dave.

"She's not cruel; she's elusive. Because out here in the soft light of the bar, in that mirror right behind your head, I look marvelous, if I do say so myself."

I re-mussed my hair and straightened my rumpled collar before continuing. "So which is it? Am I a grotesque dude with his dick in his hand or a good-looking fellow drinking a fine Irish stout?"

"My money's on the former," said Dave. He attempted to re-engage with his phone, but I wouldn't let him.

"Seriously. Have you ever walked down the street and seen a hot-looking chick ahead of you? You quicken your pace just to get a look at her, and when you catch up, it's totally not what you expect; the front of her doesn't match up with the back of her at all."

"Or even worse, she's a fucking guy," said Dave.

"Exactly! Our perceptions and expectations almost never square up with reality."

"Which is exactly why we hang out in bars drinking beer," said Dave, putting down his empty pint.

"I don't get the connection."

"Beer squares up reality. Booze is the only sane response to an insane world."

"Who said that?" I asked.

"Uh, I did. Sheesh, Jerome, you're more out of touch than I thought." He headed over to the bar for refills.

A flash of unwelcome light flooded the entrance and Graham's lanky frame silhouetted the doorway. "The usual, Davy old boy!" he yelled toward Dave's receding posterior.

Dave returned with the drinks. Graham took a deep breath. "I'm facing a bit of a dilemma. May I speak to you lads—um, 'fellahs'—in confidence?"

Dave and I nodded solemnly.

Graham pressed his thin lips together. "Well, as you know, I've been what you might call unlucky in love as of late."

"If you define 'of late' to mean since puberty, then I'm with you," said Dave.

"Go on," I said.

"It's forced me to do a bit of soul searching. Am I intimidating to women? Is it my intelligence? My wealth? My social standing?" Graham spread his arms plaintively and looked at us.

"Some women find your humility off-putting," I said.

"Oh Gray, Gray, Gray," said Dave. "I hardly know where to begin."

"Actually, I was more interested in Jerome's insights," said Graham.

"Jerome?" said Dave. "What does this dickhead know about women? He just got his first girlfriend in years, and now all of a sudden he's an expert?"

"It's clear that Gray is looking for quality rather than quantity," I said.

"You'd still be jerking off in your basement studio if not for me and my sage advice."

"Your advice was parsley."

"The problem is, Dave, you have a narrow view of womankind," said Gray. "This whole 'respect' theory of yours; it's so, shall we say, shallow."

"Oh, man, you ignorant motherfuckers," said Dave, shaking his head. "So clueless, it's frightening. I wash my hands of you two."

I looked down at my own unwashed hands and instinctively wiped them on my pants. I wondered if Dave was right. "Clueless" seemed a severe assessment, especially applied to someone who has always considered himself more clueful than most.

We simultaneously reached for our glasses and each took a draught in silence.

"Anyway," said Graham, "through a process of elimination, I narrowed the possibilities and determined it's my appearance that's holding me back."

"Shocker," said Dave.

"Actually, to be precise, it's my male pattern baldness. I don't know if you've noticed, but I'm thinning a bit up top." Graham threaded his fingers through his sandy colored hair, wispy in the front with a dollar-coin-sized denuded spot at the crown.

"Shave it off," said Dave. "I hear women are attracted to bald men."

"Urban legend," I replied. "Only athletes and actors can get away with a cue-ball head."

"Doesn't matter," said Graham. "Shaving my head is out of the question. I've got a horribly bumpy scalp that looks like a cratered moonscape. Here, rub my head and you'll see what I mean." Graham leaned toward Dave, who jumped back in alarm, toppling his stool in the process.

"I'll take your word for it," said Dave.

"You know, there are lotions and foam treatments for baldness," I said.

"I've tried them," said Graham. "The formula made my hair stiff. I couldn't blend the hairs together when I combed, so in the end, it made me look like I had even less hair. And it's alcohol based, which dried my scalp and made it flaky."

"Got to love the irony," I said. "Your hair growth treatment makes you look balder *and* gives you dandruff."

"You think that's bad?" said Gray. "There's also Propecia, that hair growth pill. Only problem is, one of the side effects is erectile dysfunction. So you take the pill to be more attractive to women, but then, when it works its magic—"

"You can't deliver the goods," said Dave.

"Oh, man, what a beautiful paradox," I said. "Dave, this is exactly what I was talking about earlier. Unmet expectations. Perception and reality."

Dave and Gray looked at me, expressionless.

"Don't you see what I'm saying?" I pleaded.

"No," said Dave. "But I hear what you're looking at."

Clearly these guys were hopeless, so I turned my attention to the menu, perusing it for some snacks. The enticing combination of four cheeses, ground beef, sour cream, jalapeños, guacamole, and salsas *verde* and *rojo* made the decision easy—nachos *el supremo*.

"Don't be obvious," said Graham after the mountainous plate was fork-lifted over, "but there's a smashing woman sitting at that table across the room."

"Ah, we saw her long before you came in," said Dave. "Jeromeo here said she's not as pretty as she looks."

"Not as pretty as she looks?" said Gray, shoving a loaded chip into his mouth. "That's an interesting concept."

Several pints later, we retired to Gray's condo for a nightcap. Gray bought his two-bedroom suite in a swanky section of town after inheriting a tidy sum when his parents died. At age sixteen, while he was away at boarding school, Gray learned that his folks perished in an avalanche while skiing in Zermatt. The bad news caught him completely off guard; he was unaware they had even gone on the trip. Graham's inheritance was put into a trust fund to be released in stages, a portion at age eighteen, another at 21, and the balance at 25.

Gray had a more-than-comfortable existence growing up, but even he was surprised at the largesse. He never shared the full details with me and Dave, being far too discreet for that, but had dropped plenty of references to the fact that he ranks himself among the idle semi-rich. A lemonade stand he set up as an eleven-year-old represented the full extent of his work experience, making for a short, if not intriguing, résumé.

His penthouse unit in the five-story building was built to spec, the space completely gutted and reconstructed from the floor joists up.

Gray's design tastes ran sleekly modern—thick glass, brushed metal, and hard wood, with clean lines and little ornamentation. A bit cold and unemotional by my way of thinking, but what do I know about interior design?

The place was kept in immaculate condition, a byproduct of Gray's obsessiveness coupled with the luxury of being able to afford a cleaning service. Yet in Gray-like fashion, he complained continuously about the inept domestic help. Or, rather, he did until Dave and I told him how elitist and off-putting his incessant ranting was.

We entered the kitchen. Gleaming cookware hung from a rack suspended above a marble-topped island: soufflé pan, omelet pan, pasta pot, various saucepans, a couple of frying pans. A six-burner gas stove with a massive copper hood squatted at the back wall. Adjacent to the stove dangled additional culinary accoutrements: egg beater, colander, grater, whisk, peeler, assorted measuring cups and spoons, sieve, tongs, spatula. A vast collection of knives sheathed in a wood block stood at the ready. I couldn't help but surmise that, like many aspects of Gray's personality, the culinary artifacts were mainly for show. Most of them looked brand spanking new, fresh off the showroom floor.

We sat in captain's chairs, drinking Pierre Ferrand cognac out of bulbous snifters. Ferrand was Graham's everyday cognac, which he once described as "a bit ostentatious, wanting to play with the big boys, but not quite in the same league." I initially thought that Gray was describing himself. Anyway, it tasted good to me.

"I've been mulling over this 'she's not as pretty as she looks' notion," said Graham, "and I think I get the gist. I came to a similar conclusion the other night. I was listening to a Wagner symphony and it brought to mind that famous quote from Bill Nye."

"The science guy?" said Dave. "I loved him when I was growing up!"

"Uh, no, the *other* Bill Nye," said Graham. "He said that Wagner's music is better than it sounds."

"That's fucking nonsensical," said Dave, swirling his cognac.

"*Au contraire*. It's perfectly sensical. Wagner's underlying musical structure is exquisitely intricate and technically brilliant. Unfortunately, it's just not that pleasing to the ear. Ergo, Wagner's music is better than it sounds."

"Whoa," said Dave, suddenly animated. "Yes! Jerome, it's like our ping-pong match at the mountain. You won, technically, in terms of the final score. But I'm actually the better player."

"Exactly!" said Gray. "Jerome isn't nearly as good as an arbitrary indicator like the score might indicate."

"The score is not an arbitrary indicator!" I protested. "It's the only way to objectively determine an outcome."

"I won on style points," said Dave.

"Here's what it comes down to," said Gray, passing around Hoyo de Monterreys but failing to provide a means of igniting them. "You're whatever you think you are. And, Dave, you're a winner."

"Come on," I said. "That self-affirming crap was discredited ages ago. Fact is, most people are delusional, so they're not reliable judges. You need an objective viewpoint. You are what others think you are."

"As usual, you shitheads are both wrong," said Dave. "You're nothing. You're a figment of your own fucking imagination."

"Dave, don't you realize that your propensity for vulgarity gets tiresome?" said Gray. "Profanity is the province of the weak-minded."

"Who said that? Des-*fucking*-cartes?" said Dave.

"Inspiring observation," I said to Gray. "How about a light?"

"I swear, therefore I am," said Dave.

"Got a match?" I asked again.

"No smoking inside," said Gray.

Just like him. He had probably passed out these same cigars to a half-dozen guests and then put them away at the end of the night after refusing to let anyone light up. If Gray were a woman, I'd call him a cock-teaser.

"You're a cock-teaser," I said. He ignored me.

"Okay," said Gray, "here's my point, and it plays into this whole appearance-versus-reality thing. Our friend Dave here is people's exhibit number one. He's Mr. Potty Mouth when he's out with the boys. Every other word is a vulgarity. Yet the minute a woman walks into the room, he transforms into Mr. Sweet Talk, who blushes at the mere thought of profanity. It's the phoniest act in the world."

"It's true, Davy-boy," I said. "You're a faker for the ladies."

"You dickheads, as usual, have it all wrong," said Dave. "Did it ever occur to you that my crude side is the act, and my suave side is the real me?"

We retreated to the living room, lit a faux log, but not our real Hoyos, and settled in around the heavy, etched-glass coffee table. Gray dealt out coasters before putting some avant-garde noise on his state-of-the-art stereo. Dissonant notes emanated from every corner of the room, if not the ceiling and floor. I'd swear my easy chair had speakers embedded in the headrest.

I noticed a three-inch rectangle of carved wood on the coffee table, hollowed out with wire mesh covering the top. "What's this?" I asked Gray, picking up the box.

"The queen's quarters," he said.

I looked puzzled.

"It's for my hive. When I got my delivery of bees last month, the queen was separated from the workers in this little box. The bees can interact through the mesh, but they can't actually get to her."

"Why keep them apart?" asked Dave.

"The worker bees need to familiarize themselves with the queen. Put a strange queen into a hive, the workers will eat her alive."

I gingerly put down the queen's quarters. "I'm sure there's a life lesson in there somewhere," I said, "but it escapes me at the moment."

"So you got your brood of bees?" asked Dave.

"That would be hens. And yes."

"You're raising hens too?" I asked.

"No, no, brood is to hens as grist is to bees," said Gray.

I didn't get it.

"The hive is out on the balcony. Want to see?" asked Gray.

"And witness cannibal bees devouring their queen?" asked Dave. "No thanks."

Being males, we inevitably shifted the conversation to sex. I took the lead. I was high on Maura and couldn't help talking about her.

"Our bodies just fit," I said. "Where I yin, Maura yangs. Where I convex, she concaves. Lying on a bed, we become a single organism, she and me."

"She and I," said Graham.

"Yeah, yeah, I know. 'She and I.' But 'she and me' sounds so much better. It's alliterative."

"It's not alliterative, you illiterate. It rhymes."

"Rhymes, schmymes," I retorted.

Dave snorted. "Illiterate, schmiterate," he said.

"Listen, you ignoramuses," said Graham. "Don't ever say that word/schmerd nonsense again. I hate that. You think it's funny and clever. It isn't. It's stupid."

Dave and I were slightly taken aback at Graham's rant, but we probably shouldn't have been. Little got Gray's dander up like improper grammar. The fact that he wound up with Dave and I as friends seemed evidence of a cruel universe.

We sat in silence, sipping our cognac.

"Stupid, schmoopid," muttered Dave into his snifter.

The fake wood crackled in the fireplace, hyper-realistic sound being the latest innovation of the manufactured log industry. No doubt laser light shows would be incorporated into the next generation.

"Anyway, let's get back to the spoons," said Dave.

"What spoons?"

"You and Maura, spooning like rabbits."

"Mixed metaphor," said Graham.

"I never said anything about spooning," I said

"Allow me to translate," said Graham. "Dave is referencing the unique physical attributes that allow your bodies to fill each other's negative spaces to create a synergistically fused entity."

"Exactly the point I was trying to get across," said Dave.

I look at him with disbelief.

"Hey, I'm not as schmoopid as I look," he said.

"I think we can all agree on that point," said Graham. He raised his snifter in a toast.

I tapped glasses with my friends and then walked behind Gray's back, leaned over the fireplace, and lit my Hoyo on the artificial log.

Chapter 9

Year 2 | Summer

Judith invited Maura and me to her apartment for dinner. Maura tipped me off that Judith kept an "unorthodox" household, intimately shared with all manner of God's creatures, both her fauna and her flora. (Maura's pronoun choice.) I planned to exploit the fact that I was allergic to virtually every living organism. A strong histaminic reaction to dander and pollen, real or staged, might provide an excuse to cut short our visit if the evening proved intolerable.

Despite Maura's warning, I was ill-prepared for Judith's abode. A pungent animal smell slapped me across the face as we entered. Deep humidity and the fecund odor of compost pervaded the atmosphere, not entirely unpleasant, but shocking in a non-greenhouse environment. I brushed past a tall overhanging fern by the doorway, wishing I had remembered my machete.

The space before me looked like a salvage warehouse store after a customer riot. The inventory included countless stacks of cardboard boxes, many up to chest level; piles of old newspapers, dated magazines, and bulging manila folders; unopened packages from catalog retailers and online stores; shoeboxes teeming with bills, statements, and receipts; boxes of photographs and decades-old letters; a 50-pound bag of pet food; another of kitty litter; several ashtrays, each with two or three unsmoked cigarettes in them.

With narrow pathways running between all the junk, the place brought to mind a cornfield maze. I wondered if Judith ever got lost in here. If the condition of a person's living quarters reflects their psychological state, clearly we were in the presence of someone completely unhinged.

Judith greeted us at the door. Her black stretch pants worked overtime, while her tee-shirt struggled to cover her beach-ball belly. Protruding from an exposed line of flesh between her waistband and her shirt hem was the most gargantuan, freakish navel I'd ever laid eyes upon, a mutant tapeworm protruding from an eyeball. I couldn't tear my gaze away from it. Judith noticed my stare but seemed unconcerned. "I used to be an inny, but since I got pregnant, I'm an outie." She playfully pushed the worm back into its socket, but as soon as she released her finger, it sprang out again, like a demented jack-in-the-box. I took an involuntary step back.

Judith tugged her shirt down. "Sorry about the clutter. My cleaning lady quit, and I haven't found another."

"Cleaning lady? She needs a haz-mat team," I whispered to Maura as Judith escorted us in.

A cat brushed my leg, nudged Maura, then leapt into Judith's arms. She cradled the animal casually. I saw another tabby sunning itself atop a cardboard box by the window. "How many pets do you keep?" I asked.

Judith listed her lodgers: two lap dogs, four felines, one parrot, scores of tropical fish in two aquariums, a turtle in a box, a pair of rabbits in a hutch, and a two-foot-long iguana in her bathtub.

Added to the biological diversity was an unquantifiable variety of plants: hanging, potted, hydroponic, seedlings, bonsais, weeds, flowering, budding, carnivorous, annual, perennial, bulbs, cuttings, and grafts, along with assorted pots apparently containing nothing but dirt.

We wended our way through the living room and passed the bedroom door. I stuck in my head. "Where do you sleep?" I asked. Maura jabbed me with her elbow.

"Oh, there's a bed in there somewhere," said Judith. "It's on the other side of those cardboard wardrobe containers that I use as portable closets. Don't have enough closet space, so I never unpacked them when I moved in four years ago."

We entered the kitchen. Four tall stools sat on either side of a peninsula counter, each with a teetering pile of paper and cardboard atop it. "I'd offer you a seat—" said Judith.

An overflowing litter box sat under the counter with an obese cat pawing at the grit, sending it flying. "Maxi! Bad girl!" said Judith, shooing the animal away. Judith removed a dustpan and brush from a sink full of dishes, swept the litter into a neat pile, and left it sitting on the floor beside the box.

A parrot perched in a gold-gilt cage suspended from a chain by the window. Judith pulled a cracker from an open box and showed it to the bird. "Hello, Glotty! You want a cracker?"

The bottom of the cage was thick with bird droppings. "I'm teaching Glotty to speak in several languages," said Judith. "Watch this. Glotty, say 'hello' in Spanish."

The bird remained mute.

"*Ahora!*" said Judith, breaking off a bit of cracker and sticking it through the bars. The bird lunged, and Judith retreated. "Say '*hola*' and you get the cracker!"

The bird screeched. Judith was elated. "Did you hear that? Spanish! Amazing, isn't it?"

Maura and I emitted appreciative noises of our own.

"Unfortunately, we aren't having as much luck with the Russian," said Judith.

"Next on our tour," she continued, "is Igor. Follow me." Judith grabbed a fresh cigarette and a wooden match from one of the ashtrays. With a nearly imperceptible move, she ignited the stick.

Holding the flame several inches away from the end of the cigarette, she drew in deeply, without actually igniting the tobacco. "I don't really smoke them," she said, glancing downward at her protruding belly. "I just go through the motions. Helps keep me sane." She blew out the match, flipped it into the ashtray, and nonchalantly waved her cigaretted hand. "Let's carry on, shall we?"

As I leaned back to allow Judith through the narrow passageway, I bumped into a pile of papers on the edge of the counter, sending them fluttering to the floor. I bent to pick up the scattered debris. "Oh, don't worry about that," said Judith. "I'll take care of it later."

The white-tiled bathroom contained an old-style claw-footed tub. Judith drew back the shower curtain to reveal a huge, scaly, green-gray iguana. With spiky spine, daggered jowl, and enormous claws, the creature lounged serenely on a plastic perch at the end of the tub above several inches of water.

"Majestically intimidating," I said. "How do you manage to bathe?"

"Oh, I shower at the lab," said Judith, referring to the medical research facility where she worked. "I used to kick Igor out of the tub each morning, but one day he lashed out and scratched my retina. Since then, he's pretty much owned the bathroom."

We navigated back to the living room and sat on Judith's cat-hair couch, surrounded by the towering piles. Maura and I sipped cheap rosé while Judith nursed a nonalcoholic cranberry concoction of identical hue. "I've found that drinking is ninety percent psychological," she said, clinking our glasses. "But, oh, what I'd give for that other ten percent."

We sampled from a bowl of marinated olives and nibbled gouda on graham crackers. "Sorry I can't offer you a more suitable biscuit to accompany the cheese," said Judith, "but the cats got into the bag."

"Well, they're definitely out of the bag now," I said as two cats prowled the room and a third leapt into my lap. I moved to dump the animal on the floor when Maura grabbed my thigh.

"You be nice to Misty now. She just wants some cuddling," Maura said.

"You know I'd be cuddling with this little ball of joy all night if I could," I replied. "But my allergies—"

"Oh, a couple of minutes of petting won't kill you."

I slid back into the folds of the couch as the cat made itself at home, nuzzling and purring with a deep guttural sound that set its entire body on vibrate mode. I sneezed loudly and pulled a tissue from my pocket.

As the women discussed epidurals and dilation, Judith picked up another unlit cigarette and puffed away. She jiggled her leg incessantly as she conversed, while flicking her imaginary ashes in the general direction of an ashtray on the floor.

Meanwhile, I was feeling increasingly uncomfortable. The cat generated a warm glow. It gently gyrated. It hummed in a low cat vibrato, all the while splayed across my genitals. This was not good. This was causing sensations that shouldn't be passed between man and animal. This was a growing problem.

I squirmed. I shifted. Maura and Judith, engrossed in chatter, noticed nothing.

Suddenly, Judith exclaimed, "My casserole!" She somehow levitated her swollen self from the couch and waddled through the maze toward the kitchen. A wisp of smoke escaped as she pushed open the door. The cat, ever loyal, dug two paws into my groin before making an Olympian leap to follow her.

Maura, bereft of conversation, turned her attention to me and immediately noticed my bulging lap.

"Well, well, well. What have we here?" She reached down, clasped my package, and gave it a squeeze. "Methinks you like the little pussy more than you admit!"

I stammered in protest.

"No need to explain," she said.

Before I knew what she was doing, Maura was kissing me deeply while simultaneously releasing my belt buckle and trouser button and unzipping my fly. I lifted my hips instinctively and in a flash she had my pants down around my knees.

"Perhaps you and I can finish what little tabby started." She flung her leg over my lap, pivoted to face me, and hiked up her skirt. Reaching behind her, Maura dipped her fingers in the olive oil, lubricated herself and me, and smoothly guided me in. She nuzzled my ear, purring cat-like and murmuring, "You beast, you."

I looked worriedly toward the kitchen door, fearing *coitus interruptus*.

"I guess we're safe," I said. "It'll take Judith ten minutes to find her way back." I fished a tissue from the pocket at my kneecap and dabbed my allergic nose.

A yell emanated from the kitchen. "Sorry, I might be a little while! I have a mini-crisis in here!"

The parrot squawked something unintelligible. I think it was in Russian.

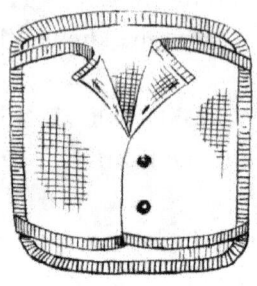

Chapter 10

Year 2 | Summer

Sunlight streamed through the dirt-streaked windows of the classroom, attracting the visually impaired students like clover draws honeybees. Minutes after their arrival in the morning, four students found their way to the sunbeam, flicking fingers and objects before their eyes to create light patterns on their compromised retinas.

I was observing the spectacle when Maura sidled up next to me. "They'll go blind if they keep staring into the sun like that," she noted. "Oh. Never mind."

I took my position at the ADL station—activities of daily living. My alcove was stocked with various teaching tools: lap-sized boards for zipper, button, snap, and velcro practice; a hiking boot mounted on a plywood square; two ends of a belt, nailed to a slab of pine; a dozen assorted bottles and jars screwed to a tray; a manual can opener and a grocery bag full of empty cans; a board with latches and knobs and handles. This was my favorite classroom activity because it was the only one even remotely tied to the real world. Once they could open the can, I figured, could heating the beans be far behind?

Maura sent the students to me in pairs for half-hour sessions, so that by the end of my ninety-minute rotation, all six students would cycle through.

I started off with Laurie and Danny, two ends of the skill spectrum. Laurie, though totally blind, could probably pick a lock. Danny, partially sighted, could pick little more than his nose. The mismatch was deliberate, as Laurie was verbal and auditory and could go through her paces with minimal cues. Danny, on the other hand, was dumb and unresponsive and pretty much needed hand-over-hand guidance to do anything.

"Okay, Laurie, today you can choose whatever activity board you want!" I said in my unnaturally cheery classroom voice.

She ambled over to the shelf, arms outstretched to avoid collisions. "Buttons! And zippers! And snaps!" she said, sounding like Dorothy in *The Wizard of Oz*. I half-expected her to add "Oh my!" to the end, but she didn't. She never saw the film, I guessed.

Laurie fingered the collection until she identified the desired items. She stacked the boards and carried them tentatively to her work table. When she lightly bumped her knee on the rounded edge, she knew she had arrived.

Meanwhile, I placed the jar and bottle array in front of Danny. His mission, should he decide to accept it (which was never a certainty), was to remove each cap and place it into a plastic container. The reverse process, recapping, presented a significantly greater challenge, due to the variable sizes. Of all the students, only Laurie could perform it independently.

Maura passed my alcove, separated from the rest of the classroom by carpet-covered, half-wall dividers. She stepped inside to observe progress.

"Hey, I discovered a fatal flaw with the button board yesterday," I said.

"Fatal flaw!" mimicked Laurie.

"Wasn't that a movie?" asked Maura.

"What?"

"Fatal flaw. A movie. Never mind. What's the flaw?"

"Manipulating buttons that are lying flat on a table isn't the same as buttoning a shirt that you're wearing."

"The theory," said Maura, "is that the skill is transferable."

"The theory is fatally flawed."

"So, what do you suggest? Strap the board to her chest?"

"Strap the board!" said Laurie.

"Quiet, you!" said Maura playfully.

"Here, let me demonstrate," I said. I rose from my child-sized chair, stood behind Maura, reached around, and grasped the top button of her blouse. "Observe the fine motor movements employed from this angle," I said. I skillfully released her first two buttons as if I'd been buttoning my entire life.

I then moved to Maura's front. "Now watch this unbuttoning technique. An entirely different sequence of muscle movements come into play." I rapidly undid her next three buttons and opened her shirt, exposing her bare breasts. In a normal school, this indecent exposure might cause a commotion. But, with a blind clientele, Maura and I were the only witnesses.

"Thank you for that demonstration," she said. "Your task analysis skills are first-rate, if unorthodox."

With rising pulse, I attempted to caress her breasts, but Maura caught my wrist. "Down, boy," she said. "This ain't no petting zoo." She refastened her shirt.

"Petting zoo!" said Laurie.

I was disappointed but not discouraged. "Perhaps you'd be interested in my analysis of the zipper board?"

Suddenly I got a whiff of an astringent odor. "What's that smell?"

Maura sniffed. "I don't smell anything."

"It's piss," I said. I started nosing around the alcove to determine the source. Danny had been known to relieve his bladder at inopportune moments, so I hovered above him at the table. He was tapping a plastic bottle against his ear. I smelled nothing.

"Found it!" announced Maura, pulling out the chair I had just vacated. A small pool of urine partly filled the concave plastic seat.

"Oh my God!" I reached for my trouser bottom and felt an unmistakable dampness. "It's me!"

"You wet yourself?"

"No, I didn't wet myself! I just sat in it," I said with disgust.

"And you didn't feel it?"

I thrust my hand into the back of my jeans. "It didn't soak through. Probably because my butt doesn't completely fit into that tiny chair."

"Okay, big boy, hands out of your pants," said Maura. "It's one thing when students do it, but when the teachers—"

"You're a riot." I fought the urge to strip down and run for the showers. "I can't believe this," I said, again feeling my backside to verify. "I knew I smelled something, but I never thought it was me."

Suddenly, Danny jumped up. The entire front of his trousers was stained dark with urine. The trail ran down his right pant leg to a shimmering yellow puddle on the floor.

Danny hated being wet, but somehow failed to make the connection that urinating while fully clothed might be antithetical to this preference. Before I could reach him, his pants were around his ankles and he was pissing on the table, the spray misting into several bottles. I grabbed him by the collar and pulled him away from the materials. He continued to urinate on the floor. I didn't know what to do. I certainly wasn't going to grab his wanker to cut off the flow. I looked helplessly toward Maura, who had moved outside the alcove, beyond Danny's firing range, and watched with an amused expression.

Danny solved my dilemma by darting off. Pants still around his ankles, he beelined toward the classroom door. Inexplicably, Maura did nothing to impede his progress. "I've never seen anyone run that fast with his pants down," she noted dryly.

"Isn't there a board meeting going on in the cafeteria?" I asked.

Maura's grin vanished. "Oh my God! Catch him!"

Danny bolted out the door and down the hall, looking like a penguin escaping from the zoo. He waddled straight toward the double doors to the cafeteria, driven by the expectation of food on the other side.

I sprinted the length of the hall. Danny was just beyond reach when he crashed through the swinging doors, advancing about ten feet into the room before sensing that something was different. He stopped in his tracks and reverted to self-stim mode, head turned toward the fluorescent ceiling lights, fingers flicking across his eyes. With his free hand he grabbed his penis and started masturbating.

I stood transfixed in the doorway, horrified at the sight. Twenty or so men and women, dressed in business attire, sat assembled at a long table in the middle of the room. Half of them stared wide-eyed at Danny, who was totally absorbed in his syncopated flicking and stroking exhibition. The other half looked expectantly at me, as if I had any conceivable idea how to terminate the spectacle.

It was a professional dilemma of the highest order, with perhaps my employment riding on the outcome. Maura came up silently behind me in the doorway, out of the view of the directors. She gasped audibly at the scene. "Do something!" she said through clenched teeth, shoving me into the room. I stumbled from the force, regained my balance and composure, and strode purposefully toward Danny.

"My apologies to the board," I said in a stentorian tone. "We've had some, uh, personal plumbing issues this morning."

Danny had attained a full erection by this time, and his tempo neared a frenzy. A female director shaded her eyes. A male turned his gaze away.

I approached Danny from behind, reached down to his ankles, and firmly grasped the waistband of his dropped trousers, yanking them up with such force that he was lifted clear off the floor. His legs flailed as I carried him bodily from the room. I turn backed toward the board members. "Please pardon the interruption. Do carry on."

Maura pulled the swinging door open and allowed me to pass while keeping herself out of sight. I plopped Danny onto the carpeted corridor floor as the door swished and clicked shut behind me. I wiped the sweat from my brow and only then realized that my hands were soaked in urine. I flinched involuntarily.

Maura moaned. "We are so screwed. He pulls this stunt on the one day of the year the freaking board is here?"

Danny wriggled like a snake on the floor, trying desperately to get out of his wet pants, but impeded by his sneakers. I grabbed the front of his shirt and pulled him to a standing position. Hand clasped on the nape of his neck, I marched him quickly back toward the classroom.

We entered and headed straight for the bathroom. There were no chairs in the room, and the toilets had no covers, so I sat him on the U-shaped plastic toilet seat. As I got down on one knee to untie his urine-soaked sneaker laces, Maura peered in from the doorway. "The toughest job in special ed—untying wet knots."

"You've been providing unhelpful commentary all morning while I deal with one crisis after another," I said.

"Just part of your continuing education."

I gave up on the laces and instead pulled each sneaker by the heel to remove it. "Okay, Danny boy, strip down," I said. He was fully disrobed before I could finish the sentence. Even his t-shirt, which was spared the indignity of the golden shower, came off. He started to bolt again for the door, stark naked, but this time I was ready. I blocked the doorway, arms akimbo. He retreated to the toilet, squatting with his feet up on the seat. I pulled the stall door shut. "Maura, will you stand guard for a minute? I need to engage in some personal ADL."

At the bathroom sink, I washed my hands three times and my face twice, lathering with copious amounts of soap. I was at a loss for dealing with my wet rump, having no change of clothes. Maura reminded me that several students kept spare trousers in the classroom. I mentioned the size discrepancy. "Beats smelling like the back alley outside a dive bar," she said.

"And you would know how that smells because—?"

I returned to the classroom, found the largest pair of jeans in the supply closet, and squeezed into them. The cuff came up to my calf; the waist couldn't be secured. I tied them off with a piece of string and pulled my shirt down as far as I could. I walked stiffly back into the bathroom.

"My God, you look like somebody straight out of Appalachia," said Maura.

I washed my hands again for good measure, then tugged on a pair of latex gloves to deal with Danny. "Aren't you glad you were born after the advent of rubber gloves?" asked Maura.

"Another extremely helpful remark," I said. "Pretty glib for someone who just let a masturbator run amok at a board meeting."

"*Oy*," said Maura, as if she had momentarily forgotten the incident. "We haven't heard the last of this."

As Maura rejoined the other students in the classroom, I gave Danny a wet cloth to wash his privates. He failed to make the connection, so I resorted to hand-over-hand washing of his genitals, wishing every second that I had taken that fry-o-later job at Mickie D's. I passed him dry clothes in proper sequence and orientation, and he somehow managed to don them.

Nudging him toward the doorway, I sent him back into the classroom. "Incoming!" I yelled to Maura.

I gingerly picked up the wet clothes and tucked them into a trash bag, then removed my gloves and stuck them in as well. I tied the bag shut, then washed my hands again.

When I returned to the classroom, I was shocked at the transformation. Maura was playing foam horseshoes with a couple of students. Two others splashed in the water table, while another pair worked with clay. It was a remarkably quiet, orderly, and, dare I say, almost studious environment. I marveled at the calm atmosphere she'd established and realized that I would never be able to replicate it. It was my discouraging epiphany; a special ed teacher I was not and never would be.

Anson, a stocky 12-year-old, totally blind in one eye and legally blind in the other, stood at the far end of a makeshift horseshoe pitch, adjacent to a bright yellow plastic post. Bruce, a lanky, mute, autistic boy of fifteen, was stationed at the throwing line, ten feet opposite. Dexterity and aim, as expected, were not among their strong points, a fact acknowledged in the soft foam construction of the horseshoes.

Bruce's throws went widely astray, hitting Anson more often than anything else. Oddly, Anson didn't react to the blows, which were admittedly mild but should have been noticeable. He stood stock still, head tilted in a manner that made him look like he was listening intently to some faraway sound, so deep in apparent rumination that the phrase "profoundly retarded" came to mind.

After about ten tosses, they switched sides. Maura directed Anson to the throwing line, with Bruce repositioned at the post. In contrast to Anson, Bruce was hyper alert. Every time a throw landed anywhere near him, he not only noticed, he tossed it back. "He's the only post that will throw back your horseshoe," observed Maura.

I wandered over to the arts and crafts area, where Laurie diligently manipulated a wad of clay. "Laurie girl, what are you making?"

Laurie cocked her head in my direction. "Spaghetti."

Indeed, on the table lay a mound of thinly rolled strands of clay looking strikingly like a heap of blue spaghetti. "Wow, you're a master chef! You must have gone to cooking school!" Laurie smiled broadly but didn't reply.

She pinched a clump of clay from a large wad and rolled it between her two palms, making it progressively thinner and longer. When it had attained satisfactory form, she added it to the growing heap and started anew. Planning, execution, dexterity, and perseverance—an impressive display.

"But there's a problem," I said. Laurie's face clouded. "Spaghetti should always be served on a plate, not right from the table."

Laurie relaxed, relieved that her culinary masterpiece was not in jeopardy. I handed her a large plastic plate, and she carefully cradled and transferred the spaghetti.

"Much-a more better," I said. "But there's another problem."

Laurie scowled. "You're a problem!" she said, trying to hide a grin.

"You can't serve spaghetti plain. Where's the tomato sauce?"

Laurie mulled that one over. Her face showed a range of expressions as she contemplated the implications of putting real sauce on her fake clay pasta. "No sauce!" she said finally.

"May I join you for lunch, madame?" I asked. I pulled plates, silverware, and cups from the cabinet, along with a pitcher and paper towels for napkins. "Perhaps madame would like a little wine with her meal?"

"Perhaps," Laurie replied demurely.

Laurie served up the spaghetti, smiling and laughing through our pretend luncheon. It was almost enough to make me forget the boardroom flasher.

My amnesia got no chance to take hold, however, as a rap came on the classroom door. "Uh-oh," said Maura. "No one ever knocks before entering the classroom."

She pulled open the heavy fire door, and a man and a woman dressed in business attire stepped over the threshold. I recognized the male—Charles Hopedale, the rarely seen executive director of the agency. He cast a lewd eye across Maura's figure before saying, "This is Elizabeth Stein, chairman of the board of directors. Elizabeth, this is Maura Wood, head teacher in this classroom."

The chairwoman extended her hand and primly, if not grimly, nodded. She didn't say a word. I slowly rose from my seat across the room, swiveling my head to scan the premises in search of Danny, fervently hoping he was fully clothed and marginally appropriate. I spotted him lying on a throw rug, which he had dragged over to a patch of sun, lazily light gazing. Not exactly constructively engaged in academic pursuits, but close enough.

Most of the other students had gone entirely off task, save Laurie, who busily prepared a new batch of blue spaghetti, and Anson, who listened to heavy metal through headphones set at maximum volume. Katie sucked on a yellow plastic triangle. Roger napped in the vibrating easy chair. Patty drank from the water table. "We'd like to have a word with you in the boardroom," said Hopedale sternly.

"Would that be the cafeteria?" asked Maura with feigned innocence. Hopedale was not amused.

"I'd love to, but we're a bit short-staffed," continued Maura, which I guess was an unintentional insult to me, since we were actually fully staffed. "And you've seen firsthand the repercussions of an inadequate student-to-teacher ratio."

"Lock them in here if you have to," said Hopedale. "Boardroom in two minutes." They turned on their heels and marched out.

"Isn't it against fire regulations to lock a classroom door?" I asked.

"He's a prick," replied Maura. "If we did and there were a problem, he'd deny he ever said it."

Maura took a deep breath and smoothed her clothes. "Hold the fort," she said.

She was gone for a worrisomely long time. I moved from student to student, trying to get them back on task, but it was like playing whack-a-mole. As soon as I stepped away, their undesired behaviors resurfaced.

I imagined the inquisition taking place in the cafeteria with a hostile audience of businesspeople who had no clue about the realities of a special needs classroom. According to Maura, most of the board members considered our students to be dumber versions of normal kids, needing nothing more than a slowed-down elementary school curriculum. I wasn't worried about Maura handling a stressful situation; rather, I was concerned over her ability to hold her tongue in the face of ignorance.

She returned after about a half-hour. The classroom door closed gently behind her. She reopened it and pulled it violently shut. The kids with hearing aids jumped.

Maura stomped over to where I was sitting at the water table with Patty. "I just had a formal warning put into my personnel file," she said. "And I have to give you one."

I looked at her expectantly.

"Consider yourself warned."

"That doesn't seem very formal," I said.

"It'll do for now. I'll warn you more convincingly in private."

"I look forward to it."

Maura paced the floor, straightened some toys on a shelf, brushed away some nonexistent dust, came back to the water table, and sat in a chair, clearly agitated. "They want progress reports from the last six months for every student in every need area."

"Shouldn't be too hard," I said. "Every graph is pretty much a flat line."

"Yeah, the *report* part is easy. It's the *progress* part that I'm worried about," she said glumly.

I looked around at our six students in various states of repose, self-stim, distraction, disaffection, and dysfunction.

"Life is just one big need area," I said.

Chapter 11

Year 2 | Autumn

After tending to his bees for a full season, Gray was primed for the honey harvest. He'd read *A Fool's Guide to Beekeeping*, a title simultaneously appropriate and worrisome, and he now carried an air of supreme self-confidence, entirely unwarranted but thoroughly characteristic. Gray had no qualms whatsoever about attempting to pilfer the golden syrup from a horde of agitated worker bees. I was dubious. Worse, I was invited to join in the fun.

Gray had grand plans for his bounty. He'd fill honey jars, bake honey cakes, concoct honey droplet candy, mold honeycomb candles, and brew mead wine. I wondered how one hive could possibly support all his sweet ambitions, but what did I know? I hadn't read the *Fool's Guide*.

I could, however, read Gray like a book, and this initiative was strikingly reminiscent of an earlier chapter of his life. It was the summer between our freshman and sophomore years. Gray, Dave, and I had been hanging out for several months, flitting in and out of various social groups, latching onto and rapidly losing girlfriends. Actually, to be historically precise, Dave was latching and holding, Gray was latching and losing, and I was fumbling with and never quite mastering the whole latch thing.

Gray and I lived in a two-bedroom rental just off campus for the summer. Dave was hunkered down in his apartment above his parents' garage. Stuck in a long drought after his last failed romance, Gray came up with a foolproof scheme for impressing the ladies— create a scrumptious meal from scratch, a primordial feast using only ingredients that he fished, foraged, and farmed himself. The women would swoon over Gray's aphrodisiacal talent for combining these masculine pursuits with culinary artistry. At least, that was the theory. Gray conscripted Dave and me to aid and abet.

First, he led us into the woods, traipsing through groves and underbrush, unearthing and plucking fungi of every imaginable shape except the one normally associated with mushrooms. Gray carried *A Field Guide to Edible Mushrooms* in one hand and a bizarre implement that looked like a cross between a spade, hoe, and hatchet in the other.

"Okay, boys, let me enlighten you," he said at the edge of the forest, flipping open his guidebook. "Based on my understanding of the local ecosystem, we're seeking a couple prevalent species, including the chanterelle, shown here." He displayed a glossy photo that looked like a negative image of a mushroom, bright yellow instead of dark brown, concave cap instead of convex.

"Snap, if that's a mushroom, I'm a potted plant," said Dave, whose profane persona was still in the pupal stage.

"Not that the two are mutually exclusive," said Gray.

Gray turned a few more pages. "Also, keep an eye out for the morel, a culinary delight." He pointed to a photo of another un-mushroom-like specimen whose cap looked like a cross-section of Van Gogh's brain.

We spread out to begin our forage, and within a few minutes, Dave had a strike. "I found a colony!" he yelled from behind a clump of bushes. As Gray and I approached, Dave maniacally cleared the area like a burrowing animal. Fistfuls of leaves and twigs flew between his legs as he crouched over his discovery.

"First of all," said Gray, "one would never say 'colony' of mushrooms. The proper terminology is either 'troop' or 'cluster.' Second of all, no you didn't." Gray kicked at the mossy bark that Dave had mistakenly identified.

"Huh! We'll see about that," said Dave, defiantly popping a small chunk of bark into his mouth.

The July sun beat down, but the thick tree canopy kept the warmth at bay. We stuck to the promising areas, cool, dark, and moist, skirting the dry, open fields. As we nosed through musky compost to extract our fungi, I kept raising alarms about poisonous toadstools, and Gray repeatedly dismissed my concerns by pointing to full-color photos of mushrooms that bore no resemblance to the specimens we held in our hands.

By the end of our four-hour excursion, we had gathered about a dry pint of questionable edibility.

The next day it was off to a nearby lake, where we pooled our funds to rent a small-bore skiff and some fishing gear for a half-day outing. As we shoved off from the dock, I realized that fishing was a depressing metaphor for my love life—quixotically casting a line into the vast murky depths in the vain hope of attracting something. Gray, however, seemed genuinely excited about the prospect of hauling in a few marlin or whatever might reside in these fresh waters. Dave shared neither Gray's gladness nor my glumness, but he did have the foresight and wherewithal to steal a six-pack from his father's fridge in the garage.

The early morning air was brisk, as the sun hadn't yet risen above the trees to take the chill off. Wispy clouds streaked the sky; a low fog hugged the glassy surface further out on the lake. We putted out of a cove toward open water.

"What time is it?" asked Dave.

Gray consulted his watch. "Just turned seven."

"Which is cocktail hour somewhere in the world," said Dave, cracking open a beer. Being underage drinkers for whom alcohol was still an illicit joy no matter the time of day, Gray and I quickly followed suit.

All was going swimmingly, figuratively speaking, when I went overboard. Having strapped a heavy lead sinker to my line to give it more heft, I was winding up for a mighty cast when I lost my balance. Beer in one hand, rod in the other, an unsteady vessel beneath my feet, I had no hope of regaining my equilibrium and gracelessly fell backward out of the boat. I panicked, not being the best swimmer, and began thrashing and flailing, losing grip of my possessions in the process.

Dave heroically dove in, but, as it turned out, not to save me but the equipment. He remained underwater for an inordinate length of time before finally bursting through the surface, sputtering and gasping for air. "I got it!" he yelled, which came as a great relief, as we hadn't taken the optional insurance on the fishing gear.

Unfortunately, Dave clambered back aboard carrying the only item he had actually retrieved—my can of beer. I didn't have the heart to tell him that the now-full can was nearly empty when it fell into the lake. He didn't seem to notice as he triumphantly drained it in a single guzzle. In fairness to Dave, it should be noted that this event took place during our neophyte, light-beer phase, before we had graduated to full-bodied ales, so the distinction between beer and water was already exceedingly thin to begin with.

Over the next few hours, Gray did manage to pull in a small lake bass, which he clumsily unhooked and threw into the cooler alongside the beer. The creature flopped around for several minutes before finally settling down. We chugged back to shore, paid handsomely for the boat and the lost equipment, and drove home.

Our final trip, a day later, was to the community garden where Gray had planted a crop in the spring—corn, cukes, green beans, potatoes, and tomatoes. Upon arriving at his overgrown plot, Gray immediately fell to his knees and started pawing at the soil, disinterring a half-dozen spuds, each about the size of a ping-pong ball. "Dang! I've never seen a cherry potato before!" said Dave.

"They're russets," responded Gray with a hint of petulance.

"Preemies," I noted.

Clearly, July was too early in the growing season to be reaping, but Gray was anxious to lay out his luscious meal. The potatoes were joined by babyish corn, gherkin-sized cucumbers, pearl-like tomatoes, and spaghetti-thin beans.

Back at our apartment, we laid out the ingredients on the kitchen table. It was a pathetic display: a pint of misshapen mushrooms, a meager fish fillet, and enough produce to yield a dollop of mashed potatoes and a single small salad.

"Just for fun, let's add up the score," said Dave. "Three guys times four hours in the woods equals twelve man-hours for a handful of fungi. A half-day's boat rental plus the lost fishing rod cost over two hundred dollars. Plus our trip out to the farm that yielded this bonsai bounty. And what do we get out of it? A single plate of food that wouldn't satisfy a dwarf."

Gray wound up canceling his feast, a mere technicality since he hadn't yet invited any comely collegiates to join us. We boiled the ping-pong potatoes and served them up with the raw mini-veggies as pre-appetizers while watching a baseball game on TV. I fried the fish in butter, stinking up the entire apartment and providing us with about a two morsels each. We decided to play it safe with the mushrooms, stashing them in the fridge to meet the usual fate of almost all produce brought into the apartment—slowly composting in the crisper drawer for several weeks before being thrown out. My curiosity got the better of me, however, and the following Monday I brought them to the food science lab at the college for testing. My suspicions proved correct—one variety was lethal. Ironically, it was the only specimen that actually bore a faint resemblance to a mushroom. The lab placed a fluorescent orange warning label on the plastic bag with the mushroom's common name scrawled upon it— "death cap."

The cumulative fiasco was typical Gray: Grandiose plans. Inadequate preparation. Poor execution.

But on the upside, we didn't get attacked by bears in the forest, sharks on the lake, or pitchfork-wielding farmers in the field. The mushrooms could have killed us but didn't. All told, not a bad outcome.

I could only hope for an equally positive result from Gray's honey harvest. I didn't care if we actually wound up with any honey. I just hoped no one got stung to death in the process.

Gray's condo smelled smoky. A grayish haze lingered at the ceiling as I made my way back toward the kitchen. I found Dave and Gray flitting around the room, not exactly like busy bees, but that's what came to mind.

A large stainless steel vat with a crank handle and a small spigot stood next to the sink. Beside it on a rolling cart was a large rectangular box covered with a wooden lid. Gray held a small metal device that looked like a miniature pig wearing a jet pack. A wisp of smoke escaped from the pig's nostrils.

A few bees hovered around the box, which I suddenly realized was the hive. "Do you think it's wise to bring the hive indoors?" I asked Gray.

"This honey extraction is messy business," he replied. "I need to be near a sink."

"And the smoke?"

"Not to worry. I disabled the smoke alarm."

"You, my friend," I said to Gray, "are a hypocrite."

Gray adopted a look that was part wounded puppy, part innocent newborn. "Whatever do you mean?"

"Aren't you the same person who bit my head off for lighting a cigar in your living room? Yet now, you could smoke a ham in here."

"There's no comparison," said Gray. "That was recreation. This is agriculture."

Turns out the jet-pack on the pig's back was a bellows. Gray gave it a squeeze and a puff of smoke billowed from the pig's snout. Gray slid the nosepiece into the opening at the front of the hive and gave a few pumps. Then he directed a cloud toward the bees that were buzzing around the outside of the hive. They retreated into the wooden confines.

Dave stood next to the hive holding a broad, flat knife plugged into an electrical outlet. "This fucker slices through wax like nobody's business," he said. "Watch this."

He lowered the edge of the knife against a squat candle sitting on the counter. It cut through smoothly, leaving a trail of melted wax in its wake.

"Impressive," I said, not truly impressed.

A white jumpsuit, leather gloves, and a mesh mask were stacked neatly on the kitchen table. "Um, shouldn't we be wearing the gear?" I asked, trying to keep the anxiety out of my voice.

"Gear is for wimps," said Dave.

"Not entirely accurate," said Gray. "Gear is certainly appropriate for novices."

"Forgive me for asking," I said, "but doesn't that precisely describe our status?"

"Only in the strictest of interpretations."

Gray nudged up the cover of the hive and a wave of bees emerged. He dropped it hurriedly, jarring the structure. The bees caught on the outside were not happy. Several alit on Gray's arms. I backed away slowly. Gray remained calm, pumping the bellows and enveloping his arms in the cloud. The insects again retreated.

A threatening buzz arose from the hive, likely in response to the dropped cover. A steady stream emerged from the mouth of the box; Gray drove them back with another plume.

Tasting smoke with every breath, I resisted the urge to soak a dish towel, cover my mouth and nose, and drop to the floor.

As Dave swatted away a couple of bees with his hot knife, Gray's tension level visibly increased. I wondered if the bees could sense his anxiety. I inched toward the sliding glass door that led to the balcony and fresh air.

"Switch on that exhaust fan, will you?" said Gray to Dave. The massive hood over the six-burner gas stove roared into action, and the smoke started migrating in that direction. A few wayward bees quickly found themselves pinned against the metal filter on the underside of the hood.

The buzz from the hive increased. "The little bastards want to play hardball, I guess," said Gray, jaw set. Grabbing a potholder, he separated the metal pig's head from its body and stuffed some crumpled newspaper inside. Flames flared as Gray quickly reattached the top.

Gray pumped the bellows a couple of times to prime it before inserting the snout deep into the hive opening. He forced a dozen blasts into the nest before pulling out. Then he gingerly lifted the top, pushed the nozzle underneath, and again pumped repeatedly, perhaps another ten times. As he lowered the top, smoke seeped out of every joint and crack of the hive box.

"That seems like an awful lot of smoke," I said as the exhaust fan cleared the kitchen air. "Aren't you worried about asphyxiating them?"

"Not a chance," said Gray with his usual dismissiveness. "They're hardy little buggers."

The hive fell silent. Only the whoosh and hum of the exhaust fan filled the room.

Gray set down the smoker and reached for the hive cover. "Let the fun begin!" he said cheerily.

He nudged the top up. No bees emerged. He lifted a bit higher. A plume of smoke escaped. He lifted it entirely off and placed it on the kitchen table. "Silence, and honey, is golden," he said.

Within the hive was a row of wooden frames encased in wax. Gray traced a putty knife around the edges to loosen the frame and then pulled out the first one. Clusters of motionless bees clung to the honeycombed exterior. "Collateral damage," said Gray, knocking the dead bees off with his putty knife. "There are hundreds more safe in the bowels of the hive."

Gray placed the frame onto a slat of wood suspended above a cheesecloth-lined tub. He took the hot knife from Dave. "I'll demonstrate the technique for you lads, then you can have a go."

The frame was filled with hundreds of tiny honeycombed chambers, each of which contained perhaps an eyedropper's worth of honey. The entire structure was meticulously sealed with a layer of beeswax, which needed to be carefully trimmed away to allow the honey to flow.

Starting at the top of the frame, Gray slowly drew the hot knife downward, separating the wax from the exterior like one might skin a fish. Thin sheets of wax fell into the cheesecloth below. "The book said a goodly amount of honey will drain from that cutaway wax," said Gray.

As Gray surgically detached both sides of the waxy exterior of the frame, honey slowly oozed from the opened chambers. He placed the frame into the stainless steel tub and then handed the knife to Dave.

I reached into the vat and scooped up a dollop of the flowing honey. "Sweet," I said. "And smoky. Good on barbecued ribs, I bet."

Over the next half hour, we removed and uncapped three more frames, placing each into the metal tub. Gray closed the lid and slowly cranked the handle. "The honey is extracted from the honeycomb cells by centrifugal force," he explained. He gradually built up speed until the extractor shuddered violently, despite being bolted to its wooden stand.

After about five minutes of cranking, Gray stopped and allowed the spinning chamber to peter out. He peered inside. "Not exactly overflowing," he said. "But we've still got six frames to go."

With the centrifuge now silent, we noticed the noisy exhaust fan still running. Dave reached up and switched it off. The room turned suddenly quiet. "The boys seem rather subdued," I said, tilting my head toward the hive.

"Not to worry," said Gray. "They're in a state of mild shock, but they'll recover."

Gray had placed a drop-cloth under the equipment, but before long our sneakers were sticking to the tiled floor. Honey and wax bits coated me from fingertip to elbow, along with numerous flecks on my shirt and a sticky spot or two in my hair.

We knifed away the wax from another four frames, tucking each into the centrifuge. Dave gave it a whirl while I tended to the final two frames still in the hive. Once we'd spun out all the honey, Gray opened the spigot at the base of the extractor. The syrup flowed with agonizing slowness into another cheesecloth-lined tub. "This is where the phrase 'sweet anticipation' originates," said Gray.

I was sure he just made that up.

"We'll pass it through the mesh a second time to get rid of any chunks of wax that may have flown off in the centrifuge," said Gray.

"Not to mention dead bees," said Dave, as several honey-coated insects oozed from the spigot.

This final step, which required no additional intervention on our part, would take hours. We decided to pass them in the pub. Our honeyed feet made sucking adhesive sounds as we padded toward the front of Gray's condo. He followed behind us with a wet mop.

Chapter 12

Year 2 | Autumn

Gray burst through my apartment door like a stripper from a cake. Dave shuffled in behind. "You'll never guess my news!" Gray said.

"You're right," I replied.

Gray wore a green linen shirt with a coat of arms emblazoned on the breast pocket. His brown trousers had such a pronounced crease, I'd swear they were wire-reinforced like a push-up bra. Dave looked his usual schlumpy self—baggy shorts, generic t-shirt, sneakers barely laced.

"Gray," I said, "I hate to be the one to break it to you, but those colors clash."

Graham's face transformed into a mixture of offended and appalled, but he quickly restored his aloof countenance. "Beg pardon? These earth tones are perfectly matched. In fact, the colors brown and green couldn't be more complementary. Would you tell dirt and grass they don't go together?"

"Um, probably not," I admitted.

Gray huffed off to the fridge in search of liquid refreshment, with Dave in close pursuit. They jostled for position in my small kitchen alcove, and each emerged with a can of Guinness. I cleared my throat and pointed to myself, wordlessly sending Dave back to fetch me one.

Picking up the dropped thread, I said, "Graham, aren't your fashion preferences just a bit, shall we say, effete?"

"First of all, the word you're searching for in the vast caverns of your mind is effeminate, not effete. Second of all—no."

Gurgling hisses filled the air as we cracked open our cans simultaneously. Dave passed around large plastic tumblers, and Gray let out an exasperated sigh. "How many times must I tell you lads? Ales and stouts should only be served in a proper pint glass. Plastic is just so gauche." He rummaged through the cabinet above the stove, found a glass, and decantered his stout into it.

Gray settled on the couch. "Here's the issue as I see it. The attention that I pay to my personal appearance is not effeminate. It's simply closer to the British ideal of masculinity than the American ideal."

"Lame," I said. "You'd be a sissy in any culture."

"Jerome, old boy, you're on shaky ground," retorted Gray. "Your sartorial style, if one could call it that, is nondescript. You wear bland colors and neutral styles. You blend into the background like a chameleon."

"Nondescript? Are you kidding me? My style is totally descript."

We turned our gazes to Dave. "What are you assholes looking at me for? I'm deliberately anti-fashion, which, I should point out, is a fashion statement in its own right."

Dave headed back into my kitchenette. Apparently succumbing to Gray's peer pressure, he decided to quaff with a glass glass. Pawing through the pile in the sink, muttering unintelligibly, he turned on the water, dug out a plastic bucket from below, and began piling plates and bowls into it, sifting through the soiled stack.

While Dave searched, the water flowed, sputtering and spraying off-kilter due to my semi-clogged aerator. I watched till the annoyance factor became intolerable. "For Christ sake, Dave, shut off the tap, would you? Do you have any clue how much water you're wasting? It's literally money down the drain."

Gray immediately rapped my knuckles, metaphorically speaking. "No, Jerome," he said in a pedantic tone. "It's *literally* water down the drain. It's *figuratively* money down the drain."

Dave squeezed a half-cup of dishwashing liquid into his found glass and swirled it around with his index finger. The water continued to flow.

"You lads have been blathering so much," said Gray, "I haven't even had a chance to tell you my news." He paused theatrically to allow the tension to build. It didn't. "I've been invited to dinner at the British consul general's residence!"

"Nice," I responded without enthusiasm, getting up to shut off the water and glare at Dave.

"Wow," said Dave, uncharacteristically impressed. "How did you ever wrangle that?"

"Wrangling was not involved. The press attaché is a member of my squash club."

"The British ambassador!" said Dave admiringly. He was so flush with enthusiasm, I began to worry that Gray's snobbishness was contagious.

"Technically, no," said Gray. "The ambassador is based at the embassy in Washington. The British Consulate General is essentially a satellite office."

"Still sounds impressive, though," said Dave.

"Indeed it does," said Gray. "They're all part of Her Majesty's Diplomatic Service, after all."

This development, of course, represented a dream come true for Graham, feeding his aspiration for a higher station in life. His social striving traced back to the upper-crust attitude he acquired in London. Upon his return stateside, he immediately purchased season tickets to the symphony, although he only attended when he was trying to impress some naïve female. He joined a country club, which he did frequent for a spell before being banned for submerging his golf cart in a pique of duffer frustration. He also made a calculated donation to a prominent local charity, which worked as intended, buying him a seat on the board. He rarely showed up for the meetings.

"I haven't been this excited since the board of governors luncheon at the Federal Reserve Bank," said Gray.

"Really, darling?" I said, eyebrow arched. "They served bullion, I presume?"

My witticism sailed over Graham's head, which I chalked up as a moral victory.

Gray beamed with pride as he took a long swig of his Guinness. He looked disdainfully at the black liquid. "I really should be drinking Bass."

"Hey, if you need a companion for this little soirée, I'm available," said Dave.

"That's actually an issue, all kidding aside," said Gray.

"Who's kidding?" said Dave.

"Seeing as how I'm, shall we say, *between* relationships, I'm in a bit of a quandary. I can't exactly show up solo."

"Not that I'm a stickler for precise language," I said, "unlike some people I know. But doesn't 'between relationships' imply both a relationship in the past and one in the future?"

Gray ignored me, as he always does when I nail him with his own hammer. He pulled out his phone and started rapidly flipping through screens. "Ah, here it is," he finally said. "Escort services."

"What?" cried Dave. "You're bringing a hooker to the ambassador's residence?"

"Not a hooker. An escort. Respectable. Attractive. Sophisticated."

"Slutty," I said.

"Gray, don't be a fucking fool," said Dave. "This would be a *pas* of unimaginable *faux.*"

"It's true," I said. "You'll tumble right off that social ladder you've been climbing if you bring a hooker—"

"Escort," said Gray.

"—to the ambassador's—"

"Consul's."

"—dinner party. When your dolled-up companion starts playing footsie with the cultural *attaché*, you'll realize too late that we're right."

Gray put away his phone, crossed his arms, and adopted a pout. "Fine. What do you suggest?"

"Well, you could take Maura," I said.

Gray immediately brightened. "Your Maura? Maura Wood?," he asked eagerly.

"Just kidding," I replied.

Gray turned toward Dave, who put up a hand in the manner of a school crossing guard. "Whoa. No way. I wouldn't subject any of my girlfriends to the tedium."

"Would that be the tedium of a stuffy dinner at the embassy or the tedium of spending an evening with Gray?" I asked.

"Tedium squared," said Dave.

"Fine!" said Gray to Dave. "You can go."

"*Moi?*" said Dave. "I'd be fucking delighted."

"But no swearing. And I get to approve your outfit."

"No effing problem," said Dave. "I don't wear 'outfits.'"

"Saturday. Eighteen hundred hours," said Gray.

Dave groaned at the remark, suffering, no doubt, from the sudden onset of buyer's remorse.

David Deng and Graham Earling had their identification papers out and ready a full five miles from the British consul general's residence. Dave nervously fingered his driver's license; Gray rested his passport on his thigh. They tooled down the leafy roadway in Graham's freshly detailed Land Rover, heading toward the diplomatic mansion in one of the city's posh outlying neighborhoods.

Firmly in his element, Graham grinned unabashedly. "You know, despite its unreliability and poor workmanship, this Rover might just be the best investment I ever made in my life."

"Slow down," said Dave. "Visiting the ambassador doesn't grant you diplomatic immunity, you know."

"Consul. And I'm only going ten kilometers per hour above the limit."

"Yeah? Well, if they don't get you for speeding, they'll lock you up for pretentiousness."

Dave read off the street numbers of the stately homes. "Should be just ahead on the right."

As they turned into the long driveway, palpable disappointment overcame the pair. They spotted nary a sentry, nor, for that matter, even a gate.

"Shouldn't there be some kind of Beefeater out here?" asked Dave.

"Safe neighborhood. No need," said Gray, hiding the letdown as he slipped his passport back into his jacket pocket. Graham guided the car up the cobblestone drive to a gabled entranceway.

The consul general maintained a stately residence, a two-story Georgian mansion with massive twelve-pane windows arrayed across the façade. White lace curtains billowed in the warm September breeze.

Graham looked around for a valet. None appeared. "Must be parking cars for the other guests," he said. They pulled into a small cutout at the side of the house. "I'll just leave the keys in the ignition for him."

Outside the doorway, Gray stopped, turned, and inspected his companion, straightening and brushing off the lapel of Dave's canary-yellow sports coat, which he wore over a black long-sleeved t-shirt and black trousers. Gray initially objected to Dave's lack of suit and tie but subsequently decided that the jet-black motif offset with shocking yellow looked sufficiently natty. Dave had gone to extremes to make a good impression, slicking down his hair, polishing his shoes, and buying a new belt.

Graham outfitted himself in a perfectly tailored gray British-made suit, woven red Pakistani silk tie, and gleaming black Italian shoes.

A tuxedoed man-servant greeted them at the doorway. Gray breathed a sigh of relief that at least one domestic was dutifully manning his post. "This way, if you please," the butler said stiffly.

The trio passed single file under a chandelier heavily laden with retina-burning crystal. Dave shaded his eyes and turned away. Gray squinted while admiring it, unable to avert his gaze. They entered a large sitting room completely devoid of furnishings, save an oriental rug so plush that each step left a footprint in the weave. Cardboard packing boxes littered the periphery of the chamber.

"Must be redecorating," whispered Gray to Dave.

Padding across the pillow-like surface, Dave couldn't contain his enthusiasm. "Wow, this is softer than my bed!" he said, a bit too loudly.

Graham put a finger to his lips and nodded toward the butler ahead of them. "Act like you've been here before."

"But I haven't," protested Dave.

They crossed a threshold into a high-ceilinged dining room dominated by a massive table covered with a gray moving pad. A dozen upholstered straight-backed chairs were turned upside-down on the surface. "How will they ever serve us dinner?" said Gray, forgetting his own admonition just seconds before.

"A moveable feast?" said Dave.

They entered a narrow hallway off the dining room, following it past a pantry, a potting room, and a storage area before entering a large, sparsely furnished room at the back of the building.

Two adults and a child occupied the space. "Graham, old chap! Glad you could make it!" A middle-aged man with a distended belly and a bad comb-over approached, hand extended.

Graham shook his hand and glanced around the room. "Are we early? Where are the other guests?"

"Oh, no one else actually RSVP'd, I'm afraid. It's just me and my girlfriend Christie." A red-haired woman approached and murmured a greeting. "And my second daughter from my third marriage." A young girl, busy at a table, looked up and waved.

"But where's the consul general?" asked Gray, voice tinged with concern.

"Oh, he moved out six weeks ago. We're selling the residence to the UAE. The upkeep was getting to be too much, I'm afraid."

"The United Auto Employees bought your mansion?" said Dave.

The attaché guffawed. "Ah, jolly good! And you would be?"

"Oh, um, this is my friend, Dave," said Gray. "Dave, this is Derek Hampel, press attaché to the deputy consul general."

Dave stepped forward eagerly. "An honor of the highest order," he said, pumping Derek's hand vigorously. "I send my greetings to your Queen."

"Ah, your significant other!" said Derek. "So nice to meet you at last! I've heard a lot about you."

Dave slit his eyes and cocked his head at Gray.

"So, ready for some stuffing?" said the attaché.

Graham looked confused. "But where will you be serving it?"

"The envelopes," said Derek. "The fundraising letter. For the unemployed, undereducated, unwed, underage, underprivileged mothers."

"Stuffing?" said Gray. "Oh my lord! When you invited me to a stuffing party, I thought you were talking about dinner! You know, the British equivalent of a Thanksgiving feast. Turkey, cranberries, stuffing—"

Derek let out such a hearty laugh that his hair became unglued. "Oh, that's priceless! But not to worry. We have plenty of food." He gestured toward a table by the back wall where several bags of take-out sat. "Wendy's," he said. "Best burger in town. Grab a bag. We can eat while we stuff."

Gray looked crestfallen as he and Dave shuffled over to the buffet table.

"Ah, yes, Wendy," said Dave, peering into a fast-food bag. "Wasn't she one of Henry the Eighth's wives?"

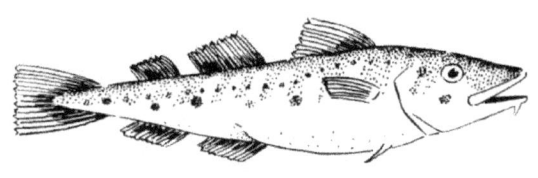

Chapter 13

Year 2 | Autumn

A voluptuous smell wafted over me as I entered Maura's apartment: welcoming, like a spontaneous smile; delicate, like the crystal wine glasses set on the kitchen table; seductive, like the sight of Maura standing at the stove wearing nothing more than one of my dress shirts, with the top three buttons undone.

"That aroma is intoxicating," I said. "Can I have a taste?"

I approached her from behind, wrapped my arms around her waist, and peered over her shoulder as Maura sautéed a medley of seafood in a large frying pan. On the cluttered counter next to the stove stood a bottle of olive oil, several cloves of garlic, two shallots, half a lemon, and a pepper grinder.

"Uh, uh, uh!" said Maura, waving her wooden scraper. "This food is off limits."

"Who said anything about food?" I slipped my hand inside her shirt and gently enveloped her breast while pressing my groin against her shirt-tailed buttocks.

"Down boy," said Maura. "Whatever it is you hope to eat, you'll have to wait. Have a glass of wine and recompose yourself."

Maura lived in a second-floor walk-up in a lively mixed-residential district. She managed to make her apartment seem simultaneously lived-in and orderly. While not a fastidious cleaner, a la Graham, Maura broke out her vacuum and duster often enough to keep the rooms respectable. While no pack rat, a la Judith, Maura did possess ample paraphernalia, but her photos, books, knick-knacks, and mementos were organized rather than stacked haphazardly. High ceilings and a front corner location gave the place a sunny, airy feel, rather than dim and dank, a la me. The furniture throughout was not coordinated in any classic interior design sense, but the quality wood, sturdy construction, and timeless design reflected Maura's sensibilities.

I realized that this feeling of harmonious contradiction that I got from Maura's flat—cozy yet spacious; casual yet tidy; mismatched yet coordinated—was not unlike the feelings I got from Maura herself: that she was a full-spectrum woman; that anything was possible; that I never knew what I'd get, but I always knew it would be interesting.

An ice bucket sat on the kitchen table. I clasped the bottle by the neck, extracted it from the icy depths, and poured myself a generous serving.

"*¿Y tú, señorita?*" I asked, holding the bottle aloft.

"*No, gracias. Mi vaso está lleno.*"

"Okay, you've officially exceeded my Spanish vocabulary. You want some of this plonk or not?"

"'No' is pronounced 'no' in most Romance and Germanic languages, darling," said Maura.

"And when a woman says 'no'?"

"She means 'no.'"

"Got it."

I took a sip of my Chablis. "Exactly what delicacy awaits me?" I asked. "If it tastes anything like it smells, I may just melt in my chair."

"My own recipe," said Maura. "I call it *ménage à trois*—the commingling of lobster, scallops, and shrimp in a simple lemon garlic reduction."

"I swoon at the thought. I can't recall having all three in the same year, never mind on the same plate."

"Just remember, Jerome, it's not the ingredients that make it special. It's the loving preparation."

"Profound," I said with full sincerity.

"It's the secret of the culinary universe. Don't ever forget it."

I savored my wine, ruminated on Maura's wisdom, and admired her form as she busied herself at the stove, shaking the frying pan by the handle, lifting the lid on the saucepans, opening the oven and peeking inside.

"So, what else do you have in store for me?" I asked.

"Is it my imagination, or is every question you ask a *double entendre*?"

"Come again?"

"Case in point."

"I did that deliberately. I knew you'd swallow the bait."

"Give it up, boy. I can out-innuendo you every time."

"Okay, I give."

"Me too." Maura switched off all the burners, sashayed over, and straddled my lap. "Time to eat." I clasped her by each butt cheek and pulled her tight. She nibbled at my ear.

Reluctantly, Maura removed herself from my clutches. She served generous portions of the seafood ménage, then dribbled the reduction sauce onto side dishes of couscous and steamed broccoli. I sliced a French garlic loaf, warm from the oven. We clinked our wine glasses and sampled the fare.

As anticipated, every mouthful tasted divine. I savored each of the delicacies separately, then in various combinations. Maura watched me with mild amusement. "You look like you're about to cream your jeans."

"Actually, I already did." I took a sip of wine, pretended to use my napkin, and surreptitiously expelled the liquid into the cloth. I then returned the napkin to my lap and squeezed a few drops on my groin area. "You think I jest?" I stood. "See?"

Maura looked simultaneously shocked and pleased. "Wow, I bet Julia Child never got a reaction like that!"

Maura ate one serving of the sumptuous meal. It took me three platefuls, but I finished everything off, then sopped up the remaining juices with several more slices of bread. The flickering candles, the ambrosial food, the copious wine, and the beautiful woman went to my head. I couldn't remember feeling more content. "Have I ever told you I love you?" I asked.

"You know very well you haven't."

"I love you."

She didn't recoil in horror. In fact, Maura smiled. "I may return the sentiment someday," she said. "If you're good."

I made a mental note to be extra specially good.

"Well, that was something to behold," said Maura as I dabbed my mouth with the napkin for the final time. "Now, what do you want for dessert?"

"Is that a rhetorical question?"

"Sorry, I'm on a different menu. Only served after 10 p.m."

"And presumably in a room other than the kitchen?"

"Not necessarily."

Maura suggested that we visit a local patisserie for dessert, which wasn't exactly how I had envisioned the evening playing out. But she was insistent and, given the effort that she put into the meal, I couldn't mount much of a protest.

She stepped into a long skirt, slipped on a pair of sandals, and fastened one button of my dress shirt in a half-nod toward respectability, leaving the top two buttons alluringly undone.

We walked arm-in-arm along the bustling street, passing by tiny eateries and coffee shops, funky used clothing stores, a cramped hardware store, imported and organic food emporiums, and several outlets unsure whether they were music stores, head shops, comic book dealers, or tattoo parlors. It was an eclectic ecosystem of entrepreneurship. The dense, compact neighborhood precluded any big box superstores from gaining a foothold, allowing local businesses to flourish.

"Hey," I asked as we pass a fishmonger's shop, "how did you ever afford that meal? Lobster, scallops, and shrimp cost a fortune on their own, but the three in combination?"

Maura reached into her bag and pulled out a piece of red, white, and blue plastic.

"You charged it?" I asked.

"Nope. Even better. Food stamps!"

"You're on food stamps?"

"Sure am! You don't think I could survive on a special ed teacher's salary, do you?"

"Sheesh, I don't know. I survive on a teacher's aide salary, which is even less."

"Yeah, and look where you live. Look at your diet. Look at your clothes."

She had a point. I lived in a tiny basement studio apartment. My diet consisted mainly of peanut butter and noodles, occasionally combined. And my clothes were what one might charitably call shabby chic, except minus the chic part. Maura outclassed me in every category.

"Wow," I said, "I've never known anyone on food stamps. I guess that makes you, well, poor."

"Which makes you a pauper."

"Hey, there's nothing wrong with being poor," I said. "There's a certain nobility in being a member of the underclass."

"There's more nobility in being rich."

We walked a block in silence.

"Anyway," Maura said, "it's not like I'm destitute. I've got $5,000 in the bank."

"You do? I know a remote little island in the Caribbean we could visit this winter."

"Sorry, it's a rainy-day fund, not a snowy-day fund."

My vision of making love with Maura under a coconut tree was instantly dashed.

"You should get on food stamps yourself," Maura continued. "If nothing else, you can upgrade to organic peanut butter instead of that jiffy crap you eat."

"Can I get organic marshmallow fluff to go with it?"

We passed an art-house movie theater advertising its retro amenities: *Single screen! Velvet rope! Real butter!* I scanned the marquee. "Since when is *Attack of the Killer Tomatoes* considered an art film?"

"It's a cult classic," replied Maura, "It's so bad, it's good."

The restaurant, a block beyond the cinema, specialized in desserts; in fact, sweets were the only items on the menu. The place bustled immediately before and after screenings, but we arrived between waves. Only about a quarter of the tables were filled. I scanned the menu, which dripped with cloying prose about the delectable wonders that await the discerning diner.

"The pastry chef is good, but the menu writer is better," observed Maura.

"I'm leaning toward the organic, fair trade, Madagascar vanilla bean ice cream hand-churned by Swedish maidens and drizzled with Hawaiian blue-ring ginger sauce," I said.

"Jerome, as part of your continuing education on the finer things in life, let me impart these words of wisdom. If the dessert doesn't involve chocolate, it's not worth your time or money."

"Huh!" I said. "And just exactly what's wrong with vanilla?"

"Vanilla is just so, well, vanilla!"

"Vanilla is my favorite flavor," I said.

"Why am I not surprised?"

I felt I'd been insulted, but I wasn't sure exactly how.

"Listen," continued Maura, "certain things in this world are inherently superior to their seemingly equal counterparts."

"*No comprendo,*" I said.

"Let's say, for example, it's hot and you want to go swimming. Where do you go? The choice you make reveals a lot about you. Do you go to the country club pool? A remote ocean beach? A freshwater pond?"

"Or my personal Olympic-size indoor pool in my fabulous mansion?"

"Exactly," said Maura.

Maura ordered a tart with three varieties of imported dark chocolate—glazed with chilled Swiss chocolate, smothered with melted Belgian chocolate, and sprinkled with shaved German chocolate. It seemed like overkill to me, but what did I know? I ordered the vanilla ice cream and a cup of coffee.

"Let's take a little quiz, shall we?" said Maura. "I'll name pairs of items, and you tell me which you prefer. Ten simple questions, and we'll have an accurate profile."

"Fire away."

Maura pulled a pen from her bag and started scribbling on her napkin. "Okay, we've already determined chocolate versus vanilla. Number two, salt water or fresh water?"

"Fresh," I said. "Tastes better."

"For swimming."

"Still fresh."

"Three, automatic transmission or manual?"

"Automatic. Easier in traffic jams."

"Four, white meat or dark?"

"White. Less gamey."

"Five, red wine or white?"

"Beer."

"Six, motorboat or sailboat?"

"Motor. Essential for waterskiing."

Maura looked up from her tally sheet. "Jerome, you don't need to explain every answer. A simple one-word reply will do just fine."

"Oh. Okay."

"All right. Seven, wheat bread or white?"

"White. Goes with fluff."

Maura shot me a look.

"Oops—sorry!"

"Eight, tuna or haddock?"

"Haddock. Not as fishy. Oh, sorry. I can't help myself!"

"Nine, chopsticks or fork and spoon?"

"Forking and spooning. You know I love them both."

Maura ignored me. "Ten, air conditioning or ceiling fan?"

"Air conditioning. It's, um, cooler."

"Okay, that's it," said Maura, tallying my score. I waited with nervous anticipation.

"Well, once I take off points for excessive explanations—"

"Hold on! You never said that would cost me points!"

"Kidding. But points off for being gullible."

I started to protest again, realized I was being set up, and held back. Maura studied her napkin. The delay proved torturous. "Well?" I asked.

"Normally," said Maura, "I would say that there's no such thing as a wrong answer—"

"Hold on. Exactly how often do you give this little quiz?"

"—but your case is, in my experience, unprecedented."

I waited for the bad news. It didn't come.

"That's it? My score is 'unprecedented'?"

"No, I'm just pulling your leg. You did just fine."

"You're not going to give me a letter grade? A pass or a fail? An 'A' for effort?"

"No, no," said Maura. "It's not that kind of test."

"I don't know," I said, dejected. "This whole test smells kind of fishy to me."

"Bluefishy? Or codfishy?"

"More like sardines. Or anchovies. Which I hate."

"This was just a baseline test," said Maura, "to determine where you are now. I'll give it to you again in a year, and we'll measure your progress."

My disappointment was tempered by Maura's implication that we'll still be together in year. That would exceed my opposite sex relationship record by approximately ten months.

Maura offered me a taste of her chocolate orgasm. I accepted eagerly.

We strolled back to her apartment hand-in-hand. I was feeling pretty happy. I had found the perfect woman, someone with refined tastes in food and sex who actually contemplated staying with me for a considerable length of time. What more could a boy want?

We climbed the steps to her flat, and Maura unlocked the door. I reached inside to flick on the light, but she grabbed my arm. "Leave it off. Time for the after-hours menu."

Maura took my hand and led me to the bedroom, dominated by a huge and inviting bed with a puffy comforter and several pillows. "Take off all your clothes," she said. I did as I was told. "Now go into the bathroom and wash any part of your body that you think might wind up in my mouth."

"What?"

"You heard me. Lots of warm soapy water."

Maura watched me pad off to the bathroom naked. As I groped for the switch, she said, "No lights."

Luckily, a shaft of moonlight faintly illuminated the bathroom. Easing my buttocks onto the cool porcelain edge of the tub, feet inside, I dutifully performed my hygiene exercise. Hopefully, I washed my penis. Imaginatively, I cleaned my earlobes. Pragmatically, though not technically mandated, I scrubbed my armpits. I tried to picture Maura's mouth elsewhere on my body, but every other body part seemed either too big to fit or too gross to contemplate. But I gave my whole torso and extremities a once-over just to be safe, then rinsed myself with the portable shower head.

When I returned to the bedroom, Maura was standing beside the bed wearing a fresh white v-neck man's undershirt that just barely covered her butt cheeks. "Okay, Jerome. Under the sheet with you." I obeyed. The sheet felt cool and fresh on my clean, naked body.

Once I was settled, Maura hopped onto the bed beside me. She knelt beside my right shoulder and placed her hands on the top of my head, riffling through my hair with alternating fingernails and fingertips, tingling my scalp. She brought her wriggling fingers to my forehead and lightly drew them down my face, creating the sensation of falling raindrops. She leaned over and darted her tongue in my ear. "You forgot to wash inside your ears," she whispered. "Salty." I started to mention my pristine lobes, but she shushed me with a finger to my lips.

With the same feathery touch, she moved down my chest, mouthing each nipple in succession, teasing them erect. "Put your arms over your head," she said. I grabbed the balusters on the headboard, half expecting her to immobilize me with handcuffs.

She didn't. Instead, Maura balled her hands into fists and gently rolled them into my armpits, kneading with her knuckles. "Just for the record," I said, "I did not forget to wash my pits."

"Shhh," said Maura.

She drew the sheet back as far as my kneecaps and mounted my thighs like hopping on a motorcycle. My penis rose between her legs, a stick-shift for her bike.

Maura reverted to fingertip stimulation, drawing zigzags down my chest, circling my belly button, and teasing the area just above my pubic hair. My erect penis throbbed and glistened at the tip with anticipatory semen.

Maura reached behind her and flung the sheet aside. She turned and again knelt beside me, this time facing my feet, playing her fingers through my pubic hair before skirting my penis entirely and moving to the top of my thighs. I moaned with aching disappointment. I attempted to caress her buttocks. "Uh-uh!" she said. "No touchy." I withdrew my hand.

She lightly scratched my thighs, knees, and calves before turning her full attention to my feet, tickling the heel, the arch, and the ball. Suddenly, I felt an unfamiliar sensation, and it took a second to discern what was happening. Maura was darting her tongue between my toes, in and out in rapid succession. The feeling was shockingly erotic. When she reached the last toe, she took it whole into her mouth and swirled her tongue around it. She moved across, sucking the ten little soldiers in succession. I attained a sexual epiphany: the foot is the second-most sensual part of the body.

By the time she moved to my penis, my head was positively swimming. Euphoria overwhelmed rational thought, and I gave in to the sensation. Maura had me completely under her spell. In the dark bedroom, I had no idea what she was doing. I only knew it was the most pleasurable experience of my life.

She alternated hands and mouth, light and firm, warm and cool, wet and dry, pulsating and steady. She tickled my testicles and my anus. I swear, it felt like three women simultaneously lavishing their attentions on me. I arched my back. My muscles tensed and released in involuntary, primordial thrusts. I was delirious.

I tried intently not to come, never wanting the feeling to end. But it felt too good. Maura broke my resolve with a grand artistic culmination of dexterity, imagination, skill, experience, and technique. She created such an onslaught of stimulation, I had no choice but to succumb. I orgasmed in a massive, throbbing release that convulsed me from head to toe. I felt like I'd just been born.

As I lay limp, helpless, spent, and moaning softly, Maura tenderly squeezed out every last pulsation and drank it down. She peeked back at me. "Ambrosia," she said sweetly.

I slowly emerged from my primal state and regained a semblance of cognition. "Maura, oh my God. You've got to tell me. What, exactly, were you doing down there? I can't for the life of me imagine."

"Jerome, my love, you know not what you ask. You expect me to reveal the secret of the sexual universe?"

The "secret of the sexual universe" sounded grandiose, if not mythological, but hyperbole it was not. Maura held the key to something timeless and mystical, ethereal and transcendent. I begged, pleaded, and cajoled, to no avail. The secret endured. Her lips, her beautiful, dexterous lips, were sealed.

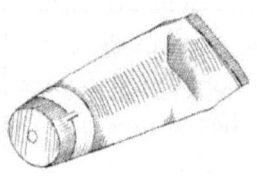

Chapter 14

Year 2 | Autumn

Two weeks later, I sat sprawled on my couch, my laptop on my lap top, watching college hoops, Gonzaga trouncing Pepperdine. Suddenly, my phone vibrated in my pocket. It felt pretty good. I decided not to answer it, instead nudging it closer to my groin. After four rings, it went into voicemail. I hoped the person would call back.

The Gonzaga point guard stole the ball and hustled down the court with one defender in hot pursuit. He faked a lay-up and flipped a behind-the-back pass to his teammate trailing the play. The big man rammed home a thundering two-hand dunk. The crowd went wild.

I couldn't decide if I was more like the speedy point guard or the muscular power forward.

The laptop warmed my groin pleasantly, and the phone's seductive vibration began again. Gotta love technology. But a sudden thought spoiled the moment: What if it was a guy calling?

Then an even more-sobering notion intruded. It dawned on me that my laptop drew a wireless signal from the router in my closet. At the same time, my phone communicated with a cell tower somewhere in the city. And all this electromagnetic radiation was concentrating itself directly onto my lap. Instinctively, I felt my testicles for lumps.

I placed the laptop on the coffee table and yanked the phone from my pocket, checking messages. It was Gray. An involuntary shudder washed over me. I called Maura.

"Hey, what are you doing?"

"My toenails," she said. "You?"

"Waxing my legs." I cleared my throat. "I'd like to try a little experiment. Are you interested?"

"I might be. What do you have in mind?"

"Well, I was sitting here minding my own business, when the phone in my pocket went off. It felt pretty good and got me to thinking."

Maura remained silent; I carried on. "Okay, so here's the plan. I want you to hang up, set your phone to vibrate mode, and place it snugly against your vagina."

"Uh, Jerome, I don't think so. Have you been surfing porn again?"

"Of course not!" I said, making a mental note to clear my browsing history. "Think about it. This could take phone sex to a whole new level."

I hoped her unresponsiveness indicated thoughtful reconsideration. I continued: "There's a setting to control the number of rings before a call transfers to voicemail. Just switch it to infinity and enjoy the ride."

"Sorry, big boy, but you're on your own."

I was crushed. My idea had me so inspired that I just had to see it through. I dialed a wake-up service. "Can you, um, arouse me from my nap in about thirty seconds?"

Friday after work, Maura decamped to visit her mother for a week, a two-hundred mile drive. After six months of dating her daughter, Mrs. Wood and I still hadn't met. Of course, Maura had never met my folks either, but they lived in San Diego, whereas Maura's Mom was just a skip down the highway. Maura didn't invite me to join her on this visit, and I didn't bring up the subject.

Maura's father, Walter Wood, died when she was twelve. And that's about the only information she ever shared about him. We had leafed through family photos of Mom, sister Monika, and Maura, but I'd never even seen a picture of Wally. Maura never characterized him as good, bad, or indifferent, a nice guy or an asshole. It was more like he never existed.

I spent the weekend alone in my gloomy basement studio, feeling as glum as my abode. I was initially overcome with ennui, which eventually gave way to a general feeling of malaise. A dull ache invaded my thighs, as though I'd been skiing nonstop for hours on end. I was mildly nauseated. And I couldn't urinate worth a damn—a weak trickle was the best I could manage. Even after dribbling at the toilet for a full minute, my bladder still felt full.

On Monday, I texted Maura to tell her I was sick. She suggested I see a doctor. I took her advice, first making an appointment, then calling in sick to work. The program director showed more annoyance than sympathy, probably because Maura was already out, thus putting two substitutes in the same classroom. I could only imagine the chaos that would ensue.

The doctor ran a battery of tests, with a painful blood draw, a cold stethoscope, a blinding light, and a splintery tongue depressor merely serving as prelude to the most loathsomely invasive procedure known to man—the rectal exam.

If the doctor had any questions about my sexual proclivities, they were quickly erased when he inserted his latexed, lubricated digit into my anus. I tensed, groaned, and inhaled sharply in an involuntary spasm. It felt like I was having a bowel movement right into his hand.

"I'm going to massage your prostate gland. Tell me if it hurts," said the doctor.

"How will I distinguish the prostate pain from this anal rape pain?" I asked through clenched teeth.

As his fingertip, submerged deep within my alimentary canal, pressed firmly against my prostate, I thought—what a miserable way to make a living. A medical doctor is supposed to be a position of prestige and respect, yet this sub-specialty, proctology, had to rank among the world's worst occupations.

The doctor finished his probe, offered me a wad of tissue, and instructed me to dress and meet him in his office. I wiped away as much of the excess petroleum jelly as I could, then slid into my underwear before finding my way down the hall.

The doctor tilted his head toward an empty chair in his small, cramped office. Medical books tumbled out of a bookcase. Several academic degrees, slightly askew, hung on the wall. None of the schools was familiar to me, nor, for that matter, the host countries.

"Your case is a bit unusual for someone in their twenties," he said. "I won't know for certain until the test results come back, but preliminarily, it looks like you've got prostatitis."

"An enlarged prostate?"

"No, actually, prostatitis involves inflammation rather than enlargement."

"Okay. What's the treatment?"

"Unfortunately, there is no treatment, per se. It's more a case of wait-and-see, letting it get better on its own. There are, however, some lifestyle changes you can make that might accelerate any improvement."

"Such as?"

"Prostatitis has been loosely associated with caffeine consumption, so giving up coffee would be a good idea. You don't need to quit outright; just switch to decaf."

"Decaf?" I said with a moan. "That's as bad as non-alcoholic beer."

"Well, funny you should mention that, because alcohol is also a potential source of inflammation. You should abstain from drinking until the problem clears up, if not for good."

"Is that all?"

"Actually, no. Spicy foods have been implicated in some studies. Eliminate them from your diet."

"So let me get this straight," I said. "I have to give up coffee, alcohol, and spicy food? You're talking about my three basic food groups."

I envisioned my new abstemious lifestyle. It was a bleak picture. "What's left to enjoy? You're not going to tell me to give up sex, too, are you?"

"Actually, there is a sexual component to this."

"No!"

"But in this instance, you may be pleased with my recommendation. For prostate health, ideally, you should be ejaculating at least once per day."

The reality took a second to settle in.

"What? Really? Once a day?" I asked, unable to suppress a grin. "Oh, wow. Can you write me a prescription for that?"

Maura texted me later that day. "How was the doctor?"

"The doctor's just fine," I replied. "I, on the other hand, am not."

"What is it?"

"Nothing serious," I typed. "I'll tell you when you get back."

I spent the week recuperating. I diligently followed the doctor's instructions by blandicizing my diet to the extreme—oatmeal, milk, bologna sandwiches on white bread. I turned down several invites for a beer and instead sat home sipping weak green tea. I went slightly overboard on the daily ejaculation requirement, but in my single-minded—and singlehanded—quest for good prostate health, who could object?

Despite my conscientiousness, progress was slow. By the time Maura returned on Saturday, I was feeling only a tad better. The aches, though diminished, still nagged. The urine flow, though improved, remained tenuous.

Maura was sitting at the kitchen table working on a crossword puzzle when I arrived at her apartment. I walked over to her chair and flung my leg across her lap, straddling her. We sat face-to-face.

She gave me a kiss on the cheek. "No lips," she said. "You might be contagious." I bussed both her cheeks, European style.

"So, what's the diagnosis?" she asked.

"Prostatitis."

"Sounds serious."

"Can be."

"What's the treatment?"

"Well, it doesn't involve drugs or surgery. He prescribed, shall we say, lifestyle changes."

"Such as?"

I got up and moved to the chair opposite.

"I have to give up caffeine."

"Geez. Sluggish mornings."

"And spicy foods."

"Adios, salsa."

"And alcohol."

"Holy moly," said Maura.

"Yeah."

"What's left?"

"Sex," I said.

"Oh my God! You have to give up sex too?"

"Well, no, not exactly."

"What then?"

"Uh, the doctor said that I should ejaculate every day."

Maura cracked a wide smile. "His medical advice is to jerk off daily?" She laughed.

"Actually, he was agnostic regarding the means. So, well, I thought that maybe this could be an excellent opportunity for us to, uh, refine our techniques. Every day."

"Whoa," said Maura, letting the magnitude of the treatment plan sink in. She jumped up. "Well, I guess we better get started. Doctor's orders!" She led me by the hand to the bedroom.

Unfortunately, despite this medical advice, sex was the last thing on my mind. My head pounded; my body ached. I doubted I could get an erection even in the face of Maura's sexual mastery. I rued the lost opportunity. It was like attending a party with an open bar but feeling too hungover to exploit it.

Standing naked with my back to the foot of the bed, my arms outstretched, I relinquished myself to the force of gravity, falling backwards like one might into swimming pool. I shuffled, crab style, toward the headboard, pulled my knees to my chest, and thrust my legs under the covers, drawing the blanket up to my chin.

Suddenly, I was aware of an odd and unpleasant sensation along my calves, thighs, and buttocks. Pressing against my skin was—what? Pebbles? Marbles? Dried beans? Bugs? Something small and hard and utterly foreign to a bed.

I switched on the bedside light and threw off the covers. There, scattered all about the sheet, were dozens of corn kernels.

"Maura!" I yelled. I pulled the blanket back up.

"What?" she said, walking into the bedroom, toothbrush in her suds-filled mouth.

"Didn't Judith stay here for a couple of nights while you were away?"

"Yeah?" said Maura.

"Well, look at this." I whipped back the covers melodramatically. "She's been eating popcorn in the bed! What a slob!" I brushed the kernels off the mattress, and they landed with a clatter on the hardwood floor.

"And when you fling garbage onto the floor, what does that make you?"

"Mmmm, good point," I said, rolling out of bed, crawling over, and sweeping all the kernels into a little pile with my hands. "I'll pick them up in the morning."

Maura left. I hoisted myself back into bed. By the time she returned, I had drifted off into the nether state between sleeping and wakefulness.

Maura climbed in beside me. "Are you asleep?" she whispered.

I stirred. "No, I'm awake."

"Why do people always deny that they're asleep, when it's obvious they are?" she asked.

"Actually," I replied, rolling over and rubbing Maura's belly, "the real question is, why would you wake someone up to ask them if they're asleep?"

Maura squirmed. "You missed a few of those kernels." She reached under the blanket to extract them.

"Take it up with Judith, not me."

"I will. It's not the first time. She has this fetish for corn in bed."

I dozed off almost instantly, overcome with exhaustion, doctor's orders be damned.

Chapter 15

Year 2 | Autumn

The medical regimen slowly yielded improvement. My general malaise lifted. The constant sensation of a full bladder dipped to the three-quarters mark. And the mostly abstemious lifestyle proved not as intolerable as expected, as the lack of literal spice was more than offset by the increase in figurative spice, courtesy of Maura's ministrations. Even sipping faux wine was weirdly intoxicating. I swore it made me lightheaded and gay, just like the real thing.

On the mend, I had the luxury of transferring my health worries to Gray. He was conflicted, depressed, and idle. His social striving had stalled. He had money, but not happiness. His vegetables and bees kept him engaged, but he couldn't putter with that stuff all day. I figured female companionship might be just the ticket to lift his spirits.

"Know any eligible women?" I asked Maura.

"I might. Who wants to know?"

"Oh, a friend."

"Don't play coy with me, buddy boy. I've got tons of female friends. I just need some background information to make a suitable match."

"I'm not sure that 'tons' of female is exactly what he's looking for. He likes his women on the svelte side."

"It couldn't be Dave," she said. "Doesn't he have more girlfriends than he can shake his stick at?"

"So to speak."

"Graham?"

"Yup."

Maura arched an eyebrow. "A good-looking, cultivated guy like him can't get a date? And isn't he a trust fund kid?"

"As trusty as they come."

"But he is a bit fussy, isn't he?" asked Maura, the matchmaking wheels spinning.

"Oh, yeah. He's a classic dork. But a lovable one."

"I might have someone in mind."

"It's not you, is it?" I asked.

She cupped me by the balls. "You're all the man I need."

Maura thought if we could get Graham and her friend into the same room, the sparks would fly. She suggested a dinner party at my apartment. We decided to invite Dave and Judith too, so the matchmaking wouldn't be so obvious.

I considered the various personality types we'd be combining and worried about those flying sparks setting off something more dangerous than romance. "Okay," I said reluctantly. "But tell Judith there's no smoking in my apartment. And she should leave the iguana at home."

A dinner party presented logistical challenges. The stove in my basement studio was just a glorified hotplate, crudely recessed into the countertop to make it seem more like an actual appliance rather than a cheap boarding house artifact. It only had two burners, electric coils covered with the charred remains of countless meals.

My microwave oven appeared to be one of the original models issued during the prior century, low powered, with an interior space disproportionately small compared to the exterior dimensions. If I had a pair of microwave detection specs, I'd likely have been appalled by the radiation leakage.

Given these limitations, I worried about my capacity to provision the party, so I asked Dave and Gray for help. They dropped by on Friday afternoon to strategize.

"I have a couple of culinary specialties that might be suitable," said Gray. "A bit too refined for the setting, perhaps, but we'll give it a go."

"I'll whip up something," said Dave. "A gourmet, organic, sustainable grocery store just opened near my house."

Gray deliberately cleared his throat, an unmistakable signal. Someone had just committed an error of etiquette or grammar, so subtle as to be nearly imperceptible to normal people, but egregiously offensive to Graham's sensibilities. I hoped I wasn't the culpable party.

"David," he said, "don't you realize that people judge you by your grammar, pronunciation, and accent?"

"Of course I do. That's how everyone knows you're a pretentious prick as soon as you open your mouth."

A flash of hurt creased Graham's brow, but he recovered quickly. "Here's a mini lesson for you," he said. "Repeat after me: gross."

Inexplicably, Dave went along. "Gross."

"Ree," said Gray.

"Ree."

"Now blend them together."

"Growsh-ree," said Dave.

"Try again. *Gross*-ree."

"Growsh-ree."

"Oh my word," said Gray. "It sounds like you have marbles in your mouth. Try this one—associated."

"Ah-so-*she*-ated."

"Ah-so-*see*-ated," said Gray, patience waning.

"Ah-so-*she*-ated."

Gray let out a sigh, removed his phone from his pocket, and tapped the screen. "I happen to know a good speech therapist. I just sent you his contact info."

"Go fruck yourself," said Dave.

"If you amateur linguists could shut the hell up, maybe we could return to the menu?" I said.

Gray agreed to prepare an appetizer: avocado halves stuffed with fresh crab meat and sprinkled with toasted pine nuts. Dave refused to commit to a particular dish, but promised to show up with something inventive.

I wanted to create a delicacy to impress Maura. She loved exotic vegetables, stuff that, prior to meeting her, I had never tasted—fresh beets, bok choy, rutabaga—so I figured I'd start there. On my laptop, I typed *recipes to impress a hot woman*, which provided my inspiration: artichoke and feta lasagna. I scrawled out a shopping list, left the boys arguing in my apartment, and headed to the *gross*-ree for my supplies.

Saturday morning; up early; time to make the apartment presentable. I gathered the strewn clothing that adorned every piece of furniture in my studio, shoved it into a large trash bag, and stuffed it into the closet. I loaded all the dirty dishes into a plastic dish bucket and crammed them under the sink. Knowing I would have neither the time nor the inclination to wash the dishes, I had picked up a stack of premium plastic plates at the supermarket—costly, but worth it.

In the bathroom, I stopped the tub, cranked the tap, and squeezed a quarter bottle of shampoo into the churning waters. Sponge mop in hand, I dunked the cellulose head, then swabbed the entire bathroom, from mirror to sink to tub to floor. I had the hygienic wherewithal to save the inside of the toilet bowl for last. Then I grabbed a dirty towel from the rack and dried everything. The room positively gleamed.

My lingering prostatitis cried out for attention. I had the irresistible urge to relieve my bladder, even though I knew it wasn't

as full as it seemed. Not wanting to sully my immaculate bathroom, I
slipped out the back door of my building and pissed in the alley.

Back in my galley kitchen, I pulled a saucepan and baking dish
from a lower cabinet and rinsed off the accumulated dust. Flipping
up a folding extension table that hung off the end of the kitchenette
cabinet, I extracted ingredients from my half-size refrigerator:
artichokes, lasagna noodles, tomato sauce, fresh garlic, canned
tomatoes, black pepper, feta cheese, and a bag of shredded
mozzarella.

In a whirlwind of activity, I adopted the persona of the culinary
artist: boiling water, plucking artichokes, mincing garlic, and opening
containers with equal parts skill and aplomb. I threw away all the
packaging, intent on using every last morsel of the supplies.

My phone rang; it was Maura. "How's it going, big boy?"

"Couldn't be better. I'm whipping up the main course as we
speak—artichoke and feta lasagna."

"Wow. Sounds impressive. You're using a recipe, I hope."

"Huh! Recipes are for wimps."

"Wimps and novices."

"Have you ever seen a TV chef consult a recipe? They have an
intuitive sense. Just like me. I'm winging it, baby!"

"Wait, what's that smell?" said Maura with an urgent tone. "Oh,
hang on. I know. It's the pungent odor of impending disaster."

"Funny," I replied, cradling the phone on my shoulder while
mincing garlic.

"Jerome, your kitchen experience starts and ends with boiling
water."

"Yeah, and you'd probably have me consult a recipe for that
too. *Place three heaping cups of water into a saucepan—*"

I hung up, considered checking online for a recipe, and
abandoned the thought as my heaping cups of water started to boil
over.

I layered the ingredients into the large glass baking dish: film of
tomato sauce; array of flat noodles; smear of feta; smattering of
garlic; shake of pepper; dose of canned tomatoes. My eyes fell on a
motley collection of herbs and spices in the open kitchen cabinet,

generously left by the previous tenant. Knowing that the true magic of fine cuisine comes from the subtle-yet-skillful application of these flavorings, I scanned the huddled mass of containers. I was savvy enough to reject the lemon zest, nutmeg, and mint. I embraced the oregano and bay leaf like old friends. I wasn't sure about the coriander, mace, and turmeric, so I set them aside.

Finally, my masterpiece was ready for the oven.

Gray showed up first, completely oblivious to the intent of the evening. He toted a shopping bag in one hand and a long, oblong item wrapped in a black trash bag in the other.

"Graham, my man, so good of you to come!" I pumped his hand vigorously. "And what, pray tell, have we here?" I gestured toward his lengthy package.

"If I didn't know that irony and satire were beyond your capabilities, I'd swear you were mocking my speech patterns."

"Perish the thought," I replied.

Gray unwrapped the item like he was unpacking a Ming vase, peeling back the plastic, layer by layer, until a dark wooden cylinder appeared: a comically oversized pepper grinder.

"For Christ sake, Gray, that thing is bigger than King Kong's schling schlong."

"Can't you come up with a less crude analogy?"

The doorbell rang. I pushed the intercom buzzer. Maura arrived carrying two heavily laden canvas bags. She was accompanied by an attractive female with a distinct resemblance. Maura gave me a peck on the cheek.

"I can't believe you two have never met. Jerome, this is Monika Wood, my sister."

"Oh, my God, you look just like Maura," I said, "only more, uh, more—"

"Careful of the thin ice," said Maura.

"Only more different!" I said.

I shook Monika's hand, gave her an air kiss, took the bags from Maura, and led them into my apartment. "What do you have in here?" I asked Maura. "These bags weigh a ton."

"Oh, just a little side dish," said Maura. "How's the lasagna coming along?"

"Great! It's resting on the counter."

"That's impressive. Where did you learn about resting lasagna?"

"The flavors need time to marry," I replied. "Everybody knows that." Maura looked skeptical. "Okay, I saw it on a cooking show."

"That I'll believe. Anyway, I need to reheat this in the oven." I tried to peek under the foil, but Maura slapped my hand. She pulled a CD from her bag and handed it to me. "Here, put this on."

I scanned the label. "Thelonious Monk? Do you really think religious music is appropriate for a dinner party?"

Graham emerged from the bathroom. "Jerome," he said, voice filled with wonder and admiration, "I've never seen your loo so spotless." He stopped short upon seeing Monika. "Well, hello!" He extended his hand. "Graham Earling." Monika accepted his mitt demurely.

"*Enchanté*," said Gray with a pretentious little bow. I almost gagged, but Monika already seemed smitten.

I was excited over the romantic prospects as I addressed the fledgling couple. "Come. Sit. You, you, you young members of the opposite sex!" I guided them to the small table and chairs under the half-height basement window.

While Maura busied herself in the kitchenette, I poured the future lovebirds some red wine. Graham twirled the glass, sniffed the wine, took a sip, and swirled it in his mouth. He looked around, as if for a spittoon, then swallowed. "Passable," he said. "What's the vintage?"

"Vintage?" I replied. "Doesn't have one." I held the bottle at eye level to examine the label. "There's no year on it, if that's what you mean."

"What's the varietal?" said Gray.

"*¿Qué?*"

"The grapes, Manuel! What kind of grape? Oh, never mind; let me see." He got up, grabbed the bottle, and slapped me upside the head. "'Three Bill Swill,'" he read. "Hmmmm, maybe 'passable' is an overstatement. Ah, well. *Salud!*" He clinked glasses with Monika.

"I have about 200 bottles in my wine cellar," he said to her.

"Uh, I hate to burst your delusional bubble," I interjected, "but you live in a fifth-floor apartment. You don't even have a basement."

"Actually, I live in a condo, not an apartment," retorted Gray, annoyed that I'd called him out on his self-aggrandizing lie. "And I do have a dedicated, temperature-controlled, light-restricted room that could colloquially be referred to as a wine cellar."

"A closet with a table fan and a bare bulb," I said to Monika in an audible aside. Then, realizing that I was undermining my own matchmaking aspirations, I backed off.

I took my empty wine glass and filled it halfway with white wine. "I hate the red stuff," I explained to Gray and Monika. "Too winey." I filled the remainder of the glass with soda water.

"That's an, um, unique concoction," said Monika.

"Doctor's orders," I replied. "I need to cut down on my alcohol consumption."

"Cirrhosis cropping up again?" asked Gray, looking disdainfully at the bubbling mixture.

"Prostrate," I replied.

"Prostrate? In other words, your medical problem is you drink until you fall face first onto the tarmac?" said Gray.

I didn't want to get bogged down on the topic when there was romance in the air, but I couldn't let Gray's ignorance of medical terminology slide. "I guess you never read that anatomy book they named after you," I said.

Monika looked impressed. "That eponymous title is merely a coincidence," explained Gray, with body language and intonation that suggested otherwise.

Gray again looked at the bubbly white-wine-cum-soda-water mixture I was drinking. "Poor man's champagne," he said with a sniff.

Gray returned his attention to Monika, and I happily plopped myself into the easy chair to watch the courtship unfold. Strains of nonsecular jazz filled the air.

He noted a class ring on her finger, sporting an ornate "B."
"Barnard?" he asked.

"Bryn Mawr," she replied. "You?"

"Oh, just a small liberal arts college that you've never heard of."

Gray's uncharacteristic sheepishness accompanied by a tinge of blush set off alarm bells. The situation could turn awkward. I jumped in. "Graham was wait-listed at Brown," I said with something akin to paternal pride. The comment seemed to restore Gray's equilibrium.

Maura leaned over and whispered into my ear. "Five years later, he's still waiting."

Gray cleared his throat and attempted to reset the conversation. "So, what do you do for a living?"

"I'm a dictionary editor," said Monika.

His heart went instantly aflutter. "Oh, my God! The dictionary is my favorite book! It's on my desert island list! The OED, naturally. What house do you work for?"

The doorbell sounded again. I hit the buzzer without bothering with intercom formalities. Multiple footsteps clomped down the basement stairs, and the door swung open to reveal Dave and Judith. "We ran into each other right outside," said Dave.

"Wow, this place is even smaller than Maura described," said Judith, brandishing an unlit cigarette. "Must have been a closet for the apartment next door."

"Or a wine cellar," I said.

Despite the fact that Maura and I had been dating for more than six months, her friends and mine had never met. Arms crisscrossed and pleasantries flew.

Dave displayed a tattered shopping bag. "My contribution to the festivities," he said, extracting cheese doodles, cheez whiz, American singles, and Ritz crackers. "Nothing goes with wine like cheese."

"That's true," said Judith. "So why didn't you bring any?"

Judith pulled a small brown bottle from her bag and twisted the lid, breaking the seal with a series of pops. "A scotch glass, please," she said to me.

"Shock therapy for the fetus?" I said.

Judith displayed the label. "Non-alcoholic scotch," she said. "Doesn't have quite the bite of the real thing, but it beats ginger ale."

Dave dumped a pile of crackers onto a plate, unwrapped an American single, folded it twice to yield four perfect little squares, and placed one on each circular Ritz. He unwrapped another slice and continued until he had garnished two dozen round orange crackers with squares of orange cheese.

"Now, for the touch of culinary genius that converts this from an appetizer to an *hors d'oeuvre*," he said. Uncapping the cheez whiz, he squirted a dollop atop each cracker. "*Voila!*"

He placed the plate on the coffee table. The anticipated food riot failed to materialize. "Fine!" Dave said indignantly, stuffing one into his mouth. "More for me."

"Step aside," said Gray, sidling past Dave. "Let me show you how it's done." He meticulously scrubbed his hands at the tiny kitchen sink. "Hand washing is the *de rigueur* first act of the master chef." He held up his hands to examine his manicure. "You wouldn't happen to have a nail scrubber, would you?"

While Gray worked his gastronomic magic, the rest of us filled every available sitting space in the room—the two table seats, the easy chair, and the closed pull-out couch. "Jerome," Gray called out from the kitchenette, "these plastic plates don't exactly do my starter course justice."

"Don't be so quick to judge, my friend," I said. "If you look closely, you'll see that the plates are both printed *and* embossed."

Maura leapt from the couch. "Not a problem!" She extracted six small china plates from her canvas bag. "Brought them just in case," she said, smiling sweetly at me.

Gray placed his avocado/crab meat/pine nut creation on each plate and distributed them around the room. "Before you start—" he said, returning to the kitchen alcove. He emerged with his massive pepper mill.

"Oh, my God!" shrieked Judith. "That thing is obscene!"

"Grinds like a dream," said Gray as he serviced the guests.

I declined. "Doctor's orders," I explained once again.

"Since when is pepper a medical issue?" asked Dave.

"Oh, you wouldn't believe his medical restrictions," said Maura.

"Yes, but they're more than offset by my medical prescription," I added.

"I don't get it," said Dave.

"No, but Maura does."

"Frequently," Maura said.

Judith snorted.

Gray placed the grinder on the floor and sat at the table with Monika.

"That contraption could be a sculpture," I said.

"Or a coat rack," said Maura.

"Or a dildo," said Judith.

Monika choked on her crab. Gray gave her a sympathetic pat on the back.

I forced down the bottom-crawling shellfish and slimy fruit; the others seemed to enjoy it, finishing off the appetizer with relish.

"All right, ladies and gentlemen," I announced. "Time for the *pièce de résistance.*"

"You'll get no *résistance* from me," said Dave. Judith laughed; no one else did.

I placed the baking dish on the small oval coffee table in front of Maura and theatrically whipped off the foil covering.

"Foiled again," said Dave. Judith cackled. She stubbed out her unlit cigarette, realized what she'd done, and cursed under her breath.

I picked up a plastic plate from the stack and Maura interceded. "Uh-uh. Use these." She extracted another six large plates from her canvas bag. I smiled appreciatively at her.

Using the edge of a metal spatula, I framed six even pieces. The utensil encountered resistance as I pushed it through the lasagna, with small cracking sounds emanating from the pan. "Geez, I hope I cooked this long enough. It was in over an hour."

"Don't misconstrue the question," said Gray, "but was the oven actually—how shall I say this—*on?*" I ignored his remark and continued dishing out the meal.

Once the final guest was served, I slid the last piece onto my plate and raised my glass in toast. "*Bon appétit!*"

It was immediately apparent that something had gone wrong. Crunching sounds filled the air instead of satisfied sighs. Faces looked puzzled instead of content. Everyone passed uncomfortable glances, like passengers on a bus where a drunk had stumbled aboard.

Dave brought his napkin to his mouth, spat into it, then stared at the output. "Uh, Jerome, exactly what is this?" He displayed the contents.

"Although I shouldn't justify such a gauche gesture with a response, that, my friend, is an artichoke leaf, boiled to perfect tenderness."

"And this?" said Gray, holding aloft a piece of vegetable matter.

"That would be bay leaf, hand-scissored."

Judith attempted to cut her lasagna. The top noodle resisted, then cracked and crunched under the pressure of her knife. "I simply must get this recipe," she said brightly. "Tell me, how long did you boil these noodles?"

"You're supposed to boil the noodles?" I asked.

Maura jumped up. "Just kidding!" She quickly collected the plates from each person and carried the stack into the kitchenette. As I sat befuddled, she emerged a second later with a square baking dish, which she placed on the coffee table, revealing a perfect lasagna, the mozzarella nicely browned and still bubbling gently.

"Jerome, prankster that he is, created a fake lasagna as a joke. Here's the real artichoke lasagna, which he's been hiding from you."

"Mildly amusing. But exceedingly wasteful," observed Gray.

I gave Maura a look of disbelief. She sent me to the kitchenette with a wave of her hand and followed, carrying the new lasagna. I quickly scraped the plates clean of the flawed food and passed them to Maura, who rinsed and reloaded each with a generous serving. Dinner party and reputation salvaged.

"May I have a word with you in your office?" said Maura, nodding toward the bathroom. She heeled the door closed behind her and clenched me in a rough embrace. We kissed so deeply that our lips formed a vacuum seal. Next thing I knew, I was feeling a strange evacuation. Maura was sucking the air out of my lungs. It was weirdly intimate and sensual, breathlessness to the extreme. I finally broke the seal and inhaled sharply.

"You saved my butt," I said once I'd caught my breath. "How can I ever thank you?"

"I'm sure you'll come up with something," she murmured, pressing against me.

"Seriously," I said, "that's the nicest thing anyone has ever done for me."

Maura stepped back and looked me in the eye. "If that were true, that would be a pretty sad statement." She gave me a peck on the cheek. "Luckily, it's not. Face it, Jerome. I know you better than you know yourself."

We were only gone a minute, but I was lightheaded upon our return, not from the embrace, but from the rush of gratitude. Her lack of confidence in my culinary skill notwithstanding, Maura had me covered.

Gray engaged in animated conversation with Monika at the table. Dave, meanwhile, consumed his second helping of lasagna. Judith fidgeted with another unlit cigarette, her lasagna untouched.

"Jerome, I misunderestimated you," said Dave. "This is actually kind of tasty. And here I always thought you were a frozen dinner kind of guy."

"What can I say?" I replied modestly.

"So tell me," said Gray, speaking intently to Monika. "Do you have vigorous debates in your office over the propriety of ending sentences with a preposition?"

"That is something up with which my boss would never put," said Monika.

Gray nearly expectorated his wine. "Winston Churchill!" he exclaimed. "Priceless!"

Judith arose suddenly. "You two are so freaking precious, I can't stand it! I'm going out for a smoke. Anyone care to join me?"

Dave scarfed down the last remnants of his third piece and raised his hand to volunteer. He stood, pulled a lighter from his pocket, and flicked open the flame.

"Dave!" I yelled. "Not in here!" He snapped shut the lid and offered Judith his arm.

"Hey, wait a minute," I said. "You don't even smoke. What are you doing with a lighter?"

"You'd be surprised what I keep in my pockets," he said. "All in the service of womankind."

Judith snorted.

"Judith," said Maura. "Give me that cigarette! Think about the baby."

"The city air you breathe every minute has more pollutants than this cigarette," Judith replied.

"That's completely false. And anyway, the cigarette just compounds it."

"Whatever," said Judith.

She and Dave disappeared through the apartment door. Ten seconds later, I saw their silhouettes through my basement casement window. They sat on the front stoop; I opened the window to eavesdrop. Gray and Monika were so engrossed in each other, they didn't even notice me.

Dave's face was suddenly illuminated by the lighter he extended to Judith. "Oh, no thanks," said Judith. "I'm pregnant."

"But didn't you say—?"

"I just had to get away from those two lovebirds or I was going to barf."

"Yeah, they seem smitten."

"And just for the record," said Judith, "I haven't had a smoke since the day they implanted the egg."

"So why do you let Maura think you're smoking?"

"Oh, I do it as a favor to her. She needs someone to mother and fuss over, so I play that role for her."

"Huh," said Dave. "She doesn't seem like the mothering type to me."

"You'd be surprised," said Judith, taking a deep draw on her unlit cigarette.

A few minutes later, Dave held the door for Judith as they re-entered the apartment. Gray's conversation drifted over: "What about relative pronouns in restrictive and unrestrictive clauses? Don't they drive you crazy?"

"Oh my God, yes! The bane of my existence," said Monika, nodding enthusiastically.

I sidled up and nudged Maura. "Looks like Graham and Monika are hitting it off."

"Yes. Good chemistry. A bubbling test tube of love. We should go into the matchmaking business."

Suddenly Gray jumped up. "Time for dessert!" he announced.

"Uh, I didn't make any dessert," I said.

"Not to worry," said Gray. "I've got it provisioned."

"Whatever that means," I whispered to Maura.

Gray extracted a foil-wrapped loaf from a shopping bag. "Platter, please," he instructed no one in particular.

Maura produced the closest facsimile she could find—a plate. Gray unwrapped the goods. "A honey cake, straight from the hive."

"Oh, wow," said Dave. "Is this made from the honey we collected?"

"Indeed it is," said Gray, slicing off large slabs and passing them around. "Normally, I'd drizzle on a lemon glaze, but I don't want to spoil the virgin experience. This is the first product from my honey harvest."

I forked a mouthful. It tasted strange, but I couldn't quite put a finger on it. The sweetness was offset by some sort of bitterness—not a pleasant combination. A feeling of *schadenfreude* arose that I couldn't suppress. My lasagna wouldn't be the only culinary failure of the evening.

Maura's sister maintained a frozen smile as she forced down a swallow. Dave quickly consumed his piece, oblivious to the flavor. Judith choked on the first bite and coughed violently.

Gray sat back at the table with Monika and sampled the fare. His face immediately clouded. He discreetly spit the cake into his napkin. "I must apologize. Something is terribly wrong with the cake."

Judith stopped hacking. "I'm glad I'm not the only one who noticed. It's weird. A flavor you normally wouldn't associate with cake."

"Wait!" said Monika. "I know it. It's, it's—smoky!"

"Oh my God, so it is," said Dave, swallowing a bite he pilfered from Judith's plate. "Reminds me of when my parents had a fire in their kitchen. Even the Cheerios tasted like smoke!"

"You ate them anyway?" I said to Dave.

He nodded. "It's an easily acquired taste."

"How could honey get smoky? Did you have a fire?" asked Monika.

"Uh, no. It's a long story," said Gray, dejected by the turn of events. "This is worse than it seems. I just casked a whole barrel of mead wine this morning."

"Serve it with smoked meat and nobody'll be the wiser," I said.

Maura surreptitiously dumped her cake in the trash. She was about to return to the main room when something in the bin caught her eye. "Jerome, what's this?" She grabbed a long-handle knife, speared something from the wastebasket, and brandished it before me.

"That? Oh, that's an artichoke core."

"Darling, it's not a core; it's a heart. You threw away the heart."

Chapter 16

Year 2 | Autumn

Running late for my squash date with Graham, I sprinted the last couple of blocks, then slowed to a nonchalant pace just before reaching the double glass doors of the facility.

I wasn't much of a player but engaged in a weekly match to help provide structure to Gray's otherwise shapeless life. He played me lefty to make our games more competitive.

Gray waited impatiently outside the glass back wall of the court. "You know what it means when a person is chronically late," he said.

"Yeah, yeah, it means that I think my time is more valuable than yours."

Gray looked miffed.

"But that's not the case," I protested. "I just forgot to charge my phone."

"I fail to see the connection."

"You know, my calendar, my clock, my pop-up reminders. It's an extension of my brain. I'm lobotomized without it."

We limbered up inside the court. The three white walls were peppered with black impact smudges, and Gray added a few more as he waited for me to finish my leg stretches. I let out a groan from the exertion, picked up my racquet from the floor, jogged a few steps in place, and pronounced myself ready.

It was never advisable to play Graham when he was angry, as he evidently was now, based on his switch to right-handed play. He vented his frustration by absolutely dominating the set. Drop shots, slams, spins, and arcs, his full arsenal was brought to bear in his quest to revenge my inexcusable tardiness.

Halfway through the first game, sweat had thoroughly soaked my cotton T-shirt. Meanwhile, perspiration had barely dampened Gray's brow.

After humiliating me for three straight matches, during which I rarely gained serve and never scored a point, Gray began to ease up. He transferred the racquet to his left hand; his stony silence broke.

"So, that was a good dinner last night. Intriguing company."

"Really? Did you like her?"

"Absolutely. She's a fascinating personality."

"Yes! I knew it!"

"Knew what?" said Gray, lobbing a serve into the back corner of my quarter court, where it curled up and died.

"Well, I guess it's safe to tell you now. It was a set-up. Maura and I were fixing you up."

"You were? Well, I have to give you credit for originality. Even I'm having trouble believing I could be attracted to a woman like that."

"What do you mean? She's a perfect match. Attractive, refined, Bryn Mawr. She's even a dictionary editor, for God's sake!"

"What?" said Gray, momentarily confused. "Oh, Monika? She's all right, I guess. A little on the boring side. I'm talking about Judith."

I stood dumbfounded as Gray's serve hit me on the forehead and dropped to my feet. "Judith? You've got to be kidding me! Chain-nonsmoking, weird cackling, egg-implanted, wound-up-like-a-cuckoo-clock Judith? I'd have thought she'd be the last woman you'd be interested in."

"One would think."

I was taken aback. Sure, love is blind. I get it, even if I don't subscribe to it. But love is stupid? Love is certifiably insane?

On the other hand, who was I to critique his choice in women? Maybe it could work. Maybe she'd be good for Gray. Maybe I was a budding matchmaking genius.

"She invited me to dinner at her house," he said.

This development I found worrisome. I imagined Gray walking into Judith's Superfund site, instantly killing any chance of a blossoming relationship. I moved to protect the emerging bud.

"Isn't that a bit premature?"

Gray arced a shot that hugged the right side wall and hopped toward the back of the court in a succession of diminishing bounces. "That's touchingly paternal of you, Jerome. I'm just visiting. It's not like we're getting married or anything."

I reconsidered my tack. "Of course; that's fine. Sounds great. But dinner's an odd choice. She never seems to actually eat anything."

"That's true," said Gray. "She barely tasted the food at your house. The lasagna I can understand, but my stuffed avocados?"

"Brings to mind that old saying," I replied. "Crazy people can't order fresh garden salad."

"Never heard that one," said Gray. "Fits the bill, though." He smashed a volley that hit the tin with an echoing report.

"Anyway, you'll like her place," I continued. "Judith's something of a fauna and flora connoisseur. She has amazing collections."

"She does?" said Gray. "Like what?"

"Oh, you know, rare plants, exotic animals, historical archives, cultural artifacts. Stuff like that. You could say that she's the curator of her own personal museum."

Gray hit a low shot with English that kissed the front wall and spun straight down to the floor, where it quickly petered out. I was so far out of position, I didn't even make an attempt.

* * *

I showered after the squash drubbing and then set out to meet Maura at the movies. We were taking in a foreign romantic flick that she'd been pining to see for weeks. I'd never been to a subtitled movie before, and I worried about my ability to keep up. I had enough trouble following plots in English.

"Oh, look," I said. "They're having a *Star Wars* marathon on the other screen. All thirteen films. Nearly twenty hours nonstop. We should go!"

"I'd rather shove that box of Raisinettes up my nose," said Maura.

"Whatever. As long as you don't do it during the quiet scenes."

I ordered a "small" popcorn from the teenage boy serving up the menu of fat and sugar products. "Can you forklift that over to our seats?" I asked. He looked puzzled.

"Actually, what I meant to say is, could I have a second empty container with that?" He handed me one full and one empty cylinder. I slipped the latter over the former. "Delicate hands. Heat sensitive," I explained.

We entered the sparsely populated cinema and hiked to seats halfway up the precipitous slope, smack in the middle. "You need to be a mountain climber to go to the movies these days," said Maura.

"Yeah, I'll be rappelling down to the bathroom later."

We sank into the plush seats. I fiddled with the arm rest between us, trying to wedge the massive popcorn container into the cup holder. Doing so, I stumbled upon a feature that enthralled lovers everywhere. The arm folded up.

"Cozy," said Maura as she sidled close to me.

The film starred an impossibly cute French girl who fell in and out of ludicrous romantic encounters. She was so freaking fetching that I found myself staring at her and forgetting to read the dialogue.

With the cup holder now up by my shoulder, I cradled the popcorn between us to share. Maura became engrossed in the plot. She took French in high school, giving her a leg up in the comprehension department. I, meanwhile, felt disadvantaged, forced to choose between reading the subtitles and thus missing the visuals or vice versa.

The story heated up. The French girl invited a bohemian man she met at an art museum back to her apartment. I took my cue from the unfolding sex scene. While the amorous couple ripped at each other's clothing, I quietly tore the bottom out of the empty popcorn container. When the French girl unzipped her lover's fly, I quietly drew down mine. When she enveloped his member inside her, I enwrapped mine as well, placing the container over my penis, already erect in anticipation of what I hoped was to come. Maura, immersed in the story, noticed not a thing.

After the sex scene, the heroine lay back with a smoke. Maura leaned back too and emitted a sigh. I waited for her to reach for the popcorn. She didn't. I offered it up. She declined. "Hot and salty," I said. "Just how you like it."

Her eyes never left the screen. "Honestly, Jerome, you're so unimaginative."

We had coffee after the movie. "So! How did you like it?" asked Maura.

I put on my best film critic air. "Intriguing plot, engrossing characters, but the dialogue was kind of stilted," I said.

"Yes," said Maura. "It was actually poorly subtitled. The translation didn't do the dialogue justice."

"Yeah, I picked up on that too."

"Jerome, you don't speak French."

"No, I'm talking about it being poorly subtitled. Don't you hate it when they put white subtitles on a white background?"

"I didn't notice that."

"Oh, uh, me neither. But don't you hate it?"

Maura shrugged.

The post-movie crowd packed the coffee shop. From our seat near the door, the queue snaked all the way to the register. I noticed a man in line wearing a sleeveless t-shirt, shorts, and sandals, despite the fall season. He was clearly one of those obstinate people who refuses to let go of summer. Virtually every square inch of his visible body was covered in a thick black matte. His eyebrows ran together and crowded his forehead. His nostril hair connected seamlessly with his mustache, creating the impression that the whiskers flowed directly from his nose. His head hair, neck hair, and upper back hair formed a continuous shag rug.

"Look at that guy," I said. "Looks like he's wearing a fur coat under that t-shirt."

"Hirsute," said Maura.

I spotted a woman wearing a business suit to whom Maura was apparently referring. "No, *his* t-shirt," I replied, discreetly pointing at the man.

Maura rolled her eyes. "Jerome, you aren't exactly Mr. Clean yourself. Have you ever looked at the back of your neck?"

I reached up and felt abundant fuzz. "No, how could I do that?" I rubbed the hair. "That's distressing. Here I am, criticizing him for a trait we share."

"Not entirely true," said Maura. "I doubt you could braid the hair on your toe knuckles, for example."

I looked over at his sandaled foot. "Impressive. Not just braided, but secured with Rasta beads."

I stirred my coffee with a plastic knife. Maura nibbled on her biscotti. "So, how was your squash match?"

"I got squashed, as usual. Gray plays me lefty, and he still routinely kicks my butt. It's discouraging."

"Why do you put yourself through the torture?"

"I don't know. It's fun, I guess." I watched over Maura's shoulder as the man in the gorilla suit poured half of his coffee into the rubbish bin and refilled the cup with cream. "But I did hear some interesting gossip."

Maura tilted her head expectantly.

"Our matchmaking scheme was a grand success."

"Did Graham tell you that?" Maura asked excitedly. "Monika really likes him! She thought they hit it off."

"They didn't. Gray is smitten with Judith."

Maura blinked in astonishment. "*What?*" she said, rising halfway out of her seat. "*Judith?* Oh, my God, that can't be true!"

"It's true."

"Wow," said Maura, settling back down. "Incredible. Interesting. So outlandish the thought never even crossed my mind. And yet, weirdly enough, I can almost see it. It could work."

"He's going over there for dinner this weekend."

Maura clasped her hand over her mouth. Her eyes widened.

"Easy, girl," I said. I gently pulled her hand down.

"We've got to stop him! One glimpse of that place and he'll flee in horror. He needs to get to know her before he wades into that."

As the week rolled forward, Maura tried several ploys to get Judith to break her date. I attempted the same with Gray. Neither of us could make a sufficiently persuasive case.

Maura and I spoke on the phone Thursday evening. "They're getting together tomorrow night," I said. "There's nothing we can do."

"I called around to get some quotes from a cleaning service. Every one was in the high hundreds," said Maura.

"I'm surprised they would take the job at any price. Wouldn't a hazardous waste service be more appropriate?"

Maura got indignant. "There's nothing hazardous about her apartment!"

"How about a stack of boxes falling over on you?"

"That's OSHA, not EPA," she said, a hint of condescension infecting her tone.

"Huh?"

"Never mind," said Maura. "We could intercept Graham at the door and whisk him off somewhere. To a surprise party in his honor!"

"Or we could put out a contract on him. Break his kneecap; put him in a wheelchair. He couldn't get past the first stack of boxes by the front door."

"Nope," said Maura glumly. "We'll just have to let nature take its course. A shame. They'd make such a cute couple."

"If by cute you mean utterly bizarre, horribly mismatched, and side-show freakish, then, yeah, I guess so."

* * *

Maura and I sat in her car outside Judith's apartment, a half block away and on the opposite side of the street. "Okay, Maura, here's how it works. If we see Gray or Judith approaching the car, we do this." I grabbed the handle that adjusts the passenger seat, yanked on it, and fell into a fully horizontal position in a split second.

"Silly boy," said Maura. "I know that trick. I've been reclining in driver seats since I was fourteen."

"But you couldn't even get a license until you were sixteen."

"Your point?"

"Uh, my point? That you were, um, precocious?"

Still prone, I rolled toward Maura and attempted to pull her closer, but she resisted under the pretext that we were on a stakeout. I reluctantly raised my seat to the vertical position.

Suddenly, Gray appeared, striding down the street in fine peacock form. He looked casually chic, with a blue blazer, yellow golf shirt, and white pants.

"Perfect posture," said Maura with admiration. I straightened up in my seat.

Gray stood for a moment under the front door light, looked at himself in the reflection, ran his fingers through his hair, and brushed his lapel. "I feel like a voyeur," said Maura.

The door opened, and an unseen person beckoned him inside. "Well, that's that," I said. "The beginning of the end."

"Don't be such a pessimist."

"Have you ever seen Gray's condo?" I said. "It's impeccable. He has a cleaning person come in twice a week, and he cleans up before they arrive and after they leave."

"Fastidious little bugger," said Maura.

We sat in silence, staring at the closed door. The hum of the street light and the sound of traffic a couple of blocks away provided the only sound.

Maura pulled out her phone. "Shall I call her? Ask her how it's going?"

"This is pathetic," I said. "We're like a couple of parents worried about their teenager's first date."

"True. Let's not obsess over that which we can't control."

"I need a drink," I said. "I'm a nervous wreck."

"Okay, let's quit this scene." Maura turned over the engine, put the car in gear, and started inching out of the parking space.

"Wait!" I said. "Look!"

We saw Gray emerge from the front door, bound down the steps, and run down the street in the direction away from us.

"Oh, my God! He's fleeing in horror!" said Maura.

Two-fifteen p.m. Saturday. Dave and I waited expectantly in Bad Abbotts, an Irish pub cum sports bar. From our vantage point by the door, a dozen immense television screens dominated the view, but thankfully, not the sound. Volume was muted in favor of scrolling captions. To fill the audio void, vintage Pogues played in the background.

No matter how I swiveled my head, I couldn't remove the sports action from view. English league soccer, American basketball, Japanese sumo wrestling, Norwegian luge, New Zealand rugby, and Indian cricket rounded out the global selection.

"You want some borscht with your burrito?" asked Dave. Another inexplicable Dave-ism. I'm wasn't eating anything.

"Damn it, where is he?" I asked. "Gray gets on my case when I'm late for anything. Yet here he is fifteen minutes late."

"Bar time is less precise," said Dave. "Anyway, didn't you say 'around' two o'clock?"

"Maybe so," I said. "But it's still rude."

The door burst open. "Gents," said Gray, nodding at us before situating himself on a stool by the wall.

"Graham," I said solemnly in reply.

He lifted a finger toward the waitress and mouthed the name of his favorite beverage. "Say, has this place changed? I don't remember this many tellies."

"Oh, my freaking word, Graham, must you?" said Dave.

"Must I what?" he replied, with *faux* innocence.

"So," I said, unable to contain myself. "I guess it didn't go too well last night, did it?"

"Why would you say that?" said Gray, handing a ten-spot to the waitress in exchange for a stout.

"A little birdie told me."

"Well, your bird is a loon. The evening went swimmingly."

"No fucking way," said Dave casually. "You two are just so—"

"Mismatched?" I said.

"Exactly!" said Dave.

"Gray, fess up," I said. "I know for a fact you didn't last five minutes in that hell-hole."

"What are you talking about?" said Gray.

"Listen," I said in a soothing voice, "you don't need to be ashamed that it didn't work out. These things happen all the time."

"Just because Judith is a little unorthodox doesn't mean we couldn't hit it off," said Gray

"Gray. A-number-one, I've been inside Judith's apartment. And B-number-two, I saw you running out of there like the place had a gas leak and your hair was on fire."

Gray looked at me incredulously. "C-number-three," he said with an edge, "what the hell are you doing spying on me? And D-number-four, I wasn't leaving; I was going to pick up our takeout."

"And E-number-five," said Dave, "why are you two using this fucking ridiculous numbering system?"

"Takeout?" I said.

"Sushi. And miso soup," replied Gray. "Judith's stove was broken."

"So why were you sprinting?"

"I was anxious to return to her mesmerizing company."

"Wow," I said, dumbfounded. My gaze landed on one of the giant screens, where a sumo wrestler was throwing a white powdery substance into the ring. I imagined the massive man rolling around in the stuff and then pictured him as titanic tempura—a disturbing mental image. I return to the topic at hand. "This just boggles the mind. Weren't you freaked out by the condition of her place?"

"I'll admit I was a bit taken aback when I first entered," said Gray. He swigged his Guinness. "I've never seen anything quite like it. It was appalling. Frightening even. Yet it was enthralling at the same time. I was simultaneously repulsed and attracted."

"But don't you realize that all that crap she's accumulated reflects her psychological state?" I asked.

"Totally," said Dave. "It's like I always say, you can learn a lot about a person from their shit."

"Your pronouns disagree," said Gray.

"Maybe," I said, "but no one else does. Dave is totally on the money. State of home equals state of mind."

"I don't deny it," said Gray. "Judith's flat is entirely consistent with her personality. She's unconventional, unruly, and impetuous."

"The exact freaking opposite of you," said Dave. "Conventional, ruly, and petuous."

"Anyway," said Gray, "she's talking seriously about decluttering her life. She wants to get rid of all that junk and make a fresh start."

"Wouldn't a relationship with you be adding to the clutter?" said Dave.

"Did you sleep with her?" I asked.

"I might have," said Gray. "But we couldn't find the bed."

Gray pulled out his phone, indicating that the subject was now officially closed. I didn't blame him. How could he credibly defend a fledgling relationship with a woman who was the absolute antithesis of his contrived persona and social pretensions? Either his life up to this point had been a sham or he was now building a relationship on a bed of hypocrisy. I was tempted to share my brilliant psychological assessment, but I thought the better of it.

A conversational void took hold. We drank our beer.

"Speaking of sex," I finally said, "did I tell you that Maura revealed the secret of the sexual universe to me?"

"That so?" said Dave with feigned nonchalance, taking a swig. Gray studied his phone with an intensity more appropriate for the Dead Sea Scrolls.

We sat in silence for a moment. "Well?" said Gray, finally looking up from the screen. "Are you planning to share the secret?"

"It wouldn't be a secret if I did, would it?" I said coyly. "Anyway, she didn't exactly *tell* me the secret; more like she *exposed* me to it."

"I don't get it," said Dave.

"She took me on this incredible sexual adventure."

"Really? Where to?" said Gray.

"Well, we didn't actually leave her bedroom."

My friends looked dubious.

"It was otherworldly," I said. "It was spiritual. It was enough to make me believe in God—or goddesses. I've never experienced anything like it."

"Jerome, didn't you once tell me that, before Maura, you had a grand total of one-and-a-half girlfriends?" asked Dave.

"Yeah. Your point?"

Gray interrupted. "How, pray tell, does one have a half-girlfriend?"

"Date-a-dwarf dot com," said Dave.

"When I was a senior in high school," I replied, "my first girlfriend was going out with someone else at the same time as me. So I couldn't really claim full credit, could I?"

"Anyway, Jerome," said Dave, "the point is, your sample size isn't large enough to draw any valid conclusions about sexual nirvana."

"Indeed," said Gray. "What you characterize as the secret of the sexual universe, Dave and I have probably experienced hundreds of times with dozens of women."

"Doubtful in your case; likely in mine," said Dave. "However, valor and discretion prevent me from disclosing."

"Fuck you guys," I said. "This was a life-changing experience, and you're just jealous."

"I don't know," said Gray. "Your life looks pretty much the same to me. In the before and after photos, I still see you sitting in dive bars drinking beer with your friends."

"To life-changing experiences!" said Dave, raising his beer mug.

"To the secret of the sexual universe!" said Gray, lifting his.

I refused to join the toast. "You assholes wouldn't recognize Epiphany if she slapped you across the face."

Chapter 17

Year 3 | Winter

Once a month, Maura and I took the "speds" on a field trip.
The term, I came to learn, was slang for "special education student."
It was used pejoratively by normal school-age children who wanted
to insult their peers, but in our school for the developmentally
delayed, it was just verbal shorthand with no negative connotations
intended.

"Attention all speds!" said Maura in a megaphone voice. "Please
grab your coats!"

Her command was deliberately ironic, since the majority of the
children were deaf, and most of those who could technically hear
didn't actually process language. No mad rush to the coatroom
ensued, also due to the fact that there was no coatroom. All the
jackets were piled on a table by the door.

"Yes, Ms. Wood!" I replied in singsong falsetto. I swept up the bundle of coats and start flipping them to the students like a dealer in Vegas.

Four months had passed since the board of directors was exposed to the seamier aspects of the school in general and Danny's genitalia in particular. Post-debacle, Maura and I spent several successive evenings compiling the detailed progress reports that the executive director demanded; months later, the stack of folders we produced remained untouched in a corner of his office. Our probationary status was due to expire in eight weeks. Not that it felt like a sword over our heads, but we looked forward to officially putting the affair behind us. And we did achieve one beneficial outcome: the next board meeting was scheduled for an offsite location.

Danny's propensity for the inappropriate and the inopportune came to mind as we prepared for our field trip. Previous excursions to a skating rink, the beach, or an amusement park were usually eventful for all involved—the students, the staff, and sometimes the occasional bystander.

Maura and I commandeered the school van for the outing, a trip to our local 3-D, gargantuan screen, stadium seating, octaphonic sound movie theater to see the Disney classic *Fantasia*. It was an ideal event with something for everyone: dazzling, techni-colorful visuals that penetrated the thickest cataracts; throbbing, eardrum-pounding sound that made hearing aids superfluous; and salty, mouthwatering snacks that, when properly wielded, helped modify inappropriate behaviors. We chose a weekday matinee to minimize the inevitable disruption and inconvenience to our fellow patrons.

Maura and I had six kids between us. Three on one was a more-than-manageable student/teacher ratio in the real world, but a bit dicey in our world. Any incident that demanded individual attention would leave the other teacher with a five-to-one ratio. If the first problem sparked a second, totally within the realm of possibility, things could quickly get out of hand.

I pulled the van up to the front door of the school. Maura had the class waiting in the lobby. It was chilly, so I left the engine running and the heater on. I slid open the passenger side door, then headed inside to help herd the group.

I took the hands of two students: Danny, whose incessant self-stimulation remained unabated in defiance of various behavior modification programs, and Katie, who in nine months had never replicated the shape-box success attained in my first week on the job.

I ushered them to the van while Maura stayed back in the lobby with the four remainders. After buckling my charges in, I pulled the van door nearly shut to keep out the cold, then turned back toward the school. Suddenly, I heard a slam and click behind me. Danny had closed and locked the van's sliding door. I was momentarily stunned. Danny had neither fine motor nor cognitive skills; suddenly he was displaying both?

I rushed for the front passenger door. He beat me to it and fisted down the lock button. The precariousness of the situation became immediately evident: A running van with two disabled children inside. Three of the van's four doors locked. Only the driver's door still openable.

Danny sat sideways in the passenger seat, with his back to the door and to me. He flicked his hand before his eyes, playing visual tricks with the sunlight that shone directly on his face.

I started to edge around the front of the van. Danny leaned in the same direction, as if anticipating my move. I was considering a mad dash for it when Maura emerged from the building, somehow guiding four children at once. "What's going on?"

"We have, um, a bit of a situation here."

I pulled a piece of hard candy from my pocket and tapped on the windshield. "Danny!" I spoke loudly to compensate for his impaired hearing. "Do you want a piece of candy?"

He ignored me. I slid to my right. He matched my movement, both of us inching closer to the driver door. I stopped. He stopped. Maura got insistent. "Jerome, exactly what's the problem?"

"Well, I left the van running 'cause it's cold, and our friend Danny here has locked all the doors, except one." I side-shuffled as I spoke. I lunged for the handle. Danny dove for the door. He brought his hand down emphatically on the button just ahead of me.

"Damn it!"

Danny swiveled himself into the driver's seat, grabbed the steering wheel, and turned it back and forth. I was astounded. During my entire tenure, I'd never seen him so dexterous, so aware of his surroundings, or so deliberate in his actions. "Does he have a full license or only a learner's permit?" I asked Maura.

"Jerome, are you an idiot? This is serious! The van is running! If he puts it in gear, we're fucked!"

I tapped the candy against the glass. "Danny, look at me!" He remained fixated on the wheel, turning it back and forth with scary intensity.

"Jerome, there's another set of keys in the classroom. I'm going to get them. Watch these four."

"What? Wait! No! I can't watch those four and deal with this crisis too! What if the van starts moving?"

"If it does, lie down in front of it!" said Maura. She started toward the door, realized I was right, and came back. Nudging the students together, she started herding them awkwardly toward the building entrance like a collie rounding up sheep.

Danny's hand passed the gearshift lever on the steering column, but didn't land on it. I swore I heard him making "vroom, vroom" noises and wondered if I'd entered a parallel universe. Standing on tip-toe, I peered through the window to see if the emergency brake, manipulated by pedal, was engaged. It was not.

I scanned my surroundings in a rising panic. A low stone wall framed some bushes at the front of the building. "Stay right here!" I instructed Danny, pointlessly. I dashed over to the rocks.

The wall was cemented together, and it looked pretty tight. The stones in the top row had a flat side, making them perfectly suited for wedging under a front tire. I spotted one with the least mortar surrounding it, turned, and gave a donkey-style kick. My foot bounced off; pain shot up my Achilles' tendon.

I looked back to the van. Katie was sitting in the bench seat behind the driver, strapped in, rocking gently, blissfully unaware. Danny appeared to be fiddling with some controls on the dash.

Suddenly, the engine roared. He found the accelerator. The RPM fell back, rose again, then dropped. The van didn't move.

I noticed a semi-loose stone in the wall ten yards away. It wasn't perfect—large and round with no flat edge—but it would have to do. I jammed my fingers into the crumbling mortar, trying to get a purchase. The van engine screamed in the background, sounding like a fighter jet. I felt the sharp edges of concrete cut into my hands as I wiggled the piece furiously to loosen it.

Maura raced from the building. "I can't find the keys! They aren't in my desk!" She ran over. "Jerome, you were the last one to use the van. Do you have them?"

"No! I put them back in your desk yesterday!"

The van horn blared. I looked over to see Danny smiling broadly. He pounded on the steering column, creating staccato blasts of sound. He stomped on the accelerator, producing syncopated engine whines.

With my butt on the ground, my feet against the wall, both hands on the stone, I gave a final mighty tug. The rock broke free and catapulted straight into my groin. I rolled on the sidewalk in pain.

"Get the fuck up, Jerome!" screamed Maura.

Moaning in agony, I struggled to my feet, grabbed the rock, and ran back to the van. It was an act of futility, as the rock was completely unsuitable as a wedge.

Suddenly, the van went silent. The horn stopped. The engine slowed to a barely audible purr. Danny sat at the wheel with a maniacal look on his face. "Uh-oh," said Maura.

Danny's hand fell to the column shift. He pulled the stick toward him and down till it came to a stop in the neutral position. The van creaked and started to roll down the street, where a gradual slope led to an increasing incline that terminated at a busy cross street. Traffic whizzed by at the bottom of the hill.

Maura jumped in front of the van, turned her back, and planted her feet, stopping the forward motion.

"Are you crazy?" I yell. "If he puts the van in gear, you're a dead woman!"

We stood for a moment, paralyzed. Suddenly, the engine screamed. Maura did likewise and jumped clear. The van again started a slow crawl forward.

I raised the stone over my head and aimed for the driver window. "No!" screamed Maura. "Are you out of your mind? You'll kill him with that thing!"

The van gained momentum. I ran to the back door and hurled the boulder through the window. Glass flew. Hopping onto the rear bumper as the pull of gravity accelerated the vehicle, I reached inside the window, popped the lock, and yanked the door open, almost knocking myself off the bumper in the process. I clambered over the seats, reaching the front of the van just as it started to veer off the road. The vehicle jumped the curb. I dove for the brake. I was face-first in the floorboards, depressing the brake pedal with my hand, when we hit something. I heard a loud crash and blacked out.

I awoke supine on the grass. The van stood nearby, its mashed front end in an awkward embrace with a tree, steam hissing from the radiator. Danny sat adjacent, waving to the sun. A staff person examined him.

Maura loomed over me. "Is he okay?" I asked, nodding toward Danny.

"He's fine," she replied. "The airbag knocked the wind out of him, but saved him from anything serious."

I closed my eyes and moaned. "How am I?"

"You'll live. Jerome, you know you'll probably get fired for this."

"Fired? I'm a frigging hero! I stopped the van from rolling into traffic, and I get fired?"

"The only reason the van was moving at all is because you screwed up so royally. You left the engine running. You left students alone. And you didn't put a seatbelt on Danny."

"Actually, I did," I said sullenly. "He must have figured out how to release the buckle."

"Well, however it happened, your ass is grass. And mine probably is, too."

A siren sounded in the distance. I reached up to touch my face. My hand came away bloodied. "How do I look?"

"You're a mess," said Maura.

"I guess this means we're not going to *Fantasia* then?"

Maura scowled.

Despite my half-hearted protests, the EMTs strapped me onto a board, plopped me onto a gurney, and shoved me into the back of the ambulance. I watched Maura through the back window, tending to the students. Then, I guess one could say, I "sped" away.

The hospital medics gave me a perfunctory check-up, took a couple of x-rays, ignored my pleas for potent pain-killers, and sent me home. A few bruises, a lump on my head, and a nasty black eye represented the full extent of my injuries.

Maura came over that night. I was spread-eagled on my couch as she entered my studio clutching a manila envelope. She gave me a dutiful peck on the cheek, which was about the only unscathed part of my face.

"Jerome, I've got something to tell you."

"So do I. I've decided to resign."

"What?"

"I'm not cut out for this work. The immeasurable progress. The frightening appearances. The bizarre behaviors."

I paused.

"And then there's the students."

Maura smiled weakly.

"Now what were you going to say?" I asked.

Maura fumbled. "Oh, uh, nothing." She tucked the manila envelope into her shoulder bag.

"This won't have any impact on us, will it?"

"What do you mean?"

"You know, us, our relationship."

"Oh. No. Of course not."

"That's a relief." I patted the couch beside me. "Come."

"Not tonight, Jerome. You need to get some rest. You look like hell."

I heard sympathy in Maura's voice, but it vanished in an instant. Something amidst the clutter on my table caught her attention. She picked up the item and dangled it before my face. "What is this?" she demanded.

As I squinted through my swollen eye, I realized her question was rhetorical. She knew full well that she held the key to the school van.

It was strange how the whole series of events—the unruly student, the runaway van, my bruised face and ego, the prospect of being fired, and my actual resignation—all seemed encapsulated in that small piece of metal. Had I returned the key to Maura's desk, as I had falsely claimed, how different the outcome. That key didn't just lock up the van; it locked up my future.

Chapter 18

Year 3 | Winter

His world made no sense. Black was white. And Gray was blue. Judith was wrong for him in every way, but, like a cloying melody, she was stuck in his head. He cringed at the thought of taking her to an opening at the art museum or an evening at symphony, yet he reveled in the idea as well. She'd wrinkle a few starched shirts.

He found her unabashed frankness simultaneously embarrassing and stimulating; her obsession with smoking, although he never actually saw her smoke, both asphyxiating and refreshing; her dusky voice repellant and sexy; the state of her apartment appalling yet fascinating. She scared him. The fact that she scared him scared him. But fear was invigorating.

Gray always imagined dating a refined and sophisticated woman—someone like Maura's sister, Monika. But when she was there within his grasp, he deliberately declined to reach out.

Sitting in his condo, Graham pulled a note from his pocket, picked up his phone from the glass coffee table, and dialed the first three digits of Judith's number. His pulse quickened. He hung up.

He paced the living room, sat back down, and pulled up *Gourmet* magazine on his reader. He leafed through it without actually looking at the pages, then put the device down.

He grabbed the phone again, dialed six numbers, then canceled. Falling back against the pillows on his overstuffed couch, Graham moaned aloud, "What's the worst that could happen?" He knew the answer: getting rejected by the type of woman he'd always rejected.

He picked up the phone a third time, determined to dial every one of Judith's digits, when his ringtone—Grieg's "In the Hall of the Mountain King"—interrupted. No name appeared on the screen, just the words "private caller."

"Graham, it's Judith," she said before he even uttered a hello. "Can you meet me for coffee?" His heart raced as he agreed.

Gray grabbed a leather winter coat from a coat rack by the door, then suddenly remembered Judith's aversion to animal byproducts and discarded it in favor of a denim jacket. He took the elevator to the ground-level garage, hopped into his Land Rover, and roared through the rising overhead door into the bright sunshine.

Judith was already at the coffee emporium, seated at a small table near the back, when Gray arrived. An unopened pack of Marlboros lay next to her cup of green tea. The place hummed with activity.

Gray slid into the seat opposite. "I can't tell you how freaking glad I'll be when I can have caffeine and nicotine again," Judith said.

"Delivered via coffee and cigarettes?" Gray asked. "Or direct injection?"

Judith pulled a plastic cigarette from behind her ear and inhaled vigorously on it. "It's got menthol and peppermint flavoring," she explained, "which isn't exactly great shakes. You wouldn't catch me dead smoking a real menthol cigarette. I use this thing more for the ritual than the flavor." She took another drag.

"I'm going to grab myself a coffee," said Gray. "Want anything?"

"See if they have any sauerkraut or pickled eggs, would you?" she asked, patting her bulging stomach. "Little Igor here is hungry."

"Isn't that the name of your lizard?"

"My iguana, yes. Do you think it would be a problem to have two members of my family with the same name?"

"Igor!" Gray mumbled on his way to the counter. "Why am I not surprised?"

Gray returned with a tall glass mug filled with a tan-colored concoction. "What you got?" asked Judith.

"It's a half-decaf, mocha latte with a double shot of espresso, topped with nonfat whipped cream."

Judith flicked a finger and snagged a dollop of the sweet stuff. "What ever happened to a good old cup of joe? What did that thing cost you?"

"Don't ask," said Gray. "Suffice to say I had to draw on my home equity line to finance it."

Judith leaned forward, bumped her belly against the table edge, cursed under her breath, and slid her chair back. She looked earnestly at Gray. "I've got a favor to ask."

Gray raised his eyebrows but said nothing.

"I'm going away to have the baby. I'll be gone about six weeks. Could you look after my place?"

"Away? Where?"

"To a commune for unwed mothers. A bunch of preggers who give birth together in a big hot tub, then bite off each other's umbilical cords."

"Really? Wow!"

"Nah, not really. I'm staying with my aunt. She lives a few hundred miles from here. Too far for me to come back to clip the iguana's toenails."

"I'd have to cut his toenails?"

"Jeez, you're gullible. No, you'd just need to water the foliage and feed the creatures. Once every two or three days would be fine. I'd ask Maura to do it but last time several plants dried out and all my tropical fish died."

"Sure, I'll take care of it."

Judith pushed a set of keys across the table. Her fingers brushed Gray's as they completed the exchange. He swore he felt a low-level electrical charge.

"Hey, it's gorgeous out. Let's go for a hike," suggested Gray. He strode over to the condiment area, took a paper cup, and poured his coffee into it.

It was one of those rare winter days when chill takes a respite. Graham and Judith headed toward the river, where a wide path accommodated walkers, bikers, rollerbladers, and skateboarders, all out in force to take advantage of the unexpected weekend gift. Bright yellow lines on the pavement attempted to create order out of the kinetic chaos, but the markings were largely ignored. The wheeled weaved freely among the shod. Gray steered Judith by the elbow toward the edge of the path. "Don't want anyone sideswiping your belly," he said.

"Hey, watch it! I'm sensitive about my bulge."

They walked silently in the bright sunshine. The warmth even brought a couple of sailboats out of dry dock; they plied the river, mainsheets luffing in the 50-degree breeze.

"Here, take my hand," said Judith. "I want to try a little experiment." Gray quickly dried his sweaty palm on his trousers.

"What kind of experiment?"

"When I walk along here by myself, I get these disapproving stares. It's the unwed mother syndrome. First they look at my belly, then they check for the ring."

They strolled hand-in-hand down the riverway. Gray observed the people approaching from the opposite direction. Some smiled. Others nodded. One guy winked at Gray.

"Seems like a decent response," he said.

"Okay, now let's disengage. You stay ten feet behind me and watch closely."

Gray fell back. The pattern exactly followed Judith's script. Notice belly. Scan hand. Register disapproval. Young women with strollers averted their eyes. Men leered. Old women shook their heads. It was uncanny.

"My God, you're on to something!" said Gray as he rejoined her.

"Yeah, I'm on to the fact that people are idiotic, judgmental jackasses."

"I wouldn't have framed it exactly that way, but you pretty much nailed it." Gray retook her hand. "I'm going to miss you when you're gone," he said.

"Don't get all sloppy sentimental on me," said Judith, pulling her hand away. "For Christ sake, we haven't even slept together yet."

Despite Gray's prodding, Judith stayed mum on her plans. She refused to provide her aunt's name and address. She remained vague on her departure and return dates. She was even evasive about the baby. As far as Gray knew, Judith had done nothing to prepare her apartment for the arrival of the newborn.

The weekend after their sociological experiment by the river, Graham got a text from Judith: "Off to the commune for unwed mothers. Don't forget about Igor!"

"Which Igor?" mumbled Gray to himself, irked but not sure exactly why.

Three days later, Gray pulled up in front of Judith's apartment in a rented moving van. Two burly, college-age men jumped out and bounded up the building's front steps like puppies let outside on the first day of spring. They sported nearly identical attire—baseball caps turned backward; athletic department sweatshirts with the arms ripped off; baggy shorts, ludicrously inappropriate for the winter season; and high-topped work boots.

Gray came around the front of the van and saw them waiting on the wrong stoop, jostling, jabbing, and shadow boxing. "Malcolm! Doug! It's number 52!" He wondered if responding to the online "Rent-a-Dude" ad might have been a mistake.

Gray opened the exterior door, and the trio tromped up one flight of stairs to Judith's apartment. He keyed the lock and pushed the door open with his foot. His helpers stood at the doorway, immobilized at the sight. Cats leapt in the foreground. The parrot squawked from the kitchen. A cairn terrier yelped ferociously while keeping a safe distance.

"Okay, you said it was bad, but I never imagined this," said Malcolm, removing his cap and scratching his shaved scalp. "You're going to have to double our fee."

"That's fine. Whatever. Let's get to work," said Gray.

They barged into the space while the dog yapped incessantly. Malcolm aimed a kick at it. The canine barely scurried out of the way, its toenails slipping on the wood floor as its legs churned, cartoon-like.

They started with the obvious stuff, disposing of overflowing trash bags, including one clawed open by the cats. They dumped expired food from the fridge; stacks of old magazines; piles of store receipts; envelopes filled with dated coupons; and mounds of telephone books, the newest more than a decade old. "Do they even make telephone books anymore?" asked Malcolm. They discarded coverless paperbacks; spent toilet paper rolls; shoe boxes teeming with paper clips, rubber bands, pen caps, push pins, and pennies. The laborers hauled it all out, filling the front end of the moving van with the unwanted items.

While Malcolm and Doug shuttled the refuse, Gray pored over the questionable stuff: folders bulging with unopened bills, many in Judith's name at other addresses; bank statements, years old, but perhaps still needed for tax purposes; notebooks filled with scrawled shopping lists, to-do lists, and doodles; college textbooks with notes in the margins. He decided to play it safe and packed all the borderline items into cardboard moving boxes.

Next, he examined the stuff that clearly couldn't be discarded: boxes of old photos. Letters bound in ribbon. Overdue library books. Knick-knacks and souvenirs. Several years of tax returns. He taped up more storage boxes.

Gray gave into his curiosity and peeked into the dresser in Judith's bedroom. Top drawer: underwear, teddies, and camisoles. Second drawer: socks, leggings, and a pair of black fishnets, the latter item sparking his imagination. Third drawer: t-shirts and jerseys. Bottom drawer: jeans, slacks, and a wooden box with a removable lid. Gray lifted the cover to find a half-dozen ears of Indian corn standing on end alongside a small jar of vegetable shortening. *Strange place to be storing food*, he thought. He dropped the lid back into place and closed the drawer with his foot.

A yowl emanated from the living room as Malcolm stepped on a cat's tail. Gray poked his head out of the bedroom door in time to see the creature jump and imbed its claws into Malcolm's bare leg, perching like an electrical worker on a utility pole. Malcolm roared, disengaged the cat one paw at a time, and flung it roughly aside. The cat scurried away. Bloody rake marks adorned Malcolm's shin and calf.

"You better wash that off," said his pal. "Haven't you ever heard of cat scratch fever?"

Malcolm grabbed a fistful of dirt from a dormant flowerpot and rubbed it on the wounds. "That's all it needs," he said, testosterone dripping from every word.

Gray scanned the apartment. They'd barely made a dent. Deciding on a new tack, he took a pad of sticky notes from his pocket and started labeling the assorted items with either "dump," "storage," or "apt."

"Guys, let's get the rest of the 'dump' stuff first. We'll fill the front part of the truck with that, then we'll fill the back half with stuff that'll go into storage." Gray moved from room to room, scrawling and sticking at a rapid clip. Twenty minutes later, everything was labeled.

While his workers carried out his instructions, Gray stomped down to the truck and returned carrying a gallon of paint, plus assorted brushes and supplies. He cleared the remaining items out of the small room next to Judith's bedroom.

A yell arose from the bathroom. "Holy shit! Doug, you've got to see this! There's a fucking dragon in the bathtub!"

Gray entered the room to see Malcolm poking at Igor with a broom handle. Gray grabbed the pole from his hand. "No taunting the pets," he said sternly. Malcolm glared at Gray for a second, veins bulging at his temple, then eased his clenched jaw.

"Yeah, whatever."

Gray returned to the baby's room. He pulled several nails, more appropriate for framing a house than hanging a picture, from the walls and applied spackle to the gaping holes. While the paste dried, he spread the drop cloth and started applying baby blue paint to the trim around the doorway and window. Sounds of horseplay arose from the other room, a loud crash followed by a moment of silence. Gray wondered if he needed to reprimand his helpers once again when he heard Malcolm's voice. "Just leave it. This place was a hell-hole already."

Seven hours, three six-packs, two pepperoni pizzas, and one missing cat later, the apartment was purged. For the first time in years, wide areas of flooring were visible and direct routes between two points navigable.

Gray paid double the original fee and sent his workers on their way. Initially, he intended to have them accompany him to the storage facility and the dump to unload, but he tired of their antics and decided to do it himself.

Gray admired the de-cluttered apartment and made a mental note about the remaining tasks: hire a horticulturist to give the plants a spa treatment; an animal groomer to spiff up the pets; a handyman to plug leaks, replace outlets, and make general repairs; a carpet cleaning service; and a chimney sweep.

He was glad Judith would be gone six weeks. It was clear he'd need every minute.

Chapter 19

Year 3 | Winter

I wasn't keen on another extended stint of joblessness, so I immediately signed up with a temp agency. Unexpectedly, an offer arrived within 48 hours, an opening for a receptionist at an insurance company. "Aren't receptionists usually women?" I asked my placement coordinator.

"That might be true," she replied, "if we were stuck in the nineteen nineties. It's a new dawn, Jerome. Today men have equal opportunities. You can be anything you want to be! Now get out there and—"

She paused.

"And—and be receptive!"

My gig started the next day—not a lot of time to prepare. In my small closet, I sought clean, presentable clothing, but found only a winter coat, a bulky knit sweater, and dozens of empty hangers. I rummaged through the pile of clothes on my easy chair, extracting a pair of dark slacks and a pale yellow long-sleeved shirt. Burying my nose in the armpit of the shirt, I quickly withdrew, repelled by the odor. I tossed the shirt in the hamper and pulled another from the heap. Same problem. On the third, I realized the cause was hopeless, so I retrieved the first shirt, turned it inside out, and applied solid-stick deodorant liberally to the armpits of the garment.

The shirt and trousers were severely wrinkled, so I grabbed a couple of coat hangers, suspended the clothes on the shower curtain rod, and turned on the hot water full blast. Closing the bathroom door behind me, I considered my hypocrisy—running an unattended shower after criticizing Dave for leaving my kitchen tap open—but summarily dismissed the thought. At least my profligate water use had a higher purpose.

While the clothes steam-pressed in my makeshift sauna, I ran out to my local chain drugstore to buy pancake makeup for my black eye. Most of my bumps and bruises from the van crash had diminished, but the shiner lingered.

Entering through the whooshing automatic door, I snatched a red plastic hand basket and strolled the garishly lit aisles, looking for the cosmetics section. It was hard to miss. A long row beckoned, stacked with a bewildering array of beauty products—eyeliner, blush, rouge, lipstick, eye shadow, mascara, eyelash thickener, nail polish, skin cream, and other stuff whose purpose mystified. I finally located the pancake makeup, dropped it in my basket, and headed for the checkout.

The teenage cashier, with a small pussy pimple on the side of her nose, a streak of shocking pink in her otherwise jet-black hair, and an attitude of barely concealed contempt toward her customers, scanned the product. As she waved the item over the electronic prism, she gave me not so much as a glance. Her aversion to eye contact allowed me to study her face closely. Doing so, I determined that the whitehead infection on her nostril was in fact a small *faux* diamond stud.

"That all?" she said. Her lack of both engagement and verb annoyed me.

"No, it's not. I'll take this, too." I grabbed the item closest to me, glittery lip gloss, and placed it on the counter. She rang it in without looking up.

"And this." I snatched a sample size bottle of red nail polish and dropped it in front of her.

"And this, this, and this." I slapped down a chocolate truffle wrapped in foil, a tin of mints, and a bottle of concentrated energy drink.

The checkout girl slowly lifted her eyelids, so weighted with mascara it was a wonder she could open her eyes at all. She appraised my face, almost making eye contact, before returning to her scanning duties. "Girlfriend beat you up?" she asked.

I passed her a twenty. "No. My boyfriend did."

She dropped the change into my hand without touching me.

The next morning, after carefully applying the makeup under my eye and donning a pair of sunglasses, I took the bus to the other side of town, then trudged a quarter mile under gray skies to a mid-rise office building. The landscaping crew had apparently been laid off months earlier, judging from the withered look of the bushes out front. A guard desk just inside the entrance was unmanned.

One of the two elevator doors was open. Before stepping aboard, I checked to make sure a car actually awaited on the other side—a nervous tic I had developed in college after a student fell to his death in an elevator shaft.

It was a memorably ugly scene. The college had a couple of five-story dorms that tended toward rowdiness on the weekends. One drunken prankster decided to amuse himself and his buddies by prying open the elevator doors, exposing the long dark shaft. A couple of unsuspecting students came around the corner, and the first one, a guy, stepped into the car that he thought was waiting. The second, a gal, just a half step behind, teetered at the brink before catching herself.

The guy might have survived the plunge—he was on the third floor—but he landed atop an elevator car on the ascent. Investigators determined that the student was probably conscious, albeit dazed, as the car rose to answer a summons from the top floor of the dorm.

The elevator apparatus had been shoehorned into an old building; as a result, vertical space was tight, with almost no wiggle room between the top of the car and the shaft ceiling. The elevator slowed as it arrived at the appointed floor, making the crushing death of the student sprawled atop even more excruciating. Legend said that his blood freshly stained the ceiling of the elevator car every year on the anniversary of his death, but I couldn't vouch for that.

I happened upon the scene just minutes afterward. A half-dozen students had dialed 911, and the wail of sirens could be heard in the distance. The girl sat slumped under the elevator call buttons, sobbing.

"What happened?" I asked a preppy looking guy standing next to me.

"I think somebody got shafted," he said.

This, it turns out, was my first encounter with Gray. I was simultaneously appalled by his callous remark and impressed with his humorous improvisation under tragic circumstances.

"George Earling," he said, sticking out his hand.

The accident occurred during our freshman year, well before the life-changing semester abroad program that transformed "George" into the bloke he became. After his stint in London, he returned stateside sporting an upper-crust accent, a fondness for tepid ale, and a spiffy new moniker—Graham, his middle name.

The "lift" incident—as Gray subsequently came to call it—had a more profound impact on me than I cared to admit. I started having recurrent elevator dreams, not quite screaming nightmares, but disquieting enough that I would wake up shrouded in anxiety and sweat. In one, my elevator shoots through the roof and crashes to earth like a doomed space shuttle. In another, the car moves horizontally around a single floor before careening through an exterior wall.

The most disturbing dream episode appeared with the greatest frequency: Alone in the elevator car, I press the button for my floor. The doors close unnaturally slowly; I peek through the narrowing aperture as the lobby vanishes from view. The car jolts momentarily, then pauses, finally lurching into its ascent. It takes only a second to realize that something's not quite right. The floor of the car is rising, but the ceiling isn't. The elevator becomes a vise with me caught in the grip. I hunch over as the ceiling nudges the top of my head. I squat. I fall flat on my back. The roof of the car looms. It touches my nose; I turn my head sideways. The ceiling clamps down on my ear. The pressure increases. My chest compresses; air is forcibly expelled from my lungs. My head feels like it will explode.

I rode the car to the 13th floor of the office building, indicated by the number 14 on the button panel. The doors slid open, and standing just on the other side was Gail, a perky administrative assistant. As we exchanged preliminary information, it was clear I couldn't match her occupational enthusiasm, so I didn't even try.

Gail eagerly showed me the reception desk that guarded the main entrance to the office. Her every sentence ended in a rising cadence, which made each statement sound like a question. "This is where you'll call home? You're taking Francesca's place? She just started her maternity leave yesterday? In fact, she broke water right here at her desk? I thought the maintenance men were going to have to deliver the baby?"

I peered over the counter at the chair on the other side. The seat cushion looked damp. "Oh, wow," I said dully.

The reception area had a jaundiced pallor of aging yellow paint under unfiltered fluorescent light. A couch, table, and two chairs looked tired and worn. A half-dozen official-looking documents hung in a row over the seats—permits, licenses, notices, all in print too small to read. A corner shelf held several cheap-looking trophies. "Our office has won the company softball championship three years in a row!" said Gail with what appeared to be genuine pride.

"Impressive," I replied, picking up one of the awards. It was significantly lighter than it looked.

"Do you play?" she asked. I mumbled something about having been a third-string catcher on my junior high baseball team. "Oh, goody!" she said. "We need a catcher!" I silently cursed myself.

Gail enlightened me on the difference between an insurance *agent* and an insurance *company*. We, it seemed, were the latter. I feigned fascination. The upshot: Most of the people who walked through the entrance were employees, rather than customers.

The stream of people ebbed and flowed, the volume dependent on the clock. Some employees didn't notice me; others nodded. One wiseass said, "Hello, Francesca!" I smiled wanly and offered a falsetto return greeting.

The day passed in interminable boredom. The phone barely rang. The workers burrowed themselves in their cubes or locked themselves in their offices. I wished I had a book.

A middle-aged guy with thinning hair approached the desk. "Make me a copy of this document, will you?"

I looked at his slender sheaf. "Don't you have a secretary to do that?"

"You, my friend, *are* the secretary. Francesca used to handle everyone's needs."

"That might explain her condition," I said. I shuffled over to the copier, a few paces away.

My "client" followed. "So, how you getting along?" he said.

"Seems alright, I guess. I haven't actually met anybody. They all seem immersed in their work."

"Don't be fooled," he said. "Everyone's surfing porn in their offices." He guffawed. "Just kidding. We're actuary very nice people here."

I continued copying.

"Get it?" he said. "*Actuary* very nice. It's insurance humor."

"Huh! Didn't know there was such a genre." I handed him his copies.

"Well, it's a minor genre. As far as I know, there's only one joke. But it's a killer!" He walked away laughing.

He turned back toward me. "By the way, your makeup's running."

The next morning, I loaded my backpack with a few *accoutrements* to personalize my reception counter: a one-inch square photo of

Maura, taken from my cell phone and printed in black and white; a mouse-pad tattooed with a picture of my parents' dog; and a small cardboard box, five inches square, to hold pens and such.

At the office, I carefully arranged my possessions, loading the box with company-logoed pens and placing it on the counter; slipping the dog-pad under my mouse; and taping the picture of Maura to the back edge of the counter so she stared me straight in the face but no one else could see her.

Maura's visage and I passed the day uneventfully. I routed a few calls, directed one or two visitors, and grunted at the arriving and departing workers. A few people took pens from the cardboard box. I conscientiously replenished the supply.

The day came and went. And so did I.

At the end of day three, administrative assistant Gail approached my reception desk. She looked uncomfortable. "Jerome," she said. "I don't know how to put this tactfully?"

"Is that a question or a statement?" I replied.

"I don't know what you mean," she said. We gazed awkwardly at each other for a moment before she continued. "Um, you know how the firm has certain standards of taste and decorum?"

I didn't, but I said I did.

She fidgeted and cleared her throat. "Well, a situation has arisen—"

I waited patiently. Finally, I could take no more. "Gail, will you just get to the point?"

"It's your box!" she blurted.

"My box?"

"Jerome, look around the office. Plush carpets, mahogany desktops, tasteful artwork."

I swiveled my head, attempting to match the worn rugs, cheap veneer desks, and tawdry prints with her description, but the differences seemed irreconcilable.

She continued, "And then you have this, this *cardboard box* plopped on the reception counter like you just reclaimed your possessions from a storage facility."

She pointed to my small square carton holding a fistful of pens. It was a classic cardboard box in every respect: tan colored, corrugated, stenciled in block letters, and assembled with packing tape.

"Gail, that's not a cardboard box."

"What are you talking about?"

I flicked my finger at the box, and my nail struck the edge with a sharp clang.

"It's ceramic; it's a sculpture. It's not a cardboard box—it's an artistic statement about cardboard boxes."

Gail stood there, mouth agape.

"That," she said after a moment's reflection, "is about the coolest thing I've ever seen."

She walked away.

"Actuary, you're right," I said.

Sitting at my reception desk, I fought off drowsiness. The brutal monotony exerted a powerful influence that countless cups of coffee couldn't counteract. My eyelids engaged in a fierce-but-hopeless battle with the forces of gravity.

A man entered the office, but in my nodding state, I didn't hear him coming. He cleared his throat; I jumped.

"I'm here to upgrade your memory," the computer technician stated, resting a double-wide briefcase on the counter.

"Memory?" I said, shaking my head awake. "Good, just what I need. The Alzheimer's is getting so bad, I don't even remember calling you."

"You didn't," he said, unamused. "We're upgrading all the machines in the company."

I vacated my chair, and he sidled past and sat down. Within seconds, the cover was off my computer. I, who could barely unwrap a CD, marveled at his technical virtuosity.

He pulled a pencil-shaped metal rod from his shirt pocket and touched the light switch behind my desk, emitting a small pop and tiny flash. "Discharging static," he explained.

The techie took a miniature vacuum from his case and ran the nozzle over the computer fan vent, sucking up a thick layer of accumulated dust. He then steered it carefully through the innards of the machine, clearing the cobwebs. Lifting two small memory modules out of an acrylic case, he inserted them into the open slots between the maze of cables, diodes, and circuit boards. He then replaced and re-secured the cover. Total elapsed time, less than five minutes.

I uttered my thanks, and he was gone as stealthily as he arrived, headed deep into the bowels of the office to perform his efficiencies on other machines.

As I lowered myself into my seat, I sensed immediately that something was wrong, terribly wrong. It was the chair itself. Something was different. I couldn't put my finger on it. It was ... it was ... it was warm! I jumped up, disgusted. The technician's body heat had transferred to the seat cushion and was now being passed to me. I felt like I was sitting in his lap.

"Don't be an idiot!" I self-admonished. I sat again. The sensation remained disquieting. I arose, grabbed a stack of copy paper, and attempted to fan away the stored warmth. Pages flew. A co-worker walked by and gave me a funny look. I didn't care. The seat remained radiant. I forced myself back into its embrace.

I knew it was stupid, but I couldn't shake the feeling that the techie and I were somehow engaged in an illicit liaison.

The phone rang. It was Maura. I gazed at her thumbnail picture and pretended the warm glow was coming from her, but the sensation dissipated rapidly.

"Jerome, I think we need a little time apart."

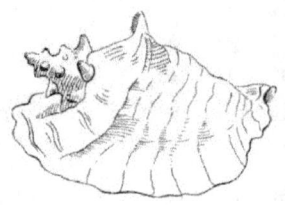

Chapter 20

Year 3 | Winter

"A little time apart," Maura's euphemism for our breakup, proved a cruel expression, filled with ambiguity and false hope. How long was a little? Was this a trial separation? Would we get back together? Would we date others? I was filled with questions. I didn't ask any.

I called Maura frequently in the days after she announced our hiatus. I usually got her voicemail. When she did pick up, the conversation was brief, with me pleading for reconciliation and her saying nothing.

After a week, I decided I was a pathetic excuse for a human being. I vowed to stop begging and moping and take charge of my life. I signed up for a lovelorn website.

I filled out the questionnaire as truthfully as I dared, knowing that complete honesty would likely result in zero dates. After leafing through dozens of profiles, I finally came across one that looked intriguing: "SWF; average looks and intelligence; non-musical but likes country; non-literary but likes chick lit; non-political but leans conservative; devoutish, but don't attend church religiously; unintentionally conformist (it's just easier); prefers 'take out' to 'go out' and cable movies to movie theaters. Seeking likeminded individual." It was signed "Sandra."

An uncommon level of self-awareness, I thought. Sandra wasn't perfect, but she was close.

I shared the profile with my friends at the pub. "Pardon my obtuseness," said Gray, "but where, exactly, is the appeal? She's so unexceptional, it's like she doesn't even exist."

"She's opinion-less," said Dave. "She's as bland as this breadstick." He jabbed me in the chest, snapping the stick in two.

"Exactly!" I said. "Maura was so intense, I need a little respite. Boring is beautiful!"

Dave snorted. Gray huffed. I quaffed.

"Anyway, this will be just a temporary fling until Maura and I get back together."

"Don't get your hopes up," said Dave. "Maura is too much woman for you."

The remark cut deeply with the sharp edge of truth. Maura *was* too much woman for me. She'd been dragging me along behind her, trying to get me up to speed on life's many pleasures. She'd exposed me to gourmet food and gourmet sex, yet I remained a cheeseburger-and-missionary-position kind of guy. I still couldn't believe she chose me, rather than some debonair bastard who could show her the good life. Only now she had un-chosen me.

"You don't think Maura's cheating on me, do you?" I asked.

"*Un*," said Gray, "it's not cheating if you've broken up."

"*Deux*," said Dave, "don't be a hypocrite. If you can go back into the meat market, so can she."

"*Trois*," said Gray, "don't worry about it. Fidelity is overrated."

"I beg to differ," said Dave. "I'm a big fan of fidelity."

"Don't misconstrue," said Gray. "Fidelity's fine." He paused. "Although Schwab is pretty good, too."

* * *

The earth's slouching posture had put the northern hemisphere at such a disadvantage that the full-spectrum lamp perched on my receptionist's counter could no longer rebalance the equation. By March, I'd had enough. I needed to get away, and the hot Caribbean trade winds beckoned. I asked Sandra to join me.

Sandra and I had gone on three dates since I responded to her personal ad. Her self-portrait was accurate to a fault, and our outings were uneventful, predictable, and monotonous. In other words, just right. I couldn't tell if she liked me, but she tolerated me. She agreed to a week-long trip to Puerto Rico, which I took as a good sign. We hadn't actually slept together yet—she rejected several of my advances—but she hinted that we might during our vacation.

Flights from our neck of the woods at high season were ridiculously expensive, so I started digging around some obscure sit-in-the-cargo-hold travel sites. I learned that a flight from Miami to San Juan was quite reasonable, as there was apparently no great demand for hopping from one tropical clime to another. To capture the savings, we just needed to get to Florida—1,500 miles south—on the cheap.

Inexplicably, Sandra was opposed to hitchhiking, so I posted a note at a local college. I got a call the same day from a student looking to split gas costs, but when I learned that he drove a tank-like vehicle that he bought at a military surplus auction, I politely declined. The next caller had a more fuel-efficient model, plus he wanted to share turns behind the wheel, allowing us to drive straight through to Florida. Fine by me. And Sandra, too.

The road trip was dull. One of us was always either driving, sleeping, or listening to music through earbuds. Not much in the way of conversation. Also fine by me.

We caught our plane in Miami thirty hours after leaving snow country behind, and we touched down in San Juan two hours after that. A bus to Farjado and a ferry to Vieques completed the journey. We jumped in a waiting cab at the dock.

"An island off an island?" said Sandra, as if she had somehow just become aware of our destination. "Could you have chosen a more obscure spot?"

"Obscure is good," I replied. "I just vant to be alone."

"Is that why you brought me along?"

My pores sucked in the humid heat like a parched field soaks up the rain. I felt my skin turning supple, my limbs limbering, my mind clearing. I could almost perceive the vitamin D surge coursing from epidermis to capillaries to veins and arteries, to be diffused throughout my exoskeleton.

"Did you go to med school or something?" asked Sandra, breaking me from my musings.

"What? What do you mean?"

"You know, all this talk about exoskeletons and capillaries."

"I said that out loud? Sheesh, I need to put up a firewall between my inner and outer selves."

"You were talking to yourself?" asked Sandra.

"No, I was thinking to myself, but the words escaped when I wasn't looking."

Sandra stared at me like I was spouting nonsense.

I paid the cabbie, thanked him for the beers, and grabbed our bags.

We rented a little villa in the town of Isabel Segunda. I keyed the door and was immediately overcome with the odor of cat urine. The interior looked nothing like the photos the landlord had posted on the Internet.

The entrance opened to a main room that comprised living, dining, and kitchen space, the latter separated from the rest by a waist-high counter. The cinder block walls, sporting beige peeling paint, were hung with random semi-artistic renderings of famous landscapes: the Matterhorn, Grand Canyon, Victoria Falls, Richmond Hill. "Not a seascape in sight," I noted. "Where's Homer when you need him?"

"Simpson?" said Sandra. "I don't get the connection."

Off the main room were two doors, one leading to a cramped bedroom that barely accommodated the double bed and dresser shoe-horned within, the other opening to a bathroom that bore a distinct resemblance to an airplane loo. The shower, hardly wide enough to squeeze a normal-sized body into, stood wedged into one corner. A miniscule triangular sink fit snugly in another. The toilet, barely a foot and a half off the floor, was parked hard by the door, which could only open 45 degrees before hitting the shower. A thick, brown, hard water scum coated the inside of the bowl.

I began to relieve myself when Sandra called out, irritated, "Would you mind closing the door?" I kicked it shut, annoyed at her prudery.

I was determined to have fun, so I subsumed my petulance. "Okay," I said brightly, emerging from the bathroom. "What you want to do? We could frolic in the waves at the nude beach. Or knock back a couple of piña coladas at an oceanside bar. Or just have kinky sex right here on this orange shag carpet."

"Must you be so crude?"

My enthusiasm dampened. "Okay, let me rephrase that. One, swim; two, drink; or three, um, you know, love?"

"I don't care. Anything but number three."

Sandra was proving something of a downer, which was doubly dispiriting since I had come here specifically to leave the depressive aspects of my life behind.

"I know! Number four—let's eat!"

Sandra murmured her assent. We exited the abode, locked the heavy metal door behind us, and then swung an ornate wrought iron grate into place.

The center of town lay a quarter mile up the road. We entered a compact commercial district, just a couple of blocks of low, mismatched buildings, variously composed of stucco, cinder block, and wood. The structures were, for the most part, run down, but the streets were lively and merchant activity appeared brisk, giving the general impression of convivial poverty.

A number of restaurants and bars dotted the streets, all of them with their shutters, bay windows, and doorways flung wide open, blurring the distinction between indoor and out. We chose Café Olé, with its huge windows, abundant ceiling fans, and small round tables, sparsely occupied at this early afternoon hour.

The barkeep ambled over, menus in hand. "You folks want a side of sunscreen with your meal?" he asked in a Spanish lilt, eyeing our pale northern complexions.

"Nah, we like everything burned to a crisp," I said.

"Sun poisoning and food poisoning. You can get it all right here!" he said.

Sandra shuddered as she fingered the greasy laminated pages of the menu.

"How about alcohol poisoning?" I said to the proprietor. "That's what I'm after. *Una cervaza, por favor, y por mi amiga tambien.*"

"*Dos cervazas!*" he yelled toward the other side of the room, which no one appeared to be occupying. "Coming right up!" he replied when he got to the bar.

"Anything look good?" I said to Sandra.

"Don't know; don't speak Spanish."

"All right, I'll order for us both."

"Okay. Just stay away from the weird stuff."

The bartender delivered our beers. I placed the food order, augmenting my pidgin Spanish by pointing at the menu items: "*Hervidos Jueyes, un lado de buñuelos de caracol, plátano asado, y una Medalla.* And likewise for the little lady."

He nodded and walked away.

"What did you order?" asked Sandra.

"Conch, plantain, and other classic Caribbean fare."

"No! I can't eat that stuff," said Sandra. "Sir! Sir!" The bartender returned. "Do you have any American food? You know, like cheeseburgers?"

"Certainly, madam," he said stiffly. "American food is readily available. Puerto Rico is, after all, a commonwealth of the United States."

As he again departed, Sandra turned toward me. "Did you hear what he just said? Part of the U.S.? The ignorance on this island is appalling."

"I've been thinking," I said. "You know how you asked me to close the bathroom door when I was peeing?"

Sandra gave me a look that implied, *I already don't like where this is heading.*

I ignored the warning sign. "When I was young and needed to urinate, I always asked my mother's permission first. I don't know why. I just did. Even with a bursting bladder, I would run all over the house looking for her to ask if I could go to the bathroom."

"Do you truly consider this appropriate mealtime conversation?" said Sandra. Since our food hadn't arrived yet, I deemed her question irrelevant.

"Finally, my mother became exasperated. 'Jerome,' she said, 'you don't have to ask me every time you need to use the toilet. Just go!'" And in my four-year-old mind I thought, Wow! What a concept. *Just go.* Who would have believed such a thing was possible?"

"Mmmm. Profound," said Sandra.

The bartender arrived with several plates and dishes balanced along the length of his arm. He distributed them around the table and retreated.

"So, anyway," I continued, "after this breakthrough, I come home from school one day. My mother's in the kitchen, peeling potatoes in the sink. I'm thirsty but can see I'm not going to get a drink there. So I head into the bathroom and fill a glass from the tap. Halfway through drinking it, I've had enough, so I pour the remaining water into the toilet bowl."

Sandra stared at me blankly, chewing her cow meat.

"'Jerome!' yells my mother. 'That's disgusting! Close the door, for goodness sake!'

"'What's disgusting, Mom?' I ask.

"'You know very well what's disgusting! Close the door when you use the toilet!'

"'But Mom, I'm not using the toilet. I'm pouring water into the toilet from a glass!'

"'Oh,' says my mother. She hesitates. 'Well, that's okay, I guess.'"

Sandra put down her burger. "Your point? Assuming there is one?"

"My point is, the sounds of streaming urine and streaming water are identical, yet one is deemed vile and the other benign. We take a perfectly innocuous sound and apply our own value judgment to it. And now I realize—context is everything."

Sandra swallowed another bite of her cheeseburger and wiped her mouth on her napkin. "Were you peeing or pouring water into the toilet back in our rental?"

"I was, um, peeing."

"And you were doing it with the bathroom door wide open?"

I nodded.

"Okay, that's the context. So now here's my value judgment: That's disgusting."

I was crestfallen. Sandra just didn't get it.

"Speaking of disgusting, are you going to eat that Mexican slop or what?" she said, referring, apparently, to my gourmet Caribbean fare. "I'd like to get out of this dive."

Later on, we sat at a beachside bar, me nursing a piña colada, Sandra sipping an iced tea. "While we're here, I'd like to live out one of my all-time fantasies," I said.

"Why do I have a feeling I'm not going to like this?" asked Sandra.

"Don't worry, I know what you're thinking, but it doesn't involve supermodel twins."

"Actually, I wasn't thinking that at all."

"My fantasy is this," I said. "Tomorrow, I want to go horseback riding on the beach at dawn."

"Horses? At dawn? I don't know, Jerome. How about we drive down to the beach at noon? I was hoping to sleep in."

I was relentless, bordering on whiney, in my quest to live the dream. Sandra finally relented, and the next morning we arrived at the stables before the sun crowned the horizon. A sleepy attendant led out two horses from the barn and hitched them to a rail fence. "The brown one is Tonto," he said. "The black, Kemosabe."

"My God, they're huge!" said Sandra.

"Why would anyone name a horse 'stupid'?" I asked.

The caballero offered Sandra a hand as she slipped her foot into the stirrup and hoisted herself up. I grabbed my saddle horn, swung my leg over the top, and settled in.

"*La playa*—that way," said the attendant, gesturing toward the only path leading away from the stable. We set off at a leisurely pace, single file, with Sandra and Tonto in the lead.

When the path widened, I jostled Kemosabe's reins and pulled alongside Sandra and her steed. The sky began to brighten and the shadows lifted. The dirt path left the wooded area, transforming into a sand trail surrounded by scrub growth. The sound of surf arose in the distance, mingling with tropical bird songs. "Beautiful, no?" I said. Sandra nodded tensely. "You haven't spent much time on a horse, have you?"

"I rode when I was a little girl; had maybe ten lessons. Haven't been on one since."

"You just need to go with the flow. Become one with the animal. His legs are just an extension of your own."

The horse snorted.

"How zen," said Sandra, with a hint of disdain in her voice.

We came around a bend to view a vast expanse of sand so white it looked like snow. The aqua *agua* lapped gently at the shore, which curved away from us in both directions to form a bay. Not a house could be seen in either direction, nor a person spotted. "Only tourists go to the beach, I'm told," I said. "But nobody goes to the beach at six a.m."

We cantered along the shore, and Sandra's face visibly relaxed. An uninformed observer might conclude that she was actually enjoying herself. I figured now was as good a time as any to pop the question.

"Um, I didn't actually go into all the details of my riding-a-horse-on-the-beach fantasy," I said. Sandra looked at me wearily and warily. "Here's the actual plan. We trot over to that grove, tie up your horse, take off all our clothes, and ride together on my horse, galloping nude down the beach, you squeezing me tight for dear life."

Sandra stared at me with disbelief. "Not happening. I'm not riding a horse naked like some sort of Lady Godiva. End of discussion."

My fantasy dashed, I belatedly realized I was in paradise with the wrong woman.

"Suit yourself," I said. I jabbed my heels and let out a staccato yell. Kemosabe tore off down the beach, clearly happy to get away from my uptight companion. I steered him toward the water's edge, and soon we were galloping through ankle-deep surf. Each hoof brought up a spray that soaked my sandals, coated my legs, and even dampened my shorts. I leaned hard over his mane, standing in the stirrups, moving in unison with the horse's undulating rhythm. The warm salt spray, the dazzling white sand, the water color more beautiful than a starlet's eyes, made me forget Sandra's rejection. This was my fantasy, almost fully realized, and it was good enough.

After a quarter mile or so, I slowed the horse back to a trot and continued up the beach. Glancing over my shoulder, I saw Sandra and Tonto, just a speck at the bend of the bay. Probably not a good idea to leave her alone, I thought. I turned the horse around.

I decided to impress Sandra with my horsemanship, so I urged the animal back into a full gallop for the last hundred yards. Kemosabe and I had already developed a good chemistry, a rhythm and responsiveness that was, in some respects, totally unlike the relationship I had with Sandra.

I yanked my steed to a sudden stop just shy of Sandra and her mount. Exhilarated from the ride, I bounded off the horse. Sandra stared at me, aghast. Admittedly, I was a sight—windblown hair; dripping wet; wild look in my eyes; maniacal grin. "What the hell is that?" she demanded.

"What's what?" I said, looking around, unsure of her reference point.

"That!" she said, pointing to my groin.

I gazed downward and saw a large bulge. "Well, lookie there!" I said, smiling sheepishly. "I had no idea."

I spoke the truth. I had no clue that my invigorating trot had produced this sort of measurable result.

"That's the sickest thing I've ever seen," said Sandra.

"What are you talking about?"

"I'm talking bestiality! I'm talking perversion! You've been sexually aroused by a horse, for God's sake! It's revolting!"

"Jesus, Sandra, get a grip. It's not sex; it's science. Action, reaction. Stimulus, response."

"Oh, so you're a freaking scientist now? Get the fuck away from me, you pervert. I'm leaving!" She started stomping down the beach, leaving Tonto tied up in the grove. I raced after her.

"You know what? You're the sick one. We've been dating over a month, and you've barely kissed me. You're repressed. You're frigid. You need to loosen up."

"Shut up, Jerome. Don't use your pop psychology on me. You're out of your league." She continued her determined march.

I jumped in front of her, arms akimbo, feet firmly planted in the sand. "For Christ sake, Sandra, get a grip. If I leaned against a running washing machine, I'd get an erection too. That doesn't mean I'm going to sexually abuse the appliance!"

Sandra burned with unbridled contempt. She roughly pushed past my shoulder and stormed down the beach, sprays of sand erupting from each footstep. I watched her till she disappeared behind the dunes. Then I went back to fetch the horses.

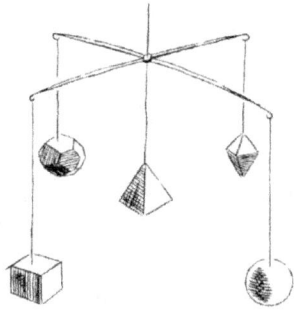

Chapter 21

Year 3 | Spring

Five weeks after Judith retreated to have her baby, Graham still hadn't heard a word. His voicemails, emails, and texts simply vanished into the void. Gray's concern rose with each passing day.

He unnecessarily hired a cleaning service to give Judith's apartment a final once-over. They didn't have much to do. The place was immaculate.

Gray called Maura. "Have you heard from Judith?"

"Yes, I talk to her almost every day."

"Did she have the baby?"

"Oh, God, yes, a week ago. A boy. He's doing fine."

"Blimey, you'd think she would have let me know. She didn't actually name him Igor, did she?"

"Well, she planned to, but she was afraid either the iguana or the child would suffer an identity crisis, so she chose the name Horatio instead."

Gray groaned. "What kind of a name is that?"

"Unusual?"

"Why hasn't she returned my messages?"

"I'm sorry, Graham, I don't know. She didn't mention them."

After another week passed—six weeks to the day after Judith left—Gray got a text: "On my way. 2 pm arrive. How's Igor?"

Gray checked his watch—twelve noon. He grabbed his and her keys and headed to Judith's.

Gray unlatched the door and entered the apartment. A cat emerged from behind a potted fern and rubbed against his leg. Noticing a browning frond on the plant, Gray pinched it off close to the base and stuck it in his back pocket. He ran a finger across a ledge; it came away clean.

At ten to two, Graham removed an artificial log from the triangular stack beside the fireplace, placed it on the rack inside, and touched a match to the ends. Flames licked at the paper wrapping.

At two to two, he stepped into the kitchen and saw that the cat had scattered some grit from the new self-dispensing, self-cleaning kitty litter tray. He cursed and grabbed a dustpan and brush from the cabinet under the sink.

At one to two, he assumed a nonchalant pose in the living room, sitting opposite the fireplace with his legs crossed. A cat leapt gracefully into his lap. He stroked it absentmindedly.

At one past two, he heard footsteps on the stairs. He took a deep breath. The door pushed open. Judith stepped across the threshold; she looked around. "Whoops! Sorry! Wrong apartment!" She backed out, pulling the door closed as she retreated.

Gray sat immobilized. Five seconds passed. The door cracked open again, and Judith stuck her head in. She scanned the room, then urged the door aside and slowly walked in. Her eyes widened. She placed a hand over her mouth. Gray jumped up; the cat scampered off. "Welcome home!" he said, walking toward her.

Judith looked disoriented. Gray took her arm. "Come see your apartment. I made, um, a few changes while you were gone."

Gray led her to the fireplace. "Turns out this was a working chimney all along. Just needed to be cleaned." The log crackled and sparked agreeably.

He took her into the bathroom. "Had the tiles regrouted. They were getting a bit dodgy."

Judith pulled aside the shower curtain. "Where's Igor?"

"Right this way," said Gray. He took her to the kitchen, where a huge aquarium sat on a long, narrow table by the window. The glass case was filled with a few inches of water, several flat stones, and a raised sunning platform, all illuminated by a small lamp. "Igor's new home. You can shower in your own bathroom again!"

Gray next escorted Judith to the bedroom, where her futon mattress had been replaced by a king-size bed with an elaborately carved mahogany headboard. Sun streamed through the window, illuminating the framed abstract impressionist prints on the wall and reflecting off the new mirror over the dresser. Judith took it all in silently.

"And now, the *piece de resistance!*" said Gray, virtually dragging Judith to the adjacent room. The baby's bedroom sported blazing yellow walls festooned with pictures of barnyard animals. Bright blue curtains framed the window. A brand new changing table sat next to a colorfully painted dresser. A wood slat crib stood ready, replete with padded bumpers and a dangling mobile of black and white geometric shapes. An oval sheepskin rug lay in front of a gliding rocker.

Judith stood stock still at the doorway. The suspense was killing Graham. "So, how do you like it?"

Judith turned to face him, jaw clenched, face reddened. "Where's my stuff?"

"What?"

"My possessions! My things! My stuff! What did you do with them?"

"Well, I, um, took some of it to the dump, put some of it in storage, and, um—

"Get out!"

"What?"

"Get out! Just get the fuck out!"

Dumbfounded, Graham didn't move. Judith gave him a shove. "Get out of my house—now!"

I'd been back from Vieques for less than a week. Sandra hightailed it off the island immediately via a puddle jumper to San Juan, a small jet to Miami, and a Greyhound north. I stayed on for the duration, getting shitfaced and sunburned and not caring.

I came home to a new trauma. Gray called me, then conferenced in Dave and asked if he could share a letter with us. He read aloud:

> *Graham,*
> *I realize that, in your unique self-delusional way, you thought you were doing a nice thing for me. But as any shrink would tell you, the "makeover" that you performed during my maternity leave was done for your benefit, not mine. It was an arrogant, narcissistic act.*
> *How could you think I'd want to live in that boring, sterile environment? Your values are not my values. The way you choose to live your life has nothing to do with the way I choose to live mine.*
> *You will bring my stuff back from storage immediately. And you will go to the dump to retrieve whatever you disposed of there.*
> *If you don't do this right away, maybe a call from my lawyer will convince you to move more quickly.*
> *~Judith*

"Wow," I commented insightfully.

"Gray," said Dave, his voice echoing faintly on the conference call line, "you didn't tell us you were rehabbing Judith's apartment. That's a total violation of her personal space. What the hell were you thinking?"

"I was thinking that she wanted to get out from under all that crap. She virtually said as much to me. I was helping her!"

"It's not help if the person doesn't want it," said Dave.

"You went overboard, laddie," I said. "You let your enthusiasm cloud your judgment."

"The great British philosopher Thomas Crapper had a saying about this," said Dave. Neither Gray nor I wanted to hear it, but Dave would not be denied. "'He who farts with vigor sometimes shits his pants.'"

We let the profundity of the statement sink in for a moment.

"First of all," said Gray, "Thomas Crapper was a plumber. Second of all, he never said that."

"Yeah, I know. I made it up," said Dave. "But it carries so much more authority coming from him."

"Okay, so what do I do now?" said Gray.

"Grovel and shovel," I said.

"I get the grovel part," said Dave.

"The shovel is for unearthing her possessions at the dump," I said.

"Or digging your own grave," said Dave.

Hours later, Gray and Dave pulled up in front of my apartment in a rental truck. I clambered in.

"So, how was Jamaica?" asked Dave.

"Vieques. And I don't want to talk about it," I replied.

Dave wisely dropped the subject. Gray was too preoccupied to notice.

At the storage facility, we loaded Judith's stuff into the van, then hauled it to her apartment building. When we rolled up the metal back door of the vehicle, a wave of papers, boxes, and assorted paraphernalia washed over us.

A note was tacked to the apartment door:

> *I'm staying at Maura's. Put everything in*
> *the baby's room—nowhere else! Stack it to*
> *the ceiling if you have to. Send me a text*
> *when you've finished. Lock the door and*
> *slide the key under it. And leave.*

"Still miffed, apparently," I said.

"You're an effing master at reading between the lines," said Dave.

I was inexplicably excited about the apartment renovation, like a kid waiting for the amusement park to open. "I can't stand the suspense," I said as Gray fumbled with the key.

We entered. The apartment was completely unrecognizable. I simply couldn't reconcile this pristine space to my memory of having dinner in the madwoman's lair nearly a year ago.

"I'm surprised," said Gray. "No clutter. No mess. I would have thought she'd have re-trashed the place by now."

"Before you sterilized the life out of it, this apartment was a work in progress," I said. "The accumulation took years. You can't expect her to recreate it in three days."

"Suppose not," muttered Gray.

"Have you seen the baby yet?" asked Dave.

"Nope. She came back to the apartment without him."

"Probably wanted to spare him the trauma," I said.

"A," said Gray, "she didn't come home expecting trauma. And B, where, exactly, is the trauma in a beautiful, clean apartment?" He made no attempt to hide his bitterness.

"Trauma is in the eye of the traumee," said Dave.

We toured the apartment. Peering into the bedroom, I spotted an ear of Indian corn at the foot of the bed. "Judith has this thing about corn," I said.

"Oh, she has a whole collection of those," said Gray, pulling open the bottom dresser drawer to reveal the multicolored ears.

"She loves popcorn too," I said. "After she stayed at Maura's for a few days, we found fistfuls of corn kernels between the sheets."

We unloaded the truck, stacking box after box into the small bedroom, filling the crib, covering the changing table, and obscuring the dresser.

"Isn't it odd that she wants you to put everything in the baby's room?" I asked.

"She'll probably have him sleep in her room for the first few months," said Gray.

An hour later, the baby's bedroom teemed with miscellany. I stood in the doorway and tried to recall what the room reminded me of. Oh, yeah—Judith's flat, prior to Gray's ill-advised reclamation project. We closed the apartment door. Gray kicked the key under it, and we departed.

Chapter 22

Year 3 | Spring

Tan, fit, and sexually frustrated, I returned to my monotonous life. My still-unpacked suitcase from Vieques sat in my dank room as I hunched morosely over my laptop, deleting junk mail. In a pique of self-pity, I deleted every item in my inbox, all 2,197 messages. I didn't care. I wasn't ever going to read them, and they were a psychological burden.

I decided to share my foul mood with Dave, so I caught a streetcar over to his apartment. He was prone on the couch watching TV. "I never knew curling could be such a gripping, glue-you-to-the-edge-of-your-seat sport," he said.

"Dave, *eins*, you're nowhere near the edge. And, *zwei*, if you were any more relaxed, the couch would be lying on you."

I grabbed a beer from the fridge.

"You still haven't told me about your trip," said Dave. "How was Tortola?"

"Vieques. It sucked."

"That's a surprise. I heard it was a beautiful little island."

"Oh, the island was fine. It was the company. Sandra turned out to be a frigid bitch."

"There's no such thing as frigid women," said Dave. "Just inept men."

"Fuck you, too."

"So this post-Maura thing isn't working out?"

"You know, I thought that a little break from Maura would be a good thing. Meet somebody else; have a nice, simple, low-maintenance relationship. Turns out Sandra is so high-maintenance, she needs her own full-time mechanic."

"You ain't exactly maintenance-free yourself, brother."

"I swear, if it weren't for this prostate thing, I'd give up women entirely."

"I don't get it," said Dave.

"My medical condition—I need to ejaculate daily."

"Listen, you fucking goon. If you're sleeping with women to treat your prostate, you're sicker than you realize."

I was tempted to put up an argument. Since I never actually had sex with Sandra, one could hardly claim that I was commandeering her vagina for medicinal purposes. Maura, on the other hand, seemed to relish the idea of helping to treat my condition, to the point where I half-expected her to accost me in a sexy little nurse's uniform. So if there was any sin here, it was in the intent, not in the act. However, mustering this self-defense hardly seemed worth the effort.

While I was mulling this over, Dave apparently continued moralizing. "This condition of yours—you need to take the matter into your own hands. So to speak."

"Yeah, funny," I said morosely.

"Not funny—serious."

A rap came at the door. Standing outside, Graham shaded his eyes and peered through the glass. "Don't let him in," I said. "I'm not in the mood for his pretentiousness."

Dave opened the door. "Graham," he said.

"Gentlemen," said Graham. "Pleasure."

"Yeah, whatever," I said

"What's with Segundo?" asked Gray as he reached into the fridge.

"He's been in a shitty mood since he got back from St. Croix," said Dave. "Moaning about the lousy vacation he had with his cranky, uptight girlfriend."

"Hard to feel sorry for a guy who just got back from the Caribbean," said Gray, taking a swig.

"Here's your problem," said Dave to me. "You've been hanging around Sandra so much, you're becoming just like her—moody, irritable, a real drag to be around."

"A well-known syndrome," said Gray. "Couples taking on one another's traits. You know what they say."

For some reason, his comment irritated me. "No, Graham, I don't know. What, exactly, do they say?"

"You are what you eat."

The remark hung in the air for a second, until suddenly Dave nearly choked on his beer. Gray smirked shamelessly at his own comment.

I didn't get it.

Dave regained his composure. "As it turns out, in Jerome's case, he is what he *doesn't* eat."

The boys burst into hilarity. Dave did a little jig and they high-fived.

I still didn't get it.

"You two are frigging fronds of wisdom," I said once they calmed down.

"That's *founts* of wisdom," said Gray. "And thank you."

Gray plopped down on the couch. "So, how's the folks?" he said to Dave. "Your dad still doing your laundry?"

A fortnight after my return from Puerto Rico, I was still depressed about my vacation. The whole time I was with Sandra, I wished she were Maura. Now, back home, I walked down the street, and every other female reminded me of Maura. I heard a woman talking, and I swore it was Maura. I turned each corner with the hope of running into Maura. Then, suddenly, I did.

She was sitting in the coffee shop when I entered. I walked over and extended my hand. She smiled and clasped it warmly. "Don't you know that tanning salons cause cancer?" she said, looking at my Caribbean-bronzed face.

"This from a woman who uses olive oil instead of sun block?"

I delivered a bravura performance of a carefree, happy, active guy. I told her about my marvelous Puerto Rican adventure. I even threw the "we" word around a few times, as in "we" rented a nice little villa, and "we" went horseback riding on the beach, hoping to make Maura jealous, but she didn't bite. Once I gave up my posturing, Maura and I had a nice, lighthearted chat over coffee.

I cajoled her into a drink a few nights later, dinner the Friday after that, and a movie the following week. Next thing I knew, she invited me to stay over. I started to think our relationship was back to normal.

Saturday morning, six-and-a-half weeks after my resurrection, Maura nudged me from my stupor. "Hey! It's a beautiful spring day. Let's go on a picnic."

"Nobody goes on a picnic at 7 a.m.," I said. "Wake me up at noon."

"If I were going to wake you at noon, I would have done so an hour ago."

I rolled over and peered at the clock. The oversized numbers were barely discernible if I squinted hard. I'd be damned if it wasn't 1:04 p.m. I flopped back over.

On second thought, damned if it *wasn't* 1:04. "Nice try," I said. "Switch it back."

My suspicion that Maura had pulled a reset-the-clock trick to rouse me from bed proved unfounded, and the time remained properly set in the present. She ripped the covers from my naked body and whisked them from the room. Left with the choice of adopting a shivering, pathetic fetal position on the bed or getting up, I arose.

I padded into the kitchen naked. "How about we invite Dave and his new girlfriend to join us?"

Maura ran her fingers through my sparse chest hair. "Sure," she said.

I gave Dave a call, and we agreed to meet in an hour.

I extracted a bag of sesame bagels from the bread bin. Unfortunately, they were beyond their expiration date and spotted with little patches of fuzzy mold. I pinched off the growths, leaving the bagels pockmarked but edible, and loaded them into a wicker picnic basket along with lox, cream cheese, grapes, carrot sticks, and a magnum of Chardonnay. Plastic cups, forks, knives, and paper napkins rounded out the provisions.

We stepped outside into the cool spring weather, so vibrant it felt unreal, like an enhanced reality video game. I placed the picnic basket into Maura's ten-year-old Saab, and we headed for the local nature preserve, which featured a moderately strenuous hiking trail leading to a grassy summit patch, ideal for picnicking.

Several dozen cars nearly filled the small lot. We parked near a fire gate that separated the dirt hiking path from the paved area, positioning Maura's car directly over the white dividing line so that it occupied two spaces, one for us and one for Dave.

A sports car pulled up, convertible top down, studly looking man driving, fabulously good-looking woman riding shotgun, her hair fetchingly mussed. "Hey, that your car?" the man yelled.

"Saving the space for a friend," I said. The couple roared off while the man uttered something vaguely obscene.

"I hope Dave shows up soon," I said to Maura, who had perched herself on a nearby rock in the sun.

A metallic green pickup entered the lot and slowly tooled over, two men inside. A magnetic sign on the door indicated they worked in the trades. The driver eyed me and nodded at the space.

"Holding it for my friend," I said. "He's just thirty seconds up the road."

"I'll be back in 35," he said, flicking a cigarette butt to the ground and briefly screeching his tires as he pulled out.

I dialed Dave's cell. "How far away are you? I'm trying to save you a space, but the natives are getting restless."

"Hold that spot!" said Dave. "Lie down in it if you have to."

"Are you kidding me? It's cutthroat out here. I'd wind up with tread marks on my spleen."

"Cutthroat would leave marks on your neck, not your spleen."

"Shut up, Dave. Just get up here. Where are you?"

"We're still a ways away. Probably twenty minutes. How, exactly, are you saving the space?"

"We parked Maura's car so it overlaps two spaces."

"Okay, then just lock the car, walk ten paces up the trail, and hide the key under the nearest rock. I'll move the car when I get there."

We agreed to meet at the top. I placed the key in the designated spot, and Maura and I began our hike upward. As we moved in and out of the shadows on the trail, the early May sun warmed us pleasantly, while the shaded areas still exuded the accumulated coolness of the winter just past. We strolled by a grove of birch, stark in its whiteness. The whole scene had a picture book quality. The air was so clear, it was almost alive. I breathed deeply.

Yet despite the overwhelming sensorial stimulation, I felt disengaged. "Look at that," I said to Maura, pointing to the scene before us. "Isn't it beautiful?"

Maura nodded her assent.

"So why can't I shake the feeling that I'm looking at a painting in a museum?"

"Detachment from reality," said Maura. "A well-documented syndrome. Electroshock therapy is the recommended treatment. Clears away the brain sludge and gets the synapses firing again."

"Kind of like a fuel additive that de-muckifies your engine?"

"Yes, only much more painful."

We continued up the trail. My flimsy low-cut canvas sneakers proved unsuited for the task. I nearly rolled my ankle a couple of times before realizing I needed to watch my steps more carefully. Maura, meanwhile, was well-equipped in spiffy hiking boots that provided all the support she needed.

"Could be worse," I said, picking up the conversation. "The recommended treatment might have been a lobotomy."

"You certainly can't afford that," said Maura.

"Are you speaking in terms of dollars or sense?" I asked. Maura didn't catch my witticism. I made a mental note that homonym humor is ill-suited to the spoken word.

Near the summit, we broke through to a clearing. I hiked over to the highest spot, a rock outcropping, to scan the view. Maura sidled up. "You can almost see the curvature of the earth," she said.

We slowly wended our away around the bald spot at the top of the hill, absorbing the 360-degree panorama. Our home city shimmered in the distance, about ten miles away. Even the brown pollution haze that usually hung over the metropolis had been dissipated by the fine spring weather.

My phone chimed. It was Dave. "We're approaching the summit. Start laying out the feast."

Maura and I spread our blanket across the grass in a semi-secluded area and started to unpack the meal. A yell arose; Dave and his girlfriend appeared at the edge of the woods and strode into the clearing. As they started to saunter over, another figure emerged from the trees behind them—Graham.

We exchanged greetings. "Where did you pick up this slacker?" I said to Dave, nodding at Gray.

Dave ignored my query as he introduced his friend Nadia—fit, attractive, brown hair smartly cut, and looking suspiciously familiar. "Did we go to college together?" I asked.

"Not unless you attended Wellesley in drag," she replied.

I liked her immediately.

"Jerome, you remember Nadia," said Dave. "That day you tagged along on my flower route. She was one of my clients."

I tried to recall. I remembered handing out daffodils by the dozen, but she looked a little young for the nursing home. Then the realization hit. "Oh, wait a minute! Nadia? Nadia with the satin sheets! Sorry, I didn't recognize you without your towel!" I gave her a hug.

"Satin sheets?" Nadia whispered over my shoulder to Dave as I embraced her. Out of the corner of my eye, I saw Dave twirl a finger at his temple.

"So, Dave brings you flowers?" Maura asked Nadia.

"Constantly," she replied. "Every room of my house is filled with them."

"And I've seen her house," I said. "It's big."

"You probably already know this," said Nadia as we settled on the blanket, "but David is a true gentleman. We first met when my rat-bastard husband—now ex-husband—tried to win me back with roses. David delivered them. I was angry and hurt. In fact, I was so mad, I was determined to have an affair of my own in revenge. I made a pass at David, but he gently talked me out of it and convinced me to take the high road."

I looked at Dave with slack-jawed amazement. He gave an aw-shucks look in return.

"We've made up for it since," postscripted Nadia.

"And the high road led to a tidy settlement," said Dave.

Maura poured us each some Chardonnay, filling the clear plastic cups about halfway. She handed Gray the bottle, as we only brought four cups.

"To satin sheets," I said, tapping cups and bottle.

Maura dealt out the bagels. I ripped mine in two and handed half to Gray. "Pretty rough looking bread," he said, eyeing the numerous spots where I had picked away the mold.

"Well, aren't you the buggered beggar?" I said. "Don't worry about it. I just, um, cut off the burnt parts."

"You made these bagels from scratch?" said Nadia.

"Actually, no. I just go to a careless baker."

"Probably out having a cigarette when the bagels got scorched," said Dave. "Lucky he didn't burn down the joint."

"Or out having a joint," said Maura.

"Burns down the joint while smoking a joint," said Gray.

"Which gets his customers all out of joint," said Maura.

"Speaking of which," said Gray, pulling a crudely rolled spliff from his shirt pocket. He ignited it, took a massive puff, and passed it on. I declined the marijuana, instead grabbing the bottle from Gray and pouring myself another glass of wine.

"Okay," Dave said. "I have a personal hygiene question for you all."

I worried that he was referring to me and resisted the urge to smell my armpit. "Dave, I thought you said you were never crude in front of the female species," I said.

"Females are not a species; they're a gender," said Gray.

"*Touché*," I said.

"*En garde!*" said Gray, who jabbed me with a carrot stick, which broke on my shoulder.

"Hygiene isn't crude," said Dave. "It's civilized. So here's my question: How many of you have used a bidet?"

Maura raised her hand. "In Paris, a few years ago."

"I always knew you had that certain *je ne sais quoi*," said Dave.

"Is that French for sanitary butt?" I said.

"My seaside resort in Portimão had a bidet," offered Gray.

"The reason I ask," Dave said, "is that Nadia was making fun of my anal cleansing methodology."

"Dave," said Gray, "number one, you must be the only person in the world who has an anal cleansing methodology. Number two, even if you have a methodology, I would hope that Nadia here wouldn't be exposed to it. And, number three, I've been to your apartment, and I know you don't have a bidet."

"That's just my point," said Dave. "Because of that inexcusable plumbing deficiency, I use the second-best method."

"Dare I ask?" said Maura.

"B.B.W.," replied Dave.

"Baby butt wipes," said Nadia. "You know, those moistened cloth wipes in a plastic tub. And, just for the record, I didn't witness him using them. I saw the container on the toilet."

"Well, that's a relief," said Gray. "But you've got to admit, it's a bit strange for a grown man to be using baby wipes."

"Not strange in the least," said Dave. "What's strange is how Americans, who are germ-phobic in every other way, are so nonchalant about anal hygiene."

Dave continued. "Let's say, for example, that you're out on a picnic."

"Easy enough to imagine," I said.

"And let's say that you're sitting on the edge of the blanket. You lean back, put your arm out to support yourself, and stick your hand right into a pile of animal dung. My question: Are you going to be content to wipe that excrement off with a tissue? Or are you going to want to wash your hand?"

We all sat silently, looking at Dave, marveling at his passion for the topic.

"It's the same way, or should be, with anal hygiene. Do you truly believe that swiping at your butt with a dry piece of tissue actually accomplishes anything?"

"It keeps clumps of shit out of your underwear," I said.

"And that's where the B.B.W.s come in. They cleanse. They sanitize."

"They refresh," I said.

"They invigorate," said Gray.

"They give you a whole new outlook on life," said Maura.

"To B.B.W.'s!" I said, raising a toast. We clinked plastic.

"You'll find over time," said Gray in an aside to Nadia, "that little animates Dave like bodily functions."

"Oh, I've found that out already," said Nadia, patting Dave's thigh.

Maura and I wandered off, hiking without a clear destination in mind. We left the well-marked path to forge our own trail through the pines. The aroma reminded me of the evergreen air freshener dangling from the mirror in Gray's Land Rover.

We walked along quietly for several minutes, our steps barely making a sound on the moss and pine underfoot. After traversing several gently rolling slopes, we happened upon a small clearing, sunny yet secluded. "Let's sit," Maura said.

A thick carpet of golden pine needles coated the ground. I lay back, supporting my head with my arm. Maura turned perpendicular to my body and likewise leaned back, placing her head on my stomach as she gazed up into the cloudless sky.

I lightly traced her hairline with my fingertips, starting at her right ear, along her temple, past the peak of her forehead and down to her other ear. I gently tugged on the lobe, then followed the contour of her ear. I repeated on the other ear so she wouldn't feel unbalanced.

I softly ran my knuckles over her facial structure—along her cheekbones, up the side of her nose, and circling the eye socket, applying soothing pressure. Maura breathed in deeply. "Clears the sinuses," she said contentedly.

Maura sat up, unbuttoned and took off her blouse. She lay her head on the fragrant pine needle bed. "Caress me, you fool," she said sweetly. I spotted a feather ten feet away and crawled over to retrieve it. Maura closed her eyes as I drew the feather around and over her face, neck, breasts, and stomach.

She unsnapped and unzipped her jeans, kicked off her hiking boots, then lifted her hips, sliding the garment off. Naked to the sun, she seemed the perfect specimen of a woman: naturally beautiful face; perfect shapely breasts; smooth, flat stomach; neatly trimmed pubic hair; long, tapered legs. I felt lightheaded just looking at her.

Kneeling at her side, I caressed her breasts with my left hand, gently nuzzled her stomach with my nose and lips, and simultaneously teased her inner thighs with the feather in my right hand. She spread her legs un-self-consciously.

I arced my face closer to her pubic hair in successive kissing sweeps, while I brushed ever-nearer her vagina with the feather. My face and hand finally meet at the labia, which I moistened, then gently engulfed. Maura moaned and arched her back.

Since she first brought me to ecstasy with her mysterious technique, I'd been trying to create the female version of Maura's orgasmic methodology. Not knowing exactly what she did under the covers, the secret of the sexual universe still being closely held, made replication difficult, but I figured through persistent experimentation I might stumble upon a reasonable facsimile.

I flicked and glided my tongue, fluttered and probed my fingers, but I couldn't get into a rhythm. Maura's sexual tension rose, but then fell. She sighed. I couldn't bring her to climax.

She reached behind her head and dragged the backpack toward her. "I've got something that might help," she said, fishing within the pack. She withdrew an ear of Indian corn.

I looked at her in puzzlement. "Why are you packing corn?"

"Judith gave it to me as a present," said Maura, "right after you and I broke up. Judith uses Indian corn to, um, satisfy certain urges."

A mental curtain lifted. "Oh my God. That's why they were in her dresser!"

"Yep," said Maura with a smile.

The curtain rose farther. "And that's why she had one on her bed."

"Indian corn is her own little declaration of independence," said Maura.

The curtain reached the ceiling. "Oh, my freaking word. That's why there were corn kernels in your bed!"

"Yes, indeed, Sherlock. I didn't want to tell you at the time."

"Why not?"

"I didn't think you could handle the truth."

Maura pulled a small jar of vegetable shortening from her pack and lovingly slathered the corn until it glistened. I'd never seen such a sexy vegetable in my life.

"It's the kernels that make this an unparalleled sexual tool. Those little nubs are, how you say? Sensational."

"If an ear of corn works so well, wouldn't a studded vibrator be even better?"

"Corn is a tool," said Maura. "A vibrator is a crutch."

"And you, my love, are a sexual purist," I said.

I gently probed her labia with the narrow end of the ear, twirling it slowly as I slipped it in and out, progressively deeper. I leaned forward to add my mouth and fingers to the mix, kissing and licking her sun-warmed vagina. I built toward a crescendo, pull back into a diminuendo, threw in an unexpected glissando, then finished with fortissimo.

Maura orgasmed with such fury that she squeezed my head in a vice grip between her thighs. The Indian corn was nearly fully inserted, locked into place under her sexual spasm. I held my breath and tried mightily to endure the tidal wave, not wanting to break her reverie. Her clitoris throbbed under my tongue.

Then the tide slowly subsided, her leg clench eased, and I took a breath. We both fell back in exhaustion. I ever-so-slowly eased the corn out of her, twirling it upon exit.

Lying there in the springtime warmth, we needed a few minutes to recover. Then, still naked, Maura rolled onto her side and placed her head on my belly, one ear stethoscoping my stomach, the other ear pointing to the sky, her eyes toward my feet. "It sounds like a mad rushing river inside you," she said.

I gently pulled on the hair at the nape of her neck as she lay there, looking comfortable enough to take a nap. "Here's a little Boy Scout quiz for you," she said. "What direction am I facing?"

"I missed that session," I said, "along with knot tying, old-lady helping, and stick-rubbing. I was off setting fires in the woods."

"Naughty boy."

"Ah, but a Boy Scout always comes prepared. You want to know which direction you're heading? My compass is in my pocket. Fish it out, and it'll tell you."

"Which pocket?"

"The, uh, zippered one."

"I should have guessed."

Maura retracted the metal zipper on my jeans with such deliberation that each tooth clicked distinctly. Reaching carefully inside the opening, mindful of the instrument's delicate nature, she extracted and caressed its fine, smooth surface. "Exceptional quality," she noted.

"Yes, a family heirloom," I replied. "So, which way are you facing?"

"I must be facing south. Because as soon as I took your compass out, the arrow sprang to life and pointed north."

"The power of magnetism," I said, eyes closed.

The sun radiated across my being as Maura engulfed me. She hummed happily, with her hand acting as the rhythm section, playing counterpoint to the tune I had performed for her.

I hated to do anything to break the magic of the moment, but I couldn't resist. "Maura?"

"Mmmmm?" she said, mouth full.

"Are you ever going to reveal the secret of the sexual universe to me?"

She stopped and turned to face me. "Well, you've just learned a little trick from the how-to-pleasure-a-female department."

"Yes, my squaw," I said.

"It's not actually the secret," she continued, "but it's a key to one of the locks."

"There's more than one lock?" I asked, dismayed.

Maura just smiled. "Anyway, I can't imagine why you'd need to know the how-to-pleasure-a-male corollary."

"Well, that's just a failure of imagination on your part, isn't it?" I said.

"I guess it is. Okay then." She got to her knees. I put both hands behind my head and gazed intently at her. She looked like an angel, pale bare skin radiating in the sun. "Off with these," she said. I obediently removed my jeans.

She retrieved the Indian corn, wiped it dry with a wad of tissue, and lightly tossed it to me. "Before we imagine that this ear of corn is your penis, let's imagine that it's an oddly shaped, soaking wet sponge. What's the most efficient method for squeezing it dry?"

I looked at her, not understanding.

"If you wanted to dry that sponge out, what would you do?"

I held the corn horizontally in front of me with two hands, palms down, then wringed it, twisting my hands in opposite directions.

"Exactly!" said Maura. She took the corn and reoriented it into a vertical position. "Now, using two hands, grab onto the corn." I clasped the ear like one might grab a pole, one hand above the other. "Okay, now repeat that wringing motion." I twisted my hands as instructed.

"Excellent! You're a fine student. Now, ease up on your grip. Instead of forcefully wringing out the corn, caress it with that same motion."

I did, and Maura smiled.

She cupped her hands at the top and bottom of the ear to hold it steady. "Now, continue that twisting caress while simultaneously moving your hands up and down the length of the ear."

I gently and lovingly stroked the corn, sliding vertically along the length, twisting horizontally across the girth. Maura watched with a teacher's pride.

"Okay, you're ready for the final step." She took the ear from me and planted it firmly in her lap, the tip pointing upward, as if it were her own penis. "Put your mouth over the end and your hands in the proper positions. Perform the motion you just learned, up and down the shaft, with your mouth following close behind your hands. Pulsate your lips and add a little tongue to the mix." My head started swimming just hearing the description.

Maura pulled my head toward her lap. The large, corny penis loomed before me. I resisted. "That's okay; I think I've got it," I said.

"Would you quit the Boston Marathon 100 yards from the finish? Would you abandon *War and Peace* a chapter from the end? Down, boy!"

I bent toward her lap. The erect ear of corn grew ever larger until it appeared bigger than my head. I took the tip gingerly into my mouth and slowly slid my lips down the shaft. The kernels tickled.

"Don't forget your hands," said Maura. I tried to answer, but my mouth was full.

I couldn't quite get the coordination. My syncopated torque was all wrong. The tip of the ear hit the back of my throat, and I almost gagged. I tried to come up for air, but Maura checked the back of my head with her palm. "Keep trying," she said. "Hand/mouth coordination can be a bit tricky."

Then it started to come to me. Up and down. Around and around. Twist and glide. Squeeze and release. So many simultaneous movements combining to produce an incredible sensation.

I got an erection of my own, which, since I was performing a simulated blow job on an imaginary male, I found embarrassing. Maura noticed, but apparently didn't consider it odd. She caressed my penis with a feathery touch. "Okay, grasshopper," she said. "You have passed the test."

I fell back. Maura parted my legs and knelt between them, facing me.

"Now watch a master at work," she said. She leaned forward and ingested me. Her hands twisted and glided in mesmerizing fashion. I was overwhelmed by her touch. I moaned. Maura moaned. My eyes rolled back in my head.

"Oh, my God," I chanted, enraptured. I clasped Maura's head at each side and gently pulled her face away from my lap, just for a moment. "You, my darling, are a sexual genius. What do you call this amazing technique?"

Maura put on a fake scowl. "Never, ever interrupt a genius at work." She resumed her stimulations, but then lifted her head again. "Bilateral stroke with a twist."

I reopened my eyes. "What?"

"Bilateral stroke with a twist. That's what I call the technique. It's another key to unlock the secret of the sexual universe."

She re-engaged my member. I returned to my euphoria, journeying toward heaven. Maura brought me close, ever closer, tantalizingly close to nirvana. It built; I resisted. It rose; I held back.

In my delirium, without even realizing I was doing it, I extended my arms, interlaced my fingers, and cracked my knuckles. A rapid series of pops cascaded through the woodland air.

Maura disengaged. "Jesus, Jerome, must you?"

"Must I what?" I asked.

"Crack your knuckles! What, you aren't getting enough stimulation?"

"Sorry. I wasn't even aware of it. It's like breathing, completely unconscious. I probably crack them in my sleep."

"Well, don't do it when I'm around. I can't stand the sound. It sends a chill down my spine."

"Right, boss," I said. A cool breeze blew across our blanket.

"Uh, speaking of sending chills down the spine," I said, nodding toward my erect member.

"Sorry," she said, standing and quickly donning her clothes. "Lost my taste for it. Let's walk."

I moaned like a man punched in the gut. She was already striding away as I recomposed myself and jumped into my jeans. Still buttoning my shirt, I hustled to catch up. We walked briskly for ten minutes or so before arriving at the lip of a hill overlooking a field. We sat on a weathered bench.

"Still mad?" I asked.

Maura didn't answer.

I got up, walked behind the bench, picked up a long branch from the ground, and broke it in two with a loud snap.

"Damn it, Jerome, I asked you not to do that!"

I moved to the front of the bench. Standing before Maura, I broke the wood again.

"Oh," she said. "Sorry. I thought—"

"So the sound of breaking sticks doesn't bother you?" I ask.

"No, of course not. Why should it?"

"Because this sound"—I broke the stick again—"is identical to this sound"—I cracked the joint of my middle finger. My skeletal pop almost perfectly matched, in pitch and tone, that of the snapped wood.

Maura cringed at the latter. "And your point is?"

"My point is, it's not the sound that bothers you. It's your interpretation of the sound. You're imposing your own meaning on the event; the sound itself is irrelevant."

"Actually, it wouldn't have mattered whether you were breaking every bone in your hand or all the kindling in the forest. Your mind was wandering. If you can't pay attention to what's happening, why should I even bother?"

"Oh, I was paying attention. You had my rapturous attention. I told you, it's like blinking."

"Actually, you said breathing."

"Whatever. You see what I'm saying. You're just being obtuse."

* * *

We rejoined the group, made a little small talk, finished off the crumbs and the dregs, then packed up. Dave, Nadia, and Gray chatted amicably on the trail on the way down. Maura and I followed silently in single file.

Though she was pissed off at me, I took solace in the fact that at least I finally learned the secret of the sexual universe.

Dave dropped back. "I forgot to mention, there was another open space when I arrived, so I never bothered to move your car. Your keys are still under the rock where you left them."

As we approached the end of the trail, we got a view of the parking lot. Maura's car listed noticeably. On closer inspection, we saw why. Her front tire was slashed.

I convinced myself that this was neither an omen nor a metaphor for my relationship with Maura. If the divine powers of the universe were inclined to send cosmic messages through automobile tires, they surely would have delivered the symbolism in the form of a slow leak.

Chapter 23

Year 3 | Summer

We put our spat behind us by not talking about it. I made a
point not to crack my knuckles when Maura was around, which
proved more difficult than expected. She seemed a bit more distant
with me, but I was confident that it was nothing that couldn't be
overcome with the passage of time.

The Friday of the long Independence Day weekend, Maura had
a dinner date with Judith. I was going to a minor league baseball
game with Dave and Gray. Maura and I planned to meet at her place
after our respective nights on the town.

I wound up having an extra beer or three with the lads. Maura
was already asleep when I arrived at her apartment. Tiptoeing to the
bathroom, I used the toilet, but forewent the flush for the sake of
silence. I quietly washed, brushed, flossed, and gargled. I crept into

the darkened bedroom, wriggled out of my clothes, dropped them to the floor at my feet, and crawled into bed.

The night air seeping through the windows made it too warm for a blanket, too cool for nothing. Maura had settled under a sheet, naked, as was her wont. As I slid beneath the sheer cotton fabric, I sidled up to her. She moaned softly and rolled from her back to her side, facing away from me. I spooned against her, my front to her back, matching the contour of her body.

I reached around her waist, then upwards to gently cradle her breast. No response. Maura was out. She was a deep sleeper, and I realized the chance of waking her to make love with me hovered around nil.

I placed my erect penis along the cleft between her buttock cheeks, where it settled comfortably, a frankfurter in a bun. I slowly rubbed against her soft skin.

Maura kept a pump bottle of lotion on her bedside table. I reached over, cupped my hand under the nozzle, and pressed the applicator a couple of times with my thumb. I smeared the cool cream over my erect penis, from tip to base.

Maura remained on her side in a loosely constructed fetal position, knees flexed and pulled slightly up. Slowly, evenly, so not to disturb her, I directed my slippery member toward the intersection of thighs and buttocks and entered her smoothly. She moaned. I wondered what kind of dream I was inspiring.

I thrusted in slow motion, trying to be gentle enough that Maura wouldn't awaken. I slowly inserted and withdrew until I came in a pulsating release.

Through it all, Maura never woke up. I pulled out, dried my penis with my T-shirt, snuggled next to Maura, and fell into a contented sleep.

Maura sat opposite me at breakfast. I studied the latest news on my laptop. It was a gray day; muted light seeped through the kitchen windows.

Maura squirmed uncomfortably.

"Got an itch?" I said. "I can help you scratch it."

"No, I'm wet. Some kind of a discharge. Not like a yeast infection, more like the morning after sex, only without the sex."

"Maybe you had a wet dream. You were moaning in your sleep last night."

"I always remember my wet dreams. In detail."

"Well, maybe you had a night visitor," I said coyly.

"What's that supposed to mean?" Her voice held just the slightest edge.

"I mean, you know, maybe the Brink's guard made a late-night deposit."

She stared at me.

"Maybe the mailman made a special delivery."

Maura got a look that signified danger. I stupidly ignored the warning sign.

"What are you rambling about?" she demanded.

I sensed I should come clean. "I, uh, slipped in for a quickie last night while you were sleeping."

"You WHAT?" She slapped her hands hard on the table, punctuating the last word. Silverware clattered. Geysers erupted from the coffee mugs.

"Well, you were asleep, and I was horny, and I didn't want to disturb you, so I just, you know—"

"You BASTARD!" she shrieked. "You fucking bastard!"

"Maura, it was nothing. It was like two minutes."

"Nothing? You raped me! You're a fucking rapist!" She stood violently, eyes ablaze. Her chair tumbled backward from the force, crashing to the floor. Her thighs hit the underside of the table, rocking it, toppling the coffee cups. The scalding liquid headed straight for my laptop. I grabbed it and pushed my chair backward just in time.

"Hold on!" I said. "Calm down!" I approached her, still clutching the laptop in one hand. I reached out, seeking a forgiving embrace.

"Get the fuck away from me!" She shoved me in the chest; I lurched backward. The laptop slipped from my grasp and hit the linoleum, the screen shattering on impact, the letter keys skittering across the floor. I stared in disbelief. Maura sobbed as she ran out of the room. The bedroom door slammed.

I stood astonished at what just occurred.

"Oh, man. She did not take that well." I walked over to inspect the laptop wreckage and stepped on a letter with my bare foot. It imbedded itself in my heel. I hopped in place as I pulled it out. "M."

The machine was clearly beyond repair. I picked it up by its screen and dropped it into the trash.

Unspooling a dozen sheets from the paper towel roll, I sopped up the spillage on the table and floor, then wadded the towels and arced a shot toward the wastebasket across the kitchen. It hit with a splat against the back wall, leaving a dripping brown stain as it banked into the black plastic bin liner.

"Score," I intoned quietly.

"She'll get over it," I mumbled to myself as I climbed into the shower. How long it would take, I knew, was another issue. I might be punished with the cold shoulder for days, even weeks.

I lathered up, mulling over the injustice of it all. How dare she call me a rapist? How could she equate me with those assholes who actually violate women? Hell, if I didn't tell her, she wouldn't even realize she'd been raped—I mean, um, visited.

I heard the bathroom door open. Ah! Maybe forgiveness would be granted sooner than expected. "Maura, I'm sorry about this little misunderstanding—"

The shower curtain yanked violently open. Before me stood two burly men in uniform. "Step out of the shower, sir."

"What?" I said as the water continued to cascade around my shoulders. "What's going on, officer?"

"Step out of the shower. You're under arrest."

"Arrest? What for?" I dropped the soap and stepped onto the bathmat.

"Put your hands behind your back." The cop clicked on a pair of plastic handcuffs, too tight around my wrists.

"Did Maura call you? Oh my God! Officer, this is a mistake. Do I look like a rapist?"

The policeman coolly appraised me from navel to kneecap. He nudged his partner. "Not exactly a lethal weapon, is it?"

Chapter 24

Year 3 | Summer

After celebrating the Fourth of July in the clink, I finally got bailed out by Graham and Dave. I was feeling chastised, if not traumatized, but was determined not to show it. I feigned nonchalance.

"What took you guys so long? Don't you know what happens to good-looking young males in prison?"

"I'm not sure how that applies to you," said Dave.

"Do you have any idea how difficult it is to get a bail bondsman over a holiday weekend?" said Gray.

"So," said Dave. "Which do you need worse, a shower or a beer?"

"I'd submit that the pervasive aroma answers that question," said Gray. He simultaneously lowered all the windows in his Land Rover.

We stopped at a convenience store for a stick of deodorant before heading to our favorite bar, 13.

Settling in at a table by the tavern door, Gray wasted no time broaching the subject. "Uh, Jerome, pardon my French, but—what the fuck?"

"What Mr. Earling is trying to say in crudely colloquial fashion," said Dave, "is how does a fine, upstanding man like you find himself on the wrong end of a rape charge? Not to imply that there's a right end."

Gray nodded in agreement. They both stared at me expectantly. I took a long draw from my beer, put it down, picked it up, and finished it off in another mammoth gulp. Gray signaled the waitress for another.

I didn't know where to begin. The story was absurdist, disjointed, jumbled in my mind. How, exactly, did I wind up in this predicament?

"I spoke to Maura," said Gray.

"You did? What did she say?" I asked.

"What do you think she said?" replied Dave. "'Work is going well, my petunias are blooming, and, oh, by the way, your buddy Jerome raped me!'"

"She didn't elaborate on the details of the sexual assault," said Gray. "And I didn't push her on it."

"First of all," I said, sucking the foam off my pint, "there was no sexual assault. There was a sexual misunderstanding. Second of all—"

I paused. Dave and Gray waited in silence.

"Yes?" Dave finally said.

"There is no fucking second of all," I said morosely.

It took another couple of beers, but I explained the full circumstances. My friends, for once, eschewed sarcastic commentary. While I appreciated their respectful attention, their somber responses underscored the seriousness of the situation. Hell, I'd seen them make humorous asides at a wake. They were being awfully quiet at mine.

"Here's what I don't understand," I said after the full elucidation. "Maura and I have had sex in every imaginable circumstance: indoors and out; public and private; manual, genital, and oral; using orifices I didn't even know existed; using implements never intended for such activity; in positions that would tax a gymnast. She's done things to me that went *way* beyond my experience and comprehension and I had to beg her to explain what happened. I would have thought that this 'night visitor' episode was simply a modest extension of our adventurous sexual repertoire. Instead, she absolutely freaked out. I mean, pressing charges? Don't you think that's a little extreme?"

We sat in silence for a spell.

"She's not going to drop the charges," said Gray.

"She told you that?" I asked. Gray nodded.

"Oh, man. I am truly fucked."

"The question that's been nagging me," said Dave, "is how you could enter her without waking her. You must have a tiny dick."

Dave and Gray fist bumped, albeit solemnly. I appreciated their semi-levity while simultaneously worrying that he might be right. "Fuck you, Dave. She's a deep sleeper."

"Listen," said Gray. "Judith is coming over to my place tomorrow. I'll talk to her."

"Judith?" I asked. "I thought you were a *persona non grata* after you sterilized her apartment."

"Well, I'm *grata* now. I ran into her at the supermarket, we got to chatting, and I invited her over for a drink."

"Jeez," I said. "After that letter she wrote I figured she'd never speak to you again."

"She forgave me," said Gray. "She still thinks my makeover project was wrongheaded, but she also apologized for overreacting. She said she realized I was acting in her and the baby's interest, not just out of self-indulgence."

"Unlike mister night visitor here," said Dave.

"Hey!" I said. "Why don't I come over too? I can explain to her exactly what happened. She can talk to Maura and convince her to drop the charges."

"Uh, I don't know if that's a good idea."

"Why not?"

"Well, Judith pretty much despises you."

The news hit me hard. I'd never been hated before. "Despises me? Why?"

"Do I really need to explain?" Gray said.

"Oh, yeah," I said. "Never mind."

"Listen, maybe it's not such a bad idea," said Gray. "But let me talk to her first. She's coming over at six. Why don't you show up at 6:30?"

The heavy oak door clicked closed behind Judith and Graham. Judith looked around with eyes wide like a child. "This place is so—so—"

"So clean?" said Graham helpfully.

"That's the word!" said Judith. "You must spend hours every day polishing your candelabras."

"Not exactly. I have a cleaning person who comes in once a week."

"I see," said Judith, separating an ivory elephant from its herd to examine it.

"In fact, I suspect she's been stealing from me. My pachyderm collection used to be significantly more robust."

The thought hit Gray that tidy apartments might not be the best topic of conversation. But Judith changed the subject before Gray had a chance to.

"You know that African elephants are an endangered species, don't you?" she said. "Don't you think it's barbaric to kill these creatures, then carve little effigies of them out of their own ivory tusks?"

Graham appeared taken aback. "Barbaric? That's rather harsh." He looked intently at his gleaming collection. "Ironic, certainly."

"Would you call it ironic if I hacksawed your jaw out of your head, then scrimshawed your picture onto your front tooth?"

Stunned into speechlessness, Graham stood frozen in place. The hallway cuckoo clock ticked loudly.

"Okay!" said Judith brightly, changing the subject and mood in an instant. She replaced the elephant on the shelf. "Give me the grand tour."

Graham quickly obliged, glad to banish the disturbing imagery. Leaving the foyer, the pair entered a large dining room dominated by an immaculately polished wood table. Judith ran a finger across the smooth surface. "Mahogany. Probably clear cut from a South American rain forest."

Graham cleared his throat. "Moving right along—" Down a short corridor, he took a sharp right. "The *boudoir.*"

"Wow," said Judith, pausing at the threshold. "Snazzy." A four-poster bed with a muslin canopy sat in the center of the room. A football field-size television screen hung opposite the foot of the bed, consuming almost the entire wall. A sliding glass door admitted abundant sunlight, opening to a balcony with a small round table, two chairs, and a view of the streetscape below.

A louvered four-door closet took up the third side. "You have more closet space in this one room than I do in my whole apartment," said Judith. She grasped a pair of painted ceramic knobs and pulled the doors open to reveal a meticulously organized closet that maximized every potential square inch of storage space.

"Claustrophobic Closets," said Graham.

"Huh?"

"My closet consultants. They designed the space."

Judith pulled out a cashmere cardigan and examined the label. "Sri Lanka." She lifted the lapel of a tweed jacket. "Bangladesh." She plucked a shoe from the tree. "Ghana."

"You are aware," she said, turning toward Graham, "of the child labor practices of these countries?"

Graham turned a shade of blush. "Uh, I guess I'm not fully cognizant of that issue." He fidgeted uncomfortably.

"Shall we proceed?" said Judith, again suddenly dropping the topic.

Graham led her to the kitchen, festooned with a vast collection of cookware dangling above the marble island and hanging next to the massive stove. Judith eyed the array. "What, no lobster pot?"

"Too big. I store it down below," he said, nodding toward an expanse of cabinets under the counter.

"Nicely equipped," said Judith. "You could open a restaurant."

"I've toyed with the idea," said Graham.

"Would your restaurant happen to serve coffee?" asked Judith.

"Why, yes! Yes, it would, in fact!" said Gray, with enthusiasm disproportionate to the request. He whipped open a cabinet housing a dozen coffee and tea varieties and rifled through the java collection. "Yes! Here it is." He pulled out a canister and brandished it. "Sustainably grown, fair trade, hand-harvested, organic, Peruvian cooperative coffee." Graham beamed like a kid showing off his new bike.

"There's hope for you yet," said Judith.

"Got it as a gift. Haven't tried it," said Graham, opening the canister with a vacuum whoosh. "Espresso, cappuccino, or Americano?"

"Um, black with four sugars."

"Ah, yes. Diabetico." Graham quickly got the coffee brewing, then said, "There's something else I'd like you to see. Come."

He directed her through a glass slider that opened to an expansive balcony. Arrayed along the rail were large earthen clay pots, each sporting well-tended plants. "My pocket garden," said Graham. As they moved along the row, he enumerated his collection. "Cherry tomatoes; kai-lan and broccolini; green, red, and yellow peppers; bush beans; baby corn."

"You actually get a yield out of this?"

"Certainly," said Graham. "Southern exposure; plenty of fish emulsion."

Interspersed between the vegetable containers were boxes of climbing vines, which extended up trellises to form walls of broad green leaves. "My grapes," said Graham. "For winemaking. In fact, I throw a grape mashing party every fall, if you're interested."

"Barefoot?"

"Indeed. We take the harvest out to my cottage on the lake, dump the grapes into a mash urn, put on some stomping music, and dance around in there. It's an age-old ritual, very cathartic."

"I have toe fungus," said Judith. "Say, mind if I smoke?" she asked while fidgeting through her purse.

"Well, I personally disdain the habit—"

"Me, too."

"But go ahead."

Judith flicked a wooden match against her wrist and ignited the cigarette in one well-practiced movement. Graham looked at her, startled.

"I cut the graphite strip off the matchbox and taped it to my watchband," she said.

"Innovative," commented Graham. Judith took a deep draw and exhaled through her nose.

"Graham, I have something to tell you."

Graham's mind raced with possibilities, none positive. She's engaged. She has cancer. She's moving away.

"I've given up the baby."

"You what?"

"I put the baby up for adoption."

"No! Oh, my God! Can we get him back?"

"Can 'we' get him back?"

"I mean 'you.' Can you get him back? How could you bring him home, then just give him away?"

"I never brought him home. The adoption was arranged months before he was born."

"But why?"

"I realized that I'd be a crappy mother. I smoke filterless cigarettes. I drink whiskey straight. My housekeeping skills are prehistoric. I keep exotic, dangerous pets. Is that any environment for a child?"

Gray leaned against the balcony rail. His head swam. Until that moment, he hadn't realized that the baby was an integral part of an imaginary threesome he'd created, and that his refurbishing project at Judith's was the male version of the nesting instinct. "I'm going to need a little time to process this," he said.

"No rush. In the meantime, why don't you continue the tour?" Judith smiled, then took another puff.

"Speaking of smoke," Gray said, "you might be interested in this." He gestured toward the far end of the balcony, where a white rectangular box sat. As they neared, a low hum gradually arose. "My hive."

A steady stream of bees approached the structure, like planes at a busy airport. The insects alighted at the lip and quickly entered the chamber.

"Ay," said Judith, stopping abruptly as soon as she realized what she was looking at. "Your hive gives me hives. I'm allergic to bees." She quickly rummaged through her purse again and held aloft an Epi-pen, as if to prove her statement.

"Not to worry," said Gray. "These are the most docile strain of honeybee. I've only been stung once, and that was my own fault."

Judith inched closer. "They all seem to be going in, with none coming out."

"That's right," said Graham. "We've caught them at the end of their workday, and they're bringing home the spoils. The hairy filaments on their legs are so laden with pollen that it affects their flight stability." He pointed to a grassy expanse halfway down the street. "See that park over there? Clover. They frolic in it."

Judith cupped her eyes and squinted through the sunlight in the direction of the park.

"Smoke is actually part of the beekeeper's arsenal," said Graham. "It has a calming effect on them. Here, give me your cigarette."

Judith handed over the lit cigarette, replete with a lipstick smear on one end. "Watch this. First, I'll get the bees ever-so-slightly agitated." He gave the hive a little bump. The bees studiously ignored their keeper, diligently continuing their pollen deliveries.

"Hmmm, unflappable today," he murmured.

Graham grabbed the rectangular hive by opposite edges and gave it a short, firm shake. The hum from within rose noticeably, like a small revving engine. Judith tensed. "Okay, now the smoke," said Graham. He brought the cigarette to his lips.

The incoming bees suddenly altered their path and went into a holding pattern above the hive. Worker bees poured out the exit.

"Not a problem," said Graham. He took a drag and then blew a puff of smoke toward the mouth of the hive. The wisps dissipated rapidly with no visible effect on the bees.

"Don't you need more smoke than that?"

"No, I made that mistake once," said Graham. "Last autumn. Killed off the entire colony."

Judith appeared not to hear his answer as she slowly shuffled backward, a look of fear washing across her face.

Gray didn't notice her departure. "By the way, don't tell Jerome and Dave that I asphyxiated the hive. They kind of idolize me, and I don't want to spoil that."

Gray looked up and saw that Judith had retreated halfway across the balcony. The cloud of bees now formed a distinct cyclone above the hive. The buzz intensified.

Still in reverse, Judith collided with a table holding a pot of wildflowers, sending it crashing; shards of clay scattered across the floor. A bee landed on Graham's arm, another on his hand. He brushed them off, panic starting to rise. Graham again drew hard on the cigarette. "Damn it! It's out!" He froze, unsure what to do next.

The buzz took on a menacing air as the whirl of bees thickened. Graham broke out of his momentary paralysis. "Run!" he yelled. Judith was already yards ahead, sprinting toward the glass doors at the end of the balcony. Graham pursued, bees trailing him like a kite tail.

Judith burst into the kitchen and didn't break stride, dashing through the dining room toward the front door. Graham raced over the threshold, stumbled, regained his balance, and lurched forward, arms flailing at the swarm. Judith dove into the front hall closet with Gray close behind. He grabbed the door handle and forcefully slid it shut, stranding hundreds of bees outside in an angry horde.

"Jesus, that was close!" said Judith. "Did I mention I'm allergic?"

Wedged between coats in the dark closet, Judith and Gray found themselves in unexpected proximity. She groped for his face, cupped it in two hands, and kissed him forcefully. Gray tasted tobacco and mint, a heady combination, he decided. He pulled her tightly against him and returned the kiss. They groped at each other, fumbling with buttons, buckles, and zippers in a frenzy of pent-up passion. Meanwhile, the bees circled the living room in a loosely formed cloud, their buzz muffled by the door.

Suddenly, a knock interrupted the closeted coitus. Gray and Judith heard the front door open. "Hello? Anybody home?"

"Who's that?" whispered Judith.

"Jerome."

"What's that bastard doing here? He should be in jail!"

"He's out on bail. He wants you to hear his side of the story."

As soon as I elbowed the door closed behind me, I sensed something was wrong. The room was simultaneously silent and noisy. A low background hum filled an otherwise hushed space, like an air conditioner in a distant window. I called out for Gray. No answer. I figured he and Judith were on the balcony, so I strode toward the back.

Suddenly, a swarm of bees came out of nowhere and engulfed my head. Blinded by the blitz, deafened by the buzz, I swatted frantically. Sharp pains stabbed at my hands, neck, and cheeks. I lurched across the dining room toward the kitchen, flailing and yelling. I slipped, careened forward, and hit my head on the edge of a kitchen chair, crumpling to the floor. The bees descended like an angry mob, alighting and stinging any exposed flesh they could find.

Judith and Gray, naked in the closet, heard my screams amidst the ferocious buzz. Judith cracked open the door. "Jerome?" she yelled. "Jerome!"

Gray dragged her back inside and pulled the door shut. "You can't leave! They'll sting you to death!"

"Graham, your friend is out there! Your fucking rapist friend! He needs our help!"

Judith burst out the door, naked, and ran toward the kitchen, while Gray stood nude, immobile, and indecisive amongst the coats. Judith peered in to see me splayed out on the floor, barely conscious, covered in stinging bees.

"Oh my God! Oh my God!" She raced back to the closet, ripped Gray's London Fog raincoat from its hanger, and donned it. She grabbed a bicycle helmet from the shelf, pulled on a pair of ski gloves, and stepped into oversized rubber boots.

"Don't just stand there!" she screamed at Gray. "Cover up!" Judith didn't wait. Running directly into the fray, she snatched a colander from the suspended rack and held it mask-like over her face. The bees continued their merciless stinging of my prone, semiconscious frame. My head and arms were covered with the pulsating insects. Red welts had already arisen.

A squadron broke rank and dive-bombed Judith. She screamed and swatted them away with a spatula. Rushing to the sink, Judith flipped on both faucets full force, yanked the spray attachment from its cradle, and blasted a stream, first at the bees circling her, then squarely at my face.

In the liquid onslaught, the bees relented. They dispersed toward the light, bumping into the kitchen windows and retreating through the open glass door to the balcony. Judith kept spraying, squirting my arms and neck to clear the remaining bees. The hum subsided.

With the majority of the swarm now beaten back, Judith dropped the hose attachment and moved to my side. Dead and dying bees surrounded me on the floor. I lay motionless, already grotesquely swollen, fully unconscious. She knelt beside me, opened her kit, and plunged her Epi-pen deep into my neck. Simultaneously, an errant bee landed on her exposed leg and delivered its venom. Judith shrieked and smacked it, gutting the insect against her calf.

Graham rushed through the door in an anorak and ski goggles, skidding to an awkward halt on the wet floor.

"You better call an ambulance," said Judith as she slumped beside me. "That was my only dose."

The needle remained jabbed in my neck.

Once the medics administered the antidote, Judith bounced back quickly from her single sting. I was less fortunate, hospitalized with 26 stings to the face and uncounted elsewhere. They say 100 stings will kill a man, so I guess I came in just under the lethal threshold.

After a week in the hospital, pumped with enough saline to replenish the Dead Sea and enough steroids to make a homerun hitter out of me, I was back on my feet, metaphorically speaking, in a courtroom. (I was actually on my butt, in a wheelchair.)

Among the worst aspects of my day in court was my picture on the local news site. My face was still bloated, so not only was I labeled a rapist, but a grotesque, malformed, apparently 300-pound rapist. The image looked so unlike me that it might have provided plausible deniability among family, friends, and associates, but I never got the chance to affirm or refute my association with the crime before they hauled me off to jail. My *nolo* plea made for short proceedings, and I was ushered from the courtroom in handcuffs.

During the long ride to the penitentiary in the back of the police van, I tried to think of it as a new experience, an educational opportunity, a grand adventure. I attempted to picture my new cellmate and imagine how I might decorate my quarters, as if I were heading off to college instead of the clink. It was a failed exercise. When I most needed an obliterating moment of self-delusion, I couldn't muster one.

~ The End ~

Epilogue I

Year 6 | Autumn

While I was in prison and out of contact with my friends, Dave completed a master's program in paleontology. Immediately after graduation, he began work on his doctoral thesis, which he claimed was entitled, "The Socio-Economic and Physiologic Markers Imbedded Within the Fecal Matter of Indigenous Peoples of Central America." Dave also maintained that the subtitle was, "*Vous pouvez déterminer beaucoup sur une personne en leur merde*," but I suspect he was, um, shitting me about that.

Dave gave up swearing in English and restricted his profanity to French. He upgraded his attire to a stereotypical professorial style, replete with tweeds and cords. He even got himself a pair of reading glasses of dubious necessity. When he wasn't studiously peering over them, he wore them on a chain around his neck. He continued to be a serial dater; the women in his life all seemed to love the arrangement. I never quite figured it out.

Gray and Judith, remarkably, solidified their relationship during my hiatus. Just after my release, she announced she was pregnant— and this time planned to keep the baby. Graham claimed, with excessive pre-paternal pride, that he was the father. He vowed they would choose a conventional name for the child; I had my doubts that he'd sway Judith. They had no marriage plans—he would, but she wouldn't—but they essentially lived together at Gray's condo.

Judith retained her apartment as a fallback in case it didn't work out with Gray. She refined her pack-rat mentality, with the apartment becoming more museum than warehouse. The old newspapers that Gray ostensibly retrieved from the dump—he actually bought replacements online—were now framed on the wall. Turns out she had some valuable editions: the JFK, MLK, and RFK assassinations; Nixon's resignation; John Lennon's murder; a bunch of popes dying in rapid succession; 9/11; the Red Sox winning the World Series after a near-century drought.

She mounted her photos, archived her papers, labeled her plants, organized her knick-knacks, racked her magazines, and shelved her books. Gray gave her a Claustrophobic Closets gift certificate for her birthday and, as a result, every available millimeter of storage space was crammed to the gills.

Gray and Judith were looking to buy a house in the exurbs, a property with sufficient space to create a small museum. Judith hoped to schedule school tours to view the fauna, flora, and cultural artifacts she'd curated. Gray's broker had heard that the former British consul's residence was up for sale and was looking into it.

Maura resigned from her job at the school for the handicapped shortly after I was jailed. She traveled the country, got married, and then divorced. Last I heard, from Gray via Judith, she was on the West Coast studying tai chi.

Epilogue II

Year 6 | Autumn

My incarceration lasted three years. And one month. And twelve days, six hours, and fourteen minutes. If they gave Lady Bing trophies or "Prisoner of the Month" awards, I would have ranked among the most honored of inmates. I absolutely didn't make waves, never complained, avoided conflict, and did what I was told. Peeling potatoes, washing laundry, cleaning latrines, I didn't care. I did it all.

Of course, it wasn't all upside. I lost my apartment, my credit rating, my possessions, my employability, my self-esteem, and my naturally sunny outlook. I wound up psychologically scarred—at least that's what the prison shrink told me—as well as physically scarred from the two dozen shots of bee venom to the face.

I took up smoking, lost weight, and developed high blood pressure. My prostatitis worsened, probably because I never got comfortable masturbating in the presence of my cellmate. In three years, I aged ten. If it weren't for writing this memoir, I probably would have gone totally insane, rather than just partially whacked.

I sent 37 letters to Maura, one per month, begging for forgiveness, pleading, apologizing. Every one came back with the words "Addressee Unknown" scrawled in Maura's handwriting. I got the message. She was unknown to me. Maybe I never knew her. Nonetheless, I kept writing. And she kept sending them back unopened.

Dave and Gray visited regularly at first. They feigned levity and talked about the things we'd do when I got out, but the humor was strained and the optimism false. After the first year, I asked them to stop coming.

Upon liberation, I found a room in a rundown boarding house. Gray offered to let me stay with him and Judith till I found a place, but I refused. I did accept a loan to cover my rent for the first few months while I looked for work.

Naturally, employment was uppermost in my mind upon my release. But I knew it would be an uphill battle. As I scrolled through the help-wanted ads, I imagined my interviews playing out something like this:

"Well, Mr. Segundo," says the driving school administrator, *"we've reviewed your résumé and checked your references. Your background in special ed and your sociology degree makes you more qualified than most applicants. But I'm afraid we can't offer you the job."*

"Oh?" I say morosely. "Would you mind telling me why? Just out of curiosity."

"It's this little matter of your criminal record. Our driver's ed program has lots of young female students, still in high school. How would their parents react if they discovered we had a sexual predator as an instructor?"

"But I'm not a sexual predator!" I say in rising cadence. "I raped my girlfriend! I'd never, ever rape a stranger!"

I realize my phraseology needs some refinement. I'm escorted to the door.

Of course, even this miserable vignette was delusional. After ten or so applications, I understood that employers were screening me out before I ever reached the interview phase.

I began to get desperate. The proceeds from Gray's loan were dwindling. I'd paid my proverbial debt to society, but it didn't seem to matter. It was the crime that kept on giving.

Finally comprehending that one misdeed inevitably leads to another, I made some inquiries among my former prison associates for identity transformation services. I completed the necessary paperwork, provided the proper imagery, and signed on the line with my new name: Jerome S. Tercero. My third name gave me a second chance.

The oddest thing about my name change wasn't that it improved my job prospects—that was my intent and expectation. Rather, it was the effect the new name had on me psychologically. Weirdly enough, it gave me some perspective and objectivity. I was able to step back and better assess what happened. I felt more like a witness and less like a perp. If I told my shrink, he might have said that this detachment was a dangerous psychological symptom, but I didn't care. I welcomed the disassociation. Anyway, I had fired my shrink because he didn't seem to be making much progress.

Of course, deep down I knew I was a perp. There was no leaving that behind. My act, while not physically brutal, was nonetheless an unconscionable violation of Maura. It was a slow realization born of many sleepless nights in prison, but I finally understood.

A spiffy new brew pub recently opened about a mile from my boarding house. Dave and Gray were already sitting by the door when I arrived. "You guys look poised to make a getaway," I said.

"Prison changed you," said Dave. "Now you frame everything as if it were a crime scene."

A two-story glass wall flanked the left side of the pub. Behind it stood several gleaming copper vats. Despite the brand-spanking-newness of the brewing side, the drinking side had an old-time feel about it. The heavy butcher-block wood tables bore chinks, carvings, and inscriptions. The dark wood around the bar looked as though it had been steeped in smoke for decades. The floor was worn along its primary walking routes; were a beer spilled on it, little foaming canals would form.

"Guys, I'd like you to meet someone," I said. They looked toward the door, then back at me. "Actually," I said, "he's already here: Jerome S. Tercero."

"Come again?" said Dave.

"It's me! I've changed my name. It's official," I said, whipping out my new ID and slapping it on the table.

"Isn't it illegal for a felon to change his name?" asked Gray.

"Oh, I didn't do it legally. Some of my, um, associates from prison helped me out."

"*Sacre* freaking *bleu*, Jerome! You've got *associates*?" said Dave, inspecting the driver's license closely.

"The crime spree continues," said Gray. "Why don't you try a law-abiding lifestyle for a while, see how that works for you?" He drew on his stout.

"The law-abiding lifestyle has driven me into bankruptcy," I said. "I can't find a job due to my criminal record. It was either get a phony ID or rob a bank."

The waitress approached. "A fake beer," I said. She winked and turned on her heel.

"I got some news about Maura yesterday," said Gray.

My pulse quickened, and I wasn't happy about it. One would think, based on my history, that I wouldn't react like a puppy every time her name was mentioned. I compelled my tail to stop wagging. "Is that so?" I said, feigning uninterest.

"Yes, Judith got a call from her—first time in months. She's in Alaska. She opened a riding stable for autistic children."

"You know, I wrote her 37 letters when I was in prison. Every one came back unopened."

"That's 38 more than I would have written," said Dave.

"Dave, that doesn't make any sense," said Gray.

"It does if your mind is capable of conceiving negative space," he replied.

"Negative space is my specialty," I said. "You'd think Maura might be curious about what I had to say. Instead, the wall of silence came sliding down, and that was it."

"It's not as black and white as that," said Gray.

"I agree. There's no white; only black," I said. The waitress returned, and I took a prodigious gulp of my alcohol-free brew.

"Well, here's a splash of gray," said Gray. "Maura put up $5,000 of your bail money."

Had he tossed his beer in my face, I wouldn't have been more shocked. Gray's statement was so contrary to my understanding of how the world worked that it didn't make sense at first. I was dumbfounded. My throat clenched. I had trouble swallowing my drink. I forced the liquid down, placed my glass on the table with deliberate care, and looked intently at Gray. "She *what?*"

"She chipped in five K for your bail."

I didn't know what to say. I couldn't comprehend what might motivate the same person to press charges and post bail.

"Why didn't you tell me this three years ago?" I asked, anger rising.

"She swore me to secrecy."

"Swore you to secrecy? That information was material to my case! Do you think I would have pleaded *nolo* if I knew that?"

I realized I was squeezing my pint glass with such force that it might shatter in my hand. "Your little secret cost me three years of my life!"

Dave, who had been a quiet observer during this exchange, spoke up: "No, Jerome, the *rape* cost you three years of your life."

"Here's another little secret that might alter your perspective," said Gray. "Maura was a childhood sexual abuse victim. Her father used to creep into her bedroom when she was asleep, slink into bed with her, and rape her."

"Which," Gray continued, "pretty much describes what you—" His voice trailed off.

A wave of nausea engulfed me. I could hardly breathe. I arose, wordlessly left my friends behind, and trudged back to my boarding house.

I didn't emerge from my room for two weeks. I shut off my phone, watched television with the volume muted, and ate nothing but peanut butter on saltines. I briefly considered suicide, but it was an exercise in self-indulgence. I knew I didn't have the courage.

I thought incessantly about Gray's revelations until they bore down on me so heavily I thought I'd be crushed by the burden. I realized I'd carry this weight a long time.

Epilogue III

Year 7 | Autumn

"Have you ever noticed the oxymoronic tendencies of certain curse phrases, an incongruity that—?"

"Holy shit!"

"Exactly, Jerome! A perfect example. The deviant juxtaposition of terms is—"

"Shut up, Dave! Did you see that?"

Dave and I sat at the bar at 13. Toward the far end of the room, a gaggle of loutish jocks slobbered over a couple of co-eds.

"No. What?"

"Those frat boys over there. One of them just slipped something into that girl's drink."

Dave swiveled for a view. He nudged his half-height reading glasses down his nose and peered over them. "The primate with the inky biceps?"

"Yeah, that's the guy."

"Reminds me of a joke I heard," he said. "How many frat boys does it take to screw in a light bulb?"

"Seriously, Dave, I swear he just mickied her drink. We're witnessing the first stage of a date rape."

"Are you sure?"

"Damn straight, I'm sure. I'm going over there to warn her." I slid off my stool.

Dave grabbed me by the shirttail. "Jerome, don't be an idiot. They'll crush you like a beer can on a forehead."

I sized up the opposition. Dave was right. These guys were cartoonishly muscular. I wouldn't stand a chance.

I watched intently as Mickie leaned over and draped his arm around his future victim, barely able to contain his drool. Dave, with his back to the action, made furtive glances over his shoulder.

"Jesus Christ," I said. "Look at them. Those guys are so hopped up they'd probably gang-bang *me* if I went over there. We've got to do something."

"Like what?"

"I don't know. Let's wait and see how the situation develops. Maybe the jocks will go off and play pool, and we'll get a chance."

"Doubtful. They appear locked in on their prey."

It had been more than five years since I last tippled at 13, and the place had changed. The layout of the narrow room was the same—a long, well-worn bar on one side, booths on the wall opposite, small tables running between, a game room and a cramped stage area out of sight, through a doorway at the back. But the quality of the clientele had deteriorated in my absence. I didn't remember the pub being a hangout for felonious frat boys.

Dave lifted the leather-clad elbow of his corduroy jacket from a small puddle of beer, wiped the patch with a napkin, then sopped up the spill on the table. We nursed our drinks—Dave, a Murphy's stout; me, a nonalcoholic brew—in tense silence, observing the unfolding crime scene. "How long before a date rape drug takes effect?" Dave asked.

"How should I know?"

"Well, after all, you are a convicted rapist."

"I never resorted to drugging my victims," I responded indignantly, as if this were a point of pride.

"Victims, plural?"

"You know what I mean." I sullenly drew on my near-beer, angry at Dave for bringing up what he knew was a sensitive topic. We sat in silence for a minute.

"We probably don't have much more than a half hour," I finally said.

Mickie and one of his brutish buddies began to get territorial about the two women, and slowly the other studs drifted away, one by one, until just the two couples remained.

The spikee attempted to stand, sweeping two glasses off the table in the process. The heavy plastic tumblers clattered and splashed to the floor. She fell back heavily into her seat.

"What do you ladies say we get out of this hellhole and find someplace cozier?" said Mickie, way louder than necessary.

His target got to her feet unsteadily and slurred something unintelligible. She wobbled in our direction while Mickie turned his attention to her friend.

"Here's your chance!" said Dave. "She'll go right past us on her way to the ladies room!"

She weaved a path toward us. I stood. "Need a guide?" I said with a smile. "It's that-a-way."

"I'm perfectly capable of finding the bathroom myself, thank you very much," she replied. She tripped over the last syllable, stumbled, and lurched forward. I caught her by the elbow, straightened her up, and whisked her around the corner, glancing back at the druggist before disappearing from view. He and his buddy were draped all over the girlfriend, virtually immobilizing her in tandem half-nelsons.

"Listen, we don't have much time," I said.

"We don't?"

"Your muscle-bound friend back there spiked your drink."

"Friend? He's not my friend! I just met him."

"No, he's not your friend. Quite the contrary."

She was flapping in the breeze like an untethered spinnaker. I leaned her against the wall just outside the ladies room door.

"I saw him put something in your drink. He's trying to drug you."

"Ha!" she exclaimed as she slid semi-involuntarily into a sitting position, her back against the wall. I squatted beside her.

"Where do you live? I can get you a cab."

Her eyes rolled upward. She blinked hard and shook her head. "Where's my drink? I had it a minute ago."

Dave stuck his head around the corner. "Jerome! *Tête de noeud* approaching."

"For Christ sake, Dave, speak English!"

"Caveman cometh!"

I genuflected before my drunken companion, tucked a hand under each armpit, and pulled her to a standing position. Then I leaned forward and hoisted her over my shoulder. The ladies room door clicked locked behind us just as Mickie rounded the bend.

He fisted the door. "Jan! You in there?"

Jan looked up from her position seated on the closed toilet. "It's Jen, you dickhead!" she screamed.

"Jan, Jen, whatever. Come out. We're leaving!"

"Fuck off!" said Jen.

"Your loss!" yelled Mickie. "We're out of here." He kicked the door for good measure, then stomped off.

"Good riddance," muttered Jen between strands of hair.

My phone rang. It was Dave. "Bad Elvis has left the building. He's hailing a cab out front."

I exhaled a breath I didn't know I was holding. "Did the other woman go with them?"

"Yes," said Dave. "The whole entourage. A cozy little *ménage a trois.*"

"Shit." I turned to Jen. "Your girlfriend just left without you."

"She's not my friend. I don't have any friends."

"She's not your friend?"

"No, she's *his* friend."

"Who? Neanderthal man?"

"Yeah, ape-man." Jen smiled, then slumped over, her head between her knees.

"Rape-man," I said under my breath.

"Mayday!" Dave's voice crackled through the phone earpiece. "He's back!"

Hairy knuckles pounded upon the door. "Hey, Joan! Open the fuck up!"

Dave's voice rose a half-octave over the phone line. "I'm going to fetch the bouncer."

"No—don't!" I whispered as sternly as I could. "I'm on probation, remember? If I'm caught locked in a ladies room with a drugged and drunken woman, how's that going to look?"

"JOAN!" yelled Mickie. "We've got a cab outside! I'm going to kick the frigging door in!"

A heavy boot shuddered the framing. I pushed my back against the door, facing Jen on the toilet. She raised her head, rolled her eyes, and projected a thick stream of coagulate in my direction. The spew arced like a rainbow, hitting my shins and shoes, creating a trail between us on the tile floor.

Mickie unleashed another kick, this time near the handle. The door trembled under his jackboot.

"We're fucked," I intoned to no one in particular. Loud music started to emanate from the far end of the bar, masking the commotion. Mickie yelled something incomprehensible to his friends.

I picked up a cylindrical chrome wastebasket and dumped its contents onto the puke-covered floor. Jen moaned, still sitting on the toilet, her head between her knees. Standing off to the side of the door, I hoisted the container over my head.

Mickie emitted a martial-arts-style yell and gave the door a ferocious kick. The jamb buckled; the door splintered and flew open. As he burst in, I crashed the wastebasket down onto his head. Mickie nosedived straight into the vomit and trash.

Dave ran in. "Jerome—let's go! His friends just went to the back room to check out the band."

I lifted Jen off the toilet and again flung her over my shoulder. She retched, and a fresh convulsion of vomit cascaded down my back, tracing a warm, wet path along my spine.

As I carried her out, Dave surveyed the scene: the crumpled body, the puke-and-trash-strewn floor, the dented can, all soundtracked to the bruising beat of rock music. Blood oozed from Mickie's forehead. "*Mon dieu*," Dave said. "This is so wrong on so many levels."

Out on the sidewalk, I propped Jen against a newspaper vending machine and flagged a cab.

"You never finished the joke," I said to Dave.

"What joke?" He looked back nervously at the bar entrance.

"How many frat boys does it take to screw in a light bulb?"

"Oh yeah," said Dave. "Just one. But he has to get it drunk first."

"Funny," I said. "But not as funny as Mickie's friends finding him unconscious in a puddle of puke."

Dave again looked anxiously at the bar and ran his hand through his hair. Power chords rolled like surf from the front door. The plate glass windows vibrated from the thudding bass.

I flagged a cab. It ignored me.

"Maybe we should walk? Or run," I said.

"What, and carry her piggyback?" Dave gestured toward Jen, slumped against the news box. "All the frat boys will need to do is follow the trail of vomit down the street."

I looked down at my shins and tried to scrape them clean with the side of my shoe.

Dave squinted toward the entrance. "Oh, *merde*! It's the posse." Several of Mickie's entourage muscled their way toward the front of the bar. The bathrooms were spitting distance from them.

"Mickie's legs aren't hanging out of the ladies room, are they?" I asked Dave.

"No, I kicked them inside and pulled the door shut."

"Remember the time I accused you of being an inept accomplice? I take it back."

"*Bouffer merde*," said Dave.

Seated at the curb, Jen couldn't be seen from the front door of the bar. Another cab approached. I waved, at first calmly, then frantically. It zoomed past.

"You need to look more nonchalant," said Dave. "Desperation is a real turn-off for cabbies."

One of the 'roid brothers poked his head out of the front of pub and bellowed his friend's name. "Malcolm! Where the fuck are you?" He looked up and down the street, then ducked back inside.

Finally, a taxi pulled over, a white sedan with the words *Green Cab* stenciled on the side. Dave and I sandwiched Jen, hoisted her by the armpits, and stuffed her into the vehicle. Dave jumped in beside her; I ran around to the other side so we could prop her up in the middle.

Just as we were pulling away from the curb, a howl arose from the pub. Malcolm came charging into the street, his buddies close behind, letting out a roar that would reverse a tsunami. He spotted us and started to chase the cab down the street. I waved and gave him a thumbs-up sign. Malcolm realized the futility of his pursuit, stopped, and kicked violently at the door of a parked car. I turned frontward and breathed a sigh of relief.

"This cab doesn't have a speck of green on it," said Dave.

"Huh?"

"It says 'Green Cab,' but there's no green."

"Have you ever noticed those big rigs on the highway?" I asked. "The ones that have the word 'yellow' on them in ten-foot letters?"

"Yes! They're *orange!*"

Dave and I had no chance to riff on this observation before a guttural moan emanated from Jen. She slumped to her left, retched, and made a vile and viscous deposit in my lap. Dave reconsidered the scene. "It's a green cab now," he said.

The cabbie was not pleased. He lowered all the windows. The warm autumn air was thick with humidity. "There's going to be a cleaning surcharge," he warned.

"Don't worry. I caught it all in my lap," I lied.

With the threat of imminent violence past, Dave relaxed. "As I was saying in the bar before that little brouhaha broke out, the term 'holy shit' is deliciously self-contradictory. The diametrically opposed elements embodied in a single phrase is a rare and fascinating characteristic. If I were a linguist, I'd be tempted to apply for a grant to study its etymology."

"You'd never catch me using 'shit' and 'delicious' in the same sentence," I said.

"There must be other phrases with similar characteristics," said Dave, ignoring me in his ponderings.

I tried to conjure up other holy-shittisms. "How about 'Sweet Jesus'?"

"Nope. Both words have positive connotations."

"'Good grief'?"

"Not bad. Has the necessary yin and yang. But a little on the bland side."

I pondered some more but was drawing a blank when, suddenly, epiphany slapped me across the face. "I've got it! 'Sweet holy motherfucking everloving delusional bastard*'!"

"Uh, yeah, I guess that qualifies," said Dave. He looked pensive for a moment. "Not a phrase you hear very often though."

Dave nudged Jen toward me and then slid in the opposite direction, hugging the door. He brushed his corduroy jacket with his hands, then caressed the length of his chinos for any signs of vomit splatter. Pulling a handkerchief from his jacket pocket, he touched up his clothing, ending with a little spiff of his shoes.

"You used to be such a *schlum*," I said. "Then I come back a few years later, and you're spit-shining your shoes."

"Rub in the puke on yours, and you'll probably get a nice sheen," he replied.

The cabbie threw a plastic grocery bag, a half-consumed roll of paper towels, and a tub of wet-wipes into the back.

"BBWs!" I said. "Since your such a fan, maybe you should do the honors?"

Dave popped the top and proffered the container. I pulled out a cloth and tried to get the chunks of upchuck out of Jen's tangled hair, but the effort proved futile. She stirred and forced her eyes open, the right side responding more cooperatively than the left. "Where are we?" she asked.

"We're in a cab. Leaving the bar. Getting you away from the goon who tried to rape you."

"Where do you live?" asked Dave. "We'll take you home."

After several halting attempts, Jen finally provided an intelligible address. "Cool," said Dave. "We'll go right past my place on the way."

"What? You can't leave me alone with her!"

"Jerome, it's one a.m., and I have to be up at 5:30 to catch a flight to my conference. You'll be fine."

"Yeah, we'll be fine," slurred Jen, who then slipped back into her coma, head on my shoulder, her hair and breath redolent of vomit. I pulled a couple of yards of paper from the roll and sopped up the mess in my lap, which had seeped through my underwear and was now uncomfortably moistening my groin area.

Dave handed me a twenty and instructed the driver to stop. "It's this housing complex on the right," he said. We pulled up to a quad of university housing for graduate students. "Remember, Jerome, you're on probation!" Dave said. He slammed the door before I could curse him.

Jen lived in a brownstone on the edge of the university district. As we arrived, I jostled her awake, jumped out, and ran around to her side, hoping to get there before she toppled back over. I put my arm around her waist and guided her to the front steps, where she slumped, exhausted as if she had just run a marathon.

As the cabbie watched impatiently, I scoured the interior of the vehicle, using up all the paper towels and dozens of wipes. By the time I finished, little evidence remained other than a bulging grocery bag filled with puke-soaked paper. The cabbie whipped out a can of Lysol and saturated the back of the cab, discharging enough chemical/antiseptic mist to annihilate a small town. Paying the bill, I sent him on his way.

I sat next to Jen on the steps. She was alert. "Feeling better?" I asked.

"No."

"Want me to help you up to your apartment, or do you want to go solo?"

"I can make it just fine." Jen attempted to get up, fell back, tried again, and slumped once more. "Okay, maybe a little help."

She handed me her shoulder bag and mimed turning a key in a lock. I fished the keys out of a side pocket. Standing directly in front of her, I offered both hands and pulled her to a standing position. She almost lurched forward into my embrace but somehow managed to regain her balance. I draped one of her arms over my shoulder and placed one of mine around her waist. We moved haltingly up the outside steps. I looked up. "I hope you don't live on the top floor," I said.

"Second," she replied.

I unlatched the exterior door, which admitted us to a small foyer with four mailboxes and buzzers. The same key opened the interior door. We climbed the flight of steps in an awkward stagger.

I unlocked Jen's door, pushed it open, and stepped aside to let her pass. "Home sweet home," I said.

Jen paused and looked at me through slightly crossed eyes and a gently swaying body.

"Would you like to come in?" she asked.

"Nah, I really must get home. Need to clean this puke off my pants and shoes."

"Oh, my God, I didn't notice! Did you get sick on yourself?"

"Um, yeah, something like that."

"Well, you can clean up in here. I do have plumbing, you know."

I started to make another excuse when Jen said, "Wait! What am I saying? I don't even know you. How do I know you aren't a rapist or something?"

"Well, you don't. Another reason why I should be on my way."

Jen moved toward the door and lost her balance. I caught her at the threshold. "Okay, Jen, let's just get you inside."

"Good idea," she said. "I'm suddenly feeling kind of tipsy."

We entered a long dark hallway. I heeled the door closed behind me. "Take your first left," said Jen.

We turned into a darkened room. She slipped from my grasp, stumbled forward with gathering speed, and tumbled headlong. I turned on the light to see her face-first on a neatly made-up king-size bed. "Just going to take a little pre-sleep nap," she mumbled.

"Before you doze off," I said, "how about getting settled properly?" Her upper torso lay perpendicular on the bed, legs hanging off. I rolled her onto her back, grabbed her calves, and pivoted her onto the mattress. She was already asleep. I tucked a pillow under her head, then took the quilt from the foot of the bed and covered her with it. I tiptoed from the room.

Outside in the dim hallway, I assessed my situation. It was approaching two in the morning. I was all the way across town. I was covered in vomit. And I was alone with a drug-overdosed woman whom I just met at a bar a couple of hours ago. Not exactly the situation my probation officer would hope to find me in.

Fatigue overcame me, equal parts mental and physical. I found the bathroom, took a leak, pulled a bath towel off the rack, and navigated my way to the living room. I spread the towel across the couch, intending to just rest my eyes for a minute or two before calling a taxi.

Next thing I knew, an early morning sunbeam stimulated my retina. I didn't know where I was. For a moment, I thought I was back in prison. My fitful dreams mixed with hazy wakefulness. I closed my eyes, reopened them, and closed them again. A bracing whiff of stale vomit invaded my nostrils, inducing mild nausea. I heard water running in the background.

Sitting up and looking down, I viewed my pants, encrusted from lap to shin in hardened bile. My shoes looked like I had spent the day dumpster diving. I feared crossing paths with a mirror to see what the rest of me looked like.

A mild panic gripped me as I heard the water shut off. Should I run? Pretend I'm still asleep? Call my probation officer? My indecision kept me frozen on the couch.

The bathroom door opened, exhaling a cloud of steam. Out walked Jen in a Japanese print robe, drying her hair. I couldn't believe it was the same woman who was slurring, barfing, and stumbling last night. She was attractive and fit, with light brown hair, still wet, a clear complexion, and eyes so big they were just shy of kitten-poster cute. She walked over, smiled, and extended her hand. "Jen Cantor."

"Um, hi. We've met. Jerome Segundo. Tercero."

"Segundo-Tercero? You don't hear that name often."

"No, I guess you don't," I said. "Never, in fact."

Jen sat in a chair opposite the couch and demurely adjusted her robe. "I want to thank you for last night."

"You do? You remember?"

"You may have to fill me in on some of the specifics, but I have the gist."

"Yeah, that Malcolm is a piece of work."

"Malcolm? He told me his name was Carl."

"No surprise. All the best date rapists use a pseudonym when they work."

"He was no date rapist because it was no date. I was just sitting at the bar minding my own business when he came over. He seemed like a nice enough guy. He introduced me to his girlfriend, so I didn't think he was out to pick me up. Or whatever he was out to do."

"Except, as it turns out, his girlfriend was his accomplice."

Jen stood suddenly. "I'm sorry. Would you like some coffee? It's the least I can do for the person who saved my life."

"Coffee sounds great."

"Okay, make yourself comfortable."

"Already have."

Jen disappeared for a spell. I looked around her living room, a neat, airy, comfortable space bathed in morning light. The furniture appeared of Scandinavian design, with blonde wood and clean lines. A reflective sheen coated the dining table. Teak, I surmised, based on my prison studies of the book, "Indigenous Hardwoods of the World." A beige fabric covered the chair and couch cushions. Muslin, I deduced, according to my jailhouse reading of "A Textile Connoisseur's Guide to Natural Cloth Fibers." The room exuded a welcoming aura, and I felt inexplicably at ease in this stranger's home.

A music library filled one whole wall, seemingly embodying every era of recorded music. On several shelves to the far left stood a collection of vinyl 78s, 33s, 45s, and EPs. A sleek modern turntable sat in the midst.

A left-center section contained tapes: 8-track, cassette, and reel-to-reel. Respective players flanked each set.

The right-center area held an array of compact disks, hundreds if not thousands of them, in clear plastic cases. A massive CD player, apparently capable of loading dozens of disks at a time, was stationed among them.

Finally, on the far right, isolated on its own shelf, was perched a small wireless music device showing the date and time in a digital readout.

"Think fast!" I turned to see a balled pair of socks whizzing toward my head. I threw up my hand and somehow managed to snag it.

"Nice catch!" said Jen.

"Nice arm," I replied.

"I played baseball in college. Second base. Only woman on the men's team."

"Wow. You don't look like a jock."

"That's because I'm not. Only batted in the low 200s. They kept me in the lineup because the novelty of it drew the crowds. I was a pretty slick fielder, though."

She underhanded me a pair of jeans, a flannel shirt, and a thick white towel. "The bathroom's thataway. We can burn those clothes once you peel them off."

I took the hint and headed for the showers. The bathroom was immaculately clean and smelled like lavender. The ceramic tiles, Italian, I surmised, without knowledge or reason, positively gleamed.

The grout had not a speck of discoloration or mold on it, unlike my own bathroom. I dropped my clothing in a heap by the toilet and spotted my naked frame in a large mirror illuminated around the edges. I had put back on some of the weight I lost in prison but still looked a bit emaciated. I pivoted to get a rear view when a knock came on the door. Before I could react, the door opened a crack and a hand bearing a cup of coffee was thrust in. "Coffee service!" said Jen.

"Thanks." Our hands brushed on the exchange. She pulled the door shut.

Classical music played softly in the background. I looked around for the speakers and finally spotted them, recessed on either side of the medicine cabinet.

The shower had one of those mega-heads with countless nipples and a lever on the side to regulate and pulsate the flow. I opted for full force, maximum pulse. The water pounded at my back at an intensity level just shy of painful. I reached for the soap, a dramatically curved, light green bar sitting in an alcove in the ceramic wall. The soap was creamy and had a delicious scent that I couldn't quite place. I lathered fully from crown to arch, hoping to erase every last trace of vomit odor. Then I turned the temperature up as hot as I could stand it and let the water cascade over me for ten minutes straight. I realized that I was sore and tired, symptoms of carrying drunks and sleeping on couches.

By the time I stepped out onto the terrycloth bathmat, the air was thick with steam. I toweled dry and put on the clothes that Jen provided. They fit perfectly.

I was about to exit when I realized I'd left the bathroom in utter disarray. I cleaned my hair from the tub, wiped the water from the floor, hung the bathmat and towel, and closed the toilet seat.

I returned to the living room and found Jen sitting there, a computer perched on her lap. She looked up and gestured toward the table. "We have bagels, cream cheese, lox, and coffee."

The smell triggered a ravenous response. I slathered a poppy seed bagel with cheese and layered on the lox.

"Do you mind if I ask you a few questions?" I said between mouthfuls. "Just stop me if I'm being nosy."

"Go right ahead," Jen said pleasantly, closing the laptop cover with a click.

"What kind of tile is that in the bathroom?"

"Italian. Marco Lanzoni."

"I knew it!"

"You know Marco Lanzoni?"

"Well, no, but I knew—guessed actually—that they were Italian."

Jen smiled.

"Okay, what kind of soap?"

"Avocado."

"Tasty," I said.

"Creamy," said Jen.

"Next, how do you happen to have men's clothes that fit me perfectly?"

"Well, the fit is merely a coincidence. The fact I have them is not—they're my boyfriend's. Or, I should say, my ex-boyfriend, as of yesterday."

"Oh, I'm sorry to hear that," I lied, looking down at the red flannel shirt.

"As you can see, he was fashion challenged."

"Is that why you broke up with him?"

Jen laughed. "No, he's the reason I happened to be in the bar yesterday. He asked me to meet him there with the intent, unknown to me at the time, of breaking up with me. He probably thought I'd be less likely to cause a scene if we met in a public place. He did the dirty deed, then left. I stayed to have a drink of mourning and celebration."

"Sounds conflicted."

"It was ninety percent celebration."

"Okay, question three. Where did you get such an incredible music collection? I've never even seen an 8-track player in real life before."

"I actually picked that up at a yard sale, along with about 100 tapes from the sixties. You name an obscure act from that era—Iron Butterfly, Strawberry Alarm Clock, Vanilla Fudge—and this person had their tape. Some of it is awful, but all of it is interesting."

She got up and walked over to the collection. "The 78s were my great grandfather's—big bands, swing orchestras, Tommy Dorsey, Billie Holiday.

"Some of the LPs were my grandfather's—jazz and blues mostly; Bird and Coltraine, Armstrong and Monk, Muddy Waters and Sonny Boy Williamson.

"The rest of the LPs, plus the 45s and the cassettes, were my dad's—classic rock, punk rock, singer-songwriter; Kinks and Stones, Ramones, Talking Heads, Television.

"And the CDs are mine—indie and alt rock, hip-hop, contemporary classical, operatic pop, plus a smattering of stuff from all the other genres."

"And the wireless music player sitting all alone?"

"I've been slowly digitizing my entire collection—about thirty thousand tracks. I've converted five thousand to digital. At the rate I'm going, I'll be done in about five years."

"Just in time for digital music to go obsolete," I said.

"No doubt. Over seven decades, there were six different means of listening to music, if you count all the forms of vinyl as one. Pretty rapid rate of change."

"So I guess we'll get direct brain-wave delivery of music within the next decade?" I said.

"Sounds about right."

Jen sat opposite me and took a sip of coffee. "Okay, enough small talk. Let's get down to business."

I wondered what she could possibly mean.

"About last night. That guy—"

"Malcolm."

"—tried to rape me. We need to report him to the police."

My brow furrowed. A condition of my probation was to stay out of bars, brothels, and brouhahas.

Jen continued. "If we don't go to the police, he'll try to rape somebody else, and someone like you may not be around to stop him."

"Well, Jen, here's the thing. We're going to have a hard time proving anything. No assault was committed. We could bring you in for a blood test, but my guess is that the drug has already left your system. Even if it hasn't, you're going to have a hard time proving that he's the one who gave it to you."

"But you saw him put it in my drink, didn't you?"

"I was across the room. I saw him reach for your glass when you weren't looking. It appeared that he put something in."

"You were convinced enough at the time that you risked your life to save me."

"That's a slight exaggeration," I said. "They probably would have just kicked the crap out of me. I'd be hospitalized, but not dead."

"From what I remember of Malcolm, you'd definitely be dead."

She was right, of course.

"We can't let him get away with this!" she said, eyes bright with anger. "*You* can't let him get away with this. Your testimony could be crucial."

"My testimony would have no credibility."

"I don't understand."

I realized that not only was I profoundly disappointing Jen, but I was disappointing myself. But it was a lose-lose proposition. If we notified the police, I'd face the prospect of going back to jail. If we didn't, a rapist remained on the loose.

"Jen, I have something to tell you."

"True confessions? I hardly know you," she said with a smile.

"I have a problem going to the police because I've had some trouble with the law."

"What kind of trouble?"

"Well, it's kind of complicated."

"You're not a murderer, are you?" She didn't look too concerned about the prospect.

"No."

"And, considering all that transpired last night, obviously you're not a rapist."

Despite the perfect opportunity to fess up, I lost my nerve. "Um, no."

"Well, what then? Littering? Fishing without a license?"

I tried to speak but couldn't form the words.

"I guess I'm not ready to talk about it. I thought I was, but I'm not. It's still kind of eating at me. But please understand—you're not in any danger when you're around me."

Jen walked over, sat beside me on the couch, and put her hand over mine. "I never thought for a second that I was." She gave me a little kiss on the cheek, then jumped up. "I'll get some more coffee. Why don't you put on some music?"

I scanned the collection, intimidated by its depth and breadth. Jen was clearly a special woman. What could I put on to impress her? Hip-hop to demonstrate my urbane cool? Classical to show off my cultural refinement? Jazz to display my *avante-gardeness*? I flipped through albums, CDs, and tapes. Finally, overwhelmed by the selection, I reverted to a time-honored tradition—the pin-the-tail-on-the-donkey method. I placed my left hand over my eyes, my right into a pointing position, and began spinning when Jen, unbeknownst to me, returned.

She stood silently in the doorway, watching me. After three rotations, I came to a stop, intending to select whatever piece of music I was pointing to. When I opened my eyes, I was pointing directly at Jen.

"I guess you'll have to sing," I said.

"Is indecisiveness a problem in your life?" she asked.

"Geez, I don't think so. I mean, sometimes it has been, of course, but as a rule, not usually. No. Except occasionally."

Jen looked at me with amusement. "You're kidding, right?"

"What? Oh, yeah, of course. Indecisiveness is most definitely not a problem for me. Watch how emphatically I choose the music."

I turned to the last items in the final row of the rock and pop section: Zappa, Zevon, ZZ Top. I opened the CD player and inserted the disc. Soon the breathy vocals of "She's Not There" by the Zombies filled the room. I thought momentarily of Maura.

Jen's phone went off, sounding like an English police siren. "Uh-oh. Trouble in the neighborhood. It's the crime notification network that I subscribe to."

She pulled up the alert. "Oh, my God—it's Malcolm! He found another victim!" She leaned close to me to share a view of the device. She smelled like flowers. A blurry video from a security cam showed a man half walking with and half carrying a woman. She appeared inebriated or drugged. As they moved closer to the camera, Malcolm looked up and stopped in his tracks. He seated his victim against the wall; she immediately slumped over. Malcolm disappeared from view. Suddenly, a shadow enveloped the lens, followed by a half-second of spider-webbed glass, then black. The phone screen flashed a toll-free "drop-a-dime" number.

This new development ratcheted up my dilemma. Malcolm was on the prowl. Didn't I have a moral obligation to stop him? I concluded I had no choice but to help.

Suddenly, my phone chimed its calendar tone—a squash date with Gray in one hour. I called him to cancel. He was atypically understanding. "Want to hear something weird?" he asked.

"I'm sure my story tops yours, but go ahead."

"I get online this morning and what pops up on the screen but a video of this guy wanted for rape. It's a bit fuzzy, but I swear it's the same bloke who helped me clean out Judith's apartment a few years ago."

"Wait! Are you talking about Malcolm?" I asked excitedly, gesturing to Jen.

"Yes! Malcolm Coventry. How did you know?"

"Oh, my God, you know his last name? Do you know how to reach him?"

"In fact, I know exactly where he lives. I picked him up at his house in the rental truck. Still have his address in my phone."

Gray gave me the street address. I scribbled it down and passed it to Jen. She called the police on her cell while I still had Gray on the line.

"You know, I'm not surprised in the least by this," said Gray after I filled him in on the previous evening's adventure.

"Why not?"

"He kicked Judith's dog."

"Always a telltale sign," I said.

The police responded with alacrity, and Malcolm was apprehended without a struggle thirty-nine minutes later.

Epilogue IV

Year 8 | Winter

Jen and I hit it off.

Every time I visited her apartment, she cued up an obscure music track for me, drawing connecting lines that I never imagined existed between genres and eras. Turned out she also played oboe in a community orchestra. I attended one of her performances, but it was hard to isolate her notes in the euphony. Her private recitals for me were inspirational though.

My fake ID worked as advertised, breaking the Catch-22 faced by every job-hunting former criminal. (I must remember to send a thank-you note to my fellow felons. The rules of etiquette apply to ex-cons too.) I finally landed that coveted position of flower boy at Dave's old job. Surprisingly, a "Nadia-and-the-satin-sheets" situation never materialized, and I was actually glad about that. Fantasies, I decided, should remain just that.

My prostatitis cleared up, due to my strict adherence to the recommended regimen. No more half measures for me: I completely swore off alcohol, caffeine, and capsaicin. And, as Dave once recommended, I took matters into my own hands as necessary to fill in any gaps in my ejaculation schedule.

Malcolm, it turned out, had a long string of sexual assaults. Women came out of the woodwork once his case was publicized. He'll be incarcerated for decades. Perhaps I'll send him a few tips for getting along on the inside.

I began spending a lot of time at Jen's place. The telltale signs of creeping cohabitation were everywhere: my clothes on hangers; my toothbrush in the rack. My room in the boarding house remained empty for many nights each week.

I still hadn't mustered the courage to tell Jen about my crime of passion. I actually expected she'd take it in stride. She's an incredible woman, and I'm lucky that she wanted me in her life. Nonetheless, reactions are tricky to predict, as I learned the hard way.

I had a near-beer date with Dave. Jen was going to a movie with two friends. We planned to meet at her place after our respective nights on the town.

Jen wound up having an extra glass of wine or two with her friends after the flick. I was already asleep when she arrived home. Tiptoeing to the bathroom, she used the toilet but declined to flush in favor of quietude. She silently washed, brushed, and gargled. She crept into the dim bedroom, stepped out of her clothes, abandoned them on the floor at her feet, and slipped into bed.

The night air seeping through the windows made it too warm for a blanket, too cool for sleeping al fresco. I was settled under a sheet, naked, as was my preference. As Jen slid beneath the sheer cotton fabric, she sidled up to me; I moaned softly and rolled from my side to my back. Jen cuddled alongside, matching the contour of my body.

She caressed my stomach, then lightly rubbed my chest. No response. I was out. I was a deep sleeper, and Jen realized the chance of waking me up to make love with her was slim.

But she was a determined lover. Jen took my flaccid penis into her warm palm, where it settled comfortably, a pig in a blanket. She slowly massaged the soft skin.

I remained on my back in a comfortable sleeping position, arms by my side and legs slightly spread. Deftly, gently, Jen ducked undercover and took my flaccid member into her mouth. She tongued it smoothly. I let out a low moan of pleasure. My dreams started to incorporate the sensation.

Jen swirled and stroked in slow motion, lightly caressing with lips, tongue, and hand, achieving the miraculous feat of teasing me erect even as I slept. She gave me a nudge. "Jerome. Are you awake?"

I heard not a word. I groaned, rolled onto my side, and remained in deep slumber. Jen realized the hopelessness of the cause. She kissed the back of my head and then turned her manipulations to herself. She attained orgasm within minutes.

Through it all, I never woke up. Jen cuddled next to me and fell into a blissful sleep.

The next morning, we breakfasted. "I had the most erotic dream last night," I said. "You were performing oral sex on me."

Jen looked up from her news reader. "That was no dream."

"It wasn't?"

"I took some liberties while you were asleep, hoping to arouse you from your slumber to make love. I managed to get you erect but not alert. I can't believe you didn't wake up."

Jen's words provoked unease. I was confused and immediately worried about the non-consensual nature of the act.

"You did that to me while I was asleep?"

"Mmm-hmm."

"You took me inside you without my knowledge and consent?"

Jen looked at me quizzically for a moment. She brushed her hair back from her eyes, smiled, and said, "I knew you'd love it."

Her simple statement lifted a mental curtain. I realized that this was exactly the reaction I'd expected from Maura—I thought she would love it. Subsequent events proved this an incorrect thought— an utterly, profoundly, completely mistaken thought. But it was not an evil thought. My act was clearly misguided, but it was not malevolent. I am not an evil person.

At that moment I felt something akin to emancipation. Like the sonic rumble of a basement furnace, only noticed when it stops, like the ambient buzz of human activity, only recognized when a heavy snowfall muffles it, my depression and self-loathing were a subconscious presence, only perceived in their absence.

Epilogue V

Year 8 | Winter

I finally did hear from Maura, oddly enough, due to this memoir. How she got her hands on the manuscript remains something of a mystery. I initially thought that Gray, whom I asked to critique the book, passed it along to Judith, who alerted Maura. However, Gray vehemently denied sharing the book with anyone. As he stated, "Why would I, when it makes me look like such a—how shall I put this?—shallow prick."

Most likely path: Gray left the book open on his reader; Judith caught a glimpse of it and emailed it to Maura. There's probably an electronic trail that could be followed, but I'd just as soon let it drop.

Maura's message arrived via postal mail, in an envelope with an uncanceled stamp and no return address. Inside was a hand-made card with a watercolor painting on it, wildflowers in a vase. She wrote:

I read your story. I'm glad you have gained some perspective. I don't think you are an evil person.

If you change my name and clearly label the book as a work of fiction,* I'm okay with it.

However, I must point out one major flaw in your narrative. Despite your description to the contrary, you have not discovered the secret of the sexual universe. Your journey was interrupted, and you mistook the milestones for the destination.

The secret of the sexual universe is not found in a mere technique. Rather, it is found in the loving application of the technique.

A technique is like a tool, and a tool is a means to an end. Why is it that men love their tools and women love what a tool creates?

The hammer enables the house. The pen enables the love letter. The bee enables the flower.

L, M.

Acknowledgements

The author wishes to thank several people for their contributions and support. You know who you are. Thanks.

www.ingramcontent.com/pod-product-compliance
Lightning Source LLC
Chambersburg PA
CBHW051413170626
46809CB00006B/2141